Praise for
Anger Is a Gift

P9-DNW-994

"An explosion of fury and revolution. Mark Oshiro's beautiful and brutal debut proves that not only can anyone be a hero, but great change comes when the heroes work together."
—Adam Silvera, *New York Times* bestselling author of *They Both Die at the End*

"Raw, unflinching, and full of heart. *Anger Is a Gift* is a masterpiece."
—Marieke Nijkamp, #1 *New York Times* bestselling author of *Before I Let Go*

"A masterful debut rich with intersectional nuance and grassroots clarity. Hella precious, hella dope."
—*Kirkus Reviews* (starred review)

"Powerful and timely debut novel. Oshiro deftly captures the simmering rage that ultimately transforms Moss from a quiet teenager to a committed activist against a brutal, menacing system."
—*Publishers Weekly*

"Part sweet love story, part social justice commentary, this title begs to be read. Give this to fans of Angie Thomas's *The Hate U Give*."
—*School Library Journal* (starred review)

"Anger is a gift, and so is Oshiro's arresting, nuanced work."
—*Shelf Awareness* (starred review)

"Oshiro's novel asks both its characters and its readers what to do next."
—*The Bulletin of the Center for Children's Books*

Reading guide available on www.markoshiro.com.

MARK OSHIRO

A Tom Doherty Associates Book *New York*

Anger Is a Gift

This is a work of fiction. All of the characters, organizations, and events portrayed in this novel are either products of the author's imagination or are used fictitiously.

ANGER IS A GIFT

Copyright © 2018 by Mark Oshiro

All rights reserved.

Edited by Miriam Weinberg

Designed by Greg Collins

A Tor Teen Book
Published by Tom Doherty Associates
175 Fifth Avenue
New York, NY 10010

www.tor-forge.com

Tor® is a registered trademark of Macmillan Publishing Group, LLC.

The Library of Congress has cataloged the hardcover edition as follows:

Oshiro, Mark, author.
    Anger is a gift / Mark Oshiro.—First edition.
        p. cm.
    "A Tom Doherty Associates book."
    ISBN 978-1-250-16702-6 (hardcover)
    ISBN 978-1-250-16704-0 (ebook)
1. Anger—Juvenile fiction. 2. Anxiety—Juvenile fiction. 3. Teenagers—Juvenile
fiction. 4. Police shootings—Fiction. 5. Anxiety—Fiction. 6. Fathers—Death—
Fiction. 7. African American teenagers—Fiction. 8. Student movements—Fiction. 9.
Police misconduct—United States—Fiction. 10. Teenagers—Fiction. I. Title.
                                                                      2017278555

ISBN 978-1-250-16703-3 (trade paperback)

Our books may be purchased in bulk for promotional, educational, or business use. Please contact your local bookseller or the Macmillan Corporate and Premium Sales Department at 1-800-221-7945, extension 5442, or by email at MacmillanSpecialMarkets@macmillan.com.

First Edition: May 2018
First Trade Paperback Edition: May 2019

Printed in the United States of America

0 9 8 7 6 5 4 3 2

For all mothers who fight for their sons

Not everything that is faced can be changed. But nothing can be changed until it is faced.

—James Baldwin

Every moment is an organizing opportunity, every person a potential activist, every minute a chance to change the world.

—Dolores Huerta

Anger Is a Gift

1

He saw the lights first. Blue and red, flashing in a regular pattern. Lots of them, scattered south of the station in the parking lot, and he couldn't help himself.

Moss had boarded the train in San Francisco that afternoon expecting nothing out of the ordinary, just a normal ride home with his best friend, Esperanza. The train was crowded, plenty of people eager to get back home at the end of the weekend. They'd been lucky to find an empty set of seats near one of the doors. Moss had leaned his bike up against the side of the car and scrambled to claim the spot next to Esperanza. But then their luck had worn off. The train now sat motionless, caught between the Embarcadero station and West Oakland, where both of them were bound. Moss closed his eyes and sighed.

"We're never going to get off this train, I *swear*."

He looked over at Esperanza, who had taken her half of the headphones out from her left ear. Moss could hear the tinny sound of Janelle Monáe as he removed his own earbud. His best friend's head was thrown back over the seat in frustration. She removed her thick-framed glasses and began to rub her eyes. "This is it," Esperanza said. "This is where we'll be stuck for all eternity."

"Well, we can't be stuck here *forever*," he replied. "They'll do that . . . that *thing* they do where they just redirect us around a train." He narrowed his eyes at her. "*Can* they even do that here?"

Esperanza sighed while putting her glasses back on. "I don't know," she replied. "I haven't ever been stuck inside the tube itself."

"It's giving me the creeps," he said. "What happens if there's an earthquake while we're down here?"

She slapped Moss's arm playfully. "Don't say that! That practically guarantees it's going to happen!"

"Then this really is like the start of all good apocalyptic nightmares," he said.

"Well, we better get used to living here, Moss. There's no escape for us. Our life as we know it is over! Which means we need to start planning out how we'll design our new home."

She stood up, grinning, her white blouse hanging loose on her body, and she gestured above the BART doors next to her. "We'll definitely have to install some curtains here," she explained. "I'm thinking . . . something that's gray. To accent the dreariness of this place."

Moss shook his head. "I am a man of high taste," he said in the most grandiose voice he could manage. This was always their game. "I cannot rest my body on this filth." He pretended to be deep in thought before exclaiming, "I've got it! *Bunk beds.* They'll save us space and give the place a youthful atmosphere."

Esperanza faked a swoon back into her seat. "Moss, you are just so full of good ideas. Plus, it speaks to the reality of the situation: We shall remain celibate for the rest of our lives, as I highly doubt that there are any cute girls for me on this train."

"Hey, speak for yourself," Moss shot back. "I'm pretty sure I saw a hella hot dude with a fixie a few cars down."

"Gonna corner the hipster market on this train, then? Smart, Moss. Very smart."

"You think so?"

"Well, they're young and ambitious. Lots of disposable income. Willing to gentrify your neighborhood at the drop of a cupcake."

Moss laughed at that. "Well, it otherwise seems like there aren't *any* cute guys in this whole city that I can stand for five minutes, so I'll take what I can get."

"That is surely a tragedy," Esperanza said. "Well, after being confined to a train car until you wither away and die, but a tragedy nonetheless."

The two of them went silent, as Moss often could in her presence.

She didn't expect him to make conversation, letting him fade back comfortably. Moss turned his attention to the vacant and detached stares about the train, a familiar sight on the BART no matter what day it was. It was late in the afternoon, though, and he saw the exhaustion on their faces, in the way they slouched their bodies. He and Esperanza had spent the afternoon at the mall in downtown San Francisco, pretending to be elegant and well-off shoppers, building an imaginary wardrobe full of clothes that they would probably never be able to afford. They had drifted from store to store, Esperanza a successful poet on her book tour and Moss a world-renowned fashion designer helping her with her wardrobe. The last time they'd gone out, Esperanza was a backup dancer for Beyoncé, and Moss played bass in her live show, and they had stopped in San Francisco on a world tour, casually drinking iced tea and wearing the most fierce pairs of sunglasses they could find.

It felt good to pretend. Like Moss had another life, a future he could look forward to living.

The sudden crackle of the speakers in their car startled him. "We apologize for the delay," said a voice that reminded Moss of his mother's, "but there's police activity ahead of us at the West Oakland station. I'm not sure if we'll be stopping there, but I will let you know once I have any information. Hold tight."

Esperanza sighed again, though her exasperation wasn't an act this time. Moss reached out and began to fiddle with the tape on the handlebars of his bike, impatience rushing over him. He just wanted to get home.

He leaned into Esperanza's shoulder, thankful that they were both the same height. "I don't want to go to school tomorrow," he said. "I know, I sound like the world's most clichéd teenager, but I'm dreading it." Moss paused. "You ever think it should be two days of school followed by five days off? That's obviously the best schedule for learning."

"Oh, come on, it's not *that* bad," Esperanza insisted, and rested her head on top of his. "We'll get through it fine."

The train jerked forward suddenly and a couple of people clapped.

Moss watched a tall, lanky kid lurch forward and grab for the hand-hold that was attached to the wall just above Moss's bike. When he grabbed the top bar instead, he balanced himself and winced. "Sorry, sorry," he blurted out. "Got surprised, that's all."

"It's okay," Moss said. "No big deal, man."

The guy ran his hand over the frame again. "This steel?"

Moss nodded, and he gave the boy a longer look. His hair was cropped short, his skin a deep golden brown, and he had that sort of lean muscle that came easy to some people through the gift of gene-tics. *He's cute,* Moss thought, *but probably tragically straight.*

"Steel's a good choice," the boy said. "Better for the messed-up streets."

Moss narrowed his eyes at that, surprised that this guy seemed to know what he was talking about. "Yeah, I know! Everyone wants those fast carbon ones, but those things hurt unless you're on the nice roads."

"Right?" The guy stuck his hand out. "Javier."

Moss shook on it. "Moss," he said. "And this is my friend Esper-anza."

While Javier shook Esperanza's hand, he stared at Moss. "That's an interesting name," he said. "Is there a story behind it?"

The sound that came out of Esperanza was a cross between a bark and a yelp, and Moss glared at his best friend and tried to clamp a hand over her mouth. "Yes?" he said, drawing it out. "Do you have some-thing to say, Esperanza?"

"Oh, please, can I tell him? It's so *adorable.*"

"Maybe Javier here doesn't want to hear adorable," said Moss, and he shot a quick glance at him. Javier was already nodding, however.

"Oh, I *definitely* want adorable," he said, and with those words, it was as if this stranger had found Esperanza's true calling. Moss watched her face light up in excitement; he dropped his hand, and she spread her own out in front of her.

"Picture it," Esperanza said. "Moss is much younger and arguably a very cute toddler."

"I dunno," said Javier. "He's pretty cute now."

Moss's mouth fell open, and he looked from Javier, who smirked at him, to Esperanza, who *also* smirked at him. "Wait, what?"

"Never mind," said Esperanza. "Y'all can have a moment in a second, I promise. I'm telling a story here, remember?"

"Exactly," said Javier. "And I wanna know what this story is!"

Moss's heart jumped, thumping in his chest. He was caught off guard, but Esperanza pushed past it, and he was thankful she did.

"So picture it," she said again. "Moss is learning to speak. He keeps hearing his parents say his name over and over—Morris, Morris!" She leaned into Moss. "And Moss here keeps trying to say it back, as any studious young kid would. But it keeps coming out without those crucial *r*'s."

"Moss," said Javier, as if he was trying it out for the first time. "I get it! Man, that *is* cute."

Esperanza stood and bowed. "It is my very favorite story to tell, and now I am gonna leave you two alone because *clearly* this is a moment."

With that, she walked away from the two of them, drifting off toward the windows on the opposite side of the train. Javier gestured to the now-empty seat. "Mind if I sit?"

Another burst of nervous energy flushed through Moss's body. "Yes," he said. "I mean, no!" He blurted it out, then shook his head. "Please sit down," he finally said, certain he had embarrassed himself beyond repair.

Javier did, his mouth curled up in a grimace. "I made you uncomfortable, didn't I?"

"No, no, it's okay, I just—"

"You're probably straight," Javier said, defeat in his voice. "I'm sorry, it just . . . I dunno, it just came out."

Moss's mouth fell open again for the second time in a matter of minutes. Then the laughter followed, and it washed away the terror of the interaction. "Oh, honey," he said. "I could not be *gayer*."

The dejection that lined Javier's face disappeared, and it was replaced with a playful grin. "Well, you never know," said Javier. "You gotta be careful sometimes."

"Oh, most def," said Moss. "Though I've never hit on someone in public like that before. You're *bold*."

"Me? Bold?" Javier laughed. "My mother would have a word or two with you about that."

"You live in Oakland?" Moss asked, and he felt the train speed up a bit as it made its way through the tunnel underneath the bay.

"Yeah, closer to Fruitvale. You?"

"Next stop," he said. "West Oakland. Well, assuming we can even *get* to that station."

Lights from the outside world then filled the train car as it rose out of the ground and climbed the elevated track. As long as Moss had lived in West Oakland, he'd never tired of this specific view, so he pointed toward the windows. "Check it," he said, and the Port of Oakland began to pass by them. The sun was already setting beyond the San Francisco coast, so the cranes gleamed from the powerful lights that illuminated the structures. "They look so silly," he told Javier, "but I love them. They look like children's toys."

"Or like a kid *built* them."

"You know George Lucas modeled those AT-AT machines after them?"

"No way! You a Star Wars fan, too?"

"A li'l bit," admitted Moss. "Minus most of the prequels. And you know I got my boy Finn's back."

"Dude," said Javier. "Poe is my *homeboy*. Latinos in space, man! We made it!"

"That's dope, dude." Moss paused and gave Javier a once-over. "You all right, Javier. I admit this is not how I expected my afternoon to go."

"Well, mine's just starting. I'm going to that rally in West Oakland. Probably why there's a delay."

Moss let a beat go by, and he worried it was too obvious. The spike plunged into him, that familiar anxiety he worked so hard to keep at bay. *A rally?* That meant one thing.

"What for?" Moss asked, hoping to smooth over his reaction.

"You heard about Osner Young yet?" When Moss shook his head

at that, Javier continued. "Older brother of some kid who goes to my school. Got shot a few blocks from the station, and police claim he had a gun pointed on them." Javier shook his head. "Of course he was unarmed. They usually are."

"Yeah," Moss said, struggling to find anything significant to say, but unsure he could. *How would I even begin talking to him about this?* Moss thought.

"So I'm going to show my support," Javier said. "I got some friends I'm meeting there." Javier put his hand on Moss's leg, and Moss wished this was all happening in a different context. "You should come!"

"Oh, I don't know," Moss said, his gaze dropping down.

"Hey, I don't mean to interrupt your little lovefest," Esperanza said, coming up to the two of them, "but Moss . . . we need to be careful getting off at this station."

"Why?" Javier said.

Esperanza looked from Javier to Moss, and he saw the worry flit across her face. The expression said it all. *Cops,* he thought. *There must be cops. How does she know?*

"Is something happening?" Javier rose and walked over to the windows, then whistled, and then Moss stood slowly.

"Is it what I think it is?"

She nodded. "You gonna be okay? I'll leave the station in front of you if you want."

Moss took a deep breath. "Lemme see how bad it is," he said, and crossed the aisle, putting his face close to the windows. He tried to peer toward the front of the train as it approached the West Oakland station, but the angle was wrong. He could see his reflection better than anything outside the train, so he pressed his hands against the glass to block out the light from inside the car.

That's when he saw them, the red and blue bolts of light, and that's when the dread filled him, overflowed, squeezed his heart to dust. His hands started to sweat, and Moss backed away from the windows, nearly tripping over Esperanza. She grabbed his right arm to steady him as he stumbled.

"What is it?" Javier said. There it was, on his face. Worry. Confusion.

"Nothing," Moss said. "It's okay."

"That's a lot of cops," Javier said, walking over to the window and shielding his own eyes as Moss had done. "Damn. What happened to the rally?"

The train began to slow down as it approached the station, and Moss sat down in the seat nearest the door, taking slow, deliberate breaths. His therapist had taught him this technique, for whenever Moss felt his anxiety getting the best of him. *All over some lights,* Moss thought. *Just red and blue lights. That's all they are.*

He knew this. It didn't matter.

The train came to a smooth stop at the West Oakland station. The platform was mostly empty, a relief. It meant a quicker exit, and that was the only hope Moss allowed himself. He stood next to Esperanza, who waited by the closest set of doors. "I'm here," she said, her hand in his. "We'll just put our heads down and get out of the station as quick as we can. That okay with you?"

He nodded to her, his heart in his throat. Moss wished he could reach inside of his brain and excise the part of it that tormented him. Instead, he had to deal with it every day. He let go of Esperanza and fetched his bike, wishing he hadn't brought it, certain it would get in the way. They waited. And waited. And waited.

But the doors did not open, and a creeping anticipation snuck in. What if they *were* stuck here? What if the cops were coming up into the station? The sweat along his hairline just seemed to appear; Moss couldn't remember it being there before.

"You okay?" Esperanza asked.

"Yeah," he said, his voice soft, gripped in the fear of the unknown. "Just wanna get off the train."

Moss caught sight of Javier, who was staring at the two of them. He saw it then, written all over him: pity. *It's starting again,* Moss thought.

The orange light above the doors flashed, followed by a short chime, and then the doors slid open. Despite the small crowd, a young man rushed into the train car, promptly dumping half of his drink on Javier's shirt. "Hey, what the hell?" Javier shouted, but the guy didn't even look back.

"Well, that was awful," said Javier, who was brushing off the front of his white T-shirt. They joined him on the platform.

"You could always call it modern art," said Esperanza.

Javier chuckled. "I like her, Moss. I can see why y'all are friends."

"He's winning me over," Esperanza said. "I hope you two exchanged numbers already. We should go, Moss."

Javier pulled his phone out, but Moss waved it away. "Let's get downstairs first," he said. "I just wanna get out of the station before . . ." He didn't finish the sentence. *How do I finish that? How do I tell him?*

They silently made their way down the stairs, the red and blue lights from the police cruisers on site bouncing off the walls. Two of the station operators stood outside their booth, their eyes locked on the scene to the south of them. Moss turned to head out of the north exit, his bike hoisted up on his shoulder, but Esperanza stopped and grabbed his free arm.

Signs were held high above the snarling crowd. One was of a photo of Osner Young, and it hit Moss: Osner could not have been more than a few years older than himself. His face was open in a joyous smile, and Moss recognized where the photo was taken: Martin's barbershop, the one not far from where he lived.

There were more signs. STOP KILLING US, read one. There was a tall white man off to the right, his messy hair gray and black, who carried a poster that read, I STILL HAVE TO PROTEST THIS? Moss frowned at that one; it left him with a bad feeling, as if the guy was more concerned with being witty than caring. But then lining the sidewalk outside the station, blocking the entrance to the turnstiles, was a row of cops in riot gear. They stood with their batons hanging at their sides, their helmets gleaming in the lights of the parking lot. Moss had to get out as soon as possible.

"Come on," Moss said, turning to walk away. "Please."

He bumped right into someone. Moss excused himself, but the guy examined him, looking him up and down. "*Morris?*" The man gave him the same look again. Was he from Martin's shop? How did this man know his name? "Yo, I haven't seen you in *years*. How are you?"

Moss backed away. "Um . . . I think you have me confused with someone else," he said. "I don't think we've ever met."

"Maybe you don't remember me," he said. "Last time was . . . damn, musta been five years ago. You were a kid still. It was at that rally outside City Hall!"

Please not now, Moss thought. He hunched down and tried to move toward the exit, but someone else stepped up, an older man with a crown of white hair. He looked more familiar, but Moss couldn't place him now. "Hey, Moss," the man said, raising a hand. "You here for the protest?"

Moss tried to form the words, but the darkness appeared. It started around the edges of his vision, it clutched at his chest, and he couldn't see an escape route. He forgot about Esperanza, about Javier, about anything other than the brightness beyond the turnstiles of the station. He reached into his front pocket and pulled out his Clipper card, held it tightly. But there were more people in front of Moss, asking him about the rally, asking him about his mother, asking him to stay and protest with the others, asking him too many questions, asking too much of him always.

A woman rushed up to his side, her cornrows a tight and intricate pattern on her head. "Hey, we got Morris Jeffries's son with us!" she shouted out. He tried to focus on her face, but it began to blur, to slide out of his vision, and then it seemed impossible to breathe.

"Please, I just need to go," he slurred out, and then he was lost, the panic slipping over his whole body. He let go of his bike, heard it clatter against the floor, the echo reverberating in his head. He felt someone grab at him as he pitched forward onto the gray concrete of the BART station, and he hoped the darkness would consume him.

2

Moss's hands slammed into the floor, and his Clipper card jarred out of his hand and flew across the concrete. He chased after it, but then couldn't pick it up. His fingers felt wrong. Too big. Too round. Irritation flared in him, then turned to rage, and then he was screaming at a card on the floor that he couldn't grab ahold of, and the terror spread. It washed out from his chest and up into his head, so total and so complete, as if he were under a waterfall that flowed the wrong way.

"Moss!" Esperanza shouted, and he felt his friend's arms under his. She tried to pick him up, but he was too heavy, and the shame of it pushed him further under. He couldn't breathe. He couldn't think. It was all too much.

"Give him some space," a voice said, deep and smoky. Moss felt a hand at the back of his head, and then an oxygen mask passed in front of him and was fastened behind his ears. "Breathe," the voice said. "Just breathe deep for me, can you?"

Moss sucked the air in, and the coolness filled his mouth, spilled down his throat and into his lungs. Someone's hand ran up and down his back, and it felt good. Comforting. He breathed deep again and slowly lifted his head, then shifted his weight backward. He sat on the cold concrete and sucked in another soothing breath. His vision was blurred; he hadn't even realized that he'd been crying.

Esperanza knelt in front of him and reached out, grasping his shoulder. "You're all right," she said.

"How do you feel?"

Moss looked toward the sound of the voice. The man's facial hair was delicately styled around his lips and chin. His nose was wide, as was his mouth, and when he smiled, Moss felt a pang hit him in the chest. The paramedic's smile was inviting. *Don't be silly,* he told himself.

"I'm okay, I guess," Moss said, his voice muffled by the mask. "Thank you."

"You get panic attacks often?" the man asked. "That one was pretty bad."

Moss shook his head. "I'm usually better at stopping them," he said, and the embarrassment pumped through his face. *Oh god, did Javier see all of this?* he thought. He began to look around him, and most of the people who had surrounded him had disappeared. But there was Javier, a few feet away, worry and concern all over his face.

"There's no need to feel ashamed," the man with the oxygen said. "I just want to make sure you're okay. Is there anyone I can call?"

Moss fished in his right pocket and pulled out his phone. *Who should I call?* he thought. Shamika might be home, and he'd relied on her before when he needed help during the day. Was his mother home? *It's a Sunday,* he reminded himself. The mail wasn't delivered on Sundays. With relief pouring over him, Moss unlocked his phone, scrolled down to "Mama," then handed it over to the EMT. When the man took it from Moss, his fingers grazed the side of Moss's hand, and he felt that childlike giddiness again. *Pathetic,* he thought. *Knock it off.*

The man pressed the button to call his mom and lifted the phone to his ear, winking at Moss as he did. His mother must have answered on the first ring, as the man began talking shortly after that. "Ah, hello? I'm sorry if this seems alarming, but my name is Diego Santos, and I'm here with your son at the West Oakland BART station. No, no, he's okay, I promise. He just had a panic attack."

Pause. Diego handed the phone to Moss. "She wants to talk."

Thanks, he mouthed to Diego, then took the phone. He lowered the mask. "Hello, Mama?"

"Moss, baby, are you okay?" Her voice wasn't pitched higher, wasn't full of terror. Just smooth. Interested. His heart rate began to slow down.

"Yes, Mama, I promise. It wasn't that bad. I just got . . . flustered. That's all."

"What happened?"

"Nothing, Mama . . ." The sentence died before he could add any more.

"Morris Jeffries, Jr., you need to be honest with me."

Damn, she used my full name, he thought. He relented. "I got recognized again."

"By *whom*?" Her voice *did* spike higher this time.

"I dunno," he said. "The first guy said he was there at that big rally at City Hall. You remember that one, right?"

There was silence for a few beats. He knew his mother was pissed. "Yeah, I do. He say anything else to you?"

"Not really. It wasn't really his fault, Mama. There's a rally here for some guy who got shot last week, and a bunch of people from the old days were here. They . . ." He paused and took a deep breath. "They surrounded me. I just freaked out a little."

She swore. Loudly. He could tell she was holding the phone away from her. "Don't repeat that, honey." A pause, and then she swore again. "Or that."

"I'm sorry, Mama, I didn't want to upset you."

"Oh, Moss, it's not your fault, I swear. I just wish people were more sensitive, you know?"

"I know."

"You need me to come get you, baby?"

"Nah, it's not far. I'll head home right now, I promise."

She was quiet again. "We can talk more when you get home, okay?"

Moss agreed, telling his mom that he loved her, then hung up. When he looked up, both Esperanza and Diego wore expressions of concern.

"You sure you're okay?" Diego asked, reaching down to take the oxygen mask from Moss. "I can stay if you need me." He handed over Moss's Clipper card.

"No, it's okay," Moss replied, and he made to stand up. Diego darted behind him and swiftly lifted him from the sitting position.

Diego clapped him on the back. "Whatever you say, jefe." The man left an awkward pause in the air. "If you don't mind me asking before

I leave . . . what was that all about?" He gestured vaguely about the station. "That crowd that surrounded you."

He saw Esperanza shake her head at Diego, and the EMT threw his hands up in a gesture of forfeit. "No worries, never mind. It's not my business."

This time, Moss reached out as Diego backed away. "No, it's okay," he said. He swallowed, hard, then cast a glance at Javier, who still stood off to the side. Moss could see the uncertainty in the other boy's body, and Moss jerked his head, gesturing to Javier to join them. *If this has to happen,* he thought, *it might as well be now.*

He sucked in a lungful of air before starting. "I guess I got this hella weird celebrity status here," he said. "Usually at rallies or protests cuz a lot of folks attended rallies for my dad years ago."

"Rallies for what?" Javier asked.

Moss looked up at him, saw that the pity was still all over his handsome face. *This is it,* he told himself. *Javier's gonna run screaming in the other direction.*

So he focused his gaze on Diego, hoping it would distract him enough. "My dad was shot by the Oakland police six years ago. They said it was a mistake."

Diego ran his hand over his mouth, which hung open a bit in shock, and then his eyes went down to the ground. Shame. Then the pity came next. Moss was used to it at this point. People stumbled into this revelation all the time. He was surprised, though, that he had not been recognized by either of the men in front of him.

"I'm sorry, man," Diego said. "I didn't know."

"Are you not from here?" Esperanza asked.

He shook his head. "Moved here from New York coupla months ago."

"Well, that explains that," said Esperanza. She turned to Javier. "But what about you?"

"Relatively new to the area, too," said Javier. "Me and my mama got here like three or four years ago."

Moss could still see the pity in Diego's eyes as he spoke. "You know," Diego said, "I lost a brotha back when I lived in Philly, in the eighties. Cops broke into the wrong house, he pulled a gun on them, they shot him right where he stood. He didn't stand a chance."

"Doesn't sound too much different from my dad," Moss admitted. "He was coming out of a convenience store, a little market not too far from here." He pointed off to the side in the general direction of his home. "Had headphones in, didn't hear the order from the cops to put his hands up. Got shot, and died right there." His voice dropped. "Turns out they were at the wrong market. Wrong end of 12th Street."

"It's a messed-up world, man, that people can die like that," Diego said.

"Yo, man, I'm sorry I asked you to go to the rally," said Javier, his eyes downturned, a portrait of embarrassment. "I had no idea, and I wouldn't have mentioned it if I'd known."

Javier ran his hand down Moss's arm, and Moss knew it was just to comfort him, but he still wanted more. That momentary connection made him feel, if even for a second, like he was less alone in the world. But it passed. Moss missed the sensation immediately.

Diego cleared his throat. "Well, I gotta get back to monitoring this," he said, gesturing behind him to the rally. "Y'all take care of yourselves."

They raised their hands to him and watched Diego disappear into the crowd beyond the line of cops, protest signs still raised, joining voices still punctuating the early evening air. Moss leaned over and picked up his bike, which had been lying haphazardly on the concrete. When he looked back up, Javier was staring, his phone in his hand.

"So, I don't know how to make a good segue here, so I'm just gonna go for this," he said. "If you're still interested . . . you wanna swap numbers?"

Responses flared in Moss's mind. *Even after all of that?* he thought. But he gave Javier a weak smile instead. "Yeah," he said. "Sure."

In another situation, Moss would have been overjoyed at the idea of a cute boy giving him his number. But he just wanted to be out of the station and in the arms of his mama. After giving Javier his number, Moss raised a hand to wave, then turned and walked north into West Oakland. Esperanza trailed behind him at first, but she caught up quickly, a sloppy grin plastered on her face.

He slowed down and shook his head at her. "What? What is it?"

"So *he* was cute," she said. "Moss, you got your first number on the train! How does it *feel*? You're practically an adult."

He chuckled at that. "I dunno. I feel weird. Still wired, I guess."

"You know we don't have to talk about it if you don't want to," she said. "We can just walk in silence, if you want."

He smiled at her. "No, it's okay," he said. "I think that talking might be a good idea."

She reached down and squeezed his hand. "What do you want to talk about? What would make you feel better?"

Moss loved this part of Esperanza. She understood that his ability to socialize after an attack was erratic at times, and she never pushed him to do anything he felt uncomfortable with. As they turned north on Chester, Moss pointed across the street. "There used to be a man there during the summer. Don't know what happened to him. But my dad used to take us over here when it got super hot and the guy sold piraguas that were *so* good. You know what those are?"

She nodded her head. "Girl, just cuz I'm adopted doesn't mean I don't know about the culture," she joked. "The Puerto Rican snow cone. I haven't had one in ages, though."

"This guy used to make ones with piña juice, and they were dope." He went quiet. "I miss them." Another beat. "And him."

"I know," she said. "And it doesn't help when people constantly remind you that he's gone."

"Right?" Moss shook his head. "It's like people want me to be this version of a person that isn't me. Like, always ready to fight and march and rally, and I don't even get to be myself."

They found a silence again for a few moments, but it wasn't uncomfortable. It was a routine of theirs, one that felt normal and intimate. How many times had Esperanza been there when Moss had an attack? How often had she helped fend off odd questions from strangers who recognized him? More than she *should* have had to deal with, but Moss appreciated it nonetheless.

He bumped into her and gestured with his head across the street.

"We used to make up stories," he said. "About all the people on the street whenever we walked home from the train station."

"What kind of stories?" Esperanza asked.

"Weird stuff, sometimes." He pointed at a flat, off-white house to his left. "Shamika lives there now, but years ago, there used to be this one dude who would always work on his cars in the driveway. And I was *convinced* that he was a robot."

"Men who work on cars all the time *are* robots."

"True," he said, giggling. "Papa never discouraged me. He *always* made the stories weirder."

He put his hand on Esperanza's back and turned her slightly to the right. "You ever see the guy who lives there?" They stared at the muted brown home, a tall chain-link fence rising up around it. It looked like a miniature penitentiary. "We used to make up all kinds of stories about him especially. My dad said he was an alien from some distant galaxy, and that's why he always yelled at everyone who walked too close to his fence."

"Isn't he the guy who got that garden up the street shut down?"

He huffed at her. "Probably. We never found out for sure. Apparently it violated some code no one's ever heard of. Can't have a garden in the hood!"

She sighed, and they fell back into a stillness. Moss examined each of the houses as he walked, trying to remember who lived in them, trying to remember the stories he used to make up with his father. There was Rosa's home, with her three boys, Rafael, Luis, and Ramon, and her trim painted bright pink, a Big Wheel long abandoned in the front yard. The two oldest boys, Ramon and Luis, were usually in the middle of the street, kicking around a soccer ball. But last week, Moss had seen Rafael put on his mother's heels on the front stoop and confidently walk down his driveway, pretending that the world was flashing cameras at him. Moss liked that memory, even if his father wasn't in it.

Rosa's family lived next door to Tariq and Eloisa, whose purple house leaned sadly but proudly to the right. They had tried to have a kid for years; then Tariq ended up putting his energy into adopting a blue-nose pit bull from the local shelter. Another memory: Morris letting Moss crouch down in Tariq's yard while Ginger jumped all over him. Moss loved dogs, and petting Ginger always lifted him up.

They continued up Chester, past the barbershop where Martin did Moss's fade, then past the only other duplex on the block, the one where a Korean family who owned three squawking chickens now lived on the bottom floor. Moss's mother's friend Jasmine lived by herself on the top floor. Moss had seen plenty of people visit Jasmine, but knew that she always lived alone. Moss liked her because she seemed so comfortable being by herself.

Over 11th now, right past the spot where a bunch of the older boys hung out. If you paid attention, you could see what they passed one another during their handshakes. Moss's mother told him to avoid that corner at all costs, but no one was hanging around that afternoon. When Moss's house finally came into view, he reached down to squeeze Esperanza's hand back. His home was small, painted like yellowed eggshells. It had two bedrooms and an attic that unnerved Moss so much that he never would explore it. It sat plainly in between two other small homes, all of them rentals and with tiny but respectable yards, a rarity in this part of town. Moss had desperately wanted a dog, but they'd resigned themselves to the neighborhood cat instead, since they didn't have time for a pet.

Moss stopped at the chain-link fence, and his mother crossed the yard toward them. Wanda Jeffries was taller than her son, and there were times he wished he had inherited her slender form. He definitely took after his dad in size, and some days, it was another reminder that Morris was no longer around. After Papa had died, Wanda had visited Martin's shop and had one of the women cut off her long locs. It was a renewal, she had told Moss. When was that renewal going to come his way?

She opened the gate, and Moss fell gently into her arms, wrapping his arms around his mama and breathing into her chest. They stayed that way for a few seconds, and then she pulled away from him. "How you feelin', baby?"

"Better," he said. He smiled up at her. "Esperanza helped."

His mother nodded at Esperanza. "Nice to see you, Esperanza. You staying the night again?"

"Yep," she said. "Just one more night. My parents get back from their academic conference tomorrow."

"You know you're always welcome. And thanks for taking care of Moss."

Esperanza beamed. "It's the least I can do," she said.

Moss looked up the street toward 12th, and his mother let go of him.

"You need to do it again?" Wanda asked.

Her face held no pity, just understanding. "Yeah," he said. "Only for a few minutes. I'll be back once I'm done."

He let Esperanza move past him into the yard, and she winked at him. His mother took hold of his bike and wheeled it up the walkway. He watched them go up into his home, and then he continued up the street to 12th, where the market sat under two streetlights. Dawit, the owner, had painted it in the colors of the Ethiopian flag, all bright green, yellow, and red, and the beaming yellow star on a blue circle sat in the middle, right above the entrance. There was usually a group of men gossiping or playing craps outside, but not that evening, and Moss was grateful for that. As Moss crossed 12th Street, he could feel the sadness settle into his bones, pulling him forward and down. The door was propped open with a cinder brick, so he poked his head inside.

Dawit waved and cracked a sharp smile, his long face full of joy at seeing him. But they said nothing. Dawit knew the routine well, and so he went back to watching the soccer match on the tiny television that he kept behind the counter.

Moss sat on the single step outside the door. He reached down and ran a hand over it, remembering the sight of his father stepping out of the market, the paper bag in the crook of his arm. He remembered the excitement he felt as he waited across the street with his mother, wondering what treat Papa had gotten for them this time. Moss tried to forget the sound of the patrol car pulling up, the cop jumping out of the passenger seat and raising his gun, the shouting, the pop and the echo of the gun, the color of the blood. He had tried for many years.

It never worked. But if Moss sat there and concentrated, he could push away the horror and find what he had lost. He tried to forget those horrible images, overlay them with other ones. Today, Moss tried to remember something new, and he shuffled through his mind like a Rolodex. His father's hugs. His smell. The way a T-shirt sat on his torso. His eyes, impossibly dark, almost black, those wells of kindness and familiarity.

His therapist, Constance, had taught Moss this technique, a way to calm himself whenever thoughts of his father or his anxiety or his terror started to get the best of him. She had gestured to the Rolodex on her desk during one of their earliest sessions, then turned the dial to flip through the contact cards. "Think of your mind as one of these," she had said, and the sound of the device pleased Moss. "Each card is a memory of your father. Now, I know you were young when you lost him, but your mind is resilient, Moss. You still have a lot of him inside of you. More than you think."

He was ten years old then, and in the six years that passed, he was still able to remember new things. It kept him going. So he focused again, turning them over in his mind, flipping from one to the next.

There. There it was.

I remember the way you used to give me that side-eye whenever I argued with Mama. You tried to get me to laugh every time. You knew it would trip me up.

He smiled. There. That's what he needed. He remained there, comforted by the memory, and he must have been there longer than he was aware of. When his mother shuffled up to Dawit's, Moss rose without a word, let her pull him into an embrace. They walked back home in silence, but just before he shut the gate, Moss looked back at the market.

His father wasn't there.

3

Moss's mother yawned as she opened the front door for them the next morning, and it was contagious. He yawned in response and then watched as Esperanza covered her own mouth. "I'm sorry to have kept y'all up so late," he said, a soft shame building in him.

Wanda squeezed his shoulder. "You know you don't need to apologize, baby," she said, and another yawn consumed her. "I think I can squeeze in a nap before my rounds this afternoon."

"Thanks for letting me stay again, Ms. Jeffries," said Esperanza. "I think my parents will be home for a longer stretch once they're back tonight."

"You know you're always welcome, honey," she said. She gestured with her head to Moss. "Would you give us a moment?"

Esperanza nodded and headed toward the gate. Moss's heart dropped when he looked at his mother's face. There was something there, not quite like pity, but a weariness. He'd seen it plenty of times before.

"I'll be okay, Mama. I promise."

"I know," she said, then shook her head. "Sometimes I don't, I guess. I just wanna make sure you feel like you're not alone."

"If it'll make *you* feel better," he said, "I'll text you. When I get to school. When I'm coming home."

"You don't need to do that, Moss. I don't want you worrying about me either."

He laughed at that. "What are the odds that we'd both be so anxious all the time?"

She hugged him and chuckled. "I'm sorry that happened to you yesterday," she said, her face nestled against his. "Just as long as you know I'm here for you."

Moss gave her a kiss on the cheek after pulling away. "Love you," he said, slinging his backpack around and stepping out the door. It closed quietly after his mother bid him goodbye, and he jogged up to Esperanza, the chain-link fence screeching as she shut the gate.

He yawned again. The grogginess in his head gave him an ache behind his eyes. How late had it been when Esperanza had passed out on the couch? When did he and his mother stop talking? He couldn't remember. He'd passed out as soon as he shoved himself into bed. He hadn't slept well either; the residual anxiety had pinged inside his skull. He had tossed and turned, awoke often covered in sweat, images of men in black uniforms dancing through his dreams.

"You know," Esperanza said after trying to hide another yawn, "I had this cute outfit planned last week, and now I don't even care. I'm too tired."

"Man, I was thinking the same thing this morning," he said. "I'd been so worried about what to wear yesterday, but it doesn't even matter anymore." He pulled his maroon fitted cap down farther on his head. "Ugh, this day is gonna suck."

"Have you texted Javier yet?"

He glared at Esperanza. "I'll get there! It was a busy night for me."

"I get it," she said. "But I think you should text him. He seemed pretty nice. And cute. *And* he called you cute, too."

Moss rolled his eyes. "Hurry up or we're gonna miss the train," he told her. It wasn't exactly true, but it allowed him to change the subject.

Their schools were up near the MacArthur BART station, so it wasn't really within a walkable distance from his home. Moss and Esperanza had been lucky enough to attend the same junior high, but since freshman year, they'd attended different high schools. Esperanza lucked out, by virtue of living in Piedmont, because it meant she got to go to one of the best public high schools in the Bay Area. Moss, however, wasn't exactly thrilled for the first day of his junior year. West Oakland High did not compare to where Esperanza went to school.

Moss pushed the envy away as he and Esperanza stood on the crowded platform at West Oakland station. She nudged him. "Remember when that cute boy hit on you yesterday?"

He stuck his tongue out at her as the train arrived. They made their way into the car and headed toward the center, squeezing past people who crowded the aisle. There was space to sit down in the middle of the car, and Moss tried to get around a tall man in a suit, his legs spread wide in an absurd stance in the aisle, his attention lost in a newspaper.

"Excuse me," Moss said.

The man did not move.

"Well, you tried," Esperanza muttered under her breath. She moved around Moss, then nudged the man aside so she could squeeze past him into the seat. "Excuse me," she said loudly. He lowered his paper. "What?" Esperanza said as she sat down. "You're in the way."

The man glared down at Esperanza. This did not have the effect that he wanted, because Esperanza refused to break her stare with him. "If you need to get by, just be a lady and ask someone to move," he said.

"I'm glad that you're now the arbiter of all things ladylike," she shot back. "Why do dudes always have to take up as much space as possible on the train? This isn't Manifest Destiny, man."

The man didn't take her bait any further, and Esperanza gave her attention to Moss as he sat down next to her. "So, Moss," she said, "tell me how you're feeling."

"About what?"

"I don't know. About being on the train. Or last night. Or *Javier*." She emphasized the name more than anything else.

"Ask me about Javier later," he said, waving it off. She gave him that look—mouth curled up on the right side—and he said, "I swear I will text him!"

"All right," she said.

"And I feel . . . okay, I guess." Moss sighed. "No, that's not right. I'm tired. But otherwise, things could be worse."

"That's . . . good? I guess?"

Moss laughed. "Look at us," he said. "We're both a mess."

"We should just get married and get it over with at this point."

"Seriously!"

Esperanza laughed. "My mom is convinced you and I were destined to be together, sexuality be damned."

"How are your parents, anyway?"

"Good, I guess. I mean, their book is doing well. Though I must confess to not understanding hereditary biology as well as they think I do."

The brakes squealed, and Moss and Esperanza attempted to stand up to leave. The man with the newspaper hadn't budged again, and Esperanza gently tapped him on the elbow. "Excuse me."

No response.

"Excuse me, sir, we need to get off here," she said, and Moss knew it was coming. Esperanza had her own brand of anger that Moss found entertaining, mostly because she didn't take shit from *anyone.* That included the businessman standing before her, who had more than enough room to move to the side. Esperanza reached up, grabbed his silk tie, and used it to pull herself upright. As Moss laughed, the man, exasperated, lapsed into a long bout of expletives about what role Esperanza should play. But he had moved out of the way. Slipping by the stranger before they could do anything about it, Moss yelled back, "Go post about it on Reddit!"

They spilled out of the train with everyone else, and Moss saw a couple of his friends exit a car a few doors down. Kaisha moved ahead of the crowd, and Reg Phillips hobbled over to Moss and Esperanza on his black crutches, a smile on his face. "Yo, dudes," he said. "What's good?"

"Same ol', same ol'," Moss replied, patting Reg on the shoulder. "You ready for school?"

"I'd rather not be," Reg said. "Hey, Esperanza! You look too happy. Did you spit on someone again?"

"Excuse me, I am a *lady*," she said. She paused, and a wicked smile appeared. "I used a dude's tie as leverage, though. Totally different thing."

"You've been missed," Reg said. "And remind me never to get on your bad side."

The four of them rode the escalator down to ground level, and Moss felt a rush of relief at the sight of the rest of his friends standing beyond the turnstiles. Kaisha was trying to navigate while texting at the same time. Njemile, Bits, and Rawiya rushed up to the others after they passed out of the station, and they all started greeting one another. He had missed them. His group was spread all over Oakland, and despite them not living all that far away from one another, their lives hadn't intersected as much as he wanted over the summer.

It was at this point that Esperanza said her hellos and then immediately followed them with goodbyes. She had a shuttle bus to take over to Piedmont High, and Moss couldn't resist having a little fun. "Enjoy your luxury limo ride to school!" he yelled after her. "Let us know if there's caviar this morning!"

Esperanza stuck her tongue out at them before parting.

The rest began their trek over to West Oakland High. They passed corner markets with fruit and vegetables overflowing from displays outside, and at one point, the group had to wait for Bits, who had stopped to buy a mango for lunch. "Perfectly ripe," they had said, the only thing offered as an explanation. Bits had gotten their nickname solely because of their succinct way of speaking. They didn't talk much, but when they did, "bits of brilliance shined through." Njemile had coined that one a long time ago, and the name had stuck.

Names were important for all them. Moss was thankful for his nickname, because it now allowed him to push away the painful memories of his father. Njemile's mothers, Ekemeni and Ogonna, had helped Njemile choose her name when she came out a couple of years prior. Njemile had wanted something that reflected her Nigerian heritage and would be her own. Kaisha was named after her grandmother; Rawiya shared a name with an aunt on her mother's side; and Reg's shortened name helped him feel like he wasn't just a copy of his older brother.

Moss was thrilled to see them all, but the previous night's confrontation still haunted him. He stayed at the back of the group, watching the others converse, anxious about returning to school. Maybe it was unfair of him to imagine this, but he saw their ease, witnessed their comfort, and he wished his head were as calm as others'.

He stayed silent as they came upon their school. West Oakland High itself was a massive structure in the northern part of what was technically *not* West Oakland at all. Moss never knew who named the school or *why*. It rose deftly from a small neighborhood of duplexes, laundromats, and mom-and-pop restaurants, mostly Korean and soul food. The building must have been a beacon of hope at one time; it was taller than everything else around it, stately, huge.

Those days were long past. Paint peeled off the doors and overhangs; the American and California flags had both torn over the last couple of years, so much so that if you glanced at them the right way on a windy day, it looked as if someone had just hung a thrift shop on the flagpole. Most of the windows on the second floor had been broken by unruly students or in after-hours fights. Some were taped over, and one of them still had a nice rock-sized hole in it. No one had bothered to patch it up.

They called it the "West Oakland aesthetic." As Moss ascended the front steps to the school, he glanced at the grease, grime, and years-old gum lining the concrete and railings. Someone had scrawled SCHOOL KILLS across the wall near the base of the front door, but SCHOOL had been crossed out with spray paint and replaced with OPD. School Officer Frank Hull stood right next to the graffiti; another year had passed, and he'd not noticed it.

Hull was young, perhaps not older than twenty-five, one of the few white faces in a sea of black and brown students. He looked at Moss and inclined his head, trying to imitate what he'd seen the other students do to one another in the hallways, across the quad. Moss never responded. Hull did it every single day, singling out certain kids as if they were the gatekeepers to some greater friendship. It was creepy, and even after two years, Moss still felt unnerved by him. He would never win Moss over, and yet he still tried. Hull had been commissioned two years earlier to take over the school's disciplinary measures by their principal, who had sought out some sort of tax break that could save the school money. Hull even had an office on campus, a place Moss had strenuously tried to avoid in his time at West Oakland High.

He remembered how his mother's family had balked at the idea that the police had a permanent presence at school when they'd heard at Thanksgiving the past year. "Honey, that's not *normal*," his auntie Briana had said.

Normal was different for Moss and everyone else who attended West Oakland High. Hull nodded again, thinking that Moss hadn't seen it the first time. Moss did not return the gesture. Instead, his eyes dropped to the hand Hull had at his hip, which rested on his holster, his black gun sitting in it. Moss shuddered. *That* was something he wouldn't ever get used to.

Ignoring Officer Hull, Moss moved inside, where the view was no better. Doors hung awkwardly on hinges that creaked and screamed. Panels in the ceiling were often missing or stained. In the center quad, where the lockers, food carts, and tables were located, the skylights cast a yellowish glow into the room, making everything look sick and rotted.

The lockers in the quad were dented, covered in graffiti and stickers, and most freshmen got stuck with locks that actually didn't close. The student body had gotten inventive, though, and it wasn't uncommon to see cables, shoestrings, and U-locks used to keep them shut. Moss had been lucky enough to score a decent locker last year, though his mom wasn't happy with the rental cost. As his friends split off to find their own, Moss pulled open his locker to drop off his bag before homeroom. He was pleased to see that Rawiya had moved to the one next to him, and they smiled at each other.

"You have a good summer, Moss?" Rawiya asked, pulling out a notebook and pen from her bag. She hung a mirror on the inside of her door and used it to adjust her beige head scarf. She wore a black X-Ray Spex shirt over dark jeans that morning. Moss loved her willingness to expose herself—she angered all the punk kids on campus just by existing. They didn't think a Muslim girl could be into hardcore, but she knew more about the genre than most others did. It was through her that Moss had discovered bands like Bad Brains and Death, and she never made him feel inferior for listening to other kinds of music. Rawiya just wanted others to enjoy something new.

"It was good," he told her. "Lazy. Lots of pretending I was doing something important with my life."

She giggled. "That's the spirit. You remember that house show we went to in July?"

"Yeah, that one out in Fremont, right? That first band was terrible."

"True, but that weird Siouxsie cover was amazing," she said. "Anyway, like a week later, my family decided that we should go to the Grand Canyon. During the first week of August!" She continued after a sigh. "You ever go to the desert in the middle of the summer?"

"Honey, I'm black," he said.

Rawiya laughed heartily. "Good point. My mom said we leveled up in whiteness because of the trip."

Moss snickered as he shut his locker. "Where's your homeroom this year?"

She looked at a small strip of paper that she'd pulled out of her pocket. "Bah, I've got Mr. Riordan. Does he hate happiness or something? I swear, that man needs a puppy."

They bid each other goodbye for the time being, and Moss began the brisk walk back toward the northern end of the building for Mrs. Torrance's class. Along the way, Moss got a few hugs and fist bumps from familiar faces, but he was mostly on autopilot. The first day of class was easy enough, but he was still distracted. *You have to text Javier,* he told himself. Moss's anxiety flared briefly, but he talked it down. *Not today, Satan. This will be a normal day.*

When he strolled into Mrs. Torrance's classroom, he saw that Njemile was there, too, towering over all the other students in the room. He nodded to Kaisha quickly. Mrs. Torrance was sitting on a desk in the back of the room, chatting with Carmela, a Puerto Rican girl whom Esperanza was deeply enamored with, but who had thus far not returned the feelings. Her long braids, striped with gray, swung every time she laughed, and it reminded Moss of the days when his mother used to have long hair.

He grabbed a seat next to Njemile just as the first bell rang and the students all slowly assembled into their seats. "We have to talk," Njemile said, leaning over to Moss and grabbing his arm. "Like . . . *now.* I've got crucial summer updates for you."

"All right, all right, after class," he said, and turned his attention to the front of the classroom, where Mrs. Torrance now stood.

Moss liked Mrs. Torrance, who was born and raised in Oakland, just like he had been. She was an acquaintance of his mother's from the days when Wanda had been more politically active. Her bright orange blouse was the color of a pumpkin, and Moss was certain that no one in the universe could pull it off *except* for her.

"Y'all calm down," she began, spreading her smile around the room. "We're just getting started, and I don't want any nonsense from y'all on the first day. We're having morning announcements in a few minutes, but I'll be marking attendance for this glorious first day of school in the meantime. I can see that Mr. Jackson over in the back row is already not paying attention, so let's all stare at him right now."

Moss turned around, and sure enough, Larry Jackson was engrossed in something on his phone, oblivious to the fact that he had just made a cardinal error in Mrs. Torrance's class. As Larry continued to stare at his phone, Moss heard Njemile mutter quietly, "Oh, he's dead."

It wasn't that Mrs. Torrance was particularly strict. She just expected a modicum of mutual respect from those she taught. She moved with the silent ease of an assassin as she swooped in, grabbed Larry's phone, and promptly leaned over to look straight into his shocked face. "You're new in my classes, aren't you?"

He muttered a reply that was largely unintelligible, and a few people muffled giggles into their hands. "Quiet," Mrs. Torrance said without looking up. The room obliged. "Mr. Jackson, I'm sure you're surprised that I even know your name, seeing as how you've never been in a class of mine."

Larry nodded, his eyes wide, his mouth open.

"All I ask is that you keep your attention focused on what's happening in my classroom. That's all. Can you do that?"

Larry nodded again, his face still frozen in shock.

"I'll be keeping this until the end of class," she said, gesturing toward his phone. "You'll see me when the bell rings, right?"

One more nod. Mrs. Torrance strode back to the front of the class with but a single glance at Larry's phone. She put it on top of her desk and picked up the Scantron attendance sheet for the day. She started out calling names of students she didn't recognize, marking those that she knew. She smiled when she got to Moss's name, and he returned it.

As soon as she got to the last name and hung the form on the door, Njemile raised her hand. "Is it true we've lost the women's volleyball team?" she asked as soon as Mrs. Torrance acknowledged her. "I was going to try out this year."

"I don't know for sure, Njemile, but a lot of things got cut this year. Which I'm sure you'll hear about, too, once Mr. Elliot does the announcements. Supplies and books are my concern, and I'm going to pay for any costs for this year's Book Club. Which, I might add," she said, pointing to a sheet of paper tacked up next to the whiteboard in the front of the room, "is something y'all should look into if you're looking for a deeper examination of the literature you'll be required to be familiar with for this year's state testing."

The room groaned in unison. "I know, I know," Mrs. Torrance replied. "We teachers don't like them any more than you do. But you're required to pass the test in order to graduate next year." More groans. "I know, we don't have money for sports or clubs, but we sure got *lots* of funding for these damn tests."

The speaker above the whiteboard beeped to life, and the voice of the principal, Mr. Jay Elliot, spilled into the room. "Goooood morning, West Oakland High, and welcome to the start of a brand-new year," he said, and with that, Moss tuned out. He heard vague announcements related to football, homecoming, the Associated Student Body, and other things that didn't concern him. He glanced around the room and saw that most of the other students, and even Mrs. Torrance, weren't paying attention, either. In fact, their teacher was casually reading a book at her desk.

Moss wished he'd brought a book to read. He was tempted to pull out his phone to scroll through his texts again, but he didn't want to risk Mrs. Torrance's ire. His eyes drifted up to the stains on the ceiling, and he tried to see if he could recognize a pattern in them. He'd almost convinced himself that one of the water spots looked like Jigglypuff when Njemile tapped him on the arm.

"Moss, did you hear that?" Njemile said.

"Hear what?" he said.

"Shhhhh," she said, and suddenly, Moss was aware that *everyone* in the class was listening to Mr. Elliot.

". . . And though there was much discussion amongst the administration here at West Oakland High, the school district decided that given some disciplinary incidents here last year, our school would ultimately benefit from a new safety program. So, beginning tomorrow, all students who have rented a locker for the year will be subject to random searches from the staff."

The classroom broke out into a chorus of groans and shouts, and Mrs. Torrance, who was shaking her head, discontent on her face, asked everyone to quiet down. Moss felt a fire in his stomach rise to his throat.

"Now," Mr. Elliot continued, "we know that this may seem like an inconvenience, but our concern is for the safety of the entire school.

If you receive a summons from Officer Hull and Mr. Jacobs, please gather your belongings and head with him to your locker. He will conduct each of the searches, and we expect *all* members of our student body to treat our resident school resource officer with respect."

Moss heard someone behind him angrily whisper, "This is *bullshit*," and he couldn't agree more. He felt a hand close on his, and he saw that Njemile was looking at him with concern. She knew why this infuriated him.

"We'll be sending more information about this program to your parents in a couple of days, so please coordinate with them to make sure that in the future, we can all have a safe experience here at West Oakland High."

It was at this point that the principal lost the attention of the room, and Mrs. Torrance didn't bother to tame the disquiet of her students. The disappointment on her face was palpable, but it was Moss who wore the most pained expression.

"Maybe they won't search ours," said Njemile, but Moss could hear it in her voice: She didn't believe what she was saying.

"Maybe," he said, "but what about the others? That man has a *temper*."

"True." Njemile frowned and her forehead crinkled up. "This sucks."

He couldn't have put it better.

4

When Moss sat down across from his mother that night at their tiny dining room table, stomach aching from stress and hunger, his mother was quick to the point.

"So, Moss, talk to me. Something isn't right."

He looked up at her, then past Wanda at Ekemeni, who had just turned away from the stove. The apron wrapped around her was covered in multicolored stains that strangely matched her red and white top. "Nope," she said. "Don't you look at me, Moss. I cannot save you."

Wanda pointed at Moss. "This is still my house," she said. "No appealing to our guests for help."

"Come to our house next time," said Ogonna, walking into the kitchen, Njemile trailing behind her. "Then you won't have to follow the rules." She walked up to her wife and planted a kiss on her cheek while Njemile dropped a big bag of greens on the counter. "Missed you."

"Missed you, too, sugar," said Ekemeni. "But don't let us get in the way of some good family drama."

Even Moss had to laugh at that one. He adjusted the silverware next to his plate, delaying the inevitable for a few seconds. His mom could see right through him, however, so he sighed.

"I just had a long day, that's all." He reached over and tried to adjust another setting, but his silent treatment didn't work very well. After a few seconds, he sensed that his mother was still staring at him. He looked up to find her soft brown eyes focused intently on him, her right hand under her chin. "And?" she said.

"And . . . not much else," Moss replied.

"Well, that's a lie."

"Mama, it's not that important, I swear. At least not yet."

"Not *yet*?"

At this point, Njemile and her moms were all staring at Moss. Njemile shrugged, as if to say, *You go first.*

He put his fork down, taking a deep breath in the process. "It's just that . . . yeah, today was kind of depressing."

"How so, baby? Because of last night?"

"What happened last night?" Ogonna asked.

Wanda waved a hand at her without looking. "Same thing. People not minding their own business."

"*Again?*" Njemile grimaced. "Over your dad, right?"

Moss nodded. "You know, I was thinking how people always want to be famous, but anyone who knows my face only sees what I wish we could forget."

Ekemeni whistled as she stirred something in the pot on the stove. "Ain't that the truth."

He shook his head. "To be honest, I managed not to think about Papa all that much at school today."

"So then what is it?" Wanda asked.

"You hear what they're doing to our school?" When she shook her head, Moss continued. "Random locker searches. At any time of the day. They can just pull you out of class whenever they want." He raised his fork. "Actually, let me correct myself: That Officer *Hull* can pull you out of class whenever he wants."

"That the same young man who caused all that trouble last year for cussing someone out?"

Moss nodded. "Yep. Been invited back for another year of overreactions. And he's still got a gun, despite that a ton of parents complained about it."

Wanda sucked air through clenched teeth. "That so?" she said. "You hear about this, Ekemeni? Ogonna?"

"I hadn't had a chance to tell them yet," said Njemile.

"So, the big question is," said Moss, "do we go to a prison or to a school?"

His mother didn't say anything, but she looked like she *wanted* to. He decided to keep going.

"And it's weird, Mama, cuz we don't have all that much funding this year, and they're cutting programs and some of the teachers are handing out copies of textbooks because we don't have enough. Look!"

He scooted his chair out and stood up, then bolted into his room. He returned with a thick stack of paper with a black spiral binding. The first page read, *New Biological Sciences*. He handed it over to her, and she began to leaf through it silently. As he sat back down, she sighed.

"This is your textbook?"

"Yep. The whole thing."

Ogonna moved over to the table and sat across from Moss, then reached out to Wanda. She examined the copy of the book after it was handed to her, then laid it gently down next to one of the plates, brushing. "Njemile, honey, you got any books like this, too?"

Njemile nodded as she came to stand next to Ogonna. "For American history," she said, and she moved her long hair out of her face. "*And* Algebra II."

"I don't remember having to deal with this when we were in school, Wanda. Do you?"

Moss's mother shook her head. "Nope." She said nothing more, and Moss could see the irritation build in her. Her jaw moved as if she were chewing, but it was just a nervous reaction she had whenever she started to get angry.

They all sat at the table without saying anything while Ekemeni chopped up some greens over on the counter. Moss watched her, hoping someone would break the awkward silence. His mother snapped her head toward Moss.

"So what are you going to do about it?"

"Me?" Moss said, surprised. "Nothin', I suppose. What can I do?"

"I don't know. You don't seem to like it, though."

"Well, I don't. Doesn't mean there's anything I can change."

"Just another day in Oakland, isn't it?" Njemile said. "I guess I can't be too surprised. Our school, they stay messin' up."

Wanda stood up without a word and walked over to the kitchen, joining Ekemeni as she began to sauté greens in bacon fat. The smell filled the kitchen, and it was a comfort at the moment, a sense that Moss was right where he should be. His mother had worked long hours at the post office the last few years, a necessary evil in order to keep the bills paid. It meant that there were some days when she simply could not cook a meal for the two of them when she got home. Moss had learned a few basic dishes by the time he was thirteen—burgers, oven-baked chicken, roasted vegetables, and, if he was feeling ambitious, a pretty dope meat loaf. Sometimes, if he got out of school early, he would attempt his mother's favorite: apple pie. He wasn't terrific at it, and so he was thankful on days when Njemile's moms or his aunties or Shamika took over duties, socializing while constructing their meals, giving Wanda a chance to get off her feet and relax.

He watched Wanda and Ekemeni switch places, saw the pork chops come out of the oven where they'd been kept warm, listened to the women speak about their days. His kitchen had always been a loud place, even in the months after the funeral, and he was glad that his mother kept people in their lives. It was a strange family assembled before him, but it was what he had.

Ekemeni placed a large steaming bowl of greens on the table. "Not my *real* recipe," she said while walking back toward the stove. "I didn't have enough time today to let them sit for a few hours."

"Please," Moss said, standing to take a bowl of rice from Ogonna. "Like I'm gonna complain about all this delicious food."

"You say that now," she shot back, "but imagine if I'd had time to make my jollof rice instead."

"Mom, don't tease him," said Njemile. "He is but a fragile man, and you know their fortitude is weaker than ours."

The five of them sat at the table, and before serving any of the food, they lowered their heads. Ogonna cleared her throat. "Thank you for this blessing of food and company," she said, then raised her head and smiled. "Amen, cuz I like to keep it short."

Even though Moss never really prayed, he still replied with an "Amen" before digging into the bowl of greens in front of him. As he passed the bowl to his mother, he felt a vibration in his pocket. He reached down and pulled his phone out. It was a text from Esperanza, and the preview read, TEXT JAVIER. NOW.

"No texting at the table, baby," Wanda said, passing the bowl to her right.

"Sorry," he said, sticking it back in his pocket. "Just Esperanza reminding me of something."

"How's she doin'?" Ekemeni asked. "I haven't seen her since last Christmas."

"She's fine," said Moss. "She was here this past weekend since her folks was out of town."

"Again?" Ekemeni shook her head. "They sure travel a lot."

"Don't judge!" Ogonna said, using a fork to stab at a pork chop and put it on her plate. "Aren't they like . . . super elite science people or somethin'?"

"I don't think any of us actually know her parents or what they do," said Njemile. "What was Esperanza reminding you of?"

He hesitated for a moment before the lie came out. "Just something I'd told her last weekend," he said. A quiet shame passed through him. He had no reason to fear that sort of conversation in this group. There wasn't a context he could imagine where Njemile's *moms* would be uncomfortable with Moss talking about a guy who flirted with him; Wanda had long ago been accepting of him being gay. But it felt like the wrong time, and he couldn't explain it to himself in any other way.

I'll tell Mama soon, he told himself.

Moss spent the rest of the meal trying to move past his discomfort. As he helped his mother clear the table, long after Njemile and her parents left, he pulled his phone out again, the unread text still on his lock screen. He dropped a plate in the sink, unlocked his phone, then went to his contacts. Moss scrolled down to Javier's name and stared at it for a few seconds, then hit the message button and began to type.

Hey man, it's Moss. How r u?

He stared at that for an even longer time. His mother came up behind him. "What you doin', baby?"

He hit send and stuffed the phone in his pocket. "Just replyin' to Esperanza," he said, and then he focused on washing the dishes while his mother dried them. He felt that familiar buzz again, but he couldn't stop to look lest he attract his mother's attention. Moss waited until she wandered into the living room, a glass of iced tea in her hand, to pull out his phone.

It was from Javier: Finally. Didn't want 2 b the 1st lol.

The relief rushed through Moss, and he felt silly that he had worried so much. They began to fire off text after text as Moss headed for his room. He let the elation swallow up his anxiety for the rest of the night.

5

Mrs. Torrance wore lavender from head to toe the next morning, and Njemile snapped at her as she walked into their third period AP English class alongside Moss. "Seriously, I want to be as confident as Teacher there when I grow up," she said. "Just look at her!"

"Good morning again," Mrs. Torrance said. "I appreciate the compliment a second time, Njemile."

"Light-years ahead of the times, Mrs. Torrance," Njemile said as she took her seat. "One day, we'll all be imitating you."

Mrs. Torrance just smiled. "And good morning to you, too, Mr. Jeffries. You were quiet in homeroom today."

"Got a lot on my mind," he said as he climbed into a seat behind Njemile and next to Kaisha, who barely looked up from her phone. Kaisha smiled briefly at Moss, flashing a mouth full of braces, before tucking the device away. More students poured into the classroom, a couple darting in just as the bell rang for the start of third period.

"Welcome back," Mrs. Torrance said. "Glad to see that you have all returned to a second day of my classes. I must've done something right." She picked up the attendance sheet off her desk. "Before we get started, I am to remind you—apparently multiple times a day— that this year's college fair is much earlier than usual. Please visit the booths in the library this Friday to pick up applications for study! I know you don't have to start applying until next year, but it helps to familiarize yourself with these forms now."

"I ain't goin' to college, Mrs. T.," said a kid in the back row. "I can barely get to your class most days."

Laughter rolled through the room until Mrs. Torrance dropped a worn box on her desk. She coughed as a bit of dust wafted up from it.

"This is our first book for the year," she announced, "and while I am certain many of you will enjoy it, we have a problem."

She came around to the front of her desk, crossing her arms. "There are thirty-four bright young minds in this classroom. I have twenty-one books."

She pulled a worn paperback book from the box and held it up for the class to see. There was a hole on the cover, and the back seemed to be hanging by a thread. "Chinua Achebe's *Things Fall Apart,*" she announced. "I hope you can appreciate the irony in that."

After a few chuckles, she put the book on the desk of someone sitting in the front row that Moss didn't know. "I am going to ask if there's anyone who can share a book with someone who lives near them. Unfortunately, after most of our library inventory was sold off this summer, there aren't any copies to check out there either."

Kaisha's hand shot up, and Mrs. Torrance said, "Yes, Miss Gordon?"

"I have another idea, if you don't mind."

Mrs. Torrance sighed. "At this point, I'm willing to do anything. What were you thinking of?"

"Well," Kaisha said, pulling out her phone, "I think there's a way that we can get a copy of the book to anyone who has a smartphone or a computer at home."

"No phones in my classroom, remember?"

"I know, I know. I promise it's necessary, though." Moss watched her tap away at her phone for a few seconds, then wait, then hold up her phone to their teacher. "Digital copies," she said. "It's not exactly . . . legal. If you're okay with that."

Mrs. Torrance walked over, the beads at the end of her braids clinking together, and examined what was on Kaisha's screen. "And this is a full copy of the text?" she asked.

"It is," Kaisha said, taking her phone back. She tapped a few more times, and Moss saw something flash open on it. "See?" She held it out to Mrs. Torrance again. "Just swipe to the left."

Mrs. Torrance did so, her head bobbing. "Well . . . okay, students. Hands up if you could read a book on a phone, tablet, or computer."

Most of the kids raised their hands. *Is this really happening?* Moss thought.

"If you don't have a device to read this file, feel free to come up and grab a physical copy of *Things Fall Apart*," she said, then sighed again. "I can't believe I have to resort to this."

The majority of Moss's peers stayed seated, so Moss stood up and walked toward Mrs. Torrance. "I prefer a hard copy," he said when she gave him a concerned look. He examined the book while walking back to his chair and wasn't surprised to see the abysmal condition it was in. While his cover was more or less attached to the binding, the yellowed pages made the book seem like it was a few decades old. He brought it up to his nose and grimaced at the smell. Ancient, old, weathered.

Njemile laughed at him. "You could join us in the modern world," she said.

"My phone is fine as it is," he said.

"Suit yourself," Kaisha said.

"Now, Miss Gordon," Mrs. Torrance said, the students' chatter dropping away once she spoke, "how do you propose to deliver this book to your fellow students?"

"Emails," she replied. "Everyone just gimme your email, and I'll send it as an attachment. Should just open up on whatever native app you use for reading books."

"My lord," Mrs. Torrance said. "I'm advocating the pirating of books. What has this world come to?"

"We got two whole basketballs on the girls' team," said Shawna Meyers, who sat in the back of the class. Everyone turned to look at her, and she pulled her beanie farther down on her head. "I expected that I'd have to deal with some hell for switching to the other team, but not like this." She sighed loudly. "I wish that joke were funnier."

"Welcome to the team," Njemile said. "We use humor to cope with this terrible, terrible world."

After a few snickers died down, Mrs. Torrance looked to Shawna. "That bad, eh?"

Shawna nodded at her. "And we lost a coupla players already. Two seniors who dropped out yesterday."

"Dropped out of school *entirely*?" she said, shocked.

"Uh-huh," Shawna said. "Got other things to take care of, I guess."

Moss felt the need to say something as irritation began to swarm his brain. "Why is it like this, Mrs. Torrance? You gotta know something, right?"

A few others added their voices in agreement, and a sadness settled on her face. "I suppose we've all known this was coming," she said. "All us teachers, I mean. I'm not the only one dealing with textbooks falling apart or supplies disappearing. You know Mr. Roberts? Science department?"

"Yeah, I got him for biology," Moss said.

"I saw him this morning in the teachers' lounge. Told me he spent nearly two thousand dollars buying what he needs for his chemistry class this year."

"By *himself*?" Moss said. "How is that fair?"

"It's not," Mrs. Torrance said. "But there's just no money. We didn't get as much from the state for the school year because test scores went down." After many students groaned in response, she shook her head. "I know. Trust me, we teachers hate them, too. But it's how the system is set up. With less funding, we've had to turn to alternative ways to get through the year."

"What if we found some way to fund-raise for the school?" Shawna said. "I don't know, something to help out so that we can have new books or more supplies. We always gotta fund-raise on the basketball team for trips and stuff."

"But why do *we* have to do that?" Moss said. "That's not our job."

"Yeah," said Shawna, defeat creeping into her voice. "I know."

"I admire your willingness to think outside the box," Mrs. Torrance said, glancing around at the students in her class. "And I know you want to help. Are any of you in the Associated Student Body this year? Maybe bring it up at the first meeting next week."

Moss felt a pulse of pain in the space behind his eyes and knew a headache was forming. *Already? It's not even noon.* He looked around the class; not a single hand was up, nor had anyone risen to Mrs. Torrance's suggestion. Why *did* they have to think about this sort of thing in school? *I bet the kids up in Berkeley don't have to worry about this shit.* The pulse turned into a pound and Moss closed his eyes, then pressed into them with the thumb and middle finger of his right hand. He blinked as the light poured into his vision again.

Things Fall Apart, he thought. *Of course they do.*

It was an uneventful class otherwise, once Mrs. Torrance reined the students in, and they began their introductory lesson to Achebe. By the time the bell rang, the class had returned to the normal state of boredom and disinterest. Moss appreciated his teacher's style, yet her enthusiasm and humor still couldn't reach a group of kids who didn't want to face the coming school year. *At least she tries,* he thought.

He caught up to Njemile as she waved goodbye to Shawna. "You going to the college fair?" Moss asked.

"Maybe," she said. "I dunno. Is it gonna be like last year?"

He winced at that. The only major university that had shown up had left halfway through the fair without explanation. "Probably," he said.

Kaisha sidled up to them. "I can just show you the applications if you want," she said. "I downloaded them all yesterday just to see what they look like."

"Always so helpful, girl," said Njemile. "How was *your* summer, by the way?"

She shrugged. "Nothing too exciting, I guess." She stopped as they stepped out of the hallway and into the quad, the massive room in the middle of campus where the lockers were located. "That don't look too good," she said.

Moss followed her gaze. On the opposite side of the quad sat the senior lockers, pressed up against the wall, the yellowed sun from the skylights casting them in a pallid tone. The ceiling was at least twice as high here, and most conversation echoed within the space. At the moment, however, only one thing could be heard: *Slam. Slam. Slam.*

There was a small crowd standing off to the side from one of the lockers, and then Moss heard another noise. The sobbing, soft and bubbly, coming from the short girl who stood next to an open locker. Officer Hull reached into it, pulled out another textbook, and ripped open both the covers, shaking the book in the air. Satisfied that there was nothing hidden in the pages, he dropped it on the floor. It was met by another muffled sob.

"Why are you doing that?" the girl said. "Please, I have to get to my next class."

Moss and his group came to a stop just near the hallway next to the senior lockers, and Hull caught them staring at him. "No gawking," he said. "Move along, or your locker will be next."

They didn't hesitate. Moss turned away and the three of them darted down the hall toward the back of campus. Njemile didn't say anything when she peeled off into one of the rooms. Was she afraid of Hull hearing them talk about him? Kaisha sighed. "Why does that man have a job?"

"Who knows?" Moss said. "He clearly hates it here."

"Well, at least in between him pretending to be our best friend," she added. "He's so creepy."

The bell rang with the sixty-second warning for the next class, and Kaisha waved as she ducked into precalculus. Moss pulled out his phone and shot off a text to Javier.

Glad we got to talk last night. You wanna chill on Friday?

He didn't know what made him feel brave enough to make the next move. *Maybe I'm inspired by his boldness,* he thought.

He saw that Javier was typing back.

Dude. Would love nothin more. My place?

He sighed. *Damn, I'll have to ask Mama.* But as he entered his next class, he rode the wave of courage he had before it dissipated.

Gotta ask mom. Will hit u up again tonight.

He thought about adding an emoji and worried he was obsessing too much over tiny details. The bell rang, and he shoved his phone into his pocket. He would have to worry about it later.

6

Shamika's gold hoop earrings jingled as she moved her head from side to side. She let out a laugh and put a plate of biscuits on the table. "Oh, Wanda," she said between breaths. "Your son *definitely* got something to say."

"I knew it," Moss's mama said, and she brought over a plate stacked high with chicken. "He always gets all quiet when he's trying to avoid something."

Moss sighed with exasperation. "Am I *always* that obvious?"

Wanda sat down to his right and then caressed his arm. "Not always," she said.

"But usually," Shamika blurted out, and then she and Wanda had a good laugh at that. Moss smiled at her and grabbed a couple of wings from the plate, then dropped them quickly because they were still hot. He hadn't seen as much of Shamika in the last few months; she'd given herself a much-needed vacation after tax season. Her afro was huge now, and he admired how well-kept it was. *I need a cut soon,* Moss realized. His hair had started getting long on top, and he needed a touch-up to his fade. He made a mental note to hit up Martin for this weekend.

"So spit it out, Moss," his mother said, breaking off part of a biscuit that Shamika had made. "What's going on?"

He stuck a broccoli spear in his mouth and chewed on it, his eyes locked with his mama's. *Just say it. Stop delaying.*

"So . . ." he said, drawing it out, his heart pumping in a familiar flopping rhythm. "I wanna ask if I can go over to a friend's house Friday night." He breathed out. "A new friend, I should say."

"Okay," his mom said, continuing to eat. "Do they live far? How long you planning to be out?"

He ignored those questions and went for the bigger issue. "It's a boy, Mama."

It took a second for this to register; her face was confused at first, and then the realization of what Moss meant grew, lighting up her eyes, her mouth slowly dropping open. "Oh," she said. Then: "*Oh.*"

Shamika, however, was not at all fazed. She leaned forward, her elbows on the table, a mischievous smirk on her face. "I want to know *everything*," she said. "What's his name? Where'd you meet him?" She paused, went quiet. "He got money?"

"Shamika!" Wanda reached across the table and playfully swatted at her.

"I'm kidding, I'm kidding!" Moss could tell she was having fun with it, though. She zeroed in on him again. "But seriously, I need to know everything."

"Actually, I *do* need to know more," Wanda agreed. "Who is this? You're not on those dating apps, are you?"

His face curled up in disbelief. "*No,* Mama, I'm not. I wouldn't dream of it."

She nodded her approval at him. "You wait 'til you're eighteen for those," she reminded him.

"I'd stay away from them *entirely* if I were you," said Shamika. When Wanda made to say something, Shamika raised a hand to stop her. "They're creepy! I got some dude on one of them telling me that he wished I would do more than his taxes." She shuddered. "Men are trash." She fixed Moss with her gaze. "But tell us about this guy anyway."

He shook his head. *She is so extra,* he thought, but it was why he loved the days when she took up cooking duty in their house. Moss adored Njemile's parents, but Shamika was somewhat younger than his mother, and he found he could relate to her more. He set down the wing he'd been working on and wiped his mouth with a napkin.

"I met him on Sunday," he began. "On BART. His name is Javier. He said something nice about my bike, and we started talking."

His mother narrowed her eyes. "How old is he, baby?"

He paused, and he instantly knew that the pause was a mistake. "Moss, how *old* is he?"

"I didn't ask," he said. "But he goes to Eastside so he can't be more than a year older than me."

"Just checking," she said. "Go 'head."

"Anyway, he seems pretty cool. We swapped numbers and have been texting—"

"So that's who you been on that phone with," said Wanda, and she smirked at Shamika.

"I swear, Mama, you and me are too close," he said, shaking his head at her.

"It's fine, Moss, I promise. Was he there for . . . you know . . ."

In the silence that Wanda let hang there, Shamika looked from Moss to Wanda and back again. "For *what*?"

Moss pushed his food around for a bit. "I had another panic attack," he said, his voice sheepish.

"Oh, honey," said Shamika. "I'm sorry. Cops again? Or something else?"

"Actually, I'm surprised it *wasn't* the cops," he said, looking up at her. "There was a rally at the West Oakland station for some dude who got killed, so the place was swarming with 'em. But no, it's cuz I got recognized again."

Shamika's cheery manner dropped off her. "Sometimes," she said quietly, "this community is too much."

"Anyway, yeah, he was there," Moss said. "Saw the whole thing."

"Wait," said Shamika. "Did you give him your number before or after that?"

"After. Why?"

"Whew," she said, throwing her hands up. "Marry that man right now."

Wanda swatted at her again. "Shamika!"

"Look, I'm just *sayin'*," she said. "This boy already knows Moss is crazy and is *still* interested?" She turned back to Moss. "He's a keeper. Trust me. I have to go through this whole routine to explain my medication to every person I date, and I hate it. Some people bounce the second I bring out one of those orange bottles."

"Really?" Moss said. "*That* soon?"

"It's already not easy bein' depressed," said Shamika. "Adding another person to that rarely makes it better. So take it from me: If he's already cool with you and your head, that's a step above most people I've met."

"She's not wrong," said Wanda. "Though please don't propose to this Javier just yet, honey."

Moss chuckled. "I won't." He crossed his hands over his chest. "So what do you think? He lives over near Fruitvale, wants me to come over and play video games and stuff."

"Will his parents be there?" Wanda asked.

"Parent," corrected Moss. "It's just his mom. And yeah, it will be supervised. I'm not *that* scandalous."

She pursed her lips, then took another bite of one of Shamika's biscuits. "Okay," she said. "I mean, it's time. I been wonderin' if you were ever going to date anyone."

"*Mamaaaaa*," he droned. "What's *that* supposed to mean?"

"It means you're hella cute, Moss, and boys should be throwing themselves at you," said Shamika, and her earrings tinkled as she laughed.

"You have any condoms?"

The question from his mama hit him square in the chest, and he actually choked on one of the biscuits. Shamika roared with laughter as she passed Moss a fresh glass of water. He swallowed it down and glared at Wanda, who looked far too pleased for his comfort.

"We are not having sex, *Mama*," he shot out. "Certainly not with his mom in the same apartment."

"I feel like I would be remiss in my parenting if I didn't bring it up," she said. "I had sex by the time I was sixteen, and your seventeenth is next month. It's not like it's unreasonable to assume it's going to happen soon."

"I don't think I'm ready yet," Moss admitted, his voice dropping in volume. "I just don't feel like I wanna hook up with someone without getting to know them."

"A true romantic," said Shamika. "You're gonna have this boy *swooning* over you."

Moss smiled at her, then his mother. "So it's okay? You don't have a problem with it?"

Wanda didn't say anything at first. She was examining his face, and he saw her eyes well up and sparkle. "Of course it's okay, Moss," she said. "I just want you to be happy." She sniffled. "*Responsibly* happy, I should add."

"I promise, Mama," he said, standing up and grabbing his plate. "I'm gonna go tell Javier, if you don't mind."

"Go ahead," she said, and she handed Moss her empty plate. He walked over to the sink to deposit them, and she added, "After you do the dishes."

She's evil, he thought. *But I love her.*

He listened to Shamika and his mama gossip as he did the dishes. Halfway through, Wanda came over and kissed him on the head. "Don't stay up too late tonight," she said.

"Where y'all headed?" Moss asked.

"I got the day off tomorrow, and I desperately need a night out," she said. "Shamika got plans but won't tell me them, so we're gonna go pretend I'm still twenty years old."

"Your mama swears she doesn't look a day over twenty-five," Shamika shot back from the table.

"Well, then you're gonna help me with my good wig tonight, girl," said Wanda. "My son's getting more action than me these days, lord help me."

Moss cackled though his face burned. "You're too much, Mama."

"Don't stay up too late, okay?"

"Be safe, Mama," he said, and he put his hands on his hips. "Don't talk to strangers."

"Oh, don't you start, Moss," she said as Shamika howled with laughter in the background.

She walked away and he called after her, "Wear your sweater!"

The sound of their laughter and conversation died as they disappeared into his mama's bedroom to get ready. Moss concentrated on the dishes as his heart began to race again, as the thought of texting Javier to confirm their first date sent an electricity through him. *Does this count as a date?*

Maybe he'd have to ask. Moss dried his hands after finishing and hung up the dish towel on its hook near the refrigerator. He dashed over to his own room and shut the door behind him. The hanging globe lights, which lined the edge where the ceiling met the wall, cast a heavenly glow over his room, but Moss needed more. He switched on the large lamp that sat in the opposite corner, and it cast his wall of posters in brightness. He had a few gig flyers thumbtacked to a board, many of them for shows he'd attended with Rawiya in the last year. Next to it, his pride and joy hung framed on the wall: a signed Missy Elliott poster that he'd gotten for Christmas the previous year. She stood proudly and defiantly in front of her own name in graffiti, and her signature was down in the bottom right. His mother refused to tell him how she'd been able to get it.

Moss fired off a text to Javier: we on for friday. What time is good for u?

He powered on his computer and brought up iTunes to play some Prince while he went through his closet. As Prince sang about controversy, Moss began to pull out shirts and flannels. Which look would be best? He assumed that he'd be coming home first, then biking over to Javier's after checking in with his mom, so he wanted to have a fresh outfit change ready.

Yet as he began to match up tops with jeans, his excitement waned. He held up a red-and-black-striped flannel to his torso and looked in the mirror on his closet door. Did it even fit anymore? He pulled it off the hanger and swung it around him. By the time he got his arms in the sleeves, he could already tell that he'd gained weight since the last time he had worn it. He could barely button one of the buttons on the front, so he dejectedly hung it back in the closet. *Maybe you need to buy longer shirts,* he thought. *At least those won't ride up if you raise your hands.*

He thought that perhaps his bike riding would help keep the weight off, but he just kept *growing. At least I'm tall,* he thought, but it wasn't much of a consolation.

He sighed, knowing he shouldn't be so hard on himself. It wasn't like his size was a mystery to Javier. The guy had seen him in the flesh. *If he thought you were ugly, he wouldn't have asked for your number,* Moss told himself.

He took another deep breath. He set out a pair of dark blue jeans and a black V-neck on his desk, hoping the simple colors would be nice enough to make it seem like he tried. Before he climbed into bed, the sound of Prince's voice still echoing in the room, he grabbed his maroon fitted cap and laid it on top of the clothing. *That's what that was missing,* he thought.

Moss turned down his music, and then snuggled into bed. He fell into a dreamless sleep.

7

They came in just before class ended.

There was no knock on the door. Mrs. Torrance had led the room in a discussion of the previous night's reading of *Things Fall Apart* for nearly half an hour, and Moss was surprised that more of the kids had engaged in conversation than he expected for a Thursday morning. *Maybe it's because most of them have digital files,* he theorized.

It didn't matter, though. Moss did his best to pay attention, but the beginning of a migraine raged in his head, making it hard to keep his eyes open in the bright classroom. One of the fluorescent lights had started flickering halfway through class, exacerbating the pain, and Moss was eager to dart over to his locker and get his medication. *Why the hell did I leave it behind?* he thought. So he listened to Mrs. Torrance speak of Achebe, his history as a writer, and the themes they should look out for while reading.

The door swung open with no announcement just before the bell. Assistant Principal Stephen Jacobs offered a curt smile to Mrs. Torrance, whose head had swung toward him, her beads tinkling again. "Sorry for the interruption," Mr. Jacobs said, and he ran a hand through his short brown hair, his eyes locked on the ground. *He won't even look at her,* Moss thought. *Serves him right.* He could see the color seep into Mr. Jacobs's face, and he was instantly thankful that he was never *that* obvious when he blushed. "I have a student who needs to come with me for . . . um . . . for a locker search." The man seemed *exhausted*.

It was then that Officer Hull appeared behind AP Jacobs. Moss almost expected the students to groan, but they were dead silent instead. A chair creaked as someone shifted in their seat, and Moss looked to his friends. Njemile held her breath, and Kaisha fixed a scowl on her face. They all watched Mr. Jacobs unfold the yellow notice he held in his hand. He cleared his throat.

Please don't let it be me, Moss said, a silent request to no one, and with everyone. He saw Hull's eyes, hawkish and focused, sweep over the classroom, and it sent a shiver down his spine.

"Is . . . uh . . . is Mr. . . . Shawna Meyers here?"

There was a collective sigh of relief as Shawna said, "Miss. I told you yesterday that it's *Miss* Shawna Meyers."

He looked down at the paper he held. "Oh, right," he said. "Yes, you did tell me that."

"I'm not going anywhere," she said, crossing her arms.

Mr. Jacobs was shaking his head. "I'm sorry, but you were randomly chosen. Please gather your things and come with me."

"No."

The entire class turned to stare at Shawna, whose black beanie was pulled low on her head as usual. Moss had never heard Mrs. Torrance's class so *quiet* before, every student anticipating the fight that was to come.

"You can't say no," said Mr. Jacobs, but even as he spoke, Moss could hear that he didn't believe the words coming out of his mouth.

"What's *that* supposed to mean?" Shawna glared at the assistant principal. "Is it against the rules to say 'no' now?"

Officer Hull pushed past Mr. Jacobs and cleared his throat. "You have to come with us now."

"Did I break a rule?"

"Please gather your things and come with us," said Hull, more forceful this time. His hand went up on his hip, right to the gun that sat in its holster.

It was like the air in the room disappeared for a moment, and Moss gripped the edge of his desk hard, sucking his breath in as he looked from Hull to Shawna. She'd seen the gesture, too, and all her anger evaporated. She didn't say anything as she slowly pulled her bag up from the floor. She stood up and shoved her copy of *Things Fall Apart* into her backpack. "What did I do, huh?" Shawna demanded, but the fire in her voice was gone. "Why me? You trying to punish me for what I told you yesterday?"

"I promise you, it's random, Ms. Meyers." He turned to Mrs. Torrance, his eyes dropping to the floor again. "Sorry for the interruption, Mrs. Torrance, I'll be out of your hair soon."

Hull stuck his hand out, taking it off the holster. "This way, please."

There was no relief left in Moss, just a tired sadness as he watched Shawna make her way out of the room. "This is bullshit," she said.

"Shawna," Mrs. Torrance said, and her usual sharpness was gone, replaced with something closer to tenderness, "please watch your language in my classroom."

She stopped by the door, and her face was full of despair as she looked back at Mrs. Torrance. "Yes, ma'am."

"If you need anything," their teacher continued, glaring at the men in her doorway, "you know where to find me."

"Thank you," Shawna muttered, and her head drooped as she left the classroom. Mr. Jacobs raised his hand in goodbye, and he was soon gone, along with Hull.

The absence left in the wake of Shawna's departure weighed heavily on the room. Moss's headache had faded a little, which he would have been joyous about under other circumstances. But Mrs. Torrance stood speechless at the front of the classroom. She had nothing witty or insightful or illuminating to say; instead, she just shifted her weight from one foot to the other, avoiding the stares her students gave her. When she looked away from the door, she happened to lock eyes with Moss.

"I don't know what to say," she mumbled, her usually clear, strong voice reduced to almost a whisper. "I'm sorry y'all have to go through this."

"What are we supposed to do?" Njemile said after a few beats of silence. She quickly had the rapt attention of the whole room. "It seems so unfair! Shawna didn't do anything."

"You know they don't care about that," said Kaisha. "Never have cared about safety or whatever excuse they make."

The bell rang out just then, and everyone began to slowly assemble their things. Mrs. Torrance did not answer Njemile. She was still looking at Moss, and he looked down to avoid her gaze as he put his stuff away. When he passed her on his way out, she smiled, soft and weary. *She saw my panic,* he realized.

"You okay, son?" Mrs. Torrance said.

He shook his head. "Not really," he answered. "Not much we can do about it, is there?"

"I don't know," she said, waving to a couple of students as they exited her classroom. "Depends on how long the school can keep up this charade before things go badly."

He shrugged at her and bid her goodbye, then caught up to Kaisha and Njemile. They all headed to the middle quad together, and no one said anything. Moss was used to Kaisha's silence. Like Bits, Kaisha did not speak unless she needed to. Njemile, on the other hand, was normally much more chatty. He couldn't blame them, though. It was as if a toxic cloud hung all around them no matter where they went.

It was Kaisha who broke the silence. "I guess I never noticed how busted up our school is," she said, and she pointed toward the ceiling above one of the classroom doors. They followed her gesture to a large rust-colored stain above them. "I mean, I knew it was messed up here, but it feels so much more obvious now."

"Like the floor," said Njemile, and Moss looked down and realized that the pale linoleum had chipped away in so many places that it looked like an intentional pattern. "I got so used to it that I don't even notice all the cracks or places where it's peeling away."

"Or the lockers themselves," Moss added. "Do any of yours lock anymore?" The others grumbled, which Moss took as a denial. "Yeah, mine either. I'm using an old bike lock to keep it shut."

"Very crafty," said Kaisha.

"Yo, you mind if we stop by mine, though?" Moss said. "I gotta get my history book."

"You know, my parents were gonna try to put me in another

school," said Njemile after nodding at him. "Actually, that same one Esperanza goes to."

"I'm sure it's better than this," said Kaisha. "You know those white schools are all fancy as hell."

"I don't know how Esperanza stands it, honestly," said Moss. "She's always complaining about all the stuck-up kids she has to go to school with."

They entered the quad, and it still looked just as yellowed as always. Moss cast a glance upward, and it was like the first time he had noticed the same cracks and plastered holes in the skylights. Dirty cobwebs hung in the corners, and a large crack ran from the frame of the southward skylight down to the area where the senior lockers were. While they walked toward the south hallway, Moss felt like a screen had been lifted. He'd gotten used to this, hadn't he? After two full years at West Oakland High, he'd stopped noticing how the lunch tables in the quad were splintered and falling apart. Or that the soda machine near the east wing hadn't been operating for over a year.

He was about to point that out to the others when Kaisha flung her arm in front of Moss. "Oh, no," she said, and Moss saw what had alarmed her.

Shawna's locker was wide open, and she was swearing up a storm. "Seriously, man," she shouted. "Why you gotta do me like this?"

Mr. Jacobs was off to the side, and Officer Hull was rifling through Shawna's locker. He seemed impatient, like he couldn't wait to get this search done. He pulled a set of books out and dropped them on the floor without even checking through them.

"Come on, man!" Shawna yelled.

"I got twenty more lockers today, kid," Hull said. "I don't got time for cleanup."

Shawna threw her hands up in exasperation, and she turned around to see Moss staring at her. "Bullshit," she said to Moss, and it was the first time Shawna had ever said anything to him directly. "You see this?"

"Yeah," said Moss, and he stuck the key in his bike lock. "I'm sorry."

He focused on opening his locker, trying to ignore each new slam, each new item dropped on the floor. Moss yanked his locker's door open right as Mr. Jacobs said, "Officer Hull, there's no need to be rude."

"Do I tell you how to do your job?"

Moss turned to stare after that, and Officer Hull was scowling at the assistant principal.

"I'm not telling you how to do your job," said Mr. Jacobs with a sigh. "But you're not making this easier on anyone."

Hull rolled his eyes and returned to Shawna's locker. She leaned up against the other lockers, rage simmering on her face. Moss shivered, the anxiety back and coursing in his veins, and he reached in his locker to grab his book.

The harsh tone in Hull's voice reeled him back in. "What's this?" Hull shouted. "Huh? You got an explanation for it?"

Moss turned. Hull held a ziplock bag up in the air, and Moss's heart dropped. White pills. Lots of them. Shawna made to grab them, but Hull yanked them out of her reach. "Mr. Jacobs, hold this," Hull said, passing the baggie to him, and Shawna was stuttering. She couldn't get the words out of her mouth.

"No, no, no," Shawna managed to say. "D-d-don't."

"What is that?" Hull shouted. "You peddlin' drugs? In *my* school?"

"No, I'm not!" Shawna shot back. "I promise! Please, let me explain—"

Hull's arm shot out, hard, and his forearm hit the spot just below Shawna's throat, and the man pinned Shawna against a locker, her back hitting the metal so hard that it buckled. Moss dropped his lock on the ground, heard it clatter against the tile, and Shawna tried to yelp. All that came out was a strangled and pathetic sound, like the spit had curdled in her mouth.

"Don't lie to me!" Hull yelled.

Mr. Jacobs, stunned for a few seconds, leapt forward and tried to pull Hull's arm off Shawna. "Stop it!" he yelled. "Let him explain!" He caught himself. "Let *her* explain, I mean!"

Moss was pushed, and he banged his elbow on his open locker door, and students poured out around them, some coming from open classroom doors, others from various hallways. The noise rose sharply, echoing, bouncing off the high ceiling and the walls. Moss held on to his locker as he watched students swarm around Officer Hull, Shawna, and Mr. Jacobs. Phones were out. Someone shouted, "Leave her alone!" Mr. Jacobs, terror on his face, raised his arms up in a sign of concession, but then lowered them and tried to push everyone away when he saw things spiraling out of control.

But Moss's focus wasn't on the assistant principal anymore. Hull had pushed his arm into Shawna even harder, had lifted her in the air, and Shawna was struggling to breathe. The yelling pitched higher, and Moss just acted. If he didn't, he knew that his anxiety would consume him. He threw himself forward, toward Hull, and was met with Mr. Jacobs's open palm against his chest. "She can't breathe!" Moss said, and he pushed back as hard as he could. "Stop it!"

Njemile was there, too, screaming at Hull, screaming at Mr. Jacobs, trying to get to her. "Get your hands off her!" Njemile yelled.

They were surrounded. There were so many people that Moss could no longer see anything but bodies. Students were kicking lockers to add to the din. A chair flew overhead and crashed against the space above Shawna's locker. It plummeted to the ground and hit another student, having left a sizable hole in the wall. The screaming collided with itself, bouncing around the quad, amplified in that space, echoes on top of echoes. Yet in all the noise, the next sound was so distinct that the mob quieted, if only for a moment.

Thunk!

Hull had backed off. Shawna was on the floor. Her head had cracked against the tile. She was shaking, twitching on the floor, her eyes rolled up. "What the hell? What the—" Hull never finished what he was saying. Mr. Jacobs shoved him to the side, and he smacked into a couple of kids who had crowded in the hallway.

"What have you done?" Mr. Jacobs shouted, his pale face red, his eyes narrowed in rage.

Moss fell to his knees next to Shawna, but he had no idea what to do. He grabbed her shoulders and tried to keep her from sliding across the floor. "What do I do?" Moss shouted, the beginning of a panic attack swelling in his throat.

Shawna sputtered, and students next to Moss parted, and Mrs. Torrance was there, screaming at Mr. Jacobs, pushing students out of the way, and the crowd let her go by, and she dropped to her hands and knees alongside Moss.

"Give me a piece of clothing," she ordered. "A sweater, something like that!"

The reaction was surreal; at least five kids handed their sweaters or jackets over within a few seconds. She took a couple and balled them up, gently pushing Moss out of the way. Shawna was still shaking; Mrs. Torrance placed one of the sweaters under her head and turned her on to her side. "Stay with me, baby, stay with me," she said softly. No one else was saying a word. There were a few camera phones out, one of them pointed directly at Officer Hull, who watched the scene with a muted horror on his face. His hands were behind his head, his eyes wide, his mouth open.

"Shawna is epileptic," Mrs. Torrance announced, then glanced down at her watch. She slowly pulled down the front of Shawna's shirt, exposing a newly formed welt on her brown skin. "What is this? Who did *this*?"

Shawna stopped shaking, and her eyes focused on Mrs. Torrance's face, her chest rising and falling rapidly. She moved her mouth, but words weren't coming out.

"Don't try to talk yet, honey," said Mrs. Torrance. "You're fine. I am here to help you." She looked back up. "No one answered me. Who did this?"

"He did," said Moss, pointing at Hull, his voice shaking.

"Over these," Mr. Jacobs added, holding up the clear bag. "An ambulance is on its way," he added.

Mrs. Torrance ignored him, turning back to Shawna. "Shawna, honey, you all right?"

It took her a moment, but she nodded.

"Can you talk or would you rather wait?"

She swallowed. "It hurts, Mrs. Torrance."

"What hurts?" She pointed to Shawna's chest. "That?"

"And my head."

"What happened, Shawna? Can you tell me?"

She swallowed again, and then her eyes shot over to Moss. "No, but he saw it," she croaked.

The anxiety spread anew, running from the center of his torso outward as Mrs. Torrance rose off her hands. She looked back at Moss. "Mr. Jeffries, can you tell me what happened?"

He couldn't ignore the staring. He glanced around, and every eye in the place was locked on him. Waiting. Even Mr. Jacobs, who should have been clearing the space out, who should have been acting like he was in charge, looked at Moss.

"He found that bag of pills in Shawna's locker," Moss said, each word a struggle to get out. "Officer Hull, I mean. He thought Shawna was selling drugs or something."

Hull stepped forward, his eyebrows arched, but Mr. Jacobs stuck a hand out. "*Don't,*" he said. "I will deal with you later."

"It broke."

Shawna's voice was hoarse. Moss saw tears form in Shawna's eyes, and his face burned with anger.

"What was that?" said Mrs. Torrance. "What broke?"

She cleared her throat and then wiped her eyes. "My prescription bottle," she said. "It broke this morning. I had to put my meds in that bag."

"Jesus," Mrs. Torrance muttered, and she stood up, moving her dreads out of her face. She strode a few steps to Mr. Jacobs, who took a step back when she got close.

"Get 'em, Mrs. Torrance!" someone from the crowd yelled, but when laughter broke the silence, she raised a hand.

"Everyone get to class," she said. *"Now!"*

As the students started to shuffle away, Moss was close enough to hear what she said to Mr. Jacobs. Her face was wrinkled up, and she leaned in to the assistant principal.

"You are going to fix this."

Moss knelt down next to Shawna, unsure what to do next. Shawna looked over at him. She reached out and grabbed Moss's hand. *Thank you,* she mouthed.

He held Shawna's hand until the paramedics shooed him away.

8

Moss barely heard the front door open. He'd been staring at a scratch on the coffee table in the living room for a long while, and it felt like he'd left his body and was staring down at it from above. The sound of the door creaking open pulled him back, and he shook away the sensation. He looked up at his mother in her postal uniform, and something on his face must have given him up.

"Oh, no, baby," she said, shutting the door quickly. "Did something happen?"

She scrambled over to the couch, dropping her bag on the floor and curling up next to him. He leaned into her and sighed. "I'm fine," he said. "Or I think I am."

"You have another attack?" She ran her hand over his scalp, something she knew helped to calm him down. But he shook his head.

"Actually, *no*," he said. "I feel like I should have. Something awful happened at school today."

He told her everything, only pausing to catch his breath when it felt like too much. He froze up again when he spoke of the holster and the gun, and Wanda pulled him into a hug. By the time he got to the end of the story, though, he didn't feel better. He started shaking, and it unraveled. All of the fear, all of the terror, it spilled out of him along with the tears.

"How can they do that to her?" Moss wailed. "How can they keep getting away with it?"

"Oh, honey," she said, pulling him closer. "I'm so sorry you had to see that. And I hope she's okay."

"It's probably just the start," he whined. "What if they call me next? How am I ever going to survive an interaction like that?"

"Maybe it's time I paid a visit to that school . . ." Wanda said, her forehead wrinkled with concern.

"No, no, Mama, you got enough to deal with," he said. "It's funny . . . you remember Mrs. Torrance? From years ago."

"Sure. She still teach at your school?"

He nodded. "She's my homeroom teacher and I got her for English." He coughed and his mother patted him on the back. "Anyway, she said today, before this all happened, that she wondered how long the school could keep this up. I wouldn't be surprised if they finally gave up on all this after today."

"I don't know, Moss," she said. "You might be surprised at how unwilling people are to turn a critical eye on themselves."

He pulled away from her and wiped at his nose. "I musta just bottled this all up," he said. "You know, my therapist said I shouldn't do this, but it was like . . . Shawna needed help, and I just kept it all inside. I just shoved all of it deep down and *now* look at me."

"I don't think that's a bad thing," she said, and she reached down to her bag to pull out her water flask. She took a sip and offered him some. While Moss gulped it down, his mother continued. "You saw someone else in peril, and you prioritized them. I think you *knew* you could deal with yourself later, so you just pushed your own needs aside to help someone else. I ain't an expert, but that sounds pretty noble to me."

He tried to smile. "Yeah, I guess if you put it that way, it doesn't sound so bad." Moss drank some more water and handed the metal container back to her. "I guess it's just hard to get over the shame."

"What do you mean by that?"

"Well. . . ." He adjusted himself and leaned against the armrest so he could face his mother. "During my last therapy session, I was talking to Constance about how sometimes I hate how emotional I am. How easy it is for me to cry or feel anxious or get upset."

Wanda nodded her head at him. "Sure, I get that. It's like you feel as if all your emotions are right on the surface."

"Exactly!" Moss exclaimed.

"Is that why you get so bothered whenever we figure out what you're thinking?"

That set him back a bit. "Wow," he said. "I guess. I never thought about it that way."

"Maybe I should lay off teasing you about that," she said. "I don't want to make you feel worse."

"No, it really doesn't bother me like that. It's just that sometimes I wish my brain worked like everyone else's. That I could get through the day without the fear of a breakdown looming over me."

She nodded at him again. "Is there anything I can do?"

"Nah, I don't think so," he admitted. "I'm just glad I can talk to you about this stuff. It's . . ." He didn't finish the sentence and his eyes dropped back down to the scratch on the coffee table that he'd stared at before.

"Moss?" Wanda said. "What is it?"

Papa got that table, Moss thought. *He found it at a yard sale down the street.* It was a new card to add to his Rolodex, he realized, and it gave him the courage to say the other thought that had come to him.

"Mama, you still think about Papa anymore?"

Now it was her turn to feel the spotlight. "Sure," she said after a few moments. "It's hard not to. There are reminders of him everywhere."

"Like this table," he said. "I remember when he brought it home, and he whacked it on the front door's knob, and that's how that scratch got there."

She laughed. "Why did he always feel the need to bring home every piece of furniture he found, like they were stray animals?"

"Hey, I wanted him to bring home *actual* stray animals, so imagine my disappointment whenever he'd come home with a *chair.*"

"Why you ask me that, baby?" Wanda leaned into her left hand, propped under her chin.

"I was just thinking," Moss said. "I was gonna say that I was glad I can talk to you because it's . . . well, it's almost like his death brought us closer."

When his mother's eyes went glassy in response, Moss felt his chest heave. "No, no, Mama, I'm sorry! I knew it sounded terrible in my head and that's why I didn't say it."

But she reached out to him after wiping a tear away. "No, baby, do not apologize. You realize how lucky I am that my son is one of my best friends?"

Heat rushed to his face. "Aw, Mama, stop it."

"It's true! I mean, of course I wish your papa was here. I'd give almost anything to have him back. But I wouldn't trade you for him."

The immensity of that swallowed him, and he leaned back into his mother as she rubbed his back, up and down. Moss cried because he missed his father, missed a misguided habit of picking up unowned furniture, missed that silly humor. And he cried because his world was split. He'd been cursed by violence and loss. He'd been blessed with love and support. He couldn't separate them, and he had to learn to live with both.

But Moss could live with all of it as long as his mother was there.

9

Moss and Njemile were getting off at the MacArthur station the next morning when Njemile said, "I declare this year over. Fin. Cerrado. Done." With each word, she threw her hands out in front of her. On the last one, she grabbed Bits's upraised hand, and she spun, her skirt twirling about her body.

"The year *just* started, and I, too, agree that this year is *o-vah*," Bits replied. They turned to Moss and gave him a once-over. "As for Moss's shirt," they began, "I declare that school is *now* in session for Moss's sense of style."

"Thanks, Bits," Moss replied.

"Purple's a good color on you, boo," Bits offered up, and then turned their attention back to dancing with Njemile across the BART platform. When they got to the stairs, Njemile demanded that Bits lift her into the air and they did so, holding her small frame aloft before setting her down. The two frolicked as best as one could frolic in a descent down stairs full of exiting BART riders, and Moss admired the effort.

They walked to school without incident, though Moss would have been hard-pressed to have noticed the detonation of an atom bomb that morning. His thoughts were scattered, jumping from one image to the next, like the Rolodex but without a purpose.

"You're lost," Njemile said to him as they turned onto their school's street.

Moss waved her off with a smile. "Just in thought," he said, "but I'm good. I guess."

Njemile thankfully left him alone, and he was glad his friends knew when not to press him too forcefully. Moss pulled his phone out for perhaps the tenth time that morning, and opened his messages to stare at what Javier had sent that morning:

Can't wait to see u tonite!!

Moss wished that conversation came easy to him, but as he read the text over and over again, every response he came up with sounded like a cliché. *How do people do this?* he wondered. He'd seen Esperanza talk to girls, and the words were so natural to her. She knew how to flirt, knew how to disarm someone with a compliment, and knew how to conquer that initial mountain of awkward that usually defeated him. *Maybe I should just ask her,* he thought. He sent a text to her first: Esperanza, 911, need help talking to boys.

A few seconds later: I'm getting off early. Meet you at WOH when you're off?

He sent her a GIF of Michael Fassbender saying, "Perfection," then went back to his thread with Javier. He stared at it some more. Couldn't he just say that he was excited, too? Was that too much?

He didn't send a reply. His phone went back in his pocket, sitting there like a stone. He'd deal with it later.

"So," Moss said at the first break in the conversation, "anyone hear if Shawna is okay?"

"No, I haven't heard anything yet," Njemile said.

"Poor girl," said Bits.

"You seen the videos yet?" Njemile said. "It was like half my Facebook feed this morning."

"How many?" Moss asked. "I only saw a few phones out yesterday."

"Dude, I've seen *hella* videos so far," replied Njemile. "From like twenty different angles."

"Damn," said Moss.

"Yeah. Are you surprised by that?" she said.

"I guess not," he admitted. "But the administration isn't going to be too happy about it."

"My Snapchat was mostly videos from it," Bits said, shaking their head. "It's too much."

"So what are we gonna do about it?" said Njemile. "I wonder if the principal will mention yesterday at all."

"Is there anything we *can* do?" said Moss. He rubbed his eye with the back of his hand and yawned. "I'm sure they'll find some way to blame Shawna for everything."

"I'm sure it's retaliation, too," said Njemile. "Since she made it difficult for the school, with her name change and all that. I remember how hard Mr. Elliot fought against letting me use the girls' lockers."

"I'm not surprised," said Bits. "Props to you, though, for actually making the school do something about it. I can't imagine talking to Mr. Elliot or anyone about being nonbinary."

Njemile shrugged. "I try not to think about that man. He means nothing to me."

"That doesn't help Shawna, though," Bits said quietly.

"Well, of course not," Moss said. "But we're powerless in this situation, aren't we? Maybe Shawna's parents will sue the district or something."

"I'm sure it won't hurt if we at least *talk* about it to other people," Njemile suggested. "Get a conversation started. They'd listen to you, Moss."

He frowned at her.

"Just *talking*," she'd said. "I mean, there are some kids who respect you, you know. Because—"

"Because my father died?" he said, cutting her off.

She grimaced, and he heard Bits gasp. "No, Moss. I wasn't going to say that," she said.

"It's true, though. Everyone thinks it. And people still tell me, 'Your father died for the cause.'" He shook his head. "Man, I'd rather have my father back than further some damn cause."

Njemile and Bits kept their eyes downward when Moss looked at them. They were quiet for a full block before Njemile cleared her throat. "Because you're a good friend," she said.

"What?"

"That's why kids respect you," she said. "You're a nice person, Moss."

"She's not wrong," said Bits, flashing Moss with a rare smile.

"Shit," he said. "I'm sorry for that, then."

"No big deal," said Njemile. "I can see why you thought I was gonna say that."

"But how is that supposed to help Shawna?" Moss asked. He turned off the sidewalk to take a shortcut over the front lawn to the steps into the school. No one said anything, so he spun around to walk backward and talk with his friends. "It's out of our hands."

They weren't paying attention to him. They were all motionless, staring behind Moss.

When he turned back around, he saw the cops at the top of the steps. None of them were Hull. All new faces, all set like stone, all surveying the students as they entered. They said nothing. Did nothing. They just stood there.

"Y'all," said Njemile. "What is *that*?"

"Maybe just to intimidate us," said Bits.

"Where's Hull?" Moss said. "You think he's gone?"

"I hope so," said Njemile. "Though I feel like having one cop permanently on campus is a lot better than . . . well, *that*."

"Let's just get to class before the bell rings," said Moss. Without another word, the three of them made their way up the steps. They passed single file between the cops—six in number, Moss counted. Their eyes washed over their bodies, inspecting them, but they didn't otherwise budge.

"Can we retire this whole week?" Njemile said once they got indoors.

Before any of them could answer, they heard the unfortunate ring of the bell that signaled that they were indeed going to be late. As they rushed off to their homerooms, Njemile grabbed Moss's arm. "Talk to someone," she reminded him. "*Anyone.* You should."

Seconds later, they both entered Mrs. Torrance's classroom. She scowled at him briefly, but otherwise said nothing. He scrambled to his normal seat next to Njemile and sat, pulling out his tattered copy of *Things Fall Apart.* He hoped that if he seemed busy, Mrs. Torrance wouldn't say anything to him.

"Didn't do last night's reading, Mr. Jeffries?"

He sighed, lowering the book. "Long night," he said. "I'll get it done, I promise."

At that, a few other students rustled in their bags and took out their books or reading devices, too, and a roll of laughter rumbled through the room.

"As long as y'all are reading, I'm happy," Mrs. Torrance said, and she began to take attendance. Moss watched her look over the classroom and settle on the lone empty seat in the back. His heart sank; it was where Shawna usually sat, both in homeroom and in AP English. Mrs. Torrance grimaced. "What a shame," she said under her breath.

"What's gonna happen to her?" Njemile asked.

Mrs. Torrance shook her head. "I don't know, Njemile," she said. "It's hard to say. Miss Stephanie in the front office stopped me this morning to tell me to pay attention to the morning announcements. Apparently, Mr. Elliot is going to address it."

Someone groaned loudly behind Moss. He looked back and saw that Carmela had her hand up. Mrs. Torrance called on her.

"Like, why do we even have to deal with this kinda stuff?" she asked. "My cousin goes to North. She don't got cops choking students. And Mr. Barre handed us all copies of textbooks." She reached into her bag, yanked out a stack of paper, and plopped it down on her desk. "This is what I gotta study from." It looked a lot like the one Moss had been given by his biology teacher.

Maybe this is my chance to talk about this, Moss thought. He raised his hand, and Mrs. Torrance pointed at him. "Yeah, and someone broke into the lab over the summer," he added, sitting up straight, speaking with confidence, "so we gotta share equipment. Like ten students to one set."

He saw a grim face settle on Mrs. Torrance, and he was certain she was irritated with him. But she looked about the class again. "Okay, let's talk about this," she said. "At least before Mr. Elliot comes on. Who else?"

"There are the stains everywhere," said Larry. "What is that stuff? It's all over the ceiling."

"Our school is old," said Mrs. Torrance.

"So is Piedmont High," said Moss, an electricity leaping through him. "So is Berkeley High. Aren't they both older than us?"

His teacher nodded. "Indeed. So why is our campus the way it is? Anyone know?"

"Money?" said Njemile, more a question than a certainty. "We just don't have any money."

"Because of those test things," Larry added. "We didn't do good, so they took money from us."

"It doesn't quite work that way," said Mrs. Torrance. "It's not that they took it *away* from us. We just got less of it for anything that *isn't* test preparation."

"But why?" said Moss, his energy turning to frustration. "That doesn't make any sense. Shouldn't they want to give us a better chance to improve test scores?"

"You would think so," said Mrs. Torrance. "But the system isn't set up that way."

It always began in his chest, a swelling anxiety that blossomed through his veins, gripped his heart, spread up his spine, pressed against his eyes, the pressure often morphing into a migraine. Anger. It was that same unwanted tourist most days, not because Moss saw no need for it, but because he was tired of it consuming him so often. The conversation turned to other topics: Team cancellations. Broken doors and windows. The way the water in the girls' locker room never came out clear. He listened as best as he could, trying to even out his breathing, but each new detail pushed him further into himself, more convinced than ever before that all of his self-doubt and hatred was the only world he would ever know. They couldn't change any of this.

Mr. Elliot's voice on the loudspeaker yanked him back, though.

He knew he could get lost within his thoughts too easily, and he wondered if he should talk to his therapist about it next month.

He focused on the words coming out of the gray box up above the peeling whiteboard.

"Good morning, students," the principal said. His voice was cheerful, *too* cheerful, really. "Welcome to our first Friday of the school year, and the Associated Student Body would like to remind each of you that elections will be in three weeks. In the meantime, nominations conclude next Wednesday, so if you would like to represent your class in any of the positions available, please declare your intent in the front office by then."

The voice paused, and Moss heard papers rustling in the background. No one in his homeroom said a word, and he glanced over at Njemile, who was chewing on one of her nails. He looked at Mrs. Torrance, who stood next to her desk, her right hand gripping it so tight that he could see the muscles flexing in her arm.

"Now," said Mr. Elliot, his voice far away at first, then closer. "I am proud of the quick response of some of our faculty members yesterday during the unfortunate altercation on campus."

This time, it was Mrs. Torrance who groaned. The class bristled in response. "'Altercation'?" she said, her words laced with acid. "That's what you're calling it?"

"We believe the safety of students at West Oakland High is of the utmost importance. Therefore, we wanted to let all of our students know that Officer Hull has been let go."

Moss heard clapping, a few whoops of celebration, and saw surprise on Mrs. Torrance's face. She held up a hand. "Quiet down," she said. "He's pausing for a reason."

As if Mr. Elliot knew there'd be a response to that, he didn't say anything for a few beats. "Now," he said. "We will be instituting a new policy for medications, starting today. You must register all medications with the school nurse, who will set up distribution throughout the day. Please stop by the office and speak with Miss Stephanie in order to set up an appointment."

Mr. Elliot cleared his throat, and the awkward silence that followed felt wrong. Unnerving. *He's not done, is he?* Moss thought. More papers rustling. Silence again. Mr. Elliot coughed. "I want to reiterate that we here at West Oakland High do not tolerate anything that risks the safety of our student body. Many students filmed yesterday's altercation and posted these videos all over social media. By the end of next week, I will announce our new policy for cell phones on campus."

Moss knew that Mr. Elliot was aware that this would not go over well. He paused again, as if he were speaking to everyone in the school's auditorium and leaving time for the groans and jeers. "And finally," he said, and he kept clearing his throat, each crackle of static a jolt of terror in Moss's body, "in order to guarantee a safe environment for all here at West Oakland High, I have signed our school up in a pilot program with the Oakland Police Department to install metal detectors at the main entrance."

The din that rose around Moss was overwhelming. Someone must have been in the office where Mr. Elliot made the announcements, because a young voice rang out in shock. "Are you *serious?*" the kid said.

It was chaos in Mrs. Torrance's room. Her face drooped; she looked numb. She must have been, because she wasn't trying to regain control in the class. Larry was swearing at the top of his lungs, and Njemile grabbed Moss's arm. "He can't be serious, can he?" she shouted. "What are we? Prisoners?"

He couldn't respond to her. His rage simmered beneath the surface.

He was going through the motions. There wasn't a class that day that wasn't sidelined by the morning's announcement. Mrs. Torrance hosted yet another discussion in her English class, instead of working on an essay she had assigned for the following week. No one seemed able to concentrate. "*Metal detectors?*" Kaisha had said.

"Yep," said Njemile. "That's our life now."

"I still can't get over it. Is Reg even going to be able to go through them?"

Moss slapped his forehead. "Damn, I didn't even think of that. When do you see him next?"

"We got precalc together," she said. "I'll ask him about his knee, but I can't imagine those pins *won't* set it off every day."

"And you know they're gonna hassle him about it *every* time," he said, shaking his head. "I don't expect we'll get reassigned a cop *better* than Officer Hull."

She clicked her tongue against her teeth, but said nothing.

"Should we do something about this?" Njemile asked. "Maybe meet up with some other people and at least talk about it. Bounce some ideas around and stuff."

"I dunno," said Moss. "Maybe. I don't know if we should draw attention to ourselves, though. Won't Mr. Jacobs or Mr. Elliot target us next?"

"I wouldn't put it past them," said Kaisha. "Think about it, though. I'll reach out to Reg."

"I could invite Esperanza, too," Moss said.

"Perfect!" Kaisha exclaimed. "Should someone invite Shawna? I feel like she might need a gripe session more than us."

"That's a good idea, but I don't really know her," said Moss.

"I got y'all," said Njemile. "Girls like us gotta stick together, so I'll see if she wants to come. Where could we meet?"

"Yo, let's go back to Farley's over on Grand," said Moss. "You know the spot, right? Next to the Ethiopian place?" They nodded at him. "Twelve on Saturday sound good to you?"

They agreed and then parted for the next period. Moss still wasn't sure if it would *do* anything, but he quietly knew it would be nice to get the whole squad together. Moss made his way to Mr. Riordan's American history class, while sending texts to both Esperanza and Rawiya. Thankfully, he was able to zone out for nearly a full hour while Riordan droned on about the colonies. Riordan never seemed to be interested in anything happening on campus that took place outside that classroom, and it seemed like he didn't even notice that not one person was paying attention.

The bell rang for lunch, and the room emptied in what felt like record time. Moss didn't feel much like socializing, so he pulled an apple out of his bag that he'd grabbed on the way out the door that morning. He wandered past the quad while munching on it and headed for the east wing to see if the college reps had decided to stick around until lunchtime this year. Even though the school's library was just one story and little more than a single room, Mrs. Hernandez had packed it full. Books balanced precariously on top of shelves, and there was a tall stack with bright, frayed covers next to her desk. She greeted Moss and turned back to helping a student with a large armful that they'd spilled over the counter. He dropped the half-eaten apple in the trash, his stomach rumbling. Moss wasn't as hungry as he thought.

The main area wasn't full of its usual students studying. The collection of tables and chairs had been rearranged into a basic U shape around the room, and multiple colleges had set up their displays on them. Each had two or three people manning a table, many of them lost in conversations with prospective students. While the turnout of West Oakland High attendees was higher than Moss expected, an unease crept through him. He saw the booth for Laney College, the community college that sat south of Lake Merritt. There was one for Merritt College, another for Holy Names, one for Contra Costa College. He made a full pass before he realized that there were some names missing.

No one from UC Berkeley. No one from Cal State East Bay. No one from SF State or UCSF. There was not one major university or college in the room. He passed by the front desk on his way out, and Mrs. Hernandez flagged him down. She pulled her long black hair back into a ponytail. "Couldn't find a book, Moss?" she said. "You know I know where everything is."

"I wouldn't dream of doubting you," he said. "Nah, I was just . . . I dunno, a little disappointed. That's all."

She lowered her voice. "We got even less than last year," she said.

"None of the academies even showed up this time around." She sighed. "If you need help with any of the state schools, you could always swing by here later."

"Thanks, Mrs. Hernandez," he said. "I'll keep you in mind."

He wandered back out of the library. It wasn't that he was surprised that things at his school were getting worse. He wasn't naive. Things just felt so *obvious* now, as if he couldn't push it into the background and ignore it.

He had the same thought as he sat on the front steps of the school that afternoon, waiting for Esperanza to show up. She was late, so he pulled his phone out again. *Maybe I shouldn't wait to hear her advice,* he thought, and he sent off a quick reply to Javier.

See u tonight. Be there around 7.

He ran his hands over the edge of the concrete steps out of habit, but it immediately felt wrong. He was so used to the specific ridges of Dawit's shop that this was like wearing someone else's clothes or putting your shoes on the wrong feet.

Esperanza walked up to him a few minutes later, a wide smile on her face and a pale folder clutched in her arms. "Sorry, Moss! Turns out I couldn't read my own schedule, cuz I definitely thought that I didn't have a sixth period on Fridays."

"It's okay," he said. "I haven't been waiting long."

She sat down next to him. "Ugh, what a week," she said. "Sorry I haven't texted you much."

"I know! I have so much to tell you."

"Me too," she said. "I have too many of these things to fill out, though."

He peeked over at the folder. "What *are* those?"

"College applications," she said. "I know, I know, we don't actually send them out until next year, but my parents want me to practice now."

"Y'all had a college fair today, too?"

"Yeah! I wish they gave us more time, though. I had a billion questions, and I feel like maybe five of them got answered."

"At least you got to talk to someone," he said. "Ours was terrible. Maybe like eight colleges showed up."

"That's not so bad," she said. "I mean, there aren't *that* many major universities here, and the big ones kinda dominate it all."

"Well, you wouldn't be able to tell if you were there today. It was kinda pathetic."

She bristled next to him. "That bad, huh?"

"Tell me," he said, turning to her. "Who were the top five schools who came to your fair?"

"Well, the obvious ones, I guess," she said. "Berkeley, UCSF, San Francisco State, Mills . . ." She stopped listing them. "Oh. Lemme guess. None of them showed up here, right?"

"Bingo," he said. "So it's not even like we get a chance to learn about them in the first place."

"Maybe there just haven't been a lot of people who have applied to those schools that come from West Oakland," she said gingerly. "Maybe there's just not a lot of interest."

He furrowed his brows at her. "Well, not if they never show up here."

"*Never?*" She shrugged. "I don't know, maybe they used to but no one paid attention to them. You could still apply yourself, though."

He felt a vicious urge to argue with her rise in him, but he pushed it down. What was she trying to say? He knew he was sensitive about this stuff, but it sounded like she was trying to blame the students for the lack of schools at the college fair. *Maybe you're overthinking this,* he told himself.

"So what was this boy stuff you wanted to talk about?" Esperanza said, changing the topic and the tone.

A pettiness came over him. He suddenly didn't want to talk to her about it. "Oh, it's okay," he said. "I just needed help figuring out something to say to Javier, but I got it figured out."

"No way! How's that going?"

"It's okay," he said. "We're just chatting at this point. He seems cool."

"You guys gonna hang out soon?"

He made the decision in an instant. "Nah, I don't think so. But I hope we get there!" He stood up and dusted off his jeans. "I gotta head home and shower. You taking BART or walking home?"

"No, my mom's gonna get me from a coffee shop up the street." She examined him a bit. "You sure everything's okay?"

He nodded. "I'll text you later. We'll talk."

"Good," she said. "I look forward to it, Moss. I've missed you this week."

Guilt surged in him, so the next words out of his mouth were the truth. "Yeah, I missed you, too."

"We're still on for tomorrow, right? At Farley's?"

"Yeah! I don't really know what we're gonna do besides rant, but it could be good."

They hugged, and Moss headed toward the train station, eager to get home and start getting ready, shoving aside any creeping suspicions he had about his best friend. *Later,* Moss thought. *I'll deal with it later.*

10

Moss pulled apart the blinds to see the sun disappearing on the horizon. If he climbed up onto the roof, he could see it slink behind Marin and the Golden Gate Bridge in the next few minutes, but he had somewhere to be. Someone to see.

He packed his Chrome bag with his U-lock, a pair of gloves, and a copy of *Overwatch*. Javier hadn't played it, and even though it was a single-player game, Moss was a bit obsessed with it and wanted *everyone* to play it. He slung the bag over his shoulder, and then adjusted it into place while staring in the mirror attached to his closet. He straightened out his shirt so that it fell into place beyond the waist of his jeans. He'd exhausted himself before his shower with push-ups, hoping they bulked up his chest, but now he was just sore and tired.

Stop criticizing your body, he said. He adjusted the V-neck again and then turned away from the mirror. If he stayed there, this could last for hours, and he couldn't let his mind convince itself that this wasn't worth it.

He sighed, anxiety coursing in his chest and stomach, the fear of rejection hanging in his mind. As far as Moss could tell, Javier enjoyed him through text, but he was so afraid that he'd hear those damning words again: "I'm just not into you like that." It wouldn't be the first time, though he supposed it wasn't as bad as when his first crush said they couldn't date because he didn't normally date black guys.

I'm gonna have to have that conversation with him, he thought, and it sank in his stomach. Had Javier ever dated a black guy? Was he just an experiment to him, something exotic to try on for size?

Moss set his concerns aside for the moment. He put the maroon cap on his head, adjusted it so that it sat perfectly, tilted just a bit to the side.

"You headin' out?"

His mother's voice rang out from the living room, and Moss sighed again. His body wouldn't change while he stood there, so he knew he had to let it go. He grabbed his phone from his desk and headed out of his room, switching the lights off as he went.

He fired off a quick text to Javier as he walked up to his mother: On my way. Biking over. See ya soon.

Moss looked up to see his mother staring at him, a slight smile on her face. "What?" he said, returning the expression.

"You're wearing that hat," she replied.

He felt heat on his cheeks. "Mama, I *swear*, you know too much about me."

She rose from the couch, laughing, and swallowed him up in a hug. "Be safe, baby," she told him, then pulled away from him to look at his face. "You are gonna be more handsome than your father, I swear."

Moss raised an eyebrow at her.

"Sorry, you just got me thinking 'bout him, that's all." She returned to the couch and picked up a book she'd been reading, something by Octavia Butler. "You got your lights?"

"Yeah, Mama. And my lock."

"You be back here by ten, okay?"

"Promise," he replied, moving to open the door. He paused before doing so, and said quietly, almost as if he were speaking to the door itself, "Thanks, Mama."

They exchanged grins, and nothing more was said.

Moss slammed his legs down as hard as he could, his quads burning, and sped through the intersection of Lakeshore and 18th, avoiding the red light. The chain whirred beneath him, and Moss felt free.

He'd picked up biking a couple of years earlier, not by virtue of its popularity, but out of necessity. Esperanza's house, on the northern end of Piedmont, wasn't near any of the BART stations, and Moss could only tolerate so much of the bus.

So now he zoomed past Lake Merritt, thankful for the wide and smooth bike lanes, the wind threatening to tear his hat from his head. He frowned as the light ahead of him flashed yellow, and Moss braked as hard as he could. This light always took forever, so he pulled out his phone from a pouch on the shoulder strap of his bag. Nothing from Javier yet, so he sent another update.

10 mins away.

As he shoved the phone back in its pouch, he wondered if he was already texting too much. The light turned green, and Moss received a curt honk from behind him. "Sorry!" he yelled, and then pushed off from the ground, pedaling through the intersection.

Maybe I'm being too hard on myself, he thought. As he continued toward MacArthur, he realized that if Javier had no interest, wouldn't he have canceled? If he didn't want to be alone with Moss, wouldn't he have invited Moss to a group activity? Moss wanted to trust his instincts, but that was the problem with his cynicism. His instincts always veered toward disaster.

He hooked a sharp right to climb up MacArthur. He floated out of his seat to mash up the growing hill in front of him and felt a bolt of nervous energy in his stomach. What if Javier wanted more than playing video games that evening?

Moss, stop it, he told himself. *Don't get your hopes up. He doesn't want you.*

Moss pursed his lips at this, and cursed himself silently for the way his mind always went to the worst possible conclusion. *If Javier didn't like you at all,* he reasoned with himself, *why would he be so excited to have you over?*

Is *he excited? Aren't you reading too much into this?*

Moss wiped a trickle of sweat off his temple before it rolled all the way down his face, returning to his seat now that he'd crested the hill. The traffic on the 580 parallel to him roared, a patchwork of red and white lights. He got lost in the ride, focusing on the cars around him so that he didn't get hit, pedaling as fast as he could. He did slow down a few blocks from Javier's house, though, because his mother's voice popped in his head: *Moss, where is your helmet?*

"Oh, hell," he said out loud. *Just this one time. I gotta look good for this dude.* He smiled as he took his last turn and pulled into the tiny driveway alongside Javier's house.

His mother had considered moving into this neighborhood at one time, and she said that it reminded her of Los Angeles. "It's like our version of Leimert Park," she had told him. The houses were like giant boxes of candy here, multicolored, bright, some even obnoxiously neon. The neighborhood had not a single chain store in it. His favorite pupusería was down the street, as was the Ethiopian spot his mother frequented. The neighborhood was familiar here, which eased his fear as he walked up to Javier's house.

It was a duplex, yellow with green trim, that stood squarely on the corner, a rusted chain-link fence surrounding it. The mesh sagged in certain places where it had come loose from its posts, a victim of the kids who used the yard to play soccer. The yard was packed thick with a dry bed of sand-like dirt. There was a dilapidated swing set at one end of the yard, towels and jeans hanging from it. Moss watched them blow in the light breeze for a bit before hopping off his bike and wheeling it up the steps to the front door.

He pulled open the screen door and was met with the sound of a child giggling from the back of the house. Javier and his mother lived upstairs, above a Guatemalan family that Javier had warned him about. "The dad's real nosy," he had told him over text. "But he's harmless."

Sure enough, the father stuck his head out of the door to his apartment upon hearing the screen open. Moss nodded to him, and the man waved back, disappearing into his own home. Moss hoisted his bike up on his right shoulder and ascended the stairs, glancing at the posters for concerts and plays from decades past in San Francisco. There was an old ad for Prince at The Stone in '81 that Moss immediately wanted to steal for his mother, but, aside from not wanting to offend the building's owner, Moss knew he'd probably just end up keeping it for himself anyway.

By the time he got to the top of the creaky wooden stairs, Moss realized that Javier was standing at the top, waiting for him. He was wearing a black tank that clung tightly to his chest, showing off his fine brown skin, and Moss felt a pang of envy at how well it fit. But the feeling disappeared as Javier reached for Moss's bike, taking it from him as he said, "It's good to see you. Thanks for coming over!"

"Good to see you, too," Moss replied, wiping more sweat away. He removed his hat to find a thick sheen of sweat there, too. Javier had set Moss's bike down against the wall in the entryway and was now staring at Moss.

"You look hot," he said.

Moss felt that nervous energy return. "Well, yeah," he replied. "Lots of hills. You got a towel or something?"

Javier disappeared around a corner for a few seconds before returning with a hand towel. "That's not what I meant," he said, grinning, after handing the towel to Moss.

"Oh yeah?" As Moss wiped the sweat away, he realized that Javier was still staring at him, an eyebrow raised, a subtle look of amusement on his face, his beanie placed crookedly on his head.

Oh, he thought.

"Oh!" he said out loud. "Really?"

Javier gave a slight nod, then licked his lips before saying, "Moss, come meet my mamá," and he gestured toward the kitchen. A shorter woman threw a dish towel on the counter and walked over to him, smiling. Her hair was pulled back tightly, and Moss could see the resemblance. Javier and his mother had the same flat, wide noses, the same deep brown eyes. "Mamá, this is Moss."

She held a hand out gingerly. "Hola, Moss," she said, her accent giving his name a softness, "it's nice to meet you. Eugenia."

"Nice to meet you, too," he said. "Thanks for having me over." He glanced behind her, saw the pile of dishes in the sink. "Necesitas ayuda?"

"Oh, no, no, it's okay," she said. "I got it." She gave him a look. "Unless you *want* to."

He laughed. "Put me to work," he said. He slipped off his shoes next to a neat line of them by the door, then put his Chrome bag down on a chair in the small dining room. "I got *Overwatch* in the bag," he told Javier. "Go ahead and load it up!"

"Already trying to win my mother over," Javier said, grinning from ear to ear. "Smart move, Moss. Smart move."

Moss pulled on the rubber gloves above the sink and began to scour one of the pots that sat next to the sink. "What did you cook in this?" he asked. "Ms. . . ."

"Perez," she said, coming to stand near him in the kitchen. "Un guisado, like . . . a stew? Soup?" She shook her head. "Stew. That's the word."

"Smells good," he said. "Or at least what's left of it."

"So you go to school con mi hijo?"

"Nah," said Moss. "I'm up at West Oakland High. We just met on the train last weekend."

"Oh, okay." She went silent as Moss moved on to the next dish, and it was the first burst of awkwardness. He wasn't sure how to *do* this. Why weren't there how-to guides on dealing with a cute guy's *mother*?

"Are you two . . ." She paused, and Moss turned to see her wrestle with a word, then look at him with certainty. ". . . dating?"

He nearly dropped the plate he was holding. "Oh, no, I don't think so," he said, his voice shaking a bit. "At least not yet. This is our first time hanging out, since we only met last weekend."

This seemed to please her, and she smiled at Moss. "Okay. Entiendo."

"Are you harassing him already?" Javier came into the kitchen. He'd changed into a red shirt with some writing on the front that Moss couldn't read. "He just got here, Mamá."

She laughed, and it was a high, joyful sound. "Just getting to know him, that's all. Thank you for doing the dishes, Moss. It is very kind of you, and is the best way to 'win me over.'" She made quotes with her fingers.

"See? I know what I'm doing, Javier."

Eugenia walked over to her son and he bent down so she could kiss him on the cheek. "Have a good time," she told him. "And behave. De vuelta en una hora."

As she headed out the door, Moss asked, "Where is she going?"

"Just picking up some dinner for us," he said. "The stew was for a get-together she hosted last night for her church friends. Plus, I suspect she wants to give us *some* privacy tonight."

"For *what*?"

"She's a bit new to this whole part of me," Javier admitted. "I only came out to her a few months ago, and . . . well, you're the first guy I've liked that she's ever met."

"Well . . . wow," said Moss. *I guess that's a good sign,* he thought.

"So feel special! You need anything to drink?"

"Yeah, yeah," he said, walking into the living room. "Water's good."

He watched Javier's tall and lanky body from the couch, mesmerized by the way he moved. A streetlight outside the nearest window to the left cast stripes through the blinds onto Javier's skin while he was in the kitchen, crossing over his shoulders and down his arms. He glowed. All this served to make Moss even *more* nervous, and he almost wished that Javier's mother was home soon.

Almost.

When Javier sat down, his hand fell to Moss's leg, where he gave it a gentle squeeze before bringing it back to his own controller. "So, amigo," Javier said, "how was your day? School started this week, right?"

Pushing aside the desire to giggle about being touched by Javier, Moss gulped and answered him. "Eh, it was okay. A bit too eventful for my taste."

He watched as Javier tried to figure out the game options, eventually settling on a practice round. But Moss was only half paying attention, not only because he knew the game backward and forward, but because he couldn't seem to focus with Javier next to him, the other boy's leg just inches from his own.

"Eventful? What do you mean by that?"

Moss grimaced. "Just . . . lots of stuff going on," he said, committing to a more vague explanation. "How's school for you?"

"Boring and *un*eventful," Javier said, choosing Tracer for his first round in the game.

"Cool," Moss said, instantly realizing what a terrible (and *uncool*) reply that was. Desperate to recover, Moss said the first thing that came to mind, which happened to be:

"So, you guys got lockers at your school?"

At this, Javier turned to Moss. "Um . . . yes? Why do you ask?"

"Ah, nothing. Just that our school is doing this thing and having them randomly searched and stuff."

"Like . . . how random?"

"I don't know," Moss replied. "I'm convinced that they're gonna make it through the whole student body by the end of the month. Don't they do that down at Eastside?"

"Not really. Things aren't so bad at my school, I guess. Why are they doing it where you are?"

"I dunno. It sucks. I mean, it's not like I have anything to hide, but I feel like my school just hates everyone who goes there. Like they want to make everything as miserable as possible for us."

The battlefield roared to life on the television, and Moss laughed as Javier began to jump Tracer around the screen, shooting at every object in the waiting room he was stuck in. He stole a glance at Javier, whose concentrated expression seemed a little angry. Without so much as turning his head, Javier said, "I'm glad I don't go to your school, then," which made Moss think, *That's too bad. I'd like to see you there.* "Of course," Javier continued, "that would mean I could be distracted by your presence all day if I did."

Moss nearly choked, and Javier laughed.

"Why are you so nervous, Moss?"

"I'm not ner—" he started to say.

"You were the second you walked into my house."

At that, Moss reached over and paused the game, fixing Javier with a searing look.

"Moss, I have to unpause the game or I'm going to die in like a second," Javier said, and he laughed.

"I'm not . . . *nervous*," Moss said with impatience. "I'm just . . . I'm just not used to this."

"Really? Am I your first real date, too?"

"*Is* this a date?" Moss questioned.

"You know, I don't actually know what counts." A bashfulness came over Javier, and Moss appreciated that he wasn't the only vulnerable one in the room. "I've talked to a few guys online, maybe exchanged a few risqué texts, but . . . yeah, man, this is new to me, too."

Moss threw his hands up in the air as he let out a breath of relief. "Honestly, this makes this so much easier," he said. "I'm always so anxious and I'd, like, convinced myself that you'd dated a ton of guys before me."

"Why didn't you just *ask* me?"

"What, in front of your *mom*?"

"Ha, not what I meant, but I'm sure she would have keeled over if you had."

"I don't know!" Moss exclaimed. "I don't know how close you are with her!"

"Well, would you tell me you found me attractive in front of *your* mom?"

Moss thought about that for a second and said, "Actually, yeah. We're pretty close."

"My mom doesn't give me a hard time for being gay or anything, but we sort of keep most of it to ourselves." He leaned over to nudge Moss with his shoulder. "She *does* like you, though." A smile spread across Javier's face, showing off his straight teeth, which Moss found inexplicably hot. *That's new.*

"Really?" Moss said. "She likes *me*?"

"It's only a theory, but that whole dishwashing thing was like . . . the most crucial thing you could have done to win her over. I wasn't joking. I think she just doesn't want me to like a total jerk."

Well, this is unexpected, Moss thought.

"You're pleased with yourself, aren't you?" Javier said. "Oh my god, you totally are."

Moss frowned. "Damn it, am I *seriously* that obvious? Why does everyone always seem to know what I'm thinking?"

Javier laughed, his eyes lighting up, and Moss wanted so badly to kiss him at that moment. "You're very. . . ." He paused. "You're expressive, Moss. It's like . . . your face says a lot in a very short amount of time."

"Is that so?"

"Yeah, because I get the sense you would like to kiss me."

Moss laughed at that, a full roar that ended when he clamped his hand over his mouth. Javier looked briefly hurt, but Moss reached out and rubbed Javier's leg. "Oh, I'm sorry I reacted like that," he said. "I absolutely want to kiss you, but you are just so *extra*, man."

Javier beamed. "My mamá says I should be an actor because I'm so dramatic." He paused. "Are you sure you're okay with this? We don't really know each other well. We kinda *just* met."

Moss knew it was time for him to be bold. "Just shut up and hold still."

He leaned forward and pressed his lips against Javier's. They were soft, full, and as Moss tilted his head to the side, he felt Javier's tongue gently run across his own lips, and then Javier's hand moved to Moss's leg, and the electricity spread along his spine, into his hands, and he found his own hand clasped over Javier's, feeling Javier's smooth skin with his fingertips. He didn't know any other way he could describe this sensation except to say that it felt *right*, as if he was *always* supposed to do this.

Javier pulled away, and Moss lost himself briefly in those eyes, those eyes that were so dark that in dimmer light, they could have been black. "Wow," said Moss. "That was my first kiss."

"You okay?" Javier asked, his eyes searching Moss for an answer.

Moss smiled, genuine joy filling his face, and said, "Yeah. Yeah, I'm okay."

Javier set the controller down and pulled Moss to him, into his chest, and Moss spun slowly over so that he was looking up at Javier's face. Javier had an arm looped over his chest, his fingers gently exploring Moss's left arm. Moss was still nervous, though the energy came from excitement instead of fear. It was the excitement of possibility, because Moss had never been touched like this by another guy, had never felt like someone could even think about him this way, so he just closed his eyes and existed right in that very moment, Javier's hands exploring him.

One hand ran down Moss's chest, lightly, fingertips just grazing his T-shirt. When Javier got to Moss's stomach, Moss reached up and directed the hand back toward his chest. "Not yet," he said. "Please."

"So, we should turn the game off, right?" said Javier.

"Oh, no," he said. "We can keep playing if you want!" Moss started to lift himself away from Javier, but Javier held him down with his right hand.

"No, stay. Like that."

Moss smiled, bashful. Javier turned the TV off, and he could see himself and Javier reflected in the screen, the light from the streetlamp falling on them both, covering them in shadows and bars of brightness. Javier began to run his hand along Moss's short-cropped hair, and then dug his fingers in, scratching, and Moss found it relaxing and soothing.

"Tell me," Javier said, "what you're going to do."

"About what?" Moss said, his voice quiet, calm.

"About your locker predicament."

"Well, a bunch of my friends and I are gonna meet at a coffee shop tomorrow and vent, but . . . I really don't think anything will come of it?"

"You're just going to let your school treat y'all like prisoners?"

"What *can* I do, man? It's not like we have the power to change anything. We live in Oakland, this is how it is. It's nothing new. No one trusts us." He closed his eyes, not to get lost in thought, but to quell the rising anger within him. *No, Moss,* he told himself. *Not now.* "Why are you so interested in this anyway?"

"Don't you care?"

"I guess, but . . . caring is all I *can* do."

Javier was silent.

Now Moss sat up, staring directly into Javier's dark eyes. "Okay, *what*? Tell me what you're thinking."

"I said something wrong, didn't I?" he asked.

Moss dismissed him with a hand wave. "Nah, it's no big deal. You're fine. It's just a sensitive subject, you know? What with my dad and protests and stuff."

Javier gripped Moss's hand tightly. "Sorry, I'll change the subject. We don't have to talk about this." While Moss was instantly relieved, part of him worried that he'd just pushed Javier away. *Am I ever going to be normal? Why do I always feel so wrong?*

But Javier pulled Moss to him again, only this time they faced each other, and Javier brought them back down on the couch. He wrapped his leg around Moss's and squeezed his hand. Moss felt moisture and thought his palms had started sweating again, but it was Javier's sweat this time. Moss went still, and he could feel Javier's heart beating against his chest.

It was racing even faster than Moss's was.

The two enjoyed the warmth of each other's bodies, and Moss realized something for the first time: It was possible for someone to *like* him. Maybe this wouldn't last; Moss didn't have that much faith in himself. But Moss believed in this single moment. He believed that Javier enjoyed him on his couch, in his arms, and in his life. For the moment.

They pulled away from each other when they heard the sound of the front door unlocking, but Moss still stayed close sitting up. He looked to Eugenia, who came into the foyer carrying two large plastic bags. He darted up to help her, and she thanked him. "What have you two been up to?" Eugenia asked. "You got that guilty look on your face, mijo."

"We have been perfect angels," said Moss, putting the food on the counter near the stove. "We were just . . . getting to know each other."

She looked to her son. He nodded at her, then looked to Moss. "Just talking about school and some stuff Moss is dealing with."

"What stuff?" Javier's mother gave Moss a suspicious look.

He started telling her about the lockers as she unpacked the Styrofoam containers, the smell of pupusas and frijoles and rice filling the room, and he realized that he had dreamed of something like this. Maybe the details were different, and maybe he hadn't anticipated the strangeness of meeting a boy's mother on their first date (if he could even call it that), but this comfort he had . . . he had wanted this for a long time.

11

"I hope people actually show up," Moss said, shuffling from one foot to the other. He and Esperanza stood outside of Farley's, and Moss felt more nervous than he had in a long time. Esperanza reached out and grabbed his arm, steadying him.

"Moss, stop moving. You're making *me* nervous," she said.

"Sorry, sorry, I can't help it," he said. "You know me: always thinking of the worst."

"Well, if no one does, we could do some sort of petition thing at the farmer's market instead," Esperanza offered. Moss leveled a look at her that made her laugh. "Okay, I know what you're going to say."

"That it's a terrible idea?"

"Well, not in general, but yeah. No one who goes to that market is going to care about metal detectors in West Oakland."

"For such a huge group of bougie hippies, they sure don't care about much of anything," Moss said. "Remember when we tried to have that fund-raiser for Reg?"

Esperanza groaned and nodded. They had set up a table on the corner of Grand and MacArthur and stacked it high with every Tupperware container they had between the four of them. Kaisha's mother had baked brownies and cookies all night, and their little fund-raiser lasted ten minutes before they were ordered to move. A younger woman who couldn't have been a few years older than them had said that without a proper permit, they couldn't be associated with the farmer's market.

"But it's for our friend's surgery!" Kaisha had exclaimed, gesturing to Reg, who was in a wheelchair at the time. "He needs it badly."

The woman had made a face. "Well, you're not going to make much money for him anyway," she said. "You should probably go across the street and sell it in the park."

"How much is a permit?" Esperanza quizzed.

"More than you can afford," the woman shot back, giving them a smile that dripped with condescension. So they had crossed the street and set up on the corner opposite where they once were. They'd lasted fifteen minutes there before the Oakland PD kicked them out for the exact same reason: lack of a permit. Esperanza had wanted to stay and yell, but Moss pulled her away. They had ended up just giving a bunch of brownies to group of homeless men and women near the lake.

Kaisha rolled Reg up to the coffee shop next. "What's up, guys?" Reg said. Moss reached out and grabbed Reg's hand, and Reg pulled him close and patted him on the back. "Good turnout, I see."

"Where are your crutches, Reg?" Esperanza asked.

"I'm wiped," he replied. "Kaisha came over and helped me get to BART."

She flashed them all a smile. "Anything for my Reg," she said, rubbing his bare head with her hand. He grinned at them, and Moss thought of Javier. *Maybe that could be us someday.*

A large group of familiar faces rounded Broadway onto Grand, and Moss's heart leapt. Njemile gracefully led the group, and she wore a stunning red summer dress, making Moss feel like maybe he should have dressed up. Trailing behind her, Bits and Rawiya were chatting, and Shawna brought up the rear. He was surprised and pleased that she'd been able to make it.

As they started to greet one another, Esperanza darted inside, making sure they could get the space upstairs before anyone else claimed it. Thankfully, she returned quickly enough, as the group's conversation had turned into a mass interrogation about Moss's love life.

"Oh, come on, honey!" Njemile said loudly. "You've got to give us something. We heard that there is a *boy* that you hung out with."

"How the hell did you find out about that?"

"Moss, do you think your mom doesn't tell everything to my moms?"

"Javier," Esperanza announced as she rejoined the group, before Moss could act scandalized. They all turned to stare at her. "His name is Javier." In the shocked silence, she gestured behind her. "Now come on, everyone. I got us a space upstairs."

As she turned back in to Farley's, her comments ignited everyone in conversation again. Njemile sidled up to Moss. "Lemme get your drink," she said, latching on to Moss. "Consider it my treat since you're finally joining the queer family."

"What's that supposed to mean?" Moss asked.

"Well, we've all been wondering when you'd actually act on your *illicit urges* ever since you came out."

Moss gaped at her. "You have?"

"That's not to say you weren't gay before," Bits said, butting in. "We just know you're a hottie, that's all."

"I *am* just trashing you," said Njemile. "You would be perfectly queer even if you never dated anyone *ever*."

If Moss could have turned scarlet, he would have. "Well, thanks," he said. "Next time, I'll bring my mama's potato salad to the gay cookout."

"You got a photo of him?" Shawna asked as the others laughed. "I wanna see."

"Actually . . . no. He's not the Facebook type. More of a Snapchat or texting guy."

Shawna pulled out her phone. "I hung out with this guy from Eastside last week," she said, flipping through her photo album. She showed Moss a pic of a light-skinned guy with a dust of a mustache and a flattop.

"Damn, he's cute," Moss said, but he frowned. "Weren't you seeing that one girl, though? The cheerleader?"

"Ah, you mean Makayla." Shawna got quiet. "She . . . well, she wasn't too into girls who aren't exclusive to girls."

Njemile placed a hand on Shawna's arm sympathetically. "She's simply not evolved," she said.

"A dinosaur," Moss added.

"A relic of a time we have since passed," Njemile said.

"Put her in a museum," Moss said. "With a placard reading, 'Cannot deal with bisexuals.'"

They broke into giggles right as Njemile gently pushed Moss forward to order. He was too anxious for caffeine, so he grabbed a lemonade. Moss carried up Reg's folded wheelchair as they then headed upstairs. "I wish this place had an elevator," Reg said, panting as he sat down in the closest chair.

"I'm sorry, Reg," Esperanza said. "I should have thought of that. We don't *have* to come here."

"You know how I feel about their cookies, though," Reg said, smiling and wiping sweat away from his forehead. "I'll be fine, promise."

"Next time," Esperanza said, pulling Moss aside, "we go to a place without stairs." He nodded at her, and they began to pull the chairs in the loft into a loose circle, making sure to leave a space for anyone who needed to go use the bathroom. Within a few minutes, nearly everyone had their snacks or drinks, and they'd gathered around Esperanza. Moss knew she was much better at organizing this sort of thing; he'd lost track of how many different clubs she had joined and/ or been in charge of over at Piedmont High. The group seemed to naturally defer to her as the leader.

Still, what good could possibly come out of this? He did a quick head count: eight. That made eight people who were supposed to stand up against the entire administration, *if* that was even their goal.

But they had to try, right?

Esperanza tapped on her mug of tea with a spoon, and the noise caused everyone to quickly quiet down. She laughed as the echo grabbed everyone's attention, then said, "I've always wanted to do that."

"Quick, it's going to her head!" Moss cried out, his hand over his heart. She stuck her tongue out at him, and he answered, "Love you, too."

"Anyway, I know that this may seem a little overwhelming to y'all. After this weekend, the metal detectors go in at your school—" She paused perfectly so everyone could boo and hiss in response to this.

"—and it doesn't seem like there's anything we can do to stop *that*. So, I think we should focus on how we can get more of the kids at school on your side."

"For what?" Njemile asked. "What's our endgame?"

"Well," Kaisha said to the group, "ideally, we should try to get enough people to stage some sort of protest." She looked back to Esperanza. "Maybe you can get some of those Piedmont kids to help."

"Ugh, I wouldn't count on it," she said. "I think you should focus mostly on your own school."

"It needs to be big enough so that they can't punish everyone without risking an enraged student body," Rawiya added.

"But *how*?" Reg asked. "I mean, I know all of you, so that's why I came." Kaisha stared at him, her brow furrowed. He quickly added, "Well, and I don't want the metal detectors in our school. That, too."

"Yeah, this is not exactly something most people are willing to care about," Shawna said. "Most people I talked to just think it's another thing we'll have to accept. Like the random locker searches." She frowned deeply at that.

"How are you doing, by the way?" Moss asked. "I haven't been seeing you at school."

"Thankfully, the bump on my head was just a mild concussion, so I wasn't hurt too bad." Her hand went to the spot just below her throat, almost instinctively. "Still sore here."

"Please tell me your parents are gonna sue the hell out of the school and the district," said Njemile. "I mean, there's so much video evidence of what that cop did to you."

"Yeah, that's gotta work in your favor," said Reg.

Shawna smiled weakly. "My pop's talking to some lawyers, but that stuff takes time. We gotta do something ourselves soon or this is just gonna get worse."

"Well, if we're going to convince people this is worth it, then we have to be able to explain *why*," Esperanza said. "So what are each of you gonna say to people?"

"They're invasive."

They all turned to Bits, who had been characteristically silent the entire time.

"Bits, breaking the ice!" Esperanza exclaimed. "Would you like to elaborate on what you meant by 'invasive,' Bits?"

"The whole system assumes the worst of everyone," they said evenly. "They got us worryin' about whether we're gonna set it off instead of focusin' on school."

Esperanza nodded her head. "It's a distraction!"

"We're not criminals," Reg finished. "We're not getting on an airplane. We're not goin' to court. We goin' to school!"

The group murmured agreements at that one.

"I bet it's against our rights or something," Rawiya suggested, then looked around the group for validation. "Right?"

Without a beat, Kaisha said, "No, unfortunately, it's not. At least not anymore."

Rawiya groaned. "I should learn not to have any optimism."

"Look," Kaisha said, leaning forward into the circle. "In a post-9/11 world, we couldn't get a single legal authority to agree with us on this point about 'safety.' Plus, we don't want to draw attention to ourselves with that battle. Our goal should be to attract the attention of the people who have the power to revoke the permits for the metal detectors."

"Wow," Esperanza said. "I'm impressed."

"I'm tellin' y'all," she said. "Find me on Tumblr. I been learnin' a lot there."

"Seriously, y'all need to follow Kaisha," said Njemile. "I wouldn't have learned half the stuff I know about asexuality if it wasn't for her blog."

Reg grabbed Kaisha's hand and squeezed. "It's true. I wouldn't have figured out that there was a name for who I am if Kaisha hadn't blogged about being biromantic."

Kaisha smiled ear to ear at that.

"But how do we do . . . well, whatever Kaisha just described?" Moss asked, shifting position in his chair. "I want to do whatever I can, but who are we going after?"

"It's gotta be Mr. Elliot," Rawiya said. "And not just because I hate him."

"Wait, I must've missed that," Esperanza said. "What?"

"Oh no," Kaisha said, looking up from her phone. "How do you not know?"

Esperanza shrugged. "Sometimes, even *I* forget I don't go to your school. I guess I just missed talk of it."

Moss looked to Rawiya, who nodded, letting him know she was cool telling the story. "At the end of our sophomore year, during a school assembly, he told me to take my hijab off. During the Pledge of Allegiance."

"And when she says 'during,'" Kaisha added, "she literally means that in the middle of it, he stopped and told her it was disrespectful to wear anything on your head during the Pledge."

"I still get shit for that day every once in a while," Rawiya continued. "But I was pleased by how many people sat down once I did."

"Maybe you should focus your attention on the principal, then," said Esperanza.

"But won't he go on one of those freak-outs again?" Moss asked. "Remember how pissed he was when a bunch of kids tried to meet with him over the assembly thing? If we push him, won't he just push back harder?"

"Probably," Njemile said. "At the same time, what if he pushes too hard? What if he does something that's so ridiculous that the school board has to intervene?"

"So, you think we can more or less *troll* him into reacting terribly, and he'll do the work for us?" Moss asked.

A smile spread across Bits's face. "That's a funny thought," Bits said.

"Damn, that's not a bad idea," Reg said. "But how?"

Moss saw that Shawna had her hand up, and he gestured to Esperanza to make sure she saw it. "What is it?" Esperanza said.

"Yeah . . . maybe we don't troll Mr. Elliot," said Shawna. "Given how badly he treated Rawiya here, and how much anger he must have towards me for upsetting his day . . . I'm guessing that won't go well."

A bolt of shame ran through Moss. *Damn,* he thought. He hadn't considered that. Rawiya nodded at her. "Yeah, I agree with Shawna," she said. "We gotta go bigger than him. We shouldn't target one person."

"Well, first of all, we *have* to get more people to agree to whatever plan y'all come up with," Esperanza said. "I don't know that we should organize *anything* until this group is a lot bigger." They nodded their agreement to her. "So, we need to branch out. And not just on campus!"

"Facebook," Kaisha said, looking up from her phone again. "Tumblr. We need to find ways to spread this in places where they're not looking. I'm pretty sure that Mr. Elliot nor a single assistant principal knows what Tumblr is, and I'm mutuals with a lot of people from school. I can post some things."

"Okay, that's a good start. What else?"

"I like the Facebook idea," Njemile replied. "Maybe a private group to reach out to people? And we can make ourselves admins so that we can approve every person who is invited. Just to make sure."

Esperanza clapped her hands together. "Brilliant, I love it. Who wants to do that?"

Reg, Kaisha, and Njemile all raised their hands.

"We've got to do stuff at school, though," Kaisha said. "We can't just recruit people online."

"I can definitely talk to people on the basketball team," Shawna said. "A lot of the girls aren't into protesting or anything, but they're all going to *hate* the metal detectors once they're in. Every bobby pin they wear is going to set it off, right?"

"That's perfect, Shawna!" Njemile said.

Shawna imitated a bow while sitting. "Why, thank you."

"I got the Book Club," Bits said.

"And I got the Anime Club," said Reg. "Nerds are gonna be pissed, too."

"Moss?" Esperanza said. "What do you want to do?"

"I don't know," he said. "I'm not in any clubs or anything."

"Well," Esperanza said, trying to defuse the awkwardness, "Kaisha, once you get the Facebook group set up, let me know the name and URL. I'll make sure everyone else has it. We should make sure to keep this limited just to students at this point, okay?"

"Of course," said Kaisha. "You want to set up one for Piedmont High or use the same one?"

They continued to hash out how Esperanza could contribute, but Moss remained silent, unsure how to help, uncertain he *should* get too involved. He pulled out his phone and saw a text from his mother.

DINNER TONIGHT AT 7. YOU GONNA BE HERE?

He texted back:

YA. SEE U IN A FEW.

He closed his phone and Esperanza was standing in front of him. It gave him a start, and she snickered. "Wow, why are you so jumpy?" she said. "Was that Javier?"

"Ha ha," he said. "Nah, it was my mom, just asking about dinner. You heading back home first, or do you wanna come over now?"

"I'm free all day, so if you don't mind, I'll come with you," she said. Moss smiled at her and the two of them grabbed their empty cups and headed downstairs, dropping the cups into the nearly full tub of dirty dishes. Moss waved to his friends as they left. As they walked out the front door of Farley's, Esperanza was quick to cut right to what she was thinking.

"So, you don't think we can do this?"

"Wow," he said.

"You were pretty quiet back there," she said softly.

"I'm fine. It's just a lot to take in, you know?"

"We're just getting started, though," she said. "It's gonna be overwhelming at the start."

"It's just so . . . *ambitious*. Do we actually have a plan?"

She pursed her lips. "No, but it's not like we're pretending we do. We just need to recruit more people."

"You say that with so much certainty," Moss said as they turned onto Grand, heading toward 19th Street BART. "Like you know it's going to happen."

"I think people are going to hate those things, after even just one day of having to use them. And I think you should capitalize off that as soon as possible if we're ever going to have any success in organizing this."

Moss sighed, and Esperanza leaned into him as they walked. "I wish I had the kind of hope you have," he said.

"Like my name?" she said, her head resting on his shoulder.

"Ha ha," Moss said. But he wondered what it would be like to be named after a concept like that, instead of a father who wasn't here anymore. Maybe his name had cursed him. That sure would explain his life better than anything else.

Moss and Esperanza descended the stairs into the BART station, and he was glad to be heading home. He pulled out his phone as they neared the fare gates and shot off a text to Javier:

I NEED TO SEE U SOON. MISS U.

Maybe that was a bit too clingy, but right then, he wanted to cling to something true. In a couple of days, he'd have to walk through metal detectors just to go to school. It was too strange to visualize, too bizarre to even consider. Yet he had no choice: this was now his life.

They boarded a train. It wasn't until he sat next to Esperanza that she broke the silence. "You realize we're right back at the same place as before," she said.

"What do you mean?"

"Back on BART. Dreading school on Monday."

"Jesus," he said. "How has it only been a week since school started?"

"How have things escalated so quickly?" She sighed. "Remember when all we were worried about was just getting through another year?"

"And now we gotta worry about so much more," he added. He sank farther into his seat in despair.

"Well, let's see how it goes on Monday, and then we'll take it from there," Esperanza said, her hand on his arm. "One struggle at a time."

Moss wished he had her optimism, too. He couldn't avoid the darkness flooding his mind. Deep down, he knew this was going to get worse.

12

Moss was surprised when he walked into Martin's shop to see Reg sitting at one of the other chairs. "Yo, man, what's up?" Moss said, claiming one of the few empty spots left in the waiting area. "You get here early?"

"You know you gotta," said Reg. "It's a Sunday. Why you crawlin' in here around noon? You're gonna sit there for like five hours."

"Guess who actually made an appointment?" Martin said, coming up behind Moss. Moss gave him a bump as he passed by.

"Wow," said Reg. "Why you gotta embarrass me like that?"

"I'll be right with ya, Moss," said Martin. He adjusted his bright red cap in the mirror, ran a hand through his thick beard. Martin had a husky build and the kind of facial hair Moss would kill to have. If he hadn't known him for most of his life, Moss probably would have found him attractive, but the man was like family to him, especially in the years after his father died. Anytime Wanda or Moss needed a ride somewhere, Martin was ready with his beat-up Honda. "Consider me your personal Uber," he said once. "Without the terrible service and business practices, of course."

He watched Martin move about the barbershop, exchanging words with the customers and the other barbers, and it mesmerized Moss. The man was so good at being social, and Moss was glad he never went to any other shops to get his fade. He'd heard horror stories from Bits before about how toxic the environments could be, but Martin was always quick to leap to Moss's defense if needed.

Martin waved him over to the chair next to Reg. "Get over here, boss," he said. "You want the same?"

"Yep," he said, sitting in the chair. "A little off the top, fade on the sides. I'm dependable that way."

Martin spun the chair around and Moss faced Reg. "How's your leg today?"

"Eh," said Reg. "Comes and goes, you know. The crash was two years ago, man! I thought I'd be better by now, but my physical therapist said that's not how all bodies work."

"Sounds like *my* therapist," he said. "You nervous about tomorrow?"

"Trying not to be," said Reg.

"What's tomorrow?" Martin said.

Moss ran the story by him quickly, and Martin whistled. "Your mom know about it?"

"Yeah." He leaned his head to the side so that Martin could get the hair that grew down by his neck. "Told her the day they announced it."

"What's she gonna do about it?"

"What you mean?" Moss asked.

Martin moved Moss's head gently to the left and ran the clippers up and down the side of his head. "Well, you know your mama's got a knack for causin' trouble. I just figured she was already camped outside the principal's office, threatening to rain down hell on him."

He heard Reg laugh and tried to keep his own head still. "I think she's just waiting this time," said Moss. "Nothing's happened yet, so it's not a priority for anyone."

"Yet," said Reg. "I'm kinda expecting a disaster tomorrow, and it will be sweet, sweet vindication."

"You think so?" Moss said. "You got more hope than I do."

"You'll see," he said. "I just hope I feel up to using my crutches tomorrow. Don't wanna take my wheelchair through those things."

"Has anyone actually been by the school to see what they look like?" Martin asked, pushing Moss's head forward to line him up.

"Nah," said Moss. "Least I don't think so."

"Sounds like a rush job," said Martin. "Shouldn't they take a few days to be installed?"

Reg's barber whisked the cape off him and shook it out. Reg shrugged at Martin. "I don't know anything about that stuff," he said. "If it ain't football, I don't know a *thing.*"

Martin laughed. "Li'l Reg here likes to think of himself as an expert," he said loudly, and some of the older men in the shop snickered at that.

"You're just mad that my fantasy-league team destroyed yours last year," Reg shot back, grabbing his crutches and limping over to the waiting area. *That* got a reaction from everyone, and Moss loved the pleasure on Reg's face.

Martin grumbled to himself as he continued to work on Moss's fade. Kaisha stopped by a few minutes later to help Reg get home, and Moss let himself relax in the chair as Martin worked his magic. He appreciated that sometimes Martin knew not to engage him in small talk, and this was one of those times. Moss found haircuts to be soothing and figured it was related to the fact that his head was so sensitive to touch. Thankfully, he hadn't fallen asleep in the chair yet; his fear of the embarrassment he would feel kept him awake.

Nearly a half hour later, Martin brushed off the last few stray hairs, pulled off the cape, and handed Moss a mirror, though Moss trusted Martin so much that he rarely gave his cuts more than a cursory examination. He handed Martin a twenty during his handshake and then made his way home, desperate for a shower to get rid of the itchy hairs that always seemed to find a way down the back of his shirt. Martin's shop was only a block and a half away if Moss went the quickest way, but that brought him right past Dawit's shop, so he usually took a more roundabout route. He was so lost in his thoughts about Javier, hoping that they'd hang out soon, that he was slow to realize he'd taken that route. He stopped on the corner of 12th, and it was impossible for him to look at anything except that stoop.

Moss had once asked his mom if they could move to another street, anywhere that wasn't just a few hundred feet from where Morris had collapsed. But they'd learned the hard way that funerals were expensive, that hiring lawyers was even worse, that when you lost a loved one, it sucked your finances dry. So they were stuck without much of an option aside from Wanda quitting the job she'd had for over a decade and uprooting themselves from the neighborhood where they'd built up a network. Of friends. Acquaintances. Activists. People and places that were important to their family.

Moss crossed over to the side of the street where the market stood, and he knew that there was a part of him that *didn't* ever want to leave. He'd attached so much of himself to those three concrete steps, and he couldn't imagine moving somewhere far away. What if he unraveled? What if he couldn't visit those concrete steps and remember what he had lost?

The calm and comfort Moss had found in Martin's shop slid away, replaced with a nagging terror and panic. He headed straight home. He rushed inside, shouting a quick greeting to his mother, who must have been in her bedroom. Moss bolted into the bathroom and peeled off his clothes, started the shower, and then jumped in before it warmed up. The cold water shocked him, jolted his emotions, and sent a chill over his skin. He let it pour over him and he wiped at his face, desperate to push this fear away from him. *Not now!* Moss thought. *Please go away.*

He'd learned to talk to his brain as if it were a person, and there were times when he couldn't accept that it *was* a part of his body. If he thought of it as an invader, he could conceive of it. Compartmentalize it. Fight it. But standing in the shower, the water temperature rising faster and faster, he knew the darkness was here to stay for a while. He let the water wash off the excess hairs and then shut it off. He toweled himself off and put his boxer briefs and jeans back on, but headed to his room for a fresh shirt. He pulled out his phone and sent Esperanza a text. You around? Could use the company.

By the time he threw on a Beyoncé tee that he'd bought at the swap meet across from the Ashby BART station, Esperanza had already replied. Sure, she had texted. Fentons in thirty?

He knew he shouldn't have ice cream for lunch, but he sent her back a confirmation. *I deserve to feel good,* Moss thought, channeling his therapist.

He found his mother curled up in bed reading the same Butler book she had been a few days before. "Gonna go get some ice cream with Esperanza," he said, pulling on some socks while in the doorway. "You want me to bring you back anything?"

She shook her head. "I'm good. You'll be back for dinner, right?"

"Yeah," he said. "And I finished all my homework last night, so I am responsibility-free for the rest of the day."

"Glad you take after me," Wanda said, then returned to her book.

He grabbed his lock and shoved it in his bag, then attached his helmet and slipped into his biking shoes. He was about to dart out the front door when he heard his mother call out to him. "Make sure to take the trash out before you leave!"

Apparently not *responsibility-free,* he thought, then headed back into the kitchen to the sound of his mother chuckling to herself.

Piedmont was to the northeast of their house, and it took just about twenty minutes for Moss to bike there. There were more cars out than he expected, so navigating around those that decided to sit in the bike lane on Broadway added a couple of minutes to his time. He cut a sharp right on Piedmont Avenue to head up to Fentons, and the neighborhood changed within a few blocks. The tall businesses of downtown Oakland morphed first into blocks of condos and apartment buildings, then into the quaint, small-town feel of Piedmont. Esperanza's house wasn't far from the main drag, but he was glad she'd chosen a neutral location for them to meet at.

Well, relatively *neutral,* he told himself. As he pulled up next to Fentons and saw the line stretching outside the shop, it was like he was in a different world. Piedmont was full of people who liked to tell outsiders that they lived in Oakland. A certain amount of street cred came with that, at least if you weren't from here. But these people would probably *never* come to his neighborhood. Moss locked his bike up in front of a baby-clothes boutique, one of those shops where an afternoon's shopping spree might be worth more than his mom paid in rent for a month. He stared at the clothes in the window. *Who needs a fashion-forward baby? Wouldn't they just throw up on the clothes anyway?*

A white couple pushing a stroller gave Moss a wide berth, and he had to laugh at them. What else could he do? Whenever he came to this part of town, *someone* clutched their pearls so hard that it was impossible not to notice it. It gave him a little thrill, knowing that his very presence could upset someone's walk or their afternoon searching for craft toilet paper holders and heirloom tomatoes.

He would make the best out of a terrible situation, and that included eating at Fentons. The first time Esperanza had taken him there, Moss gave them props. "White people know how to do ice cream," he said. "I will give them that."

"Ice cream and colonization," she had added. "A winning combination."

Now, Moss didn't yet see Esperanza around, so he pulled his phone out. Nothing from her. *And nothing from Javier,* he realized. He looked up the street, then in the other direction, and didn't see her. He wandered closer to Fentons, unsure whether or not to get in line. What if someone got all twisted because Esperanza joined him later? Could he risk that?

Thankfully, Moss heard Esperanza call his name out, and then he saw her approaching from the east side. He waved to her, and she pointed to the end of the line, so he quickly made his way there to join her.

"How ya doin', Moss?" She shielded her eyes from the sun with her hand. "Everything okay?"

"As good as can be, I guess," he said. "You?"

"Boring Sunday. Mom and Dad are arguing about some plant thing, so I was more than happy to get out of the house."

"Seriously," he said, "your parents have some of the strangest arguments."

"Tell me about it," she groaned. "Your mom doing all right?"

"Yep! Day off again, so she was reading in bed when I left her."

The line inched up some, and Esperanza didn't waste time. "So what's up? Something I can help you with?"

He shrugged. "I don't know about that, but I just started freaking out earlier. And you help calm me down so . . ." He spread his hands out. "Here I am."

She reached out and rubbed his right shoulder. "Talk to me, Moss. What's freaking you out? Is it about our meeting yesterday?"

"Kinda?" He sighed loudly. "I was getting my hair cut today, and Reg was there, and everything was fine. I guess I was distracted on my way home, and I didn't realize I was right by the market and . . ."

Esperanza was already nodding her head. "This is a lot for you, isn't it?"

"Yeah," he said quietly. "It's hard for me not to assume the worst once the police are involved with anything, so there's a part of me that wants to run away from all this. To just wash my hands of it and not deal with it at all."

The line moved forward again, and Esperanza looked a bit panicked. "I hope I haven't been pressuring you to do this," she said. "I know I kinda just took charge yesterday, but I was thinking that since I don't go to your school, that might be a good thing."

"Nah, you're fine," he said. "I think that's why it feels so good to talk to you about this stuff sometimes. You're not exactly connected to it, so I can get, like . . . I dunno. An outside perspective, I guess?"

"Sure," she said. "I try to understand what's going on with you. And it seems perfectly reasonable to me that this would cause you a lot of anxiety."

"To be perfectly cured with some dope ice cream," he added, raising himself up on his tiptoes to see how many more people were in front of him.

"Exactly," she said. They dropped into silence for a few seconds, and then Esperanza said, "Sometimes, I wish I just went to your school."

He balked at her. "*Really?* Isn't your school like, all high-tech and stuff?"

"I suppose," she said.

"You *suppose*? Y'all got like Wi-Fi and stuff, right?"

"Yeahhh," she said cautiously, turning her body away from Moss.

"And you were telling me about your college fair, and *that* was definitely better," he said, building a momentum. "Plus, y'all get catered lunch, and you have off-site dances, and you have real-ass textbooks and . . ."

He stopped. Maybe that was shame on her face, but Esperanza did not seem all that interested in committing to the point she'd tried to make. "What is it?" Moss said.

"I just meant that it would be nice to go to the same school as everyone else," she said, bashful. "It's kinda lonely over here in Piedmont. I can't relate to *this*." She swept her hand in a grand gesture. "This is not where I would choose to live if I had the choice. But I never got a choice in all this."

Something nagged at him, poked his heart, but he pushed it aside for the moment. "Oh, yeah, of course," he said. "Yeah, that *would* be cool if we were all together."

He let the moment pass, and Esperanza seemed satisfied that they'd smoothed things over. Yet as she began to talk about her newest attempt to chat up some cute girl in her gym class, the thought Moss had shoved away came back to haunt him.

She doesn't understand how good she has it, Moss thought. *I don't think she'd last a week at our school.*

He loved Esperanza. She had been there for him during some of the most difficult years of his life, right when Moss first became a teenager. They'd been attached at the hip by the end of seventh grade, partially because Esperanza was preternaturally talented at dealing with Moss whenever a panic attack hit him, whenever he was on the brink of a breakdown. Esperanza's parents were well-meaning, but occasionally clueless, certainly unprepared for the complications of adopting a brown girl and raising her in a white home. Moss was often a sounding board for her as she worked through her issues. He had even helped her during her first breakup, at the end of summer the year before, and it felt like they'd cemented a mutual bond that couldn't be broken by anything.

Yet every once in a while, Moss was reminded that her adoptive parents came from money. That they'd raised Esperanza in a world very different from his own. Perhaps right now, Moss was more sensitive than usual and that was why her comment hit so hard. But as the two of them ordered their cones and Esperanza paid for it, Moss knew he needed to get away, take some space. He ate his chocolate-chip cone and told Esperanza that he had more to think about. By himself. Moss was on his bike and flying back to West Oakland a few minutes later. When he biked past Lowell Park, saw the men playing chess at the park benches, saw the complicated graffiti on the side of one of the apartment buildings, he began to relax.

He had just needed to get back home.

13

The four of them—Moss, Njemile, Kaisha, and Reg—stood entirely motionless, staring in horror at the nightmare before them.

They couldn't even see the steps of West Oakland High, nor could they see a shred of the concrete path that led to the stairs at the front of the school. There was a persistent din in the air, a combination of excited and angry voices clashing with one another. Every so often, someone in the rear of the group would shout toward the front, but it was a futile act. You couldn't make out a single voice in that hive. Moss watched as a few balls of paper were launched forward out of the surging mass.

And at the top of the steps, just in front of the group of students, sat the two metal detectors.

They were a slate gray, shiny, intimidating. They stood nearly eight feet high, locked together with a set of cables that crisscrossed from one machine to the other, making it impossible to move between them. They were placed perfectly within the doorways, as if the school had been built around them.

Mr. Elliot was nowhere to be seen, which surprised Moss. He figured that the man responsible for signing the school up for this would want to be there on the first day of implementation, but that didn't seem to be the case. Was he in hiding, desperate to avoid this disaster? *I wish I could do the same,* Moss thought.

They stared at the throbbing mass ahead of them, and Moss realized it was the closest thing to a school-wide riot that he'd ever seen. It made the incident with Shawna pale in comparison. When Moss turned to look at his friends, they all had their mouths wide open.

"I'm glad I didn't bring my wheelchair today," Reg said. "Something tells me I'd never get to class if I had."

"You sure your leg feels okay?" Kaisha asked, her face full of concern.

Reg took a few tentative steps forward. "Yeah, it's not so sore today," he said.

"This is so much worse than I thought," Njemile said.

"Well, it'll work in our favor, won't it?" Moss said.

She looked at him, impressed. "Look at you! Seeing the positive side of things."

He grinned. "Well, I have to admit. This looks like a disaster. I guess I couldn't imagine how bad it would truly be."

Kaisha had her phone out and was snapping photos from multiple angles. "Oh, this'll be perfect for Instagram," she muttered. "Quick, what's a good hashtag?"

"What?" Moss said.

"You know, something catchy I can tag all these photos with." She paused, thinking, her hand twisting one of the knots on her head. " 'WestOaklandTrafficJam'? Nah, too long."

" 'SpaceJam'?" Reg said.

She cocked her head at him. "I'm giving you bonus points for a *Space Jam* reference, but no, that's too weird."

As she continued to type, the four of them inched forward. In the minutes they'd been there, the crowd didn't seem to have moved at all or in any particular direction. Some students were crowding around the edges, hoping to slip in on the side and get in before anyone else.

Rawiya joined them a couple of minutes later, and in that time, they hadn't budged at all. She then whistled before saying, "Well, we're missing homeroom." She looked at her watch. "In three, two, one. . . ."

The school bell rang loudly over the courtyard, and the students' voices rose to drown it out in frustration. "Come on!" Moss heard someone yell near to him, and a bunch of people began to shove forward. They didn't move with them; Reg turned around, his limping more pronounced. "Would y'all mind waiting until this calms down?"

he said, worry in his voice. "I don't have the strength to fight through this."

"Yeah, I'm with Reg," Kaisha said. Moss nodded his head and the six of them sat down in the yellowed, dying grass of the courtyard. Soon after, Bits wandered over their way, nodding their head at Moss before sitting next to him. They all sat there for nearly forty minutes, spending the majority of that time silent in awe of the unreal situation unfolding in front of them. More students arrived to school on foot, and Moss noticed a group of them collecting across the street, their voices loud and exuberant, but not more so than the pulsing, formless entity outside the school. The students pushed against one another, scrambling to fill any available space. It was at least twenty minutes before the people a few feet in front of them appeared to have moved forward at all. By the time Reg felt safe enough to stand and join the remaining stragglers, Njemile had managed to finish a piece of homework left from the night before, and Rawiya had gotten forty pages ahead in one of her books for Senior Lit.

Is it always going to be like this? Moss wondered.

"You're worried," Njemile said, standing at Moss's side. "And I don't really blame you."

"I don't like this," Reg said, and Moss noticed that his right arm was shaking. Was he nervous? In pain?

"None of us do," Moss said, still staring at Reg's arm.

Reg used his other hand to stop himself. "I'm okay, I promise. Just a little on edge, that's all."

"You know," said Rawiya, "if everyone's late to homeroom tomorrow, how long will it be before they start writing us up for being tardy?"

Bits stood and swore. They walked away from the group for a second, then returned, shaking their head.

But Moss stood. "Nah, I think we're fine," he insisted. "How can anyone blame us for *that*?"

"Moss makes a good point," said Kaisha. "Does Mr. Elliot think that he can ask students to be here over an hour before school starts *every day*?"

"He probably *would* do something like that," said Rawiya bitterly.

"Maybe, but imagine how many parents he's gonna piss off," Moss said. "Look, I know I'm negative all the time, but I really think he's shot himself in the foot with this." He sat back down. "I say we wait it out."

And so they did. Moss pulled out *Things Fall Apart* and laughed to himself at the new irony that the title represented. He thumbed through the book for a few minutes before stashing it back in his bag and just watching. The blob of students became a twisted version of a line after ten minutes, and not long after that, there were only a handful of people left waiting to get into school.

Which had started forty minutes prior.

Kaisha put her phone in her pocket and sighed loudly. "Shall we try this?" she said, moving ahead of them. The crowd had thinned down to less than twenty students, and the courtyard was far quieter than it had been an hour before. They all nodded at Kaisha and let Reg set the pace for them. He took his time, making sure each crutch was placed properly before continuing. As they made their way closer to the machines, Moss got his first glimpse of the cops that had been sent to work what arguably must have been their worst assignment ever. A tall officer was on the right side, in front of one of the metal detectors, telling each student what process they were to follow. His sandy blond hair was drenched in sweat; it could not have been pleasant to stand on those steps for as long as he had with no promise of shade.

On the far side of the detector on the left, another officer—brown, dark hair, angular features—was monitoring a screen of some sort, gesturing every so often for the next student to come through it. If the machine did not beep, the student continued on. But one of the cheerleaders set it off, and the blond cop roughly pulled her to the side. A third cop gathered the stuff left behind and gestured for the cheerleader to enter the main office. The girl was quick to show emotion, her tears springing out in a matter of seconds, and Moss didn't blame her. But the source of the disastrous line to get into school now made sense:

They only had *one* of the machines running. If this weren't such a dire scenario, Moss would have broken out into laughter.

They finally made it to the stairs. Reg struggled with the first few steps, his forehead gleaming with a new sheen of sweat. Kaisha had a hand on his back, her bulging backpack slung on the opposite shoulder. Moss took one side of Reg while Kaisha stood on the other; their friends were behind them. As Reg struggled up the steps, Moss's heart raced in his chest. This felt wrong. That was the only thing he could think, over and over. *This isn't what school is supposed to feel like.*

They reached the top step, and a couple of students ahead of them prepared to pass through the machines. Moss watched them empty their pockets and place the contents of them into small, round plastic containers. Their backpacks and the bowls went on a faded portable table and were slid across so the guards on the other side could have them ready in case of a possible search. While Moss watched this process unfold a couple of times, he became aware of a distinct hum from the devices, low and subtle. It made his skin crawl.

Reg moved up to the table and placed a single crutch on top of it. He used his now-empty right hand to clutch the table, and put the other crutch on the table. He placed his wallet and a ring of keys in one of the bowls, which he then slid across to the guard on the other side. The cop rolled his eyes at Reg, a sign of his impatience, and began to question him.

"Do you have any weapons on you?"

Reg glared at him. "No," he said, out of breath. "No, I don't."

"Have you emptied your pockets?"

"You just watched me do that."

Moss heard Njemile snicker behind them. The cop didn't find it amusing, though, and his scowl deepened. "Look, man, I gotta ask these questions. To everyone."

"Sorry," Reg said, his hand still on the table. He stared at the device, and Moss watched him inspect it, tracing the edge of it with his gaze. He looked back at his friends, but Moss wasn't sure what he wanted.

Moss stepped forward. "What's up, man?"

Reg shook his head, subtly at first, then much more furiously. "No," he said. "I can't do this."

"Hurry up, dickwad!" someone shouted behind them, and Kaisha turned to give them a murderous stare.

"This is *wrong*," said Reg. "And I don't trust this thing, y'all." He backed away from the devices. "You guys got some pat-down lane or something? Because I am *not* walking through this."

"Yes, you *are*," said the blond cop, and he took a few steps forward, his hands at his hips, a scowl on his clean-shaven face. "No exceptions."

It only seemed to convince Reg more. "You know if this is safe for me?" He directed his question to the cop behind the metal detector. "I got six pins in my knee. Is this thing gonna aggravate me?"

"Come on," said the one who was operating the scanning device. "I don't got all day."

"So you know for *sure* that this isn't gonna mess me up, then?"

The cop raised a hand to his head, running it through his hair. The tough demeanor evaporated in an instant. "Oh man, I don't know about that," he said, almost as if to himself. He continued to rub his own head, his face scrunched up in concentration. Moss's instinct kicked in and his eyes darted down to the cop's badge: TORRES.

"Can you wait a second?" Torres said. "I'll be quick."

The man jogged away from them. "Jesus, is this going to be okay?" Njemile said, shifting from one foot to the other, restless.

"I hope so," Reg replied. "But I can't do this, guys. I thought I'd play along for a day or two, but this is ridiculous."

"All your other friends have been fine with it," said the blond cop. "You're not special. Go through *now*."

But Reg stuck to his decision, backing up into his friends and crossing his arms. "You're gonna have to force me to," he said, "because I'm not going through that thing."

The cop lunged. It happened so fast that Reg stepped back and missed the step behind him, plunging down and into both Moss and

Kaisha. The cop's hands were on his shoulders, and he lifted and Kaisha cried out as Reg tried to thrash free. "Let *go* of me!" Reg yelled, and Moss saw Torres running back, his hands in the air, waving at the others, and then he ran a flat hand across his throat in a desperate attempt to signal to his partners, to get them to stop, but *no one else was looking.*

Reg reached out and grabbed the edge of the metal detector, but the cop yanked him free. Moss instinctively reached out, and Reg clasped his hand, harder than he'd ever felt someone grab him. His eyes pleaded with Moss, told him not to let go, and then the cop pulled again with a guttural yell, and Reg followed, slamming into the older man, who was nearly twice Reg's size, so he did not so much as stumble. Instead, the cop put both hands on Reg's back, and he shoved him through the metal detector.

The hum deepened right as Moss heard Torres scream, "Don't! It's not safe!"

Reg didn't make it through. His right knee jerked to the side, and the metal detector seemed to respond to Reg. *Thrum!* His body hit the frame hard, hard enough that it made a hollow ringing like a steel drum, and Moss saw that Reg's breath had been knocked out of him. As his hands went to his chest, Njemile and Kaisha shouted, scrambling to reach their friend as he doubled over, his arms shooting out to the ground to catch himself.

"What's happening to him?" Njemile shrieked. "Stop it!"

Torres rushed forward, his hands up in front of him. "No, no, don't!" He tried to keep people from coming through the metal detector, and so Moss bolted forward and dropped down on his knees. The blond cop had grabbed Bits and hauled them away as they screamed. Moss grabbed Reg under the arms to lift him up and—

"Turn it off," Reg wheezed. "I can't move."

Reg's face was covered in sweat, and he looked up at Moss, eyes wide in terror. Moss pulled upward on Reg, who let out an earsplitting yelp. Moss dropped his friend, who crumpled on the floor, a whimper leaving his lips. He reached over to pull Reg's leg away from the device and his hands grazed Kaisha's. She had the same idea. He ran them over Reg's black jeans and he knew what was wrong as he did so.

Reg was stuck to the metal detector.

"What is it doing?" Kaisha screamed, her eyes locked on Reg now. "How can it do that?"

Moss stood quickly and looked at the confusing screen on the machine. There was a flashing error message, and he tapped it repeatedly to no effect. "How do you turn this off?" he shouted.

He watched as Kaisha ducked under one of the cop's arms and burst through the device, leaping over Reg and dropping down on her hands and knees where Moss had been. "Moss, you have to turn this off," she said. "I don't understand how, but the internal magnet in this thing is out of control."

Reg's breathing was ragged, staccato. He had slumped over, leaning his weight into the machine. Even if Moss hadn't known that Reg was in pain, the position he was stuck in was so unnatural that it was bound to hurt. Moss heard footsteps behind him and twisted to see Mr. Jacobs sprinting toward them. He looked back to his friend, whose leg was awkwardly twisted up and behind him, rigid against the side of the metal detector. "Stop it," Reg begged. "Please."

Moss stood up and ran his fingers along the doorjamb, trying to find any indication of how this monster was wired. Mr. Jacobs was now alongside him, watching him for a few seconds before he gasped. "I know what to do! Get away from that machine!" he shouted.

The assistant principal dashed away and over to the ground near the entrance to the front office and pried a metal compartment in the wall open. Moss backed away from the detector, as did those on the other side. Reg pulled himself upward and struggled to remain that way; tears streamed down his face. "Just do it!" he yelled.

When Mr. Jacobs pulled a thick black cable out of the wall, the hum dropped out. Reg pushed himself away from the metal detector with a scream. His voice was a hellish bleat as he dropped on the ground. Kaisha rolled him over on his back, a hand on his wound.

Blood, Moss thought. Where had that come from? How was that possible?

Something must have broken through the skin, Moss realized, and as he watched Kaisha agonize over her partner, his rage rushed over him, suddenly and completely.

All Moss could picture was his father lying outside the store, the blood pooling behind his head, his mother crying as she held Moss back and away from his papa's body. Moss's own blood heated his body in anger, and it give him the strength to finally move forward, toward the blond cop, glare set on the man, who was now backing away with his green eyes full of fear. He felt the tingling in his hands, the lightness in his head, the heaviness of his heart, and it consumed him, filled him to the brim with a bitterness and voracity that burned his throat.

And Njemile stepped right in front of Moss. She held a hand to his chest, and he looked straight into her dark eyes, and he heard her say, "*No.*" Just that, nothing more, and he saw how she stared at him, a mixture of pity and her own fear.

Moss glanced down at Reg. His friend shook his head. "Not now," Reg whispered, and his voice sounded so lost, so young, that Moss deflated, the rage rushing out of him, the river of anger gone.

Reg smiled at Moss, and then he passed out.

14

Moss drifted.

Mr. Jacobs carried Reg's limp body off to the school nurse, and he saw Kaisha and the others chase after him. But Moss remained behind, and he felt a distinct sensation pass over him: This was not his body. Not his world. None of this belonged to him. He was watching a movie of someone else's life now, and he saw the cops get on their cell phones, probably to notify their superiors of what had happened. It wasn't until Moss felt pressure on his hand that he came back to himself, and he turned to find Bits by his side.

"The man can't keep me down," they said, and smiled softly. "You okay, Moss?"

Moss could only shake his head, and he felt his legs tremble. He stumbled forward, and Bits directed him toward the front of the school. Moss collapsed in exhaustion on the steps, the concrete cold against his legs. He didn't know where the blond cop had gone, but Moss suspected that the man had not stuck around to see what would happen. He brushed his fingertips over the steps themselves. They weren't as worn as the steps outside Dawit's, but the grooves felt familiar. Bits remained silent as Moss picked at the concrete, pulling tiny bits of it off and running it in his fingers. He concentrated on the texture, the way it crumbled if he pressed it too hard.

Moss couldn't forget the blood. There was so much of it that Reg had left behind at the base of the metal detectors.

He said nothing to Bits for an eternity, and it wasn't until he saw the black sneakers in front of him on the steps that he felt conscious again. He followed them up to the blue slacks and the sharp uniform shirt his mother wore.

She pulled him up and squeezed him tight, then pulled away to examine his face. She ran her fingers across his cheek, making sure that he was still here, still real. It was a familiar routine for them.

"Miss Stephanie called me," Wanda said when she pulled back. "Told me you were out here."

"I'm fine, Mama," Moss tried. "I'm fine."

"That's all I wanted to know," she said, and she grasped him tighter to her own body. This. This felt real. It was all he needed, too.

They sat in the living room. A glass was on the table. It sparkled from the condensation that lined the edges, the television reflecting off of it.

The lights were dimmed, and Moss couldn't bother to get up to make them brighter. His mother, Esperanza, and Njemile were packed onto the couch, Esperanza's hand in Wanda's, their eyes locked on to the TV as Kaisha appeared on the screen.

"It was awful," she said, her eyes red, her face puffy. "I've never seen anything like it."

The broadcast cut to images of West Oakland High, the front steps cordoned off with police tape. The reporter's voice was shocked, dramatic. "School officials believe that a malfunctioning magnetic band is responsible for today's accident, and they'll be taking further precautions to prevent this from happening in the future. Principal Jay Elliot was not willing to say if these new metal detectors, installed last week, will be used again."

"They better not be," Njemile said. Moss saw that she was twisting one of her thick dreads in her hand, something she did when she was anxious. "How could they possibly turn them on again?"

"I wouldn't be surprised, honestly," Esperanza said, removing her glasses with her free hand and setting them in her lap. She started rubbing the bridge of her nose. "I still can't even believe it happened. I mean, I thought it would be a disaster, but . . ." She never finished the sentence.

Wanda had been quiet as she took in all the new information from the broadcast. "You talk to Kaisha yet?" she said to Moss.

"Yeah," Moss said. "She said Reg is out of emergency surgery. He'll be fine, but I'm guessing he's gotta start over with his physical therapy."

She clicked her tongue against her teeth once, and then fell silent again.

Njemile picked up the remote, flicking through a couple of other channels. "I wonder if the other networks are covering it," she said, stopping on another local broadcast. They watched a few stories. One of rising gas prices, another of a shooting in East Oakland, and then a piece on the upcoming city council election.

Esperanza took the remote from Njemile and switched the TV off. "I can't watch this anymore," she said, sounding ashamed. "What are we going to do?"

"Is this what it's going to be like every day?" Njemile wondered.

"What are they going to do about Reg?" Moss added. "He's gonna have to use his wheelchair for a while until his leg heals again."

"And isn't there that other girl who uses a wheelchair? The senior?"

"Ramona," Moss said, nodding. "How'd she get into school today?"

"It doesn't sound like they would care," Wanda said. Her lips were pursed in concentration.

"Mama?" said Moss, concerned.

"They don't care," she repeated, pulling her hand from Esperanza's and rubbing her temple. Her voice was even, deliberate. "They don't care about your safety, first of all. They didn't care when that poor girl got assaulted and had a seizure, and they won't care about Reg's injuries."

"See!" Esperanza said, leaning forward to stare at Moss. "I told you. We just gotta reach out to more people, get 'em on our side."

"What do you mean?" Wanda said. "On what side?"

Moss and Njemile exchanged a glance as Esperanza's gaze drifted away from Moss's mother. She said softly, "We were just thinking of organizing something at their school."

"Really?"

"I mean, nothing too serious, you know, nothing that would break the rules or anything," Esperanza added, her hands up in a gesture of innocence.

"Well, why not break the rules?"

Esperanza scoffed. "You're not serious, are you?"

"What did you have in mind? A protest? A petition? Maybe some sort of demonstration outside the school?" Wanda asked.

Esperanza was so shocked that she threw her hands up. "Moss, is she for real? I can't tell if she's joking."

"Yo, my mom's legit," Moss said, nodding his head. "I have seen her get *down*."

Wanda laughed. "That's one way of putting it," she said, a gracious smile spreading across her face. "Me and my husband used to be involved in politics 'round here. Years ago, that is." She went quiet. "And after he died, too. I haven't been as involved lately, but it has been a large part of my life."

"Well," Esperanza said, encouraged to continue, "we're definitely thinking that there needs to be some sort of protest. But we just need to reach out to as many people as possible first."

"What do we even protest at this point?" Njemile said, bitterness in her voice. "Our school? This country? Our whole lives?"

"Well, what if Reg had been hurt worse than he was?" Moss asked.

"It's just the start," said Esperanza. "I really think it is. So, a protest is a good idea! Right, Wanda?"

"I think y'all could do better than that," Wanda said. Moss tilted his head, confused, and his mother stood up and walked across the living room toward the kitchen. "Moss, you seen my phone? I gotta make some calls."

"Why?"

Wanda peeked back around the entryway to the kitchen. "You kids are right. We need to organize people. I think we should get more than just students, however."

"What are you talking about?" Esperanza asked.

She came back into the room and sat on the armrest of the couch.

"Sorry, just getting ahead of myself," she said. "We need to take care of this now. I worry enough as it is whenever Moss leaves this house. Who knows what else those things at the school are capable of? Are the police trained well enough to use them? Based on what I heard from y'all, it doesn't even sound like anyone knew how to operate those monstrosities."

Wanda disappeared back into the kitchen, and Moss's friends looked to him for an explanation. He'd seen his mother go into this mode before, but it was a long time ago. She went to every rally after Morris died, organized as many of them as she could, spent hours on the phone trying to connect with as many people as possible. A few minutes later, the three of them could hear her rapid chatter, and a familiarity washed over Moss. He hadn't seen her like this in a long while.

It was strangely comforting.

Njemile switched the television back on and Esperanza groaned at her. "Aw, come on," Esperanza said. "The news depresses me."

"I just wanna see if they say anything more," Njemile said. "Just a few minutes, I promise."

Moss pulled his feet up to sit cross-legged on the couch now that his mother's seat was empty, turning his face away from the television. But he couldn't keep his attention away from the news, even though he wanted to. Njemile turned the volume up once an image of their school flashed on the screen. "That's us!" she said, but her excitement quickly evaporated.

The anchor read the story without any interest or passion. "Local residents in West Oakland are concerned about the installation of metal detectors at West Oakland High after a malfunction in the equipment momentarily harmed a student," the man said.

"Momentarily?" Njemile whined.

"While we haven't received a statement from the Oakland Unified School District, the Oakland Police Department has reported to NBC4 that no crime was committed, so no arrests have been made."

The three of them groaned, and Moss felt a spike in his chest, a surge of rage. "Damn it," he muttered. "Of course they're quick to say that."

"I mean, I'm not surprised," Njemile said. "What would you even charge someone with? *Who* would you charge?"

"Shhh," Esperanza said. "It's not over."

There was a shot of the front steps of the school, yellow tape strung across the entrance. The newscaster continued. "A school official, who spoke with us under guarantee of their anonymity, said that the metal detectors were installed after a fight broke out on the second day of school."

Then the video flashed on the screen. A chair flew over the heads of a mob, and it was impossible to make out what was happening. *Unless you happened to be there,* Moss thought. He could make out the row of lockers and even saw Shawna for a brief second, but his heart sank. This was not an angry response to a fellow student being assaulted; this looked exactly like what the newscaster said it was.

"That wasn't a fight!" Njemile said. "Why are they making it seem like one?"

"It's easier for them to categorize it that way," Wanda said from the doorway, startling them all.

"Jesus, Mama, how long you been standing there?" Moss said, his heart thumping.

"Just a few seconds, actually."

"Categorize it how?" asked Esperanza. "What do you mean?"

"Notice how they called what happened to that Meyers girl a 'fight,'" she said. "And it certainly looked like one, right?"

"So now that they've established that there was a danger," Moss said, following his mother's logic, "it makes it seem like the metal detectors were justified."

"Exactly," said Wanda, smiling at her son.

"You done your phone calls?" Moss asked.

"No, got quite a few more," she admitted. "But I've got something for y'all."

Esperanza smiled. "Ooooh, a surprise?"

"A meeting place."

They were speechless at first, and Njemile tilted her head, her eyes narrowed in suspicion. "Meeting for what?"

"You remember that old church we used to go to over on Oak, Moss?" Wanda asked. When he nodded, she continued. "I called up the reverend. He said we can use it."

"For . . . ?" Moss said.

"For us. For the students, for the parents, for the community. Anyone who wants to stop this from happening again."

"You're serious, aren't you?" Esperanza said, her eyes wide.

"Why wouldn't I be serious?" Wanda said. "My son wasn't exaggerating. I have connections. People I used to rally with. Many who helped us after things went bad."

"Mama, that's great," Moss said, the tension in his chest slowly receding. "You think you can actually get people to help?"

"Yeah," she said, nodding to him. "You get who you can to show up, I'll handle the rest." She sat back down on the couch and leaned forward, her attention on Moss and his friends. "So what are y'all doing for outreach?"

"We're mostly using the internet," Njemile said. "Kaisha's got that down, but we'll be talking to kids at school, too. But we were worried about *how* to organize all these people. We can't meet in school; the staff would get too nervous. And it would be too obvious."

Wanda nodded. "You gotta get this message out as clandestinely as possible," she said, "without letting the administration know what you're doing. How will y'all communicate with folks online?"

"We're thinking a private Facebook group," Moss said. "That was Kaisha's idea. She probably already set it up." He laughed. "She's already mad as hell. We won't need to tell her twice."

"Good," she said, her eyes alight with warmth as she looked at Moss. "Anger is a gift. Remember that." She stood. "You gotta grasp on to it, hold it tight and use it as ammunition. You use that anger to get things done instead of just stewing in it." She sighed. "Trust me, y'all."

For a moment, she seemed to be looking at something else. "Mama?" Moss said.

"When Morris died," she said, still staring off in the distance, "there were days when I couldn't even get out of bed. You remember that, baby?"

He nodded. "I missed a day of school once, back in fifth grade."

"I felt so terrible about that," she admitted, her gaze back on Moss, "not because I was sad or angry. But because I didn't channel that anger *into* anything. I just let it grow until it consumed me."

"Aw, Mama," said Moss, his heart sinking.

She smiled gently at him. "I'm not saying you shouldn't grieve. Or just give up and let the sadness or anger take you over. But what's the step after that?"

"That's when you started organizing those rallies, wasn't it?" Moss said. "I remember. You used to be up hella late calling people." He laughed. "I used to sit at the edge of my room, y'all. Ear pressed to the door. I told myself you were talking to the president."

Wanda whooped at that. "Really? You never told me that."

"Well, that's because I grew up and realized you probably weren't talking to Obama every night."

"Oh, Moss," said Esperanza. "You are my absolute favorite."

"So, Facebook group," Wanda said, wiping at a glassy eye. "How y'all gonna get that passed around without raising suspicions?"

Njemile's face lit up. "A party," she said.

"What you mean?" Moss said.

"Make them party invitations. For a party this Friday night. We can tell people in *person* what the invites are really for, but we should design the cards and the Facebook group so that it *looks* like it's really a party."

Wanda whistled. "That's good, Njemile. That's real good."

"I'll tell Kaisha about it tonight," Esperanza said, standing up. "I'm gonna swing by the hospital on my way home. My parents are actually expecting me home tonight, so I need to be there."

"You tell Rebecca and Jeff I said hello," Wanda said. "And you keep us updated on Reg, okay?"

"Will do," Esperanza replied. Before she left, she snapped her fingers. "Come over Wednesday, Moss, Njemile," she said. "Invite the others, too. Let's do some more planning."

"At *your* place?" Moss said. "Are you sure your parents are gonna be okay with that?"

"Yeah," she said. "I mean, they're pretty liberal. I'm sure that once they hear the news themselves, they'll want to get involved."

"That okay, Mama?" Moss said.

"Of course, baby," she said.

"And bring Javier," Esperanza said, and she shut the door before Moss could disagree.

"I should probably get going, too," Njemile said, stretching out before putting her sweater on. "Thanks for lettin' us come over, Wanda."

"Anytime, honey," she said, and embraced Moss's friend in a hug. "You make sure Ekemeni knows I'm coming over for her suya this weekend, okay? I ain't missing that. And tell Ogonna I said hello, too!"

Njemile laughed and flashed her bright smile at Wanda, her face aglow with joy. "I will, I promise." She planted a kiss on Moss's cheek before she bounced out of their home, the door slamming shut behind her.

Wanda plopped down on the couch next to Moss, draping an arm around him. "How you doin', Moss?"

He sighed. "Better, honestly. It's been . . . a weird day," he admitted. "A weird week, actually."

She reached up with her left hand and stroked his scalp with her nails, and it calmed him down instantly. "I know," she said. "Weird and scary."

"I'm just glad Reg is okay. Well, relatively okay, I suppose." He paused and looked at her. Her eyes sparkled with affection, adoration. "Why are you doing this with us?"

"Because," she said, "I'm not going to lose someone I love again."

She kissed him on the temple, stood up, and walked into the next room. Moss sat there and listened to her call up one person after another, asking how they were and if they had any time this upcoming Friday evening to help her out. She called Shamika. Then Martin. Then Dawit. He sat there, the TV muted in the background, and he felt at home again, a strange sensation after such an intense day.

He pulled out his phone and gasped at the missed-call notification from Javier. He hadn't even felt his phone ring! He opened his phone and called him back, and Javier picked up on the second ring.

"Hey!" Javier said, and he was clearly out of breath. "Glad you called me back."

"Sorry, I was just . . . lost. In conversation. I didn't feel my phone vibrate."

"No worries," he said. "I figured you might be busy."

Moss paused at that. "Why?"

Javier sucked in his breath. "I saw the news. About your school. That guy your friend?"

"Ah, *that*," he said. "Yeah. Pretty good friend, actually."

"I'm sorry, man." Javier fell into silence. "Look, I know this might be a bad time, but I'm in the neighborhood. One of my biking buddies lives off 11th. Can I stop by?"

Moss leapt at the chance to feel something other than dread or fear. "Yeah, man, come on over. Anything to get my mind off all this. I'll text my address."

"Sweet! See ya soon."

Moss sent over his address, but then immediately second-guessed himself. He got up from the couch and found his mother about to dial another number on her phone. "Hey, Mama . . ."

She looked up. "I know that tone," she said. "What is it, Moss?"

"So, I kinda didn't think this through," he began, "and I probably should have asked you first, buuuuut . . ." He sighed. "I kinda invited Javier over just now?"

She put her phone down. "You sure you're up for that, baby?"

"Oh god, *yes*," he said. "Even if he's just purely a distraction, I just need . . . I dunno, something *good* to happen."

"Then if it's good for you, I'm all for it." She stood up, stretched her arms up above her head. "It'll be nice to finally meet him." She shook her head. "Already," she added.

"Don't worry, Mama," he said. "Me and him aren't really moving that fast. I promise that he won't ask you for permission for my hand in marriage next week."

She laughed as there was a knock on the door. *That was fast, though,* Moss thought, and he maneuvered his way to the living room as quickly as he could. There Javier stood on the stoop, a giant grin on his face. "Honestly, I really *was* in the neighborhood," he said. "Where should I leave my bike?"

"You can leave it here in the entryway," Wanda said as she came into the room. "We don't have much room otherwise, and I wouldn't advise leaving it out front."

Javier laughed, and Moss loved the way his whole face lit up when he did. It was pure, real. "Don't worry, Ms. Jeffries," he said. "I already had a bike stolen outta my yard a couple years ago." He stuck his hand out. "Javier. Nice to meet you!"

She shook it and smiled back. "Nice to meet you, too, Javier."

Javier reached out and ran his hand up and down Moss's arm. "Hi, amigo. Good to see you, too."

That familiar heat ran to his face, and Moss stuttered a reply. "S-same to you," he said. He couldn't believe this was happening, and he had not prepared himself for Javier and his mama to be in the same room.

"You need anything to drink?" Wanda asked. "Come into the dining room."

"Just water," said Javier, and as Wanda turned, he darted over and planted a kiss on Moss's cheek. "Didn't want to miss a chance to do that," he said quietly.

Moss grabbed Javier's hand and led him into the next room.

"What you doin' in the neighborhood, Javier?" Wanda asked, handing him a glass of water.

He took it and gulped down half of it. "Spent the afternoon riding bikes with my buddy Jamal," he said. "I just dropped him off down the street, figured I would check in with Moss here."

"Well . . . it's been a weird day," said Moss.

"Yeah, I can imagine. Your friend doing okay?"

Moss shrugged. "He's out of surgery now. I'm just glad he's alive."

"Man, that's so scary," said Javier. "I know you were worried about those machines before, but I'd be terrified of them now."

"Hopefully, the school won't turn them back on," said Wanda. "But we'll have to see."

She gestured for Javier to sit down at the table, and he followed her, sitting down on the far side. "I did actually have something to ask about tomorrow."

Moss winced. "I don't know how tomorrow will be, what with all the stuff happening at school."

"You think you'll be free for dinner?"

Moss looked to his mama. "Isn't Shamika coming over tomorrow night? I don't want to skip out on her."

"Oh, I meant both of you."

Moss and Wanda looked from Javier to each other, and then back. "Wait, what?" Moss said.

"Look," Javier began, "my mamá is pretty excited about you, but I think she'd feel a lot better about us hanging out if she met your family, too. I explained that it's just the two of you, and she suggested making a meal for all four of us."

Wanda smothered a giggle, and Javier glared at her. "Sorry," she said, "it's just that Moss was saying that you two weren't rushing things yet, and here you are, inviting us to dinner at your place."

"Oh, I'm sorry," said Javier, his gaze dropping down. "You know, you're right, maybe it is too—"

"Of course we'll come," interrupted Wanda.

Moss gaped at her. "Really? You're okay with it?"

She nodded at him. "What did you just say? Something about wanting good things to happen?"

"So I can tell my mamá yes?" Javier said, his eyes alight with excitement.

He looks so cute when he does that, Moss thought. He watched Javier wordlessly as he called his mother, and Moss sent out a silent thanks to the universe, to whomever might be listening. He didn't expect this gift, but he wasn't going to refuse it, either.

15

Moss wasn't sure if what coursed through his body was excitement or dread.

They were near the back of the bus, the one that ran down Mac-Arthur alongside the 580 freeway. It wasn't as bumpy a ride as it used to be, so Moss wasn't worried that he'd get a headache. He felt fine otherwise, but there was a tightness in his chest.

"Mama, I'm nervous," Moss said. He leaned into her arm as the bus took a turn a little too sharply, and she wrapped it around him, pulling him in close.

"I know," she said. "I'm sure it feels awkward that I'm coming along."

"No, it's not that," he said, smiling. "I think you'll like Ms. Perez. She's nice. And funny. She doesn't think she's funny, but she is. Don't let her fool you."

"Then what is it?" Wanda asked.

"I dunno," said Moss. "Maybe I'm just nervous in general. I just want him to like you." He paused. "And me."

"Ah, Moss, to be young and in love again," she said.

He frowned at her. "I'm not in love, Mama. Least not yet."

"I know, I know. But I remember how huge everything felt when I was your age." She swiveled to the side so that she was now facing him. "I'm sure this feels like one of the biggest moments of your whole life, right?"

"Yeah, I guess," Moss said, his heart still pounding.

"Good. Don't forget that. That kind of excitement will keep you alert."

"Maybe," he said, "but I wish I could calm down about these things."

She pursed her lips. "You talk to Constance about that?"

He shook his head. "Not yet. To be honest, it's been hard to talk about this with anyone. I keep finding ways to avoid the subject with Esperanza, and I usually tell her *everything*, Mama."

Wanda reached up and pressed the button to call for a stop. "It's new for you," she said. "Your father was my first love, you know. And even though I like to portray myself as calm and collected, he kind of sent my heart into a tailspin. It's not a pretty thing to deal with."

They both stood up and headed for the rear doors. "What do you mean?" Moss asked.

The doors opened, and Wanda waved at the driver and shouted a thanks. They stepped out onto MacArthur Boulevard, the sound of traffic on the nearby freeway roaring in their ears. "Well, you ever feel like Javier has invaded your heart and mind?"

"Well . . . yeah," he admitted. "And it feels weird because I don't know if it's the same with him. He always comes off as so carefree whenever we hang out, and I'm always a nervous wreck."

They hooked a right on Park Street and headed toward the Perez residence. "What you're going through is honestly quite common, Moss. I promise you. And he might very well be nervous, too, but he just shows it in a different way."

"I guess." His head hung down. "Thanks for talking me through this. And coming with me. I hope this isn't too weird for you, either."

"I suppose they don't tell you about this when you find out you're going to be a parent," she said, and then chuckled. "But I just want you to be happy. Whatever that takes."

They didn't speak again for the remainder of their walk. Moss felt a burst of relief, knowing that his mother supported him. He knew that Esperanza's parents had reacted much more strangely when she had told them that she was a lesbian. On the surface, they were accepting, but they didn't ever seem to want to *talk* about their daughter's interest in girls. As long as she kept any details to herself, Esperanza was tolerable to them.

That didn't seem fair to Moss.

His relief gave way to a wave of nervous energy as they turned onto Javier's street, and the sight of the rusted swing set sent a pang through Moss. He suddenly felt self-conscious. He worried that his mother would judge the yard, the lack of grass, the condition of the neighborhood. When the man from downstairs waved a greeting at them as they ascended the stairs, Moss was desperate to know how his mother felt about it all. But she remained silent behind him. She just placed her hand on his lower back as Moss rang the doorbell, and the moment of comfort washed over his thorny nerves.

I'll be okay, Moss told himself.

Eugenia opened the door, a smile spread across her face. Smiling made the lines in her forehead deeper every time she did it. "Come in, come in," she said, stepping to the side, and Moss darted into the room. "Eugenia Perez," she said, stretching her hand out to shake his mother's.

"Wanda," she said, and his mother's face glowed when she said it. "Nice to meet you finally."

Javier walked out of the kitchen, a dish towel flung over his right shoulder, and Moss's heart fluttered at the way the white undershirt clung to his chest and shoulders. "Don't mind me," Javier said, and he flashed a grin at Moss. "I just gotta clean up real quick." He placed a gentle kiss on Moss's cheek before heading off to his room.

His mother and Eugenia were staring at Moss, and there was no pity or sadness in their eyes. No, they were *smiling,* their faces bright with joy. His own face burned with embarrassment. "Okay, okay," Moss said. "The show's over."

"He was like this last time," Eugenia said. "Que cute."

Wanda laughed at that. "Moss wears his heart on his sleeve," she said. "It's one of his best features."

"Wow, you two have already started talking about me as if I'm not in the room," Moss said. "Great."

That sent them into an uproarious bout of laughter, and they slipped past him into the kitchen to finish up that night's meal. Moss sat down on the couch, running his hand over it, remembering the last time he'd been over, the feel of Javier's hands on his body. For a moment, Moss relaxed. The apartment was alive, the sounds of gossip coming from the kitchen as his mother and Eugenia hit it off. He could hear the shower running from down the hallway, and the thought of seeing Javier again filled him with excitement. He let it all wash over him. He was used to his mind betraying him, taking a moment of joy and turning it sour and grim, spinning it about in his head until it was all he could think about.

The calm was new. And maybe it was a sign that things would be all right.

The bathroom door creaked and Moss glanced over toward the hallway. Javier appeared, a gray towel wrapped around his waist. "I'll be done in a minute," he said, and Moss was lost in the water droplets, the way his brown skin gleamed under the hallway lamp, the ease with which his muscles flexed. He was gone as quickly as he arrived.

Moss didn't know if it was envy or sadness that jolted through him, but it could have been both. *I wish I had a body like that,* he thought, and he immediately felt pathetic for even allowing the moment to happen. *You can't give in to those thoughts,* he reminded himself, and then he stood and darted into the hallway. The door to the bedroom was ajar, so Moss moved into the bathroom, the humidity instantly clinging to his skin. He closed to door behind him and switched on the light.

The mirror was coated in condensation. He grabbed a hand towel off a hook to his left and ran it over the glass, his reflection appearing in the clear streak he made. He wiped away enough of it to see the upper half of his body there, and that awful feeling swept through him again.

"You can do this," he said, just louder than a whisper, and he ran through the ritual that his therapist had taught him. "This body is mine, and it is perfectly fine." He breathed in deeply. "I am not ugly. I am *not* ugly."

Moss smiled at himself. There. He liked that, the way his face curled up, the wideness of his mouth, the scruff growing evenly around his chin and above his lips, the way it provided contrast against his dark skin. Constance had advised him to latch on to these moments, to cherish them, to remind himself that his brain was *constantly* betraying him. If Moss could remind himself of the good, he could start to push away the bad. He puffed his chest a bit, ran his hands over it and down across his torso, then pulled his black polo down over his waist.

"You can do this," he repeated, then ran the water and splashed some on his face, thankful for the rush of alertness it gave him. He dried himself off with a hand towel and took one last lungful of air in before he headed out to dinner, to his fate.

When he entered the dining room, they were all there, his mother and Eugenia laughing at some joke Moss had missed, Javier finishing up setting the table. A new burst of energy jolted through Moss, but it felt good. Thrilling. Intoxicating. "Need any help?" he said to Javier.

"Nah, I'm just about finished," he replied, then gestured to a seat opposite him. "Sit."

The smell of Eugenia's cooking—pollo guisado, she told them—filled him with comfort. When he sat down across from Javier, he didn't panic. Instead, he smiled as his mother reached under the table to grab his hand, a quiet sign of support. *This is real,* he reminded himself. *I wouldn't be here unless they wanted me to be.*

Moss dug in, slurping down the hot stew, and he listened to Eugenia and his mother swap stories, comparing the life of single motherhood, then rising rents in Oakland, and he just watched them, admiring how effortless they made this seem. Eugenia helped run a beauty supply store farther down in East Oakland, out past Fruitvale, and she'd been there for over a decade, they learned. Moss was so transfixed by her that he was startled when he felt Javier's foot rub up against his leg. His eyes dashed over to him, and Javier tried to act like he was innocent. Courage spread through Moss, and he winked at Javier.

"You'll have to tell me how you two met, though," Eugenia said, reaching out to stroke her son's arm. "Javier's been quiet about it."

"Really?" Moss said. "I'm surprised by that. He's usually so bold."

"Am I now?" Javier replied, arching his eyebrow.

Eugenia laughed. "Oh, you know it's true." To Wanda, she said, "He can be so full of himself sometimes. Isn't that true, mijo?"

He waved a dismissal at her. "It isn't that big of a deal. I saw him on the BART. His bike was pretty sweet, so I told him so. His friend Esperanza was with him."

"Esperanza?" Eugenia said. "Pretty name."

"Pretty *girl*," said Javier. "Even I can recognize that."

Moss nudged him. "He just came up to me, all full of swagger and arrogance, and just interrupted our conversation so he could flirt with me."

Javier acted horrified. "No, no, that's not how it—"

"I'm just playin'," Moss said. "I'm glad he talked to me. Though you're right, Ms. Perez. He's totally full of himself. Came up to me and hit on me within sixty seconds."

"Hey, I'm not the one who was oblivious to the fact that he was getting hit on," Javier said. "You thought I was some straight boy until the first time we hung out."

"Moss *can* be a bit oblivious," Wanda interjected.

Embarrassment rushed into his face, but he didn't hate it. As Wanda and Eugenia began to talk about how no one had ever taught them how to raise gay sons, Moss realized how lucky he truly was. This wasn't the nightmare he had expected it to be. His mother and Eugenia seemed to truly get along, and they were already cackling together within the hour.

Moss learned more about Javier and Eugenia, learned about when they'd come to the States, how long she'd worked in a laundromat before getting a better job at a beauty supply store. Wanda shared stories of growing up in Oakland, and all the while, Javier kept rubbing his leg up against Moss's. They stole glances when they thought no one was looking, but by the end of the night, Moss was sure his mother had caught them once. Maybe twice.

By the time dinner wrapped up and they were bidding the Perez family goodbye, Moss was more certain than ever that he'd stumbled onto a good thing. It was a rarity for him, and he wanted to cherish that.

He kissed Javier good night at the top of the steps. He was sure he floated all the way home.

Moss woke that night in a terrible sweat, his mother cradling him, shushing him and telling him that everything was going to be all right. He gasped for air, his heart raced, and the darkness of his room was suffocating. But instead of fighting the attack, he let it take its course, and it soon passed. His mother's face was all creases and lines of worry, and he reached out to stroke it. "Please, Mama, I'm okay," he said between breaths. "Thank you."

"The dream again?"

It was all she had to say. He nodded at her, then pushed himself upright, wiping away the sweat from his temples. "Same one."

She passed him a glass of water and he gulped it down. "I'm sorry, baby. I wish I could take it away from you."

The images came rushing back into his mind: the men in dark uniforms, their guns raised, bursting into his room, dragging him out of his bed, promising to finish what they started with his father. His mother was always there at the doorway, screaming at them, but unable to stop them as Moss was pulled through the window, away from her, away from safety. He'd lost count of how many times he'd had an iteration of this same dream, and while some of the details changed, the effect was the same. He awoke in a panic, the shrieks and screams spilling into the conscious world.

"It's been a while since you last had it," Wanda said, and she put her hand on his forehead. "Did something trigger it this time?"

He shook his head. "I don't think so. I had a good night, Mama. I wasn't thinking about it at all." He sighed. "Maybe that's why I had it. My brain had to remind me that I'm broken."

His eyes hadn't fully adjusted to the darkness, but he knew his mother's eyes were full of sadness. "Oh, honey," she said. "You know that isn't true."

"I can't help but think it," he said softly. "How is Javier ever going to like me once he finds out how bad I am?"

"That's not fair," she said. "To yourself or to Javier. I'm sure you'll have to talk to him about these things, but if he truly cares about you, he'll accept you for who you are. It's that simple."

"Even if that means I might wake him up at night with my messed-up head?"

He could see her nod, just barely. "You know, your dad snored. Badly. Some days, I just wanted to put a sound bubble around him so that I could sleep. But he couldn't control that. He wasn't doing it to torment me, and I accepted that. That's what love is about, you know? And if Javier really does come to love you, he'll love your mind for what it is, too."

He swallowed hard. He hoped she was right. But he couldn't trust that right at this moment. So while his mother sat there, her hand running up and down his back softly, he cycled through his memories. He needed this, and he cycled from one to the next. *The shape of your hands. The smell of the cologne you'd wear when we went to the Grand Lake Theater.* He knew these memories, and while they comforted him, they weren't enough.

The bicycle I got for my ninth birthday, and the horribly tied bow on it. No, that wasn't it. *The night you brought arroz con pollo home and dropped it on the front steps.* Moss laughed at that one; his father had been furious. And that led Moss to something he'd not thought about in many years, and it was finally enough:

I remember that time we went over to Lake Merritt, and you chased the Canada geese away from our picnic spot, and they chased you right back. You fell into the lake when you thought you were farther from the edge than you were. You smelled for almost two days, of stale water and rot, and you hated it.

Moss clung to the memory as he fell asleep, his mother curled up next to him.

16

The metal detectors were still off when Moss arrived at school on Wednesday. Their principal had not made any sort of announcement about them the day before, but that morning, in homeroom, he finally addressed them. "They will be recalibrated and tested until next week," Mr. Elliot's voice said over the PA, "and we'll have another test run then. I promise that we'll have no more unfortunate incidents like the one on Monday."

That elicited a set of groans from Moss's homeroom, and Mrs. Torrance was the loudest of the bunch. When some of the students laughed at her, she replied tartly, "What happened to Mr. Phillips is no laughing matter."

No one brought it up again.

Moss caught Kaisha in the hallways between his first and second class. Her face was slack with exhaustion and she stood motionless in front of her locker, the door open. Her face lit up, however, when Moss placed a hand on her shoulder. "Hey!" she said, and snapped to attention. "Reg is already at home now."

"Really? That quick?"

She beamed. "He's a trooper, that one," she said, pride in her voice. "I admire him a lot."

"What do you mean?"

"You know, it's just that . . . I dunno." She was deep in thought for a moment. "I think I would have given up a while ago," she continued. "Nearly losing my parents in a car accident, having my leg smashed, the drunk driver getting off . . . and now this."

"It's a lot for one person to deal with," said Moss.

"But he's got so much energy, Moss!" Kaisha's eyes were wide. "I don't understand it. All the stuff he's been through, and . . ."

She slammed her locker shut and locked it. "How did you get me to talk about things, Moss?" she said, laughing. She started to walk away, but Moss shouted her name.

"Before you go!" he said. "Tonight. Esperanza's house? Six P.M.?"

"We doing it?" she said.

He nodded his head.

"I'll be there," she said, smiling.

Moss cornered Rawiya during lunch, her attention lost in her iPod, and got confirmation that she was attending. Then, after school, he found Bits in the library. He pulled up a seat next to them and began to go over his notes from Mr. Roberts's biology lecture.

"You going later?" Moss whispered.

Bits subtly nodded their head, their attention buried in a book.

"I'm picking up Javier on the way over, so I'll see you there."

Bits inclined their head once. That was all Moss needed. They returned to their work again, and neither of them spoke. Moss did his best to keep his mind on the intricacies of cell replication until four, when Mrs. Hernandez had to close things up. As he stuffed his notebook into his messenger bag, he felt a hand on his shoulder. "We'll figure this out," Bits said. "All of us together."

Moss smiled in affirmation to them, and then Bits was gone.

Moss sent a quick text to Javier: omw.

He slung the bag over his head and let it rest on his back. It was a good day for a ride, and he was eager to get back on his bike again. It had been chilly on his ride to school that morning, and he knew that winter would soon drop over the Bay. He wanted to take advantage of the clear skies and sunshine that afternoon.

So Moss pushed himself faster as he pedaled south toward Lake Merritt. There wasn't too much traffic on Broadway that day, so he took the lane, drifting downhill smoothly, the wind cooling his face and passing through the air holes in his helmet. He came to a stop at Grand after moving over to the left-turn lane, and he felt his phone vibrate in its protective case on his shoulder. He figured that Javier had beaten him to their meeting place, so Moss left the phone alone, his attention focused on traffic.

When he rolled up to Splash Pad Park, he saw Javier's black bike on its side in the grass, and Javier himself was hanging from one of the pull-up bars, next to a much younger boy who was being held up by someone older. "Are you ready?" he heard Javier say as he pulled up next to him.

The boy nodded his head. Moss didn't recognize either of them, but they seemed to know Javier well.

"Three . . . two . . . one!" Javier cried, and the two of them raced at pull-ups. The boy's father did all the work for his son and lifted him in sync with Javier. Moss watched them, and his eyes drifted to Javier's biceps, which bulged with every pull-up, and his heart fluttered in his chest. Seconds later, Javier began to slow down and struggled to lift himself up while the young boy laughed wildly. "I'm beating you, I'm beating you!" he screamed in between giggles. Finally, Javier dropped off the bar, panting, sweat dripping down the sides of his head.

"You got me, Manuel," he said, breathless. Manuel's father put him down and he waddled over to Javier. Manuel raised a hand and Javier gave him a high five. "One day I'll beat you, I swear."

"I wish I could do that," Moss said when Javier turned to look at him.

"You wanna give it a go?" Javier said. He waved to his friends as they left.

"Nah," Moss said quickly. "We should get going soon anyway."

Javier leaned over and planted a kiss on Moss's cheek. "Then let's go."

Moss watched Javier pick up his backpack and his bike, one after the other, and wondered when he would discover the catch. It was inevitable, wasn't it? Maybe Javier had police officers in his family and thought that bad cops were a rare occurrence. Maybe his mother was a lot more religious than he previously thought. Or was Javier just waiting until they had sex, and then Moss would never see him again?

He watched Javier wrap a thick, heavy chain around his waist. "What's that thing?" Moss asked.

"My lock," he said. "Got it for my birthday earlier this year."

"You lock your bike with *that*?"

"Dude, it's safe! Thieves can't cut through this thing. Plus, it's quite fashionable, wouldn't you say?" He posed for Moss, his hands on his hips. "Tim Gunn would be proud."

Moss climbed back on his own bike, shaking his head, and Javier pranced about before getting on his. *Well, at least he's a little weird,* Moss thought. Then Javier was off, far ahead of Moss enough that he had to slam his pedals down in order to catch up to him. With a quick look behind him, he passed by Javier, taking the lead as the two of them smoothly coasted up Grand. Moss had suggested they take the back way to Piedmont, since the hills weren't as steep as they were on the shorter route. As Moss rode, he kept glancing to see that Javier was still behind him, and each time, Javier flashed him a quick smile. *Maybe I am overthinking it,* he thought. *He still seems to want to be around me.*

They pulled up to the Miller house a few minutes later. Javier deftly swung his right leg back over his seat and came to a stop with his left leg still in the cages of his pedal. Moss had seen other people do that before (he hadn't even bothered to attempt it himself), but watching Javier do it . . . he felt inexplicably attracted to him. Javier turned, a goofy grin on his face, and Moss desired him so wholly that it frightened him. He'd fostered crushes for as long as he could remember, but as he watched Javier unlock the chain at his waist, sweat glistening on his arms, Moss wanted this one to be real.

"You okay?" Javier said. "You're welcome to lock up with mine."

Moss nodded his head. "Yeah, just thinking." He slung his bag to his front side and pulled out his own lock, and Javier grabbed Moss's bike and leaned it up against his.

After Moss finished, he rose to see Javier staring up at the Miller residence. "That's a big house," Javier said, his voice soft with awe.

"You have no idea," said Moss. "Wait until you see inside."

There was a sense of symmetry, of order, to this part of town. The houses here towered over the people. He supposed the neighborhood was quaint in its own way, but he thought it felt too safe. There were no bright colors anywhere, no dirt lots in place of lawns, no rusted chain-link fences.

And the Miller house was a prime example of that. It was light gray with white trim, all sharp angles and expertly painted wood tiles. The front yard—a rare thing in *any* house in the East Bay—was freshly manicured, the blades of grass practically uniform in height. Peonies and roses sat lining the flower bed, almost equidistant from one another. Esperanza had told him that a man named Guillermo was responsible for that; her parents could study the science behind those plants, but were horrible at any gardening themselves.

"It can be intimidating," Moss admitted. "I also feel like I should give you a heads-up."

"About?"

"Esperanza's adopted. Her parents are white, and they're . . . well, they're nice people. Just kind of intense sometimes. They mean well, though."

"Ah. Got ya. I'm sure I'll be fine." Javier gave him a smile. "I mean, I'll be with you."

"Oh, stop it," Moss said, rolling his eyes, but he couldn't help smiling back.

They made their way inside, through the massive eight-foot door that felt like it weighed a ton. Moss moved to the side in the foyer and slipped his shoes off and gestured at Javier to do the same. There were three potted plants hanging from the high ceilings in the front room, and it made the house seem impossibly larger than the outside led you to believe. Moss could hear voices coming from the next room and, feeling unusually bold, he reached out and grabbed Javier's hand before leading him into the dining room where their friends were. Javier looked at him, surprised.

"You gonna be okay here?" Moss said softly. "I know this place is ridiculous."

Javier squeezed Moss's hand. "Yeah," he replied. "Promise."

They walked into the dining room. Rawiya and Kaisha lit up when they entered the room, and the others—Bits, Njemile, and Esperanza—turned around to greet them. As Esperanza got up, her gaze resting solely on Javier, Moss spoke up. "Hi, y'all. This is my friend Javier." His heart rate sped up, a nervousness coursing through him, but when he saw how excitedly Javier was greeted, he figured that there wasn't a need for him to worry. Esperanza slid up next to him, her face close to his.

"He's still hot," she whispered.

"I know, right?" Moss whispered back.

She flashed him a grin and returned to the table. As Moss and Javier took the only empty spots, Esperanza's mother came out of the kitchen, a large Crock-Pot in her hands. Bits rose to get out of the way, and Rebecca Miller placed it on the table. "Is everyone here?" she asked her daughter. "I thought it would be a good time to bring out the chili I made." She beamed at them, and her dangling emerald earrings sparkled alongside her smile. She kept her brown hair tied back from her face, and Moss thought the earrings looked good on her.

"I'll get bowls and spoons," Esperanza said, rising from the table and then making a silent count of those at the table. When she left the room, Rebecca smiled at the group.

"I think I've met all of you at one point!" she said excitedly. "But if not, I'm Esperanza's mother, and you can call me Rebecca, please."

They all nodded their heads or said hello to her, except for Kaisha, who had her attention directed solely toward her laptop. She simply raised a hand to acknowledge her. Seconds later, Esperanza returned with her father, Jeff, who carried half of the bowls for the table. His hair was lighter than Rebecca's, but they both looked like all the scientists that Moss had seen in the sci-fi films he'd grown up on. They both had long hair tied back and a fashion sense that hadn't been updated in twenty years. "Hello, everyone," he announced loudly. "Welcome to our home!"

Rebecca continued talking. "Now, I didn't know what everyone liked, so I figured that some chili would be filling. It's vegetarian, so you should be fine, Rawiya."

Rawiya beamed at her. "Thank you for remembering."

"We've got some cheese or sliced onions if you want, but feel free to ask for anything if you need it." She ladled chili into the bowls and passed a steaming dish to each of the people at the table. Jeff had popped back into the kitchen and came back with a tray of corn bread. "My mother's recipe," he explained, setting it down on the table. "And she grew up in the South, so I swear it's good."

"That's what I like to hear," said Moss. "Nice to see y'all again. I feel like I haven't seen you in forever, Jeff."

Jeff waved a hand dismissively at Moss. "You know how it is with our academic work. It takes over our lives."

Bits didn't even wait for the chili to cool down before they stuffed a spoonful in their mouth. Moss watched them chew it for a bit before they spoke. "Not very spicy," they said, and then they promptly took another bite.

"Would you like some hot sauce or something?" Rebecca asked. "I'm sorry, I didn't want to make it too spicy or anything."

Bits pursed their lips. "You got Crystal's?"

Rebecca snapped. "Yep! I'll go get it now."

Bits smirked at Esperanza. "Your mom knows what Crystal's is," they said.

"We are only clueless some of the time," Jeff joked. He leaned in toward the table. "Though she picked up the food habits from me," he whispered.

Once the chili was passed out, Jeff lingered behind his daughter. "So what's the plan, then? Esperanza has given us an idea of what's happening."

"And it's just awful what happened to your friend the other day," Rebecca added, returning with the hot sauce, which she dropped off next to Bits. "Just awful."

"Well, did your mom give you an address?" Esperanza asked, looking at Moss.

Moss pulled his phone out of his front pocket. "This one," he said, sliding it across to her. She took it and nodded.

"That's over near 27th, isn't it?" she said.

Moss nodded. "We've got to get these out before Friday, since the meeting is going to be that night. Kaisha?"

She took that as her cue to stop working. "Okay," she said, and she turned her laptop to face them all while pulling a bowl of chili toward her. She shoveled a spoonful of it into her mouth. She swallowed and began again. "The Facebook event page is done, and it's disguised as best I could as a party invitation." She gestured toward the computer, and they all leaned forward to get a better look.

"So, we invite people we know to the page?" Njemile asked. "That's all we're doing?"

"No, but it's a start," Kaisha said. "I mean . . . I'd like it if all of you started using Tor, maybe set up some two-factor authentication on your devices, took some steps to protect your own privacy."

They all stared at her, silent in confusion.

Kaisha sighed. "Baby steps," she said, more to herself than the group. "The event is set to invite-only; you can't find the page unless you've been invited. I've made myself and each of you an admin on the event page so you can invite anyone you trust."

"How do we know who to trust?" Bits asked.

"Do you really think that the administration is going to care about this?" Rebecca asked. "I'm not even sure that *I* know what you are planning to do, and I'm standing right here."

"The point is to get everyone to meet at the Blessed Way Church on Friday evening," Moss explained. "We're not planning what to do about the metal detectors tonight; we're hoping to use the meeting itself to do most of the planning. And we'd just like to do what we can to make sure that the school doesn't know about it until they can't ignore it."

"Think of it like a meeting of spies," Rawiya said. When they all turned to look at her, mostly amused, she added, "What? It's exciting to think of it like that!"

"We're not *spies,* Rawiya," Njemile said. "At least not yet."

Rawiya raised a finger. "But we *might* be," she retorted.

"Nah, it's more like we're Dumbledore's Army," said Kaisha. "You know, organizing in secret to fight off the Dark Lord."

"Now *that* is a great analogy," said Moss. "Wait, but which one of us is Dumbledore?"

"Ew, can *no one* be Dumbledore?" Rawiya said. "I'd rather not have one of you secretly planning to let us die to beat some snake-faced dude."

They all laughed at that, but Esperanza's father stepped forward. "Why not just make it a public meeting?"

"The element of surprise," Kaisha explained. "Moss's mother was right about this plan. I think this would be a lot more shocking if they didn't know what we were planning."

"Think about how every protest goes down in this city," Njemile said, looking at Esperanza's mother. "The police know it's happening, they show up in droves, it lasts an hour, and it always ends terribly."

"You think the police will show up?" Rebecca said. Moss heard it in her voice for the first time that night: hesitation. "I don't want you doing anything dangerous, Esperanza."

Esperanza frowned. "Exactly *how* dangerous do you think this meeting will be?"

Moss jumped in before Rebecca could answer. "It's just a meeting, y'all, I promise. It's not even the actual protest. Even then . . . we should probably wait to overreact until we know what it is this protest will even be."

Kaisha pulled her laptop back to her, swiveling it around. "I also designed some party invitations with the address that we can print out and give away in person," she said quickly, hoping to move the conversation in a new direction. "To anyone who doesn't know, it looks entirely normal. That's how we'll get people who aren't on Facebook."

"Make sure to email that to my mom," Moss said. "She'll get people in the neighborhood to pass it around."

"Can't she hand it out on her mail route?" Rawiya suggested.

Moss shook his head quickly. "Oh, no, no, no," he said. "That's like . . . super illegal. I don't think my mom wants to lose her job over this."

As the group shifted the conversation to the logistics of getting the invitations out as quickly and efficiently as possible, Moss reached under the table again to grasp Javier's hand. "You doing okay?" he whispered softly to him. "You haven't said much throughout this."

"I'm good," Javier replied. "I'm just getting used to everybody. Watching. Observing."

Moss gave his hand a squeeze, and Javier returned it. When Moss turned back to the group, he caught Esperanza's smirk; she'd been watching them. He felt heat rush into his face, but he was pleased it didn't bother him.

The conversation moved along. They spoke about Reg for a bit and Kaisha provided updates about his progress, which wasn't much different from what they knew that morning. More therapy loomed in his future. "What about Shawna?" Kaisha asked. "I haven't seen her since last weekend."

"Apparently her dad's filing a lawsuit next week," Njemile answered.

"Good," said Rebecca. "I hope they get everything they ask for *and* more."

"Amen," said Bits.

"Esperanza," said Jeff, and he turned to look at his daughter as if he was asking for permission. "If you don't mind . . ."

"What's up?" She removed her glasses and set them on the table in front of her. "Is it getting too late?"

"No, not at all," he said. "You all can stay as long as you need to. I obviously haven't talked it over with your mother, but . . . can we come to this meeting?"

Moss tilted his head. "Really? Y'all wanna help?"

"We've been out of town a lot this year," Jeff explained. "And this seems like a good opportunity to get more involved."

"I agree," said Rebecca. "Plus, I'm intrigued. I want to help plan if I can."

Moss traded looks with the group. Kaisha nodded subtly, and no one else seemed to indicate that it was a bad idea. "I think that would be cool," he said. He then added, "If you're cool with it, Esperanza."

"This isn't your fight," she told her parents. "You have to understand that."

"But we care about it, too, dear, and—" Rebecca began.

Esperanza cut her off. "I'm not saying you can't care. I just don't want a repeat of my science project in eighth grade."

Moss tried to hide a giggle, but heads swiveled in his direction.

"See?" Esperanza said. "Moss knows exactly what I mean."

"Don't throw me under this bus!" he shouted.

"Oh, come on, Moss," she said, smiling. "You probably would have told them the same thing."

Javier raised his hand. "I'm sorry, I'm new here," he said. "What are y'all talking about?"

"Yeah, even *I* don't know this story," said Kaisha. "What's up?"

Moss had never seen the Millers act bashful, but they gazed at one another, scarlet cheeks and tight lips, and they looked like shamed children. "We . . . we may have gone overboard for Esperanza's project once," Rebecca said slowly.

Jeff winced. "We may have projected a lot of ourselves into it."

"'May have'?" Esperanza sighed. "You took it over! My teacher was convinced I cheated for the rest of the school year!"

"They're all being modest," Moss explained. "That was the most complicated eighth-grade science exhibit on soil in the history of the world."

"I'm serious, though," she continued. "If you two get involved, you have to sit back and listen. You have to make sure not to make it about you."

Moss experienced a flash of a memory then: Esperanza, days earlier, making the college fair about herself. *She takes after them and she doesn't even realize it,* he thought. He said nothing.

Jeff had his hands up in conciliation. "We promise," he said. "No going overboard."

Rebecca made an X gesture over her chest. "Cross my heart," she said.

"Thank you," said Esperanza. "So please tell me that someone has any gossip aside from all this serious stuff, because I have the *best* story about this guy in my Algebra II class."

The conversation swirled around the table as Njemile, Kaisha, Rawiya, and Esperanza all swapped the latest info they had on their fellow classmates. Jeff and Rebecca seemed to have understood that there wasn't much they could contribute, and they drifted away from the table and headed upstairs. Javier brushed Moss's hand with his fingertips, then turned toward Esperanza and cleared his throat. "Sorry to interrupt," he said, "but I was wondering if I could maybe ask a question?"

"So polite," said Njemile. "Please tell me you're marrying him soon."

Moss rolled his eyes. "You're the second person to say something like that to me," he said.

"Second?" Javier said. "Who was the first?!"

He dismissed Javier with a wave, but Esperanza jumped in. "What did you want to know?"

"Well, Moss here says I'm bold, so lemme fulfill my destiny: What's it like having white parents?"

Njemile gasped in the most dramatic manner possible. "Javier! You can't just ask someone why they have white parents!"

He laughed. "There's no tactful way to ask that question! I guess I just never met someone like you."

"Man, you *are* really forward," she said. "I respect that." She sighed, however. "I mean, it's got its positives and negatives. I was adopted pretty young. My parents immigrated here by not-so-legal means before I was born, but . . . well, what little I know is that I got separated from them not long afterwards. By . . . the government."

Javier shook his head. "Can I guess? ICE?"

She nodded. "Again, I don't know much. Adoption washes away a lot of history, especially from kids like me who were put in the system so early. But my parents adopted me from a state agency, and they're really the only parents I've ever known. I love 'em a lot, and they've been pretty awesome to me."

"I feel like there's a 'but' coming next," said Javier.

She shrugged. "I mean, they can be ignorant like any white people, and I had to teach myself the sloppy Spanish I do know. People question my identity all the time cuz of my last name or the way I talk, but all in all, it's not the worst thing. I'm lucky to have them."

"Cool," he said. "I'm probably a jerk for asking that, so I'm sorry for putting you on the spot."

"*And* he apologizes before he's asked?" Njemile said. "Moss, where did you *find* this fine specimen of a man?"

"Stop it!" Moss said.

Esperanza smiled back at Javier, a thankful expression on her face. "No, I appreciate you asking," she said. "It's complicated, but I *do* like talking about it." She leaned forward. "So what are *your* parents like?"

"Yeah, we don't know much of *anything* about you," Kaisha said, leveling Moss with a stare.

"My mom's great," Javier replied, smiling. "Dad hasn't ever been part of the picture. He left a long time ago. It's just me and her. And she just *loves* Moss," he added, reaching over and rubbing him on the back.

Moss leaned away from him briefly in embarrassment, but it was enough that the others caught it. The questions came in an unending stream.

"So how long *have* you two been hanging out with each other?" Kaisha asked, leaning forward.

"Is Moss a good kisser?" Rawiya asked, her eyes flashing with humor.

"Is it true that he likes it if you rub his scalp?" Esperanza offered.

"Do you foresee marriage in your future or are you just testing the waters?" asked Kaisha.

"You gonna break Moss's heart?"

They all turned to look at Bits. "What?" they said. "It's an important question."

Javier didn't seem to know who to look to, and yet Moss was surprised when he locked eyes with him. "I won't," Javier said, a warmness in his face. "Promise."

And without any hesitation, Javier began to talk to Moss's friends, answering their questions as each was launched at him. Moss knew they were being difficult because they cared. But Javier didn't seem to mind. *God, he's so attractive,* he thought.

The interrogation was still going strong when Jeff and Rebecca returned. Moss was familiar with this particular dance between Esperanza and her parents. It meant that they felt it was time for Esperanza's friends to head home, but they were so hopelessly awkward that they couldn't bring themselves to say it, lest they seem uncool. Moss knew what to do, though.

He pulled out his phone and said, "Damn, I should probably get home. Anyone else headin' out?"

It was like falling dominoes. Within a few minutes, they had all helped clear the table, Rebecca urging them not to stay and try to help with the dishes. "I've got it, I promise," she said, shooing them toward the front door. But she lingered as they gathered their belongings, and Moss caught her gazing at him. "Thank you," she said, quiet enough that he knew it wasn't to the whole group.

He stepped up to her. "For what?"

"Letting us help," she said. "You know, we try to get involved in the community, but it gets hard to fit it in with my schedule and my husband's."

"No problem. I'm just stoked y'all want to help."

"And I really am sorry about your friend Reg. Give him my regards and tell him he's welcome here any time."

He offered Rebecca a thankful smile. It was times like these that he appreciated how gracious she could be.

They all bid the Millers goodbye and began to separate at the end of the walkway from the front stoop. Bits and Rawiya left together to catch a bus, but Kaisha and Njemile hung back.

"Well, that was not a complete disaster," said Javier. "Y'all have the Facebook plan set up, and it sounds like you got the details worked out. You mind if I send some people from my school your way?"

"Come to the meeting," said Kaisha. "On Friday. Listen to what we plan. If you're in, I say we go for it."

"You really want to help out?" Moss said. "Honestly?"

"Of course, dude! I wouldn't dream of missing it."

"Uh-oh," said Njemile. "They're gonna do cute stuff. *Everyone run away.*"

The nervous laughter rang out on the street, and Javier pulled Moss toward him and kissed him, hard, deep. "To planning your own little rebellion," he said.

Moss kissed him back for just a little bit longer, pushing back against the awkwardness that tried to conquer him. He had never kissed anyone in front of his friends, but he focused on how it made him feel. Warm. Secure. Admired.

"I'm leaving before y'all get cuter," said Kaisha.

Moss waved goodbye to his friends, then swung a leg over the top bar of his bike. "You ready?"

Javier nodded. "I was born for this," he said. "Race you down to Grand?"

Javier kicked off before Moss could agree, and Moss chased him down the street, a joy in his heart.

17

Moss's family had never really been a religious one; they'd attended church a few times when his father was still alive, though even then it was out of obligation to his papa's side of the family more than anything else. So it was always a strange experience to step inside a church to begin with, but that wasn't why he was so bewildered. He had pulled the tall wooden door of Blessed Way Church toward him and was greeted by a wave of noise, all of it echoing off the high ceilings. Marvin Gaye was blaring out of the speakers on the stage. He stepped inside, his eyes jumping from one thing to another. The dirty stained glass, still colorful but muted by dust; the arches stretching across the space of the church, eager to greet the walls; the concrete pillars that supported the weight of the cobwebbed ceiling above; the flickering light off to the left that caused shadows to dance upon the opposite wall.

And the room was utterly full of people.

He thought he might have heard someone shout a greeting at him over the din, but the moment passed. He saw Njemile talking to someone he didn't recognize, both of them animated and expressive. There were people standing about in the rows of pews, some off to the side, nearly all of them engaged in some sort of conversation. He heard pockets of laughter and thought he heard Esperanza's voice, but upon rushing toward it, he realized it was from an older Chinese woman, gray streaked in her hair like a stripe, her voice an eerie resemblance to his best friend's.

He knew a lot of the faces in this room: People who had been to rallies and marches over the years. People who had protested his father's death. People who kept this community alive. The very man who had accosted him in the West Oakland station raised his hand to Moss, and he lifted his chin quickly, a silent hello. Shamika rushed up to him and grabbed him into a hug, but before he could say anything, Mrs. Torrance sidled up to him.

"Nice to see you here, Mr. Jeffries," she said. "Have you met my partner, Walter?" She gestured to a tall black man who stood next to her. He wore relatively conservative clothing on his stocky frame, at least relative to what Mrs. Torrance normally wore. She had on a white dashiki etched in purple, blue, and black designs over white pants, and she looked stunning.

Moss shook her partner's hand. "Nice to meet you," he said, but he leaned over to Mrs. Torrance. "What are *you* doing here? Aren't you worried about being seen?"

She raised an eyebrow and laughed at him. "Not at all, Moss. Your mother asked me to show up, and I didn't hesitate."

"Well, I won't tell anyone you're here to break the rules," he teased. She just laughed at him.

Behind Walter, Moss spotted Shawna, who stood next to her parents. He excused himself and darted over. He'd seen Shawna's parents before, but hadn't actually met them. Her father raised a hand to Moss. *Well, he recognizes me,* Moss thought tightly, but he still went to shake hands with Mr. Meyers.

"Nice to see your mother still has a pull," the man said. "I don't know that we've formally met before. Franklin Meyers. This is my wife, Teresa." He paused and he pursed his lips. "Thank you. For my daughter. You know her well?"

"A little," said Moss, shaking Franklin's hand. He glanced at Shawna and smiled. "And it's no problem. I didn't even do anything."

"Sorry to hear about your friend," Shawna said. "I guess we're both in the same boat."

Moss sighed. "Yeah, it's . . . unfortunate." The word still felt wrong. He directed his next question to Franklin. "How'd you find out about this? My mom?"

"Most definitely," he replied. "My wife knows her, too."

"From what?"

Teresa laughed. "Too many things," she said. "We actually went to high school together. West Oakland High, too. Solidarity is important," Teresa said. Her eyes sparkled when she said it. In her, he saw the same eagerness that he'd witnessed in his mother, a hunger that he was beginning to understand, too.

Filled with excitement, Moss pushed past them, brushing up against other people in the crowded space, and then he cut through the pews back to the center of the church. He looked toward the front and caught sight of his mother, but only briefly. He ducked under someone's outstretched hand, quickly gave Dawit a fist bump, shouted at Rawiya, and stumbled up to the stage where his mother was standing, helping someone with a tangled mass of electrical cords and cables.

"Mama, what are you doing?" Moss said, out of breath as he came up beside her.

She reached out and pulled him close, planting a kiss on top of his head. "Pretty good turnout, no?"

"That's an understatement," he said. "I guess I didn't expect you to still have the same pull as you used to."

"To be honest, neither did I," she said, uncoiling another knot in the cable she held. "It's been years since I did any organizing."

"Clearly you're still good at it," he said. He walked to the edge of the stage and looked out at the crowd again, saw his friends and many of his classmates chatting with people he hadn't seen since his father had been killed. *Two worlds colliding,* he thought. He never imagined a reality where these two groups of people would ever meet, but here they were, all to support Shawna and Reg and the kids at West Oakland High.

Wanda came to stand beside Moss, her face dancing with mischief. "I told you I was gonna help," she said.

"Help?" he said. "This is beyond helping, Mama." He looped his arm around her. "Thank you. Honestly."

She kissed him on the forehead. "We won't let them get away with it," she said.

And with that, she walked away and down the steps, stopping to chat with Reverend David Okonjo, who had managed Blessed Way for as long as Moss knew the place existed. Both he and Wanda had roots in Nigeria, and many of Moss's mother's friends joked that Reverend Okonjo could have been her father in another life. As Reverend Okonjo and Wanda walked off into the crowd, an energy zapped Moss. *This is really happening.*

He hopped off the stage, hoping to find anyone else he knew. Reverend Okonjo held out a hand and Moss gratefully took it. He then moved past the reverend toward someone he thought looked like Reg. But before he could cross the length of the church to greet him, he felt a hand on his arm stop him. "Moss!" Esperanza said excitedly. "Look how many people are here!" She pulled him into a hug as so many others had.

"Seriously, my mom really came through," he said, and saying it out loud again made him feel a bit better about the future. "You sure you're okay doing this?"

"Don't worry about me," she said, waving a hand to dismiss him. "So we need to thank Kaisha and your mom, cause I'm pretty sure we couldn't have done this without them."

"Oh, I will," he said. "Where are your parents?"

She gestured behind her. "Somewhere in the back, chatting with someone. Turns out they *do* have friends outside of Cal Berkeley!"

"You're not worried?" he said, struggling to be loud enough for Esperanza to hear him.

"Worried about what?" she asked.

"Well . . . your parents being here. Them getting involved."

"Maybe a little bit. I had a talk with them on the way over, and I think they understand that they're here to support y'all, not turn this into some crusade."

"I just hope we can count on everyone here," he said, scratching his head out of nervousness. "I mean, how can we be sure that these people want to help?"

"We don't, I suppose. But that's the whole point of this, right?"

"I guess," Moss said, "but I still don't even know what we're planning to do. I mean, most of the people here don't even go to school anymore, so how are they supposed to help?"

Esperanza ran her hand up and down Moss's arm, trying to comfort him. "Look, I think you're asking good questions, but you *are* nervous a lot. I don't want to tell you that you worried for nothing, but I'm hoping that your mom can help direct all this chaos. She *did* volunteer, didn't she?"

"True," he conceded. Moss led her back to where he'd last seen his mother. "I guess I just don't want us to lose again," he added, more to himself than to Esperanza. She didn't hear him over the noise, though. She had rushed to Wanda's side, her voice cheery and carefree, and Moss took a moment to give a long look to the church hall. The door opened and more people squeezed in, filling the space around the pews and at the back of the room.

Javier shouted a greeting, and Moss couldn't help the wide smile that grew on his face. A joy washed over him, a spark without the other complications he felt in that room. He planted a kiss on Javier's cheek when they hugged. "Hurry up," Moss said, and he guided Javier to a spot on the edge of stage right. "It's about to start."

"Glad I got here when I did," he said. "Hey, before this gets all out of control . . ." He paused, looked down, then back up. "You busy Sunday morning?"

"I don't think so. Why?"

"Come to breakfast with me. You ever been to Brown Sugar Kitchen?"

Moss scoffed at him. "I'll put aside the offense for the moment," he said, "because how *dare* you assume I haven't been." He kissed him on the cheek again. "But yes. Lemme ask my mom if it's okay first, but I'd love to."

He wanted to say more, but his mother ascended the short set of steps to the stage, Reverend Okonjo behind her. She allowed Reverend Okonjo to pass by her and step up to the pulpit, and as he did so, the room hushed almost immediately. The electricity of that transition sent a chill through Moss, and he watched as the whole room changed. People sat down quickly and quietly. The joking stopped. The laughter ceased. The entire crowd was now focused on the man on the stage. Moss stood off stage right so he didn't block anyone's view, and Javier locked his fingers with his. *This feels right,* he thought, and he gripped that hand with purpose, with happiness.

"Thank y'all for coming out tonight," Reverend Okonjo said, his voice booming in the church. "I know we got a lot to talk about. I've had Jermaine there"—he gestured to the middle aisle, toward a lanky black man adjusting a stand—"put up a microphone so y'all can talk with Miss Jeffries here. So *we* can have a conversation about our community." He looked toward Moss's mother and smiled. "Now, Miss Jeffries here has been a longtime resident of Oakland, born and raised here, and she chose to raise her son here, too. Me and her, we go way back," he said, which elicited a soft laugh from the crowd. "We been in this community, trying to make it better, for a long, long time.

"So when she came to me with a story about one of our own—Mr. Reginald Phillips, a bright young man who goes to this very church—I knew I had to help. Now, the Phillips family could not make it tonight; they're taking care of their son right now, making sure he is loved. It's our job, my friends, to take the burden on ourselves when they cannot. It is our duty to lift them on our shoulders and raise them above their circumstances."

A few people hollered and clapped. Moss was fixated.

"I see a lot of familiar faces tonight," Reverend Okonjo continued. "I see Martin Tremaine, who was responsible for the food drive last year to help feed those who could not afford a holiday dinner." A sizable portion of the crowd clapped after that one. "I see Tenaya back there!" He waved to her. "She was responsible for helping the city council pass that domestic-violence initiative in the spring." More applause.

"I see a community that cares about those around them, so I am asking y'all to listen to Miss Jeffries. Listen to her, and ask her questions. Speak your mind. Honesty and integrity shall guide us, as it always has."

He raised his hands up, and most of those in attendance lowered their heads. Moss kept his raised, his eyes open. "Lord, please guide us today as we seek the truth," the reverend said. "Help us to know your ways. Teach us your paths. Lead us in your truth and teach us, for you are the Lord of our salvation, and for you, we shall wait. Amen."

The crowd echoed the amen, and Reverend Okonjo stepped aside, offering the pulpit to Moss's mother. She looked over at Moss before speaking, and a wave of affection swept over him as she smiled. He knew that smile was for him alone.

"Good evening, y'all," Wanda said, and a few people muttered a response or waved to her, some shifting in the pews, and the rustling echoed loudly in the otherwise silent church. His mother continued and introduced herself, spoke of all the years she'd spent in Oakland, and Moss's gaze drifted to the crowd itself. His mama had always been so good at this stuff. She never seemed to hesitate, as if she always had the right words waiting on the tip of her tongue. But a prickling ran over his skin as he watched the people in the church, their attention focused on his mother, all of them awaiting whatever it was she was going to say.

They would nod their heads on cue when she spoke of the problems this neighborhood had gone through before. When she mentioned how they'd defeated the last fare raise on AC Transit a couple of years back, a group of people whooped and cheered in response. No one seemed bored or disinterested in what she had to say. He was so used to the wandering attention of his fellow classmates that the phenomenon here thrilled him. He felt nothing like Esperanza must have felt toward her own parents; he was glad his mother was as involved in his life as she was. That creeping doubt, that deadly fear, began to slide away.

He turned his gaze back to his mother as she continued.

"I'd like to take a moment here to pass things along to someone who is better qualified to tell this story," she said, looking to her right. Moss glanced behind himself and did a double take when he saw that Kaisha was standing off to the side. He let go of Javier's hand and moved up next to her.

"How's Reg?" he whispered after hugging her.

"Okay," she said into his ear. "He's back home now. He was gonna come to speak, but his doc didn't want him using his energy tonight."

"So who's gonna speak for him?"

It was then that Moss felt the silence in the room, aware that his mother was staring in his direction. "I am," Kaisha said, moving away from him after squeezing his arm. She walked up the steps to the stage to scattered applause, each step purposeful. It was clear that the attendees didn't know whether or not they should be clapping at this moment, and so it petered out rapidly as Kaisha approached the mic. She embraced Wanda, then pulled out her phone, propping it up in front of her, sucking in a deep breath before looking up at the crowd. Moss could see her gripping the edge of the pulpit, her fingers tense and rigid, and he moved back to stand next to Javier.

"My name is Kaisha Gordon," she said, her voice quavering on her last name. She took another deep breath, and Wanda came up behind her, a hand on her back. Moss saw his mother whisper something to her, and she nodded her head. "I'm sorry, I'm just a little nervous," she said, leaning in to the mic. "I'm used to doing this online, and no one is actually staring at you when you're typing stuff up."

A few people laughed, and the nervous energy seemed to comfort her. *You can do it,* Moss thought.

"I was at West Oakland High when my boyfriend, Reginald Phillips, was brutally harmed by the recently installed metal detectors." She said this with clarity as her quavering voice began to even out. "He is currently at home with his family, and wishes he could be here. He did write something that he'd like me to read to y'all, and I hope you'll listen."

She paused again, her eyes drifting over to Moss, who nodded to her in encouragement. The only time he had ever seen Kaisha speak in front of a group was for a presentation in an English class the year before. She had spent the entire time with her eyes glued to a piece of paper, her voice monotone and rushed, and she had later confessed to Moss that she felt miserable about it. He could see her gaze keep falling down to her phone, and he knew she was trying. A woman from the back of the crowd shouted up at her, "Go 'head, baby!" This was followed by a number of shouts and some applause, and she smiled briefly in response, then returned her focus to the phone.

"'To my friends, family, and community in Oakland,'" she began, reading from her phone. "'This was not an easy thing to write, but I wanted Kaisha to have something to say to you about what happened with me. She also helped me with my writing 'cause I'm not very good at it.'"

The crowd laughed at that one, and Kaisha took another breath. "'When I woke up that morning, I just wanted to make it to Ms. Edmunds's art class because I love to draw. It's what I'm good at, and Ms. Edmunds makes me feel good, too. When I tried to enter school that day, I ended up experiencing the worst thing I've ever gone through.'"

Kaisha paused for a few seconds. "'When I was fourteen, a drunk driver hit our car, and I almost lost my parents. It shattered my leg, and I've been goin' to rehab since then to get better. I'd even started being able to walk on crutches a couple times a week this summer. I was proud of my progress.'"

She turned her head to the right, and Moss saw the tears running down Kaisha's face.

"'What happened to me,'" she said, her voice cracking, "'ruined that chance. The doctors expect that with the bone and muscle damage, I'll never be able to walk normally again.'" The crowd gasped, but Kaisha's head jerked upward, and she dealt the audience a fierce glare. "Please don't feel sorry," she said, and Moss knew she wasn't reading from her notes. "He doesn't want your pity, he wants your *anger*."

Someone whooped from the back of the crowd. "Damn right!" they said loudly.

She bowed her head and continued reading. Her voice carried through the room, and Reg's words, simple and straightforward, captivated them. But it was Kaisha's delivery, so nervous and sincere, that broke Moss's heart. *She really loves him,* Moss realized, and he knew that this whole affair had taken a toll on Kaisha, too. How often had she put Reg before herself? How was *she* coping with this nightmare?

He looked to his mother, whose arm was locked around Reverend Okonjo's, her chin up, her face proud. *I want to make her proud, too.* The thought flashed through Moss's mind, and he felt a determination spread in his chest.

Kaisha folded the paper up and pushed it aside on the pulpit. "I know y'all don't know me," she said, and she wasn't looking down anymore. Her eyes were jumping from person to person. She gave Moss a quick glance and smiled. "And many of you don't know Reg, either. But we just want to go to *school.*" Her voice broke again. "I'm sixteen. I shouldn't have to beg for that. But we just want to get to class without fearing for our lives."

She stepped away from the pulpit to applause, but it wasn't celebratory. Moss felt the ripple through the crowd. Anger. *Rage.*

His mother took Kaisha's place as she came to stand next to Moss. He pulled her close to him in a side hug. "You did real good," he said as quickly as he could.

She wiped another tear off her cheek. "Thanks," she said.

"I wanted to bring up another young woman to speak to you," said Wanda, and this time, she gestured out into the crowd. Moss watched Shawna stand up, saw her mother and father cheer her on. She took her beanie off as she got onstage, and Moss realized he'd never seen her without it off. Her hair was as short as his own, and he thought she looked incredible with her fade. She grabbed the sides of the pulpit as Kaisha did, but the poor girl looked even more nervous.

"Yoooo," she said into the mic, then chuckled nervously. "Sorry,

I don't do this kinda shit often." Then she clamped a hand over her mouth. "Oh, shit, man, I'm sorry, Reverend."

That brought another round of laughter from the crowd, and Reverend Okonjo smiled. "Continue, Ms. Meyers," he said.

She breathed out, a little to close to the mic, and it popped. "My name is Shawna Meyers," she said, "and I also go to West Oakland High. I wasn't there when Reg got hurt, but I was also a victim of my school's policies."

She looked out to the crowd, and Moss saw that she had locked eyes with her father, who gestured at her to keep going. Another deep breath, another burst of air let out over the mic. "The reason the metal detectors were installed was because of me," she continued, "but it's important that you know that it wasn't my fault. When one of our campus police officers overreacted and assaulted me, the other students came to my defense."

Shawna glanced over to where Moss, Kaisha, and Javier stood off the stage. "You know, I feel the same way," she said, and she was speaking to them. "I just wanna go to school. Get to basketball. *Play.* And now I gotta worry about cops running free over our school. How many of us knew that Officer Hull had a temper?"

The response from the students in the crowd was instantaneous, a raucous bout of yells and cries of anger.

"And it sounds like this other cop who hurt Reg had just the same type of temper. So when we gonna say that this is *enough*?"

More applause, more rage. Moss's heart *soared*.

"That's all I gots to say," said Shawna, and she hopped off the stage and sauntered back to her family, who welcomed her with open arms.

Reverend Okonjo strode up to the pulpit right as the crowd broke out in applause and cheers, the group agitated and eager to do something, *anything*. "What we gonna do?" a man shouted out, and Moss couldn't even tell where it came from.

Reverend Okonjo raised his hands as people shouted out suggestions. "My friends, we must do this one at a time," he said, and that seemed to work. The crowd quieted down until the only sound was the reverend's breathing, amplified by the microphone just inches from him. He lowered his hands, grasping the edges of the pulpit. "I want Miss Jeffries to lead this part," he said, inclining his head slightly in Wanda's direction. She walked up to him without a glance behind. The reverend stepped to the side, and then Wanda took control of the entire room.

She would point to people, call them out by their first names, sometimes throwing in a last name if it was too common, and she seemed to know who *everyone* was. They'd shout, speak their piece, make a suggestion, and then sit down, the crowd roaring to life whether they disagreed or agreed with whatever someone said. And yet, Moss's mother always managed to get the crowd silent enough so someone else could speak and get their turn.

The suggestions themselves came pouring out of the people from this community. Boycotts. Demonstrations. Letter-writing campaigns. Someone suggested that some of the more industrious members of the community "uninstall" the machines after hours. Wanda shot that down quickly, though, pointing out that the school would most likely have extra security after hours.

"What if we take it to the news?" a woman holding a newborn suggested from the front row, bobbing up and down to soothe her child. "It's already being reported."

"They're not going to be on our side!" Njemile shouted. Wanda nodded her head at her, a gesture meant to tell Njemile to continue. "Did you see the stories that *already* aired since this happened?" she asked loudly. "See how they're already shifting the blame?"

"Maybe the blame is right where it belongs," an older man shot back from the other side of the room. That response sent a rustle through the crowd, but they quieted upon the reverend's upraised hand. Moss tried to see who had said such an awful thing, but it was coming from too far away.

The man cleared his throat. "I just don't understand why this younger generation can't just respect the process," he said, and *that* was met with a number of boos and hisses. Moss squinted, hoping his eyes would adjust to the darkness in the back of the church. The person rose, and he stood out for one reason only: He was one of the few white men in the room. The guy was tall and one of his arms was raised up above his head. "Why are we even talking about this?"

Wanda did not miss a beat. "Because we care about what happens in this community," she shot back. "West Oakland High is in *this* community. It's our school, filled with our students, one of whom happens to be my son. So I think it's pretty damn relevant that we talk about it."

"And what's the problem with just *talking* about it?" Moss saw who had stood up and said it: Shamika. "We just talkin'."

"About what?" The man had moved out into the aisle. "Why are we assuming that there was anything done wrong here? Wasn't this just an accident?"

"What do we do if there's another accident?" Shamika said. "What then? Do we always just write it off as an accident?"

"If it is one," he said. "You call a spade a spade."

The crowd murmured again, some in anger, others in frustration, but Moss was disturbed to see others nodding their heads.

"You really gonna use *that* phrase, aren't you?" Shamika said.

"If I may?" Moss looked back to the pulpit and saw that Kaisha had returned. His mother gestured her to take her place. She pulled the small microphone back down to her height. "Since y'all are talking about my friend, perhaps I should explain."

"Look, I'm sorry your friend got hurt," the man shouted, shaking his head, "but it was an accident. What's the problem here?"

"The problem is that there never should have been a situation like this in the first place," she said, the anger creasing her forehead. "Why does our school need metal detectors?"

"That's not the question at hand—" he began, but Kaisha cut him off.

"No, that's exactly what I'm asking. Why should my school even *have* metal detectors?"

He didn't answer at first. He shuffled from one foot to the next.

"For safety," he said, his words echoing in the church. "Especially after that brawl your friends got in last week."

More voices of affirmation this time. Moss felt the roiling anger under the surface, and he was envious of how calm Kaisha seemed up there. She took a deep breath and smiled, and he knew exactly what was about to happen: She was going in for the kill.

"Do you go to my school, sir?"

The question was met by silence. The man scoffed, his shoulders up in a shrug, and he looked about the audience as if he needed validation that Kaisha was absurd. No one said anything to him, so he turned back to her. "Are you serious?"

"Completely."

"No," he answered. "Of course not!"

"Since you don't, then you couldn't possibly know that last week, Shawna Meyers, who you just heard from, was assaulted by Officer Frank Hull, who suspected her of bringing drugs on campus. Instead of taking *five seconds* to learn that it was her medication, he nearly killed her. Whatever video you might have seen was taken out of context. Did students overreact? Probably." She stopped and shook her head. "I don't know who threw that chair, but your aim was *terrible*."

Some laughter at that. Kaisha pressed on. "I'm just saying that I understand *why* that happened. It was the last straw. We are *tired*, sir, and what you saw was a reaction to that."

He started to sputter out a response, but she held up a finger. "No, sir, I'm not finished." A few people in the audience giggled or gasped at that, but Kaisha pushed on once more. "Let's assume that you're correct, that there *had* been a brawl, and that it had not been a reaction to a security guard choking a student against the lockers. No weapons were used in that altercation. We do not have a history of weapons being brought into campus. There was nothing that could possibly have justified Mr. Elliot and the other administration bringing in the Oakland Police Department to have full run of our school. *Nothing*. And that's the problem you can't see. To you, it's an answer, but to us, it's a question that never existed in the first place."

She sighed, and she rubbed her temples with her left hand. "I'm trying not to be personal, but it's hard not to take this personal. That's my boyfriend whose leg was hurt. That's *my* boyfriend who is gonna have years of trauma to deal with. And some of us go to that school, and we're going to wonder every day if we're next. *Are* we next?"

Moss stood up, the energy of Kaisha's words flowing through him. "And why should we worry about something like that just for goin' to school?"

"What's wrong with caring about the safety of our kids?" A woman near the unnamed man stood up, her hands on her hips. "Why are we demonizing this man for speaking his mind?"

"Who's doing that?" Moss said. "No one did anything of the sort."

"My son goes to the same school, and I hear the things he brings home with him," she yelled. "The music, the language, the way you kids wear your clothes. I think it's a good thing that someone is willing to protect him from hooligans like you and your friends."

The chaos that followed drowned out any single response; people stood, shouting angry responses at the woman, while side conversations began to spring up, too. But Moss kept his focus on her.

"She sounds pleasant," Javier whispered in his ear.

"Please, *please*," Reverend Okonjo said, and his voice boomed over everyone. "Please, we have to do this one at a time." The crowd began to quiet down and return to their seats, but Moss remained standing, glaring at the woman who spoke, hoping she saw the look he was giving her.

The reverend continued. "I'd also appreciate it if we did not insult other people in this community. We want everyone to speak, but we cannot treat each other with such suspicion and anger. *Please*. Now, Wanda, would you like to continue?"

She stepped back up to the microphone. "I know I shouldn't be surprised, but I didn't think any of us needed to justify our feelings on this new pilot security program at the school." She tapped the side of the pulpit while scanning the crowd. "There's a history in this city, one that y'all should know, of law enforcement agencies treating our youngsters with disrespect, disdain, and mistrust. Now, we can argue all night about how we feel about the police, but that's not the point of this meeting. I hope that we all agree that we want these dangerous metal detectors out of the school as soon as possible, police involvement or not."

A round of applause passed through the audience at that, and Wanda smiled. "So, again, the topic at hand: What are we going to do about it?"

"Well, I work at the local NBC station," said an Indian woman off stage left, her hand in the air. "I know some of the staff writers."

Wanda nodded her head. "You should come speak to us"—she gestured to herself and the reverend—"once we're done. What's your name?"

"Kripa," she shouted. The woman sat down, and Wanda kept the conversation moving. It was a spectacle to Moss, seeing his mother's eyes wash over the people in that church, jumping from one raised hand to another, always knowing when to shift the conversation to the next person. Esperanza came up to the stage to join him on his right as he sat down on the edge, her head resting on his shoulder. Javier followed and snuggled up against him without a word. Moss put his left hand on his leg, and Javier looped his fingers into Moss's. A jolt of nervous energy filled him; he had never held hands with anyone in front of so many people.

But it felt right.

The three of them watched Wanda for a while, transfixed. The suggestions felt nonstop. Like the woman who said that she knew someone close to one of the superintendents of the Oakland school district, which opened an administrative avenue they had not considered. Or the Haitian couple who lived a couple of blocks over from Moss, the ones who had the Siamese cat who intimidated passersby from the window. The wife suggested that they find some way to get the permit pulled from the school, so then they'd *have* to keep the metal detectors off.

But the consensus came about through this conversation: This community needed to stage a demonstration outside the campus *during* school hours, something that would be dramatic, distracting, and unable to be ignored. "There *is* that student parking lot across the street," Bits suggested when they got to the microphone, their voice low and even. "What if we ask people to leave a couple of rows empty near the front so that we can gather there later in the afternoon?"

Wanda nodded her head. "That's a fine idea, Bits." She turned to Kaisha. "We can use the Facebook group to let students know about that, right?" Kaisha excitedly nodded back. "So what time works best for a rally?"

"I think we gotta do it before school ends," Bits continued. "Most classes are out at three, but it's not gonna be effective if we wait until after that."

The idea came to Moss suddenly and he thrust his hand in the air from the side of the stage. "Mama," he said, and she bowed her head gently to him, and he said, as loudly as he could, "we should stage a walkout."

There were a lot of people talking after he said that, and he felt that charge run through him again. His mother motioned for people to quiet down, and they obeyed her. "Come here, baby," she said. He looked to Javier, whose face was full of excitement. *Go,* he mouthed. Moss moved to her side and she scooted out of the way so that he had the microphone. His heart leapt as he looked out at all the people whose attention was directed to him. He cleared his throat, and the microphone carried it through the room.

"I just think that if we're going to do something that will make the school think twice about these metal detectors, we need to disrupt class. Like, *really* disrupt things."

More murmurs from the crowd. More rustling from those moving about. Moss was onto something, and so he pressed forward, more certain than he was before that this was the best idea. "I think we should organize a time for the entire student body to walk out of class next week. Sometime in the middle of the day. Everyone just picks up their stuff and leaves. It'll be eerie, right?"

He looked out at the crowd. "It's happened before, hasn't it? Maybe not here but in other schools. Walkouts are pretty effective, aren't they?"

His mother beamed admiration at him, and she nearly lost control of the conversation once again. Moss felt like the ignition for a fire, and as the people in Blessed Way began to talk strategy and logistics, he looked at Esperanza. His mother. Javier. His friends scattered about the room. All the anger and anxiety gave way to something new: hope. Maybe it wouldn't last long, but he wasn't going to fight it. Not this time.

18

"You nervous?" Javier asked. He stuffed his phone back in his pocket and sat down next to Moss on the bench outside Brown Sugar Kitchen. There were still at least a few parties ahead of them, so he settled in for the long wait to be seated.

"I know you haven't known me long," Moss said, "but I'm a pretty nervous guy in general. You're gonna have to be more specific."

Javier laughed. "I just got a message on Facebook from a friend of mine over at Eastside. Apparently news of your little protest thing has gotten over there."

"Ah, *that,*" Moss said. "It's barely been twenty-four hours, and it's kinda taken on a life of its own." He pulled out his own phone. "You're not on Twitter, are you?"

"Not my thing. Snapchat, you know."

"I noticed. You Snap *everything,* man. I'm surprised you haven't sent me one from the shower."

Javier's eyebrow curled. "Would you like one?"

"We can talk about that later," he said, then laughed. "And yeah, maybe."

"You're so nasty, Moss. If only people knew the truth!"

Moss rolled his eyes at him, then scrolled down his timeline on Twitter. "Kaisha came up with a great hashtag. 'EverybodyWalksIn-Oakland.' It's pretty funny. Everyone's referencing the walkout without actually being specific."

"Pretty clever," Javier admitted. "So how are you surprised this has gotten so big?"

"I don't know. I guess I'm not used to people caring. These things come in waves, you know?"

"What things?"

"Like . . . look, my mom's been involved in a lot of stuff over the years. Protests, rallies, that sort of thing. And that was *before* my dad, too. I'm pretty sure her parents were involved with the Black Panthers here in Oakland. And it's not that I don't care about any of it, because I do. Maybe too much."

"But it all comes and goes, right?" Javier said, scrunching up his face. "Yeah, I get that."

"I know you won't remember it, but my dad's death was a phase, too," said Moss, and he was a little surprised at how easy it was for him to talk about this with Javier. "Not for me, of course, but most people just stopped caring after a while. He was just another story, another unfortunate bit of history." Moss paused, his gaze focused on the sidewalk. "You ever know what it's like to be a statistic? Or part of one?"

Javier sighed. "Maybe not in the same way as you, but yeah. Mom came here when I was like . . . eight? Right after my father disappeared. I still don't know where he went. He just left one night. My mom thinks it was with someone younger than her." He shook his head. "It's not important, but the point is that I'm not actually a citizen. We never managed to get citizenship for either of us."

Moss didn't know how to respond to that, so he just said, "I had no idea."

"It's okay," said Javier. "It's not something I should advertise, you know?"

"And your school has no problem with it?"

"Ha!" Javier slapped his own knee. "If they did, they'd have to eject half of the student body. Lots of kids there are just like me."

"Wow," Moss said, leaning back into the bench. "I feel like I learned your deep, dark secret."

"Oh, you have no idea," Javier joked. "A gay immigrant from Guatemala. Wait until you see my agenda."

Moss laughed, and it filled his spirit with a joy he'd not felt in a long time. He reached over, grasped Javier's hand, and then brought it up to his mouth. He planted a kiss on it, delicate but purposeful. "You're a national treasure, dude."

"Thank you, Moss. The feeling is mutual."

Moss smiled at that, and a boldness came over him. "It is, isn't it?" he said.

Javier balked at that, and his left eyebrow shot up. *God, I love when he does that.* Javier studied his face. "Man, you're serious, aren't you?"

"Yeah, I am. Do you know how hard it's been to just believe that you want to spend time with me?"

"I've noticed," Javier said. "Why, though? Why would I want to hang out with you if I didn't actually like you?"

"I don't know," Moss said, leaning into Javier. "Maybe you just wanted me for sex. We're gay men. That's not exactly an unbelievable suggestion."

"Yeah, but I haven't had sex either. I'm in the same boat as you."

"The U.S.S. *Sexual Frustration*?"

"Ha ha ha," said Javier. "We *could* take care of that if you wanted."

Moss winced. "I don't know. I don't know if I'm ready yet."

"It's okay. I don't know if I am either. But this hasn't been about sex, has it? You always seemed bewildered that I even found you attractive."

"Yeah." He watched a couple get ushered into the restaurant, and the hostess gestured to him and Javier, letting him know they were next. He waved to her, and then looked back at Javier. Eyebrow raised. *He really is too much.* "What? Why you givin' me that look?"

"Are you avoiding the subject at hand? Using social obligations to ignore the uncomfortable issue?"

"Maybe! Also, I'm starving, and I really need some chicken and waffles in my stomach soon."

Javier leaned back against the building. "So what's the problem?"

"I guess it's hard to talk about," Moss admitted. "But I really am a lot more cynical than people realize. At least in my head."

"I get that. I mean, again: We're gay men. And we're not white."

"That's one part of it, but . . ." Moss nearly dropped the point he wanted to make, but he turned, positioning his body in Javier's direction. He *had* to be honest with him about it, and now seemed like the best chance he was going to get. "I'm just gonna say it, man."

"Say what?" Javier said. Moss saw the worry flit over him.

"Have you ever, like . . . dated a black guy?"

He furrowed his brows at first, looked away, then back at Moss. "Um . . . well, not a date. I was talking to some guy earlier this year. Nothing came of it, though."

"I know it's an awkward question, but it's something I have to think about. All the time."

Javier was nodding. "That's fair," he said. "I can't imagine it's easy. You know, asking that question *or* having to worry about it."

"I have to ask because . . . well, it's not just a white thing, if that makes sense. I've had people who weren't black say creepy things to me, and I gotta protect myself."

"So that you don't feel like a fetish, right? Like you're just some experiment or something?" He shook his head. "Please tell me if I'm not getting this right."

"That's pretty much it," Moss said. "Man, this is awkward. I'm sorry."

"Nah, don't apologize," he said. He grabbed Moss's hand. "You're not the first, I guess, but still, I'll also do my best to treat you right."

"Thanks," he said. "It's one reason why I have a hard time believing you liked me," he admitted, "but it's not the only one. My brain just . . . doesn't cooperate."

"You mean like a self-esteem thing?"

"Well, it's sort of like that," said Moss. "But just imagine that no matter what you see or hear, your mind tells you it's wrong. That's what I've got working against me. Like, you can tell me that you find me hot, and my brain will literally tell me that you don't mean it, that you're lying to me, that you're just stringing me along in order to hurt me later."

Javier didn't say anything at first, and the silence was worse than if he'd said something terrible. He stared forward and remained still except for the slight movement from his breathing. *Oh no,* Moss thought. *Have I found the breaking point? Is this where he leaves me?*

But before the panic could settle in, Javier squeezed Moss's hand, then raised it and kissed it much like Moss had done minutes earlier. "That helps me understand you," he said. "And I *want* to understand you better."

"Really?" Moss turned his head to face Javier, and not even his cynical brain could deny what he saw. Javier's eyes were aglow with interest. It was genuine. *Real.*

"If you need me to say it, over and over again, I will." Javier stood up then, his hand still locked in Moss's, and he pulled him up and into an embrace. "Even if it's corny," he said into Moss's ear, then he kissed him on the cheek. "Even if it's repetitive." He kissed him on the other one. "Morris Jeffries, Jr.: I think you're pretty awesome."

Moss didn't care that there were other people waiting for lunch, that some were staring at the two of them, that in any other situation, he'd probably be embarrassed to death. He kissed Javier, deep and hard, for a few seconds, then pulled away. "Thank you," he said. "It means a lot to me."

"Excellent," Javier said. "And good timing, too. I think your name is up next."

Moss looked behind him to see the hostess wave in his direction. "Let's go, then."

"You ready for our first official date together?" Javier teased. "Let me make sure to mark down this date on my calendar. I'll celebrate it every year."

A year. The idea was new to Moss, and it scared him a little. But he sat at a small table across from Javier, and he could imagine himself doing this again and again. *Maybe that's what Mama was talking about,* he thought. *Maybe this is what love feels like.*

He sure hoped so.

They placed their order for food a few minutes later—Moss went with his standard, the cornmeal waffles and fried chicken, and Javier decided to try the BBQ shrimp and grits—and let the sheer chaos of noise settle in around them. Moss had only been here once when it wasn't packed, early on a weekday during the summer when his mom had a day off. It was generally worth the wait, though, and he started salivating as he watched plates get delivered to every table that wasn't his.

"You ever been out on a date before?" Javier asked as Moss gaped at a bowl of grits with envy on his face.

"Me?" He shook his head. "Never got to that point with anyone before."

"No one? I find that hard to believe."

Moss blushed as the waitress refilled his water. "It's true, though," he said. "There was a guy last year at my school. I had had a crush on him for most of my freshman year, and he came out at the start of our sophomore year."

"And you made your move then, right?"

"Oh, *god* no," said Moss, laughing. "I waited in silent terror for at least a month before I even spoke to him."

"And how did that go?" Javier asked.

Moss grimaced. "Well, let's just say he wasn't very interested in guys who had my *luxurious* skin tone."

"You're kidding," said Javier. Then he shook his head. "Of course you're not."

"Welcome to the Bay Area," said Moss. "Liberal bastion of progress."

"I've had my fair share of guys who made taco jokes at me or asked to see my . . . ahem." He cleared his throat and looked around at the tables near them, then leaned closer to Moss. "My *burrito*," he whispered.

Moss squinted. "I don't get it," he said. "Did they think you just carried a—" His eyes shot open. "Oh. *Oh my god.*"

"Indeed," said Javier. "Not my most dignified moment."

A plate of biscuits and jam was dropped off then, and Moss pulled it toward him. "Sorry, I'm *starving*," he said, and he spread some boysenberry jam over a warm biscuit. "I think some people think being gay here in the Bay means that all our problems are solved."

"That's because they don't see us as anything else," said Javier, grabbing the other biscuit and buttering it. "It's like we're a single, solitary identity and nothing more. The world is hella complicated! There's more to it than that."

"Amen," said Moss, wiping some crumbs off his patchy facial hair. "By the way, I could eat these every day of my life and never tire of them."

"I gotta have my mom's cooking, though. I can't live without it."

Moss put his elbows on the table and leaned on them, a smile growing as he examined Javier's face. "Thanks for this," he said. "And I don't just mean the date."

"No problem, man," he said, smiling back. "This has been a pretty wild couple of weeks."

"You realize we, like, skipped over the whole awkward Dating 101 shit, right?"

Javier put the other half of his biscuit in his mouth and chewed for a few seconds. "What do you mean?"

"You know . . . like, 'Hi, what are you into? What do you do in your free time?'"

"Ugh," Javier groaned. "'What are you into?' I hate that question. You know they're trying to ask about sex without outright saying it."

"Right? And as soon as you call a dude on it, they get all hella defensive about it." Moss leaned back into his chair and stretched his leg out, rubbing it up against Javier. Javier smirked at Moss. "Well, I like video games. Comic books. Reading. Finding a good record and disappearing into it. I hate long walks on the beach, by the way. All that damn sand in your shoes." He shuddered.

"You read comic books?" Javier asked, pointing a butter knife at him. "You never told me that."

"Some," he said. "It's hard to keep up with everything, and they keep messing up the stuff I like. Like Captain America or Miles Morales."

"Don't even get me started," said Javier. "I stick to indie stuff, mostly. Lots of comics online." He paused, pursed his lips.

"What is it?"

It looked like Javier had *grimaced*. "I kinda like *drawing* my own comics," he said, his voice lower than before.

Moss whooped. "No way," he said. "Lemme see some! You got any on your phone or anything?"

Then it washed over Javier's face: redness. *He's blushing.* Suddenly, Moss didn't feel so bad about being sensitive and easily riled. He reached over to put his hand on top of Javier's. "Dude, I'm sorry, you don't have to show me anything. I promise."

"Nah, I wanna," he said, his eyes darting up to Moss, then back down to the table. "It's just that I'm still learning. I'm not very good."

"Girl, I can barely draw a *circle*. I'm sure you're very talented."

Javier finally gave Moss a full gaze. "Okay, soon, then. My friend Carlos is teaching me stuff . . . this kid is *wild,* man." His eyes were lit up again, the embarrassment gone from his face. "I have to introduce you to him. He's this tiny little guy from Chile; his parents came here not too long after me and my mamá did. Hella quiet, but he can do these unreal pieces. The teachers had him paint a mural at our school!"

"You know," said Moss, "I actually feel really excited by the idea of meeting your friends. I can't say I expected that."

"Well, I couldn't imagine getting to know someone like you," Javier said. "You're so damn cute. And you care about the world, too. That's . . . well, that's rare."

Their waitress returned and dropped two steaming plates of food in front of them. The smell of the spices on the chicken wafted up, and a pang of hunger hit Moss again. But it couldn't even touch the surge of affection he felt for Javier.

"Y'all need anything else? Maybe some extra syrup," the waitress said.

"Please," said Moss. Javier shook his head and thanked her, then looked back to Moss. He raised his glass of orange juice to him. "I know I gave a toast the other night outside Esperanza's house, but we didn't actually have drinks in our hands, so it doesn't count."

Moss raised up his water. "To . . . new possibilities," he said.

"To good food and even better company," said Javier.

"And to dismantling a system of violence in my school," said Moss playfully, and they clinked glasses and laughed. They dug into their food, and Moss savored the mixture of the cornmeal waffles with the sweetness of the syrup, the kick of the chicken, and watched Javier's eyes bulge as he took his first bite of the grits. They devoured their food quickly and quietly, but the moment seemed to last forever. Moss would not have cared if it really hadn't ended. He could stay in this restaurant, across from this handsome boy, for an eternity.

19

The news passed from person to person.

Moss saw people whispering in homeroom when he arrived on Monday morning; one was that girl Njemile currently had a crush on, and there were two guys on the football team on the opposite side of the room who glanced at Moss quickly, then looked away, their voices hushed and husky. Mrs. Torrance had her eyebrows raised when he looked her way. Would this plan get back to the other teachers at some point? Mrs. Torrance was at the church, but what if the less-invested administration got wind of it beforehand?

Stop thinking of the worst, Moss told himself as he sat down. *We'll deal with that if it happens.* He looked over at Njemile, and she was already smiling at him. "What?" Moss said.

She shook her head. "It's kinda cool, isn't it? The way everyone seems so excited."

"I hope they're excited," he said. "I still don't believe it's happening."

"Oh, Moss," she said. "How little faith you have in others."

"Do you blame me? I don't have much faith to go on these days, what with the world ending around us."

"You know, sometimes it *does* feel like we're in one of those trendy dystopian novels," she admitted. "Except a lot less white."

He laughed, but Mrs. Torrance cleared her throat at that moment, so he didn't get to continue. The class focused their attention on one another as she began to take attendance. When Mrs. Torrance got to Moss's name, he could have sworn she winked at him.

This is going to be a very strange week, he realized.

———

Tuesday morning. A searing sun already sat in the sky, and Moss wiped the sweat off his hairline before putting his fitted cap on his head. "You ready for this?" Moss said.

Reg shuffled in his chair, his right hand massaging his thigh just above the spot where the gauze ended. "I hope so," he said. "I don't want to sit at home any longer."

"We got you," Kaisha said. "Anything you need."

"I'm just glad those detectors are off," he said, and then he sighed loudly. "I wish they weren't even here, though."

"Maybe they'll come to their senses," said Moss, "and *actually* get rid of them."

Kaisha and Reg scoffed at that simultaneously, then fell into a fit of giggles. *Those two are made for each other,* Moss thought.

"Well, no sense delaying this," said Reg. He put his hands on the wheels on either side of his chair and gave himself a forceful shove forward. Kaisha stood behind him to help him up the makeshift ramp, and Moss stayed to the right. A crowd of students still milled about on the front lawn of campus, but Reg had wanted to give himself extra time to get inside, just in case he needed it.

He never made it to the ramp. Moss heard the applause first; then someone yelled out Reg's name. The students of West Oakland High converged on Reg, and before Moss could react, they had grabbed ahold of his wheelchair. "What are you doing?" Reg yelled, but he was drowned out by the chants of his name, repeating over and over. He was lifted up the stairs and deposited at the top, and the applause rang out again.

Moss scrambled up the stairs after him, shoving his way past people he'd never interacted with before at school. Kids were patting Reg on the shoulder. "Welcome back," one of the guys said before darting into the building. Another sprinted up the steps to get next to Reg. "We'll fight for you," they said. Then they were gone.

"Well, I didn't expect that," Kaisha said, her breath ragged. "Though I wish they'd kept their hands off his chair."

Reg reached up and grabbed Kaisha's hand, but said nothing to her. Moss watched him as he acknowledged each person who came up to him in the hallways as he slowly rolled toward his homeroom.

Maybe this won't be such a bad turnout, Moss thought. Given the circumstances, it was strangely comforting, and Moss felt better by the time he entered Mrs. Torrance's classroom.

"Sorry I couldn't make anything tonight," his mother said, tearing open the plastic bag that held their Thai takeout that night. "I didn't expect this promotion would suck up so much of my time."

Moss grabbed his red curry and a box of jasmine rice. "Don't worry about it, Mama," he said, walking back to the dining room table. "I'm surprised you *ever* have the time or energy to cook."

"Finally, someone appreciates me," she said. "Shamika has her hands tied with one of her bigger clients, and Ogonna said she's got to spend the night calling people for the rally, so we're on our own." She grabbed her pad thai and flipped open the container. The steam rose rapidly, and she breathed in the sharp scent. "You know that one lady down on Adeline I'm always talking about?"

He groaned. "Oh god, the one who gets mad at what mail you deliver?"

She picked at her pad thai with her chopsticks, mixing it up. "Yep, that's the one. Guess what she yelled about today?"

Moss tried to spoon some curry into his mouth, but spat it out. Too hot. "I dunno," he said. "The possibilities are endless."

"You would think so, but no, Moss. Today, she spent five minutes shrieking about junk mail. Why I deliver it. How I'm *personally* wasting trees and am dooming the world to ruin. All by myself, Moss!"

"It's good to know that you're ending the universe, Mama. Maybe we *do* need to start from scratch."

She laughed and took a huge bite of noodles, slurping up a stray one. "God, I don't think I'll ever get sick of this place," she said. "Enabling my laziness one noodle at a time."

"Says the woman who worked twelve hours today."

. She grunted in response to that. "Don't remind me. My feet already have been."

The conversation ceased as the two of them shoveled food into their mouths. Moss was nearly finished with his curry when his mother pointed her chopsticks at him. "I meant to tell you," she said in between chewing. "Spoke to a lot of folks since this weekend. I think the administration at your school is gonna be overwhelmed on Friday."

"What d'you mean?" Moss said. He tipped the bowl up and drank down the last of the curry at the bottom of it.

"Well, Martin, Dawit, and Shamika have all been telling anyone who's been in their businesses about the rally. And I reached out to a lot of my old activist friends. They'll be there, too."

"No way!" Moss said. "They really want to help?"

"Yeah, they do. This community matters to them, too."

"I guess," said Moss. He pushed his empty food containers away from him. "It's just weird to think that people could care about someone they don't know."

Wanda scraped at the sauce left. "I know," she said. "But what happened to Reg, to Shawna . . . I'm worried about what comes next. What happens if we don't stop this now."

"You really think it'll get worse?"

She raised an eyebrow at him. "If your school has no problem hurting its own student body over and over again, they'll never learn."

"Well, then we gotta teach them," said Moss, standing to gather their empty containers. "And soon."

Only three days left, he thought. His nerves rattled his stomach in a brief burst, but he dismissed it. Breathed through it. *This is happening,* he told himself. He couldn't stop it if he tried, and he knew he just had to let the momentum take him forward.

His mom kissed the top of his head as he stuffed the containers in the trash. "Your father would be so proud of you," she said before she disappeared into the living room.

Moss believed her.

20

Moss picked at the steps again in front of West Oakland High on Wednesday afternoon. "How do *your* parents feel about all of this?"

Rawiya leaned back on her elbows and sighed. "You know, my dad was pretty excited to move here last year," he said. "We'd been in Detroit for so long, and he just wanted to move somewhere warm."

"Is that why y'all went to the desert in *August*?" Moss asked, laughing.

"Uggggghhh!" She drew the groan out. "Don't remind me. Dad loved it so much, but I'd rather be *anywhere* but the desert in the height of summer."

"So what did they say about the walkout? You told them, right?"

"Of course," she said. "I can't keep anything from my mom. That woman lives in my head." She paused. "They're . . . nervous. And I'm sure you get this, but they just don't want me getting into trouble."

"Trust," he said. "You don't have to convince me."

"My dad is just worried because this place isn't what we thought it was," she said, and she sat forward, her elbows on her knees, her hands under her chin. "Like, isn't this supposed to be one of the most progressive cities on the planet?"

"Yo, I was *just* talking to Javier about that this weekend!" Moss exclaimed. "It's wild, isn't it?"

"He still on his way?" Rawiya asked. "I didn't really get to talk to him at Esperanza's house."

Moss nodded. "Yeah, we're getting boba over on 40th. You wanna come?"

"Nah, I gotta get home," she said, and she stood up and brushed off her skirt. "I have a paper for Mr. Riordan due on Monday. Already!

The year *just* started." Rawiya sat back down and sighed. "Yeah, my parents are glad I'm getting involved with something, but they are also convinced that the school is gonna single me out."

"Well, it's not an entirely irrational thought," Moss admitted. "Given that Mr. Elliot did that once already."

She shook her head. "I know, I know," she said. "You just try to be yourself and get through your day, and punks always gotta hassle you." She gave him a look of concern. "How do you do it, Moss?"

"Do what?"

"Exist. When the world hates you so much."

He whistled at that. "Well, that's a hella deep question, girl. What is this, my NPR interview?"

She cackled and held up a pretend microphone to Moss's mouth. "Our listeners would love to know what you, a gay black teenager, do to make it through each and every day. Please, Morris Jeffries, Jr., describe for them in detail all the pain that you go through."

"Well," he said dramatically, "if that will placate your white listeners and make them feel as if they're not personally complicit in any corrupt systems, then why would I *ever* dream of keeping my life to myself?"

They fell into each other laughing. "What's so funny?" Javier said as he approached them. "What did I miss?"

"Oh, this is too good," said Rawiya. "We're practicing for Moss's inevitable NPR interview. He'll become a superstar of tragedy porn."

"Hey, as long as they're paying you. . . ." He shrugged. "Get that white money, Moss."

Moss stood and kissed Javier. "How you doin', boo?"

Javier smirked. "Am I your boo now?"

"We can talk about that later," said Moss, winking at him.

Javier turned around and glanced across the street. "So that's where the rally is gonna be, right? That parking lot?"

Rawiya nodded. "Pretty weird to think about, isn't it?"

"And you're all coming out the front here?" Javier asked.

"Yep," said Moss. "Right at two P.M."

"I don't know how we're gonna last through classes on Friday," said Rawiya. "I'm *already* impatient."

"Well, you can count me in," said Javier. "Me and some of my friends are ditching school to come support y'all."

"Wait, *really*?" Moss put a hand to his chest.

"Moss, this dude is hella punk rock," said Rawiya. "Props. That's legit."

"You're serious?" Moss asked.

"Yeah! Of course." He shuffled in place. "Look, I care about you, and my friends think that what happened to Reg and Shawna was bullshit. So . . . we'll be here."

"Have you already proposed marriage to him?" Rawiya said. "I know I'm like the millionth person to say this, but maybe you two should assimilate as soon as possible."

"Shut *up*, Rawiya," Moss said, but it was playful. He gazed at Javier, saw that bashful sincerity on his face, and knew he wouldn't trade it for anything. "Come on," he said. "Let's go get boba."

They bid Rawiya goodbye and left her behind. Javier slipped his hand in Moss's and they walked away from the campus, the impossible now real. This was his life now.

Not bad, he thought. Now he just had to get through classes on Thursday and Friday, but with Javier at his side, it seemed all the more possible.

21

But when Friday morning rolled around, that hope had dissipated. "I hate how I'm feeling," Moss said to Njemile. "Like everything is going to go wrong."

They could see Kaisha at the end of the block, her face buried in her phone, and Moss wasn't sure he wanted to voice his uncertainty in front of her. This week had been bad enough for her, he guessed. She'd spent a lot of time with Reg and his family, running errands when they couldn't, sticking by Reg's side otherwise. *She has to be exhausted,* he thought. But there she stood, typing away on the touchscreen keyboard, and she seemed as energetic as ever. Moss couldn't take that away from her, despite the dread that had sunk deep into him.

It must have been all over his face. Kaisha smiled briefly at him. "I'm sure it'll go fine," she said, and then she looped her hands into the straps of her backpack. She greeted Esperanza. "We convinced a lot of people to participate. You should be proud of that."

"I almost can't believe it," Moss said. He removed his black snapback and wiped away at his sweat. "I guess I won't until I see it happen. Where's Reg?"

"His mom dropped him off early," she said. "He didn't want to deal with the stress of getting on campus."

They headed toward school, but Moss welcomed the sight of Memo, the man who made fruit cups from his cart on MacArthur. Njemile skipped over to him and greeted him in Spanish, and soon Moss's favorite part of the morning began. Memo chopped up mango, honeydew melon, strawberries, and orange slices, some with intricate patterns. He coated them in chili powder in a clear bag, then arranged them all delicately in a paper bowl. There was a purpose to the way he moved, a sense that this was all second nature to him, and Moss admired how quickly he was able to carve those pieces of fruit.

"I swear, that man is an artist," Kaisha said. "Mind if I take a photo for Instagram?"

Njemile was more than delighted to. "Just make sure to credit Memo! And maybe mention that he's at Jack London Square on the weekends."

"I got you," Kaisha said. "I always give credit."

By the time they were finished with their impromptu photo shoot, Bits and Rawiya had found them. They said their hellos, but conversation was clipped. Sporadic. The tension flowed between all of them, and so their walk to school was not as cheery or social as it could have been. The dread began to fill the vacancy. What if this was a mistake? What if they came to regret this?

He didn't vocalize his concerns, out of fear that he'd just make everyone else feel as miserable as him. But as the group came in sight of their campus, Moss no longer had to worry about that. The image they saw outside their school guaranteed that misery would have some company.

"We're screwed," said Njemile.

Two men in jet-black uniforms were patting down a student who stood outside of the metal detectors. There was no exposed skin on any of the men. Their gloves were black, their long-sleeved undershirts stretched tight over large arms, and their boots glistened, even in the shade. Their heads were adorned with matte black helmets, and they reminded him of characters in one of those shoot-'em-up military games. They wore leather utility belts about their waists, and Moss couldn't recognize a single object attached to them. He thought one was a billy club, but it was too short, too thin. He saw the holster, and the anxiety threaded into his veins, pulsed from his chest up to his throat, and he couldn't breathe. Guns. Lots of them. Each cop had one. His mind took the image and transported him back to Dawit's store, to the guns raised upon his father, and he froze. The fear was like cement blocks on his feet.

He could see OAKLAND POLICE DEPARTMENT across the back of one of the uniforms. He knew then that it was over.

The hum of the metal detectors could be heard from the bottom of the steps. The machine on the right blared loud and clear as a young black girl—some underclass student he'd only seen a couple of times before—went through it. Within seconds, she was pulled off to the side and pushed up against the wall, her legs spread, arms pinned, the cops ignoring her cries of protest.

"Oh, no," Kaisha said. Moss could hear the dread in her voice, too.

"What is it?" Moss said. "What?"

Kaisha stuffed her phone in her pocket. "They know."

"What?" said Njemile. "What do you mean?"

"They know," she repeated. "They figured it out."

"But *how*?" said Njemile. "How could they possibly know?"

"I don't know, but they know about the walkout. That has to be why they're all here. They're just trying to intimidate us. Right?"

There was an uncomfortable pause, right when Moss heard a student shout loudly, "Man, stop touchin' me there!" The yell continued—it was Lewis, one of the running backs for the football team. Lewis swatted one of the cop's hands away as another went in for the student's leg. "Don't do that, man. *Don't.*"

Lewis's hands were forced behind his back in an instant. Two cops had him in cuffs a moment later, and pulled him off toward the front office. "Man, leave me alone!" they heard Lewis yell, and then he was gone.

"Well, this looks bad," said Njemile. She sucked a gulp of air into her lungs and let it out with force. "But I don't care. We have to do this."

"I'm not letting them stop me either," Kaisha said, and she marched up to the stairs, defiant. Moss looked at Bits, who shrugged and followed her.

Rawiya locked her arm in Moss's and led him forward. His heart

raced, a constant pounding underneath his sternum, and he felt his
mother's waffles from that morning surge up his throat. Moss wanted
to call her now and have her come get him, and yet the thought filled
him with a weird sense of shame. Was he a coward for wanting to bail?
Was he weak because of the terror that washed over him whenever he
saw a cop or a gun? His legs wobbled as he took another step toward
the school.

"You got this," Rawiya told him, and she led him closer.

He watched Kaisha. She looked so fearless, and he admired that.
She dropped her bag on a folding table, and one of the cops immediately began to search through it. She passed through the metal detector without a sound, but the cop on the other side put a hand up.
"Additional screening," he said.

Kaisha delivered one of the most vicious glares Moss had ever seen
from her, but she said nothing. She raised her hands above her head,
her face a mask of disinterest and quiet rage. They all watched as a
cop roughly ran his hands over Kaisha's body, lingering far too long
on her chest and on her legs. But the men said nothing to her, and
the eeriness of their uniformity finally crept under Moss's skin. They
all looked like the exact same person. Their build was identical, they
all stood around six foot, and there was not a single detail anyone
could have used to differentiate them at all. No badges. No names.
No numbers.

And then Moss realized that was probably by design.

Kaisha angrily grabbed her bag without saying a word, and she
stood a few feet behind the line of cops, waiting for everyone else.
Njemile went through next, and one of the cops asked her to take off
her wig to show him what was underneath. When she refused, they
tried to cuff her, too, at least until Kaisha angrily shouted at them.
"It's not a wig, you pigs! Don't y'all know anything about hair?"

The same one who had searched Kaisha released Njemile, turning
to look at Kaisha, and for a moment, Moss thought that there might
be an escalation. But he said nothing and resumed patting down the
next student.

Moss sucked in his breath, relieved, but still miserable. He finally approached the detector, put his backpack down on the small table, and then passed through the machine uneventfully. The cop stopped Moss and gestured for him to put his arms up. He raised his hands and the cop ran his hands over his body. A memory dragged up in his mind: the Alameda County Fair. Moss was eight, and his father took him to watch the judging of the animals, and Moss remembered crying because they were all too rough with the pigs and the sheep. He hadn't thought of this memory in a while, and he wasn't thrilled that this was the time his mind decided to turn to that page in its mental Rolodex.

Moss felt the gloved hands run over his chest, down his sides, and then his shirt was lifted up, exposing his stomach to everyone, and he felt shame and terror rush through him anew. His own hands instinctively bolted up to pull his shirt down, but Moss stopped halfway, raising them again. *Don't draw attention to yourself,* he thought fiercely.

His eyes watered as the cop ran a finger around him, *inside* Moss's waistband, rubbing against the part of his stomach that stuck out over the belt. The cop pulled Moss's shirt down and then knelt next to him, running hands down each of his legs, starting at the top, just inches from his crotch, and squeezing every so often.

"Take your shoes off."

When he spoke, Moss thought he was imagining it. The man spoke again, this time more forcefully. "I said, take off your shoes. You deaf or something?"

The anger conquered everything else in that instant. It pushed the anxiety and fear away, and it pumped through his veins. "No," Moss said.

The cop stood and moved in front of Moss. "What did you say?"

"No," Moss repeated, his eyes locked on the tinted visor of the guard. He focused on it, hoping he could see *something* behind it. "You don't need me to do that."

The man reached out quicker than Moss expected and wrapped the front of Moss's shirt inside a fist, and he lifted. Moss was not a small guy, a fact he had frequently lamented to himself, but he was shocked when his own feet began to dangle, unable to reach the floor. He brought his right hand up to his neck to free himself, and the guard swatted the hand away. Moss was aware of his own breath—struggling to escape, then struggling to enter—and the yelling around him. Was that Njemile? Kaisha? He couldn't make it out enough, and it scared him, fear surging into his heart. Who was yelling? What were they saying?

He was lowered slowly back to the concrete, and the pressure around his neck was gone. He gasped for air, and Rawiya's face appeared in front of his, blurry at first, then in focus. She had her hands on either side of his face, caressing him, and then she pulled him into a hug. "Just breathe, Moss," she said. "You're okay."

"What do you think you're doing?" The voice was loud, above Moss and to his left. He and Rawiya turned together to see Mr. Jacobs standing toe-to-toe with the cop, his own nose just inches away from the helmet. His eyes were red with rage as he continued shouting at the man. "You are not to assault my students! We don't need them to take their shoes off unless we have a reason to suspect there is something *in* their shoes." He paused, and Moss saw his chest heave up and down as he breathed in and out forcefully. "Did the screening tell you that this student had something suspicious there?"

There was a long silence. "I'll ask you again: Was there a reason to ask this gentleman to remove his shoes?"

Another pause. The cop didn't move at all; he stood statue still. "No, there wasn't."

Mr. Jacobs turned to Moss, laying a hand upon his shoulder. His eyes changed, communicating warmth and concern. "Are you okay? Do you need anything? Would you like to see the nurse?"

The questions poured out of Mr. Jacobs rapidly, and Moss struggled to find his voice to answer them. "I think I'm okay," he croaked, standing up. His friends and a huge crowd of students stood behind the assistant principal, their faces a mix of shock and worry. "I'll be okay," he said, quieter this time, and his eyes drifted from one student to another. How many were there watching him? A hundred? More? They were crowded in the hallway, some trying to climb up on others to get a better view, some of them on tiptoes. Phones were raised up high, too, poking up above the crowd, their owners desperate to get a good shot.

"Do you need to see the nurse?" Mr. Jacobs repeated, and he tried to direct Moss toward the main office by the shoulder. Rawiya, who had ahold of Moss's other arm, jerked him back, and Mr. Jacobs threw his hands up in concession. "Please, if you need anything, you can come to me."

Rawiya guided Moss forward to their friends, and as she did so, Moss turned his head around to see Mr. Jacobs speaking to the cop, who remained as still and passive as before. He could not hear a word coming from the man's mouth, but Moss could tell he wasn't pleased. But it was little comfort to him. He swallowed, his throat still raw and sore, and it reminded him that he wouldn't be the only student roughed up that day. How could they have known? How long had they had to prepare for this? Would anyone even be *able* to leave the campus that afternoon?

Kaisha darted forward then and hugged him, hard. "You sure you're okay?"

"Yeah, yeah. We have to do this," he announced, rubbing the side of his neck. "We have to walk out of class."

"I'm there," Kaisha affirmed. "Ain't no way I'm letting them get away with this." She held up her phone. "I'm sorry I didn't get video or anything. My phone is acting weird. I was trying to post it to Snapchat, but I can't seem to open any apps." She shook her head. "It's just weird."

Njemile moved in next to him. "Mine's the same way," she said. "It just seems to have turned off and won't come back on." She sighed. "I'm in regardless, though. They can't stop me."

"Same here," Bits offered.

He gave Rawiya's hand a squeeze. "Thanks for that," he said. "My ride-or-die chick," he added, and they shared a laugh, a nervous reaction as much as an act of desperation.

Moss looked about the group gathered. He didn't recognize most of the faces. Some were younger, some older. He heard a number of them say the same thing: They'd be leaving at 2:00 P.M., too. Others confirmed with nods and pats on the shoulder. He still had a nervous fire running through him from his confrontation, but he couldn't process it. It was almost as if the incident had happened to someone else. But it *had* happened to him, these people had witnessed it, and they *still* wanted to risk their own safety, all for some idea. And what would they accomplish today? Moss wasn't sure; fear struck him as his brain told him that this would be worthless, that they'd never get anything done.

"I have to do this," he said out loud. "I can't let them stop me."

The group walked to their morning classes, splintering as they broke off to find their homerooms. Some of them bid Moss goodbye and reminded him of their commitment to the walkout, while others just quietly departed. As they came to the hallway where Rawiya and Moss would have to separate, she grabbed his arm again. "This is about you now, too," she said.

"It shouldn't have to be," he said, hanging his head.

"But it is. We're doing this for Reg and Shawna and for you and for anyone else who's going to have to deal with this bullshit here. For all of us."

He smiled at her, grateful for her support. "Thank you."

"We'll make you proud," she said, and then she walked off to class. Moss stood there for a few seconds, his mind swimming with thoughts and anxieties. The bell rang loudly above him, and he bolted down the hall to Mrs. Torrance's homeroom. *I hope this works,* he thought, his neck still sore and his heart still racing.

22

It was 1:46 P.M.

Moss sat in his biology class, not far from Rawiya, who glanced at the clock every so often while taking notes. He didn't understand how she could concentrate for as long as she was. His mind swung between panic and hope, fear and exhilaration. He stared out the window, his attention on the students jogging and walking around the track beyond the baseball field. Moss didn't envy them as he wiped at a drop of sweat that ran slowly down his right temple. In every class he'd had that day, the air had not been running. None of the teachers knew why. By the time he got to Mrs. Torrance's English class, she had turned her small desk fan out toward the classroom. It didn't help much. The heat stuck to his skin and now made it too hard for him to listen to Mr. Roberts's lecture.

Moss suspected that this was intentional, too. The other kids in the class fidgeted, and even Mr. Roberts stopped every so often to dab at his forehead with an off-white handkerchief before continuing to lecture the disinterested, overheated students about biodiversity. There was sweat glistening off his bald head, too. His dark beard was cropped close, and Moss often felt brief bursts of desire when he spent too long staring at the man's face. In last year's astronomy course, girls would often giggle and ask Mr. Roberts any asinine question they could just so he'd speak to them. But Moss wasn't daydreaming about this handsome teacher today. Instead, his eyes were constantly jumping up to the clock out of the hope that more time had passed than Moss was conscious of.

It was 1:48 P.M.

He looked over at Rawiya again and she shot a quick smirk at him before writing down something else. He didn't have any other friends in this class, but Moss still let his attention wander, desperate to get out of this room. He watched as Carmela passed a note to one of her friends, a light-skinned girl whose name Moss didn't know. They both caught him looking at them, but didn't break the eye contact. Both of them nodded while smiling, and the message felt clear. *We got your back.* How did they know? he wondered. Had Kaisha reached them? Was it just word of mouth?

A folded piece of paper—it looked like the same one Carmela had—was slid onto his desk, and Moss quickly tucked it under the edge and out of view of Mr. Roberts, who droned on about the Amazon rain forest. He unfolded it as quietly as he could and read:

> Are you okay? We saw that guy hurt you. We're leaving class at 2.

Moss looked back toward the two girls and nodded his head. *Thank you,* he mouthed at them.

It was 1:50 P.M.

He shifted in his seat and examined his fingernails, then ran a hand over the welt that had formed around his neck. He couldn't stop touching it, the skin raised and tender. It hurt to swallow, but he found it hard to stop himself. He had wanted to text his mother about it, to warn her so she wasn't surprised when she saw him at two. His phone, however, had no service whatsoever. If he tried to open any of the apps, it would freeze, and he'd have to restart it. He had repeated this process over and over again without any success. Had they done something to all their phones?

Moss hated the thought. His mouth was drying out quickly, and whenever he glanced up at the clock, it made him nervous. *Don't look at it again,* he told himself. *You'll only make it worse.* So he tried to focus on his teacher, but the words sounded wrong. They were all hard angles and harsh tones, and he soon felt his tongue stick to the roof of his mouth, everything dry once more. Why didn't he bring any water with him? He stole another glance at the clock.

It was 1:52 P.M.

It was the scuffling outside in the hallway that pulled his attention away from the sluggish journey of the second hand. Moss heard the squeak of sneakers on tile, then voices raised in alarm, incoherent and high-pitched. Then the entire class heard a large *thump,* and Mr. Roberts stopped talking, all their eyes now locked on the classroom door. Through the glass, they could see bodies passing by quickly, just blurs of color and shadow.

"What in God's name . . ." Mr. Roberts said. His exclamation died as he moved to the door. When he pulled it open, they could see students streaming past, many of them shouting at one another. "Move! Move!" a young man called, and Moss and many of the others in the classroom got out of their seats. But no one made a move to leave.

"What's going on?" their teacher shouted into the hallway, his own body positioned to keep the door open. Moss was unsure who he was yelling *at,* since the students passed by so quickly that it was impossible to get anyone's attention. "Is this that walkout thing?"

"You know about that?" a kid in the front of the class said with alarm.

"Well . . . yeah," Mr. Roberts said, shuffling away from the door, which shut loudly. There was more shouting from the hallway, but their teacher ignored it. He grabbed a messy stack of papers on his desk until he found the yellow memo. "They sent us this thing this morning, dropped it in all our mailboxes," he explained. He held it up and read, " 'Please be aware that many students are planning a walkout at two P.M. You are not to let students out of your class unless it is an emergency.' "

Moss felt his heart freeze, and then it leapt up into his sore throat. *Oh god, they're really going to stop us,* he thought.

"Are you not going to let us leave, Mr. Roberts?" Rawiya asked, her own raised hand shaking.

Mr. Roberts looked over to her, his dark eyes shining. He ran a hand over the top of his head, a tic of his that meant a student's question had stumped him more than usual. He surveyed his classroom after sitting on the edge of his desk, holding the memo. He glanced down at it, then crumpled it within his hands. He dropped it in the wastebasket next to his desk before returning to his desk. "I didn't receive any memo about anything happening today," he announced. "So there is no reason to stop you from doing as you choose."

In an instant, the class began to move about, but not *out* of the room. Moss realized that they'd all turned to him, as if he was meant to lead them on. "Moss?" Carmela said. "What do we do?"

"I don't know," he said sharply. "I didn't organize this."

"You helped," Rawiya said quietly.

"And we're doing this for you and Reg and Shawna," someone else said, a black kid behind him whose name Moss did not know but whom he recognized upon the invocation of Reg's name. Weren't they cousins? James? Jerome? Moss wasn't sure, but he felt a responsibility regardless. He thought of his friend, who had been so close to his rehabilitation goals, and he stood up.

"Let's go now," he said. "At least we might catch them by surprise."

The mood changed then; students scrambled to collect their gear and bolt out of the classroom. Mr. Roberts shouted a warning to them all to be careful, but it was drowned out as the remaining students all joined the flow of people heading toward the main entrance of the building. Some people passed by and patted Moss on the back, while others cursed the very existence of the school. "We gettin' a day off from this!" someone shouted as they pushed on by, and Moss frowned at him. It was inevitable that some people would just look for an opportunity to ditch class, but he supposed it didn't really matter in the long run. Weren't they all walking out of class together? Wasn't that the whole point?

Rawiya locked arms with him as they paraded down the hallway, passing more classrooms, students emptying into the stream like the loosing of a dam. Someone whooped and jumped on Moss's back, and he carried them for a few feet before they jumped off. "We're really doing this!" Moss didn't recognize the student who exclaimed this, and then he jolted forward, lost in the surge. Rawiya and Moss found

Reg when they turned right into the hallway leading to the main door. He was at the threshold of one of the English classrooms, his eyes wide with shock, and Kaisha stood behind his chair, a smile on her face.

Moss patted him on the back. "This is for you," he said, pride in his voice.

"And you, too, I hear," Reg said, his lip curling up in a goofy grin. "Apparently these jerks can't keep their hands off people."

Moss's hand went up to his neck. "I'll be fine," he said. "And I guess it means we converted more people to our cause today anyway." He gazed up to Kaisha. "I meant to thank you most. Honestly. We couldn't have done this without you."

"You know you can count on me," she replied. "You okay?"

"Yeah. Y'all ready?"

Reg leaned back in his chair. He placed his right hand on Kaisha's left, running it down her skin and looping his own fingers in hers. "As long as she is."

Kaisha smiled and gripped his hand. "Let's go," she said.

The four of them walked out into the hallway together, Kaisha and Reg in front, Rawiya and Moss in sync behind them. Reg wheeled himself smoothly toward the front of the school, and Moss realized that most of their peers had left class already. Some of the doorways were occupied by fascinated teachers in their empty classrooms. The group of friends passed by Mrs. Torrance's room, and she said nothing to them. She offered them her pride instead. Her hand was clutched to her chest, and her face beamed.

But then Moss's heart dropped—a thick band of students clogged up just feet from the entrance that contained the metal detectors. People were pushing or scrambling to get a better view, so the four of them stopped where they were.

"Oh god, what's going on *now*?" said Rawiya.

"A bottleneck?" Kaisha observed. "Maybe they can't all exit the school at once."

"A traffic jam," Reg added, grinning. "Cool."

Moss laughed, but it was cut short by the sound that rose sharply from in front of them. It was difficult to discern individual phrases or words in the din that echoed down that long hallway, but they knew something had gone horribly wrong when the kids at the back of the pack turned suddenly and began sprinting toward them. "Oh, shi—" Moss uttered before he felt someone jerk him into a nearby office. He fell to the floor, knocking his funny bone against the tiled floor. Pain shot down his arm to his fingers.

"Sorry!" Rawiya shouted. Moss swore and scrambled back to his feet in time to see Kaisha shove Reg's chair into the room after them, right as the first group of stampeding teens surged past. He couldn't even make out what the sound was that roared into his ears. Feet on tile. Shouts and yelps. Whoops of excitement, terror. Moss and his friends watched, frozen in place, as two cops clad in all black chased after the fleeing students, one of them with a baton raised in the air.

Another student dove into the room, scrambled to their feet, and shut the door behind them. It took Moss a few seconds to realize it was Njemile, who sat with her back to the door, her breath heaving her chest up and down. When Moss took a step forward, she raised her hand. "No," she said. "Don't. Don't go out there."

"What's going on?" Rawiya said, her hands on her head, terror in her eyes. "What's happening?"

"They knew," Njemile said. "They *knew*."

"Well, that's not a surprise," Kaisha said. "We figured that out this morning when those stormtrooper dudes were posted up in front of the school."

"But they knew when we were walking out—which exit we'd take!" Njemile shouted. "There were so many of them, just lined up in front of the entrance, and I think only a few people slipped past them before they started firing."

"*Firing?*" Moss exclaimed.

"I don't know what it is," she said. "It's not a gun or anything I've ever seen. It hurts so bad."

Njemile raised her hand up, her whole arm shaking, and they all saw that the skin on the back of her hand was raised and swollen. Rawiya cried out in alarm and rushed to her side, but Njemile gestured her friend away again. "No, no, don't touch me!" she said forcefully. "It was some kinda liquid, and it burns like hell."

Moss crumpled into a chair placed in front of a desk. *This must be one of the counselors' offices*, he thought, and he looked around for anything they might be able to use to get out of there. He pushed papers around on the desk, then stood up and rushed around it, pulling open a drawer. A stapler. Post-it notes. Pens. Standard office fare.

"What are you doing, Moss?" Reg said, his own voice cracking in fear.

"I don't know, man, I don't know. Looking for anything." He spied a small container of hand sanitizer sitting on the right side of the desk and grabbed it. He tossed it over to Njemile, who caught it with her uninjured hand. "I don't know if that'll work, but it can't be worse, can it?"

Njemile struggled to open the bottle before Rawiya took it from her, flipping the cap open and liberally pouring its contents all over the other girl's swollen hand. Njemile yelped at first, trembling in pain, but she breathed a sigh of relief. "It's working," she said. "Don't know why, don't care."

Kaisha had her face buried in her phone, and her fingers flew across the screen. Without looking up at Moss, she said, "I'm letting everyone know what's going on. You know, updating Twitter and the Facebook group that—"

She began tapping her screen harder and hard. "No, no, no!" she screamed. "Not now, *please* not now!"

"What is it?" Reg asked, his face lined with worry.

"Of *course* this is exactly when service drops out on me. Of course!"

Rawiya pulled her own out and handed it over to Kaisha after standing up. "One-oh-two-seven," she said.

Kaisha didn't even get to enter the passcode before she also swore louder than Moss had ever heard her speak before. "No service on yours," she said.

Reg reached into his own pocket and examined his phone as well. He didn't say anything, just shook his head at them all. Moss knew what his phone would say, but he still pulled it out of his pocket, his hand shaking.

NO SERVICE.

They all remained silent for a few seconds, the sounds of students running and shouting outside the office haunting them. "What's happening?" Rawiya said, her voice soft and afraid. Moss saw the tears that brimmed in her eyes. They sprang to his own, his mind filling in the blanks. *It's happening again. They're going to do the same to us.*

"This is exactly what my parents were worried about," Rawiya said.

Moss stood from the desk, heart thumping, mind reeling, and the solution came to him suddenly. "We need to get out of here *now*," he stated.

"Why on Earth would we do that?" Njemile said. "We safer in here."

"No, we're not," Moss insisted. "They're gonna come down that hallway, open this door, and see five students *trespassing* in a counselor's office. What you think they're gonna do to us then?"

"But how do we get past them?" Reg asked.

"We don't. We go out the back," said Moss.

"What?" Rawiya said. "The back what?"

"You know that hallway down by the science labs? The creepy one where the football players always take their girlfriends to make out?"

As most of them nodded their heads, Njemile quickly stood up. "There's an exit there for the janitors," she said excitedly. "It lets out right by the dumpsters."

"Exactly," Moss said. "Let's not even try to go out the front."

"But what about those *things* they have?" Kaisha asked. "I ain't about to get sprayed by what they got Njemile with."

Moss quickly surveyed the room, then began ripping the posterboard displays off the wall. He handed one to Reg, who inspected the front.

" 'Five Ways to Tell You're Depressed'?" Reg said. "Seriously, man?"

"Okay, it's not the best idea, but it could work as a shield," he said. He grabbed some masking tape out of the desk drawer and began to create makeshift handles looped on the back of the poster.

"I'm not taking my chances again," Njemile said, ripping down a poster about the stages of grief. "I'm taller, so let me go first."

"I'll take the back," Moss said. He finished looping tape into a handle on the back of the first poster and handed it to Kaisha. "You remember how to get there, Njemile?"

She nodded. The noise outside the hallway was no longer a roar, so after they assembled in a rough line—Njemile, Reg, Kaisha, Rawiya, then Moss—Njemile gently opened the door, pulling it inward. She peeked out, then turned back to the others. "There are still some students down at the front exit, yelling and stuff. We gotta go *now*."

Njemile slipped out the door, and the rest followed. Moss left the door open, unwilling to risk the sound it might cause if he shut it. They crept down the hall, then headed back down the English wing. Moss found it unnerving that every classroom he passed was either fully empty or had its door closed. Where was everyone? Even the teachers. Where had they gone? He hoped to see Mrs. Torrance in her classroom, but the room was just as vacant as the others.

They hooked a left at the next wing and found chaos. Students darted from one hallway to the next—Moss realized that they must have known how futile it was to get out of the school through the front entrance. Two students—young women, one of them Carmela— sat near a door, tears streaming down their swollen faces. Moss wanted to stop and help them, but Rawiya pulled him along without any hesitation. "Keep moving!" She only briefly looked at Moss as she yelled, then continued to run.

He glanced back at Carmela. Her face was wrong, misshapen. What the hell had caused that?

They passed one person after another, crouched in the hallways or in doorways, their bodies red and puffy, some of their eyes swollen shut, while others clutched arms and legs, wailing in terror. When they reached Mr. Roberts's classroom, they saw him on the floor, his mouth on some kid's face, then pulling away, his hands on the young man's chest, pumping up and down. He looked up, his face covered in sweat, his bald head gleaming. "Go!" he shouted. "Get out of here now!"

They darted away from that doorway and picked up the pace. Kaisha was now pushing Reg as fast as she could, but she was losing ground on Njemile. "Lemme help," Rawiya said as she grabbed hold of one side of Reg's wheelchair. Together, they glided Reg toward the end of the science wing as Moss himself struggled to keep up.

"Moss!"

He nearly tripped trying to stop. He whipped around and saw Javier's beanie-clad head pop out of one of the labs.

"Javier?!" he exclaimed. He shouted back at the group, "Hold up!"

Moss jogged back to the classroom, confusion slowing his steps. "I thought you were meeting us at the rally point," he said. "How did you even get *in* here?"

"I snuck in," Javier said, his face a vision of joy as he smiled. He kissed Moss, hard and quick. "We were just going to meet you outside, but the back gate wasn't locked. Figured it would be a fun surprise. We found your friends, by the way!"

We? Moss thought.

Javier stepped aside and Moss saw what he meant. Bits and Shawna were huddled together near the back of the room, and they lit up when they saw Moss, rushing to his side. As they hugged him and shouted greetings, he saw three other kids standing awkwardly in the room. "Who are they?" Moss asked once his friends gave him some breathing room.

"My friends," Javier replied, stepping aside. "I'd make more introductions, but I get the sense that we gotta get out of here *now.*"

Moss glanced at the others, the kids from Eastside. There was a short black girl, her hair in tight braids, her hand interlocked in someone else's. They were Filipino, dark, with silky black hair. And behind Javier, a shy boy, young and mousy, his hair black, his skin a light brown, peering out at Moss. He nodded his head. "Hello," the boy said, so soft that Moss barely heard him. "Javi has lots of good things to say about you."

That must be Carlos, he thought.

As frightened as Moss was, he felt an affection for Javier fill him completely. Moss looked upon the boy he'd become so enamored with, and he suddenly felt that everything was worth it. "Thank you," Moss croaked, the emotion getting the best of him. "For this."

Javier smiled and planted a kiss on his cheek. "Anything for you." He turned to gesture at his friends. "Okay, real quickly: This is Carlos, and that's Chandra over there, and that's her partner, Sam."

"This is super cute," Rawiya said, standing in the doorway, Kaisha and Reg just barely behind her, "but can we go?"

Moss laughed at her, a bashful smile spreading over his face. "We're close, everyone," he announced. "At the end of the hall, you'll follow the others through the service exit. It's a quick sprint to the back gate."

"Nobody move!"

Moss hadn't even seen the cop slide up next to Rawiya, Kaisha, and Reg. The man pushed her into the room. "All of you, on the floor now!" he ordered, his voice muffled by the helmet. "Now!" the cop repeated.

Moss stood as still as he could, but he motioned for Rawiya to move closer to him. He knew this was her worst fear. It was his, too, but Moss *had* to help his friend.

The cop pushed her forward, and she stumbled a few times before gaining her balance back. The man reached to his belt and grabbed a bullhorn that hung from the right side, raising it in front of him. "Get out of the way!" Njemile yelled, and instinctively, a few of them raised up their pathetic poster-board shields that they still carried. Moss dropped into a squat behind a desk right as the cop pressed a button on the front of the device, and he shut his eyes tight, hoping that whatever he was about to be sprayed with wouldn't hurt him.

Nothing happened.

He opened his eyes after a few seconds, and that's when one of Javier's friends groaned and dropped to their knees. "Chandra!" Sam rushed to her side, only to pitch forward and start groaning, too, their hands clutched to their head, their black hair brushing against the ground. "Make it stop!" they shouted.

"Make what stop?" Bits yelled. They were still in the rear of the room, their face in an expression of bewilderment.

Chandra threw up. It was violent, loud, and her wrenching caused Sam to do the same, and it was in their hair, all over the floor.

Moss stood up, looking at the two kids writhing and vomiting on the floor. "What did you do to them?" he yelled at the cop, advancing on him. The man raised the device and pointed it directly at Moss, and despite wanting to appear fearless, Moss still flinched. The man kept firing it at him—

But nothing happened.

The cop held the gadget up to his face as if inspecting it. "No, this is supposed to *work,*" he said. "Why isn't this working?" He banged it on his hand a few times, then tossed it to the ground. He reached to his utility belt and pulled out a canister. He fumbled with it for a second and then it slipped out of his hand and dropped to the floor. The cap flew off and rattled across the floor. The cop took a step forward, but the canister had rolled towards the man, and he stepped on it. It sent him airborne briefly, and Moss knew this was their only chance.

"Go, go, go!" Moss yelled, and his feet obeyed his own order. He sprinted toward the doorway as the guard, dazed by the shock of the fall, struggled to stand upright. He reached out for Moss, and Moss danced away.

And they all ran. Their steps echoed in the empty hallway, the groans behind them growing softer and softer. Moss glanced to the side to see Javier keeping pace. "That was a close one," Javier said in between breaths. They darted for the doorway that Rawiya now held open and Moss burst out into the sunlight, his eyes overwhelmed by the sudden brightness. Moss stopped and rested against the dumpster, desperate to catch his breath as his friends poured out of the doorway. Njemile, then Reg and Kaisha. Reg's laugh was infectious and loud as Kaisha wheeled him out the door.

"Did you see that jerk hit the ground?" Reg said. "I'd be so embarrassed if I were him."

Out came Rawiya, then Carlos, then everyone else in a brief flood of panic. Everyone had made it except for Chandra and Sam. They'd been left behind. "Should we go back for them?" Javier asked, Moss's hand still clutched in his. More students dashed out of the open door; the silence was terrible.

"Don't," a guy answered, his skin darker than Moss's, his breath wheezing out of his mouth. "That dude is on his way, man. We all gotta keep movin'."

No one spoke after that; they simply turned and jogged down the alley between two different wings of their school and out into the practice fields. In the distance, a crowd had formed beyond the back gate. Who were they? Had the rally moved out already?

Moss experienced a jolt of excitement as they picked up the pace and crossed over the baseball field. They each ducked through a passage in the chain-link fence that surrounded it. Moss glanced over his shoulder briefly. He saw a few more students scrambling out of different parts of the building, and he was certain he saw someone climbing out of a window on the first floor. But there was no sign of the cop who had cornered them, so he kept going. They were less than a hundred feet from the back entrance of the school, less than a hundred feet from freedom.

It was not a terribly fancy entrance, but it still gave Moss a sense of grandeur when he saw how many people stood outside of it, clogging up the entire block that sat behind West Oakland High. There were so many faces struggling to catch a glimpse of someone they knew that Moss himself could not recognize any of them. Some people clutched signs. "NO DETECTORS AT SCHOOL," one read. A long banner strung on two large poles said, "STOP CRIMINALIZING STUDENTS," and it was bookended by sets of handcuffs. People were shouting, but Moss couldn't make out the words. His focus was now on the group of people he'd not been able to see from so far away: a line of imposing cops in riot gear who stood in front of the gate. On the *inside*. Moss made a quick count: eight of them, batons held at the ready, their faces unseen, their motives unknown. Would they dare harm anyone in front of so many witnesses?

Moss slowed down, then came to a stop, and the rest of the students who had been following him did the same. Javier squeezed Moss's hand. "Dude, what do we do?" he said.

"I don't know," Moss answered. Louder, he added, "Anyone have any ideas?"

"You're not going anywhere," a voice said from behind him, and Moss whirled around in time to catch a baton on his shoulder, instead of somewhere much more painful. The cop from earlier shoved Moss to the ground, and the roar from everyone around them seemed deafening. Moss heard Rawiya shout, "Leave him alone, you asshole!" and he felt Javier's hands grab him under his arms and yank him to his feet. There was a figure sprinting toward them from the school, hands in the air. Moss couldn't hear—was it Mr. Jacobs?—because there was simply too much noise coming from behind him.

"Get your hands off him!" the cop shouted at Javier. "He's mine."

Javier laughed, his voice full of mirth. "You can't do anything to me," he said, amused. "I don't even go here."

The cop twisted his head to the side, and a low groan left Moss's mouth.

"Oh, *damn*," Javier said, and Moss felt Javier droop against him.

The cop covered the last few feet between them in no time. "What was that?" he demanded, raising the baton to point directly at Javier's face. Moss positioned himself so that Javier remained behind him, their hands still locked together. "What did you say?"

"Stop it, stop it!" Mr. Jacobs shouted as he arrived, his face red and sweaty. "You have to stop this."

"I don't answer to you *or* this school," the cop sneered. He pointed the baton at Mr. Jacobs this time, waving it just inches from him. "I've had about enough of your interference anyway."

Moss felt Javier gently pull him backward, and he obliged, realizing that this might be the only chance for them to escape. His eyes darted over to his friends, and it was clear that they had the same thought. All of them began to slowly back up, and Moss hoped desperately that they could find a way past the cops who still stood motionless in a line by the gate.

"Mr. Elliot has already declared this a bust," Mr. Jacobs insisted to the cop, still out of breath. "And I'd appreciate it if you got that damn thing out of my face."

There was no hesitation before the response. The baton swung hard and cracked Mr. Jacobs across the jaw. The collective gasp Moss's friends couldn't smother betrayed their escape, and the cop turned to see them slipping away. He sprinted after them. The cop looked so awkward with all that gear, Moss thought, but his brain wouldn't react otherwise. Moss, too, wanted to run, but his own legs were jelly, wobbly and uncertain.

The baton came up. Moss reacted then, cowering in front of the man, and it was the wrong reaction. The baton started to come down, but then he swooped it to the side. The baton hit Moss's left knee, making him crumple to the ground in an instant, overwhelmed with pain, with shame, the burning agony. The baton came up again, and Moss had no time to block it. The pain from the blow on his shin made him cry out, and he curled up, an instinctual reaction, an attempt to make his body as small as possible. But Moss felt huge. He felt like the most obvious target in the world.

Javier was on him then, trying to help, so the next blow connected with one of Javier's hands instead. Javier swore but he wouldn't move. He was smothering Moss, using himself as a shield, and it was the only comfort Moss found in that terrible moment.

"Are you okay?" Javier said, right in his ear, and Moss turned his tear-streaked face up to Javier. Javier's expression broke Moss's heart. Why did Javier have to see him like this?

"We need to go!" Rawiya screamed. "They're coming!"

They both stared in the direction Rawiya was looking. The line of cops was now advancing on them in unison. Moss cast a glance back behind him. Mr. Jacobs was on the ground, sobbing something terrible with his hand over his face, and the cop who had struck them stood frozen and uncertain. He gazed toward Mr. Jacobs, then back at Moss, then back again at the assistant principal. Why? Why had the cop stopped hitting them?

The cop belted out something close to a groan. It sounded like he was *frustrated*. He tore off his helmet, chucking it at Moss and missing.

"Daley, don't!" someone shouted from behind Moss. He risked a glance; it was one of the advancing cops, their hands up, their focus not on any of the students, but on Daley.

Daley had a face full of rage. His brow crunched up in the middle, and his cheeks were a deep beet color, sweat pouring down his face. Moss realized that it must have been agonizing in those hot suits, but he had no time to feel any sympathy for this man. The cop growled at Moss and struggled to free something from his belt in the process. "You little shits never learn," he snarled, pulling at his holster, at a stout, rectangular object. "You have no respect for *anyone,* do you?"

Daley swore as something fell to the ground. *Was that a Taser?* Moss thought, and he was gripped by an overwhelming need to *move*. His reluctance, his fear, his terror, it all slid away in that instant. Moss had always heard a lot about the fight-or-flight instinct, but he had never experienced it; his mind had always channeled fear into stillness. Now, something else took control of his body. He had to get away. He had to *survive.*

Moss scrambled to get to his feet. He would risk running. He would risk anything to escape this man, to flee from the vengefulness radiating from his body. He glanced up at Daley as he pushed himself into an upright position. Rage flared in Daley's eyes, and Moss's stomach dropped.

Moss yanked at Javier, pulled him up alongside him, kept his own eyes on the the advancing cops and his back to Daley, but then Javier stilled. Moss saw Javier's eyes go wide, saw that his mouth slightly open. His gaze was not on Moss, though. It was *behind* him. Moss spun around.

The beet-faced cop had a gun trained on Javier. And then he fired.

It wasn't the first time Moss had heard the pop of a gunshot. Nor was it the first time he'd heard the sickening sound of the air leaving someone's body. The sound that meant the worst. Javier curled into himself; his brown hands jerked up to his chest, and blood squirted out between his fingers. Moss screamed, again and again, and pitched himself forward as Javier crumpled to the ground, the life too quickly draining out of him.

"No, no, no!" Moss shrieked, his own hands pressing over the hole in Javier's chest, the blood gurgling in Javier's throat, the hot liquid spraying everywhere, and Rawiya was there and screaming as well, as was Njemile and then someone else, and finally there was an ungodly roar coming from the gate, but Moss couldn't look at any of it. He watched Javier's eyes roll about wildly, trying to focus on something, anything.

"Please stay with me," Moss begged. "Please don't leave me now."

Someone yelled the cop's name, and Moss didn't want to look away, but he couldn't help it. The man stood off to the side, the gun still in his hand, just staring. He said nothing. Did nothing. Offered no reaction at all.

Moss looked back toward the cops who had been coming their way. "Someone, help us!" Moss yelled so loud his voice cracked. "Please, *help him!*"

None of them came to his side. One of the cops had his hands on the side of his head, swearing over and over again. Another was rushing toward Daley, his own hands up in front of him, and he called out. "Holster your weapon, Daley!"

Javier heaved and moaned. But he said nothing, his throat offered no words. His mouth was agape and the blood was pumping out of him slower and slower, and Moss couldn't stop screaming. "Someone, please help!"

The color was draining from Javier's face, his lips were the wrong hue, they were so wrong, it was all wrong. Moss pressed harder on the wound, and Rawiya laid her hands on top of his.

"Keep putting pressure," Rawiya shrieked, "and don't let go!"

Don't let go, Moss begged. *Please don't let go, Javier.*

Javier stopped kicking about. He stopped looking at Moss. His beanie had come off, sat forlorn beside his head. There was no life left in his eyes. Moss knew Javier was gone.

It had happened again.

Moss slumped back and nausea rushed up into his throat. He saw a pair of black boots next to him, and he followed them up.

Daley had holstered his gun and stared at the body of the boy he'd shot. His head tilted to one side, like a dog's did when you said something they did not understand. Without a word, the man turned and walked away.

Moss reached over and grabbed Javier's beanie and he clutched it hard; then he fell over Javier's body and shook him, begging him to come back.

Again. Again. Again.

But there was no response.

23

He washed his hands.

Again.

The hot water was wrenched on high and Moss left his hands underneath it, the heat stinging his skin. He didn't move them. He left them there and stared at them, viewed them as if they were attached to some other body in some other place.

There was still blood. Around his cuticles, tucked in the corner on his left thumb and forefinger. He pulled his hands back and squatted down, ripped open the cupboards below the sink. He found a sponge in the back, grabbed it, and stood up. Steam rose from the basin and it made Moss sweat, but he couldn't stop. He began to scrape at his hands, running the rough side of the sponge over his fingers. It stung. He scrubbed harder, but he couldn't seem to get the spot to go away. He had to make it disappear, to make it stop reminding him of everything all over again.

The spot got bigger. It bloomed, spreading down his fingers, and there was more red, and it wouldn't stop coming. It dripped down into the sink, red on white, spreading out into the water that poured from the faucet. Moss dropped the sponge and held his bleeding hand still, watched the drips disappear down the drain, wished he could follow them and disappear himself.

He couldn't. He couldn't disappear. Not now. No matter how badly he wanted to.

Moss rinsed off the blood as best as he could, shut off the faucet, then wrapped the hand towel around his finger. He had to face them, he knew it. His legs were lead but he forced them to move, one after the another, down the hallway and toward the living room. He heard the newscaster speak. Something about an upcoming traffic report. An awkward cough. The squeak of the leather couch. And there was an overbearing silence that hung over everything, a massive hole that no one wanted to acknowledge.

But they had to.

Moss stepped into the living room, glanced at the others. His mother. Esperanza. Reg. Kaisha. Njemile. Rawiya. They looked to him, but it was brief. They avoided staring too long, and Moss hated it. It was happening all over again. When everyone treated him as if he was fragile, as if he would crumble any second.

Moss despised himself because it was true.

He limped to the couch and sat in the vacant space. Esperanza stole a look, but Moss didn't return it. His mother looped her fingers between his and squeezed once, but he was lost in the news broadcast. It was looping back again, and Moss couldn't tear himself away. The helicopter shot of their school, the gates with yellow police tape like party streamers, the shots of students huddled in tears on the front steps. The same images repeated and the newscasters babbled the same nonsense. No one knew much of what had happened, not unless they'd been there and seen that man raise his gun and fire it at Javier and saw Javier crumple and then . . .

The images on the TV set blurred, and Moss's eyes filled with tears. He didn't even bother wiping them away.

His mother did it for him. "I'm going to get you some tea," she announced, rising from the couch, letting him go. "Would anyone else like some?"

"I'll have some, if you don't mind," Esperanza said.

No one else answered her, so Wanda slipped into the kitchen. Moss heard the water running; he heard the thump of a cabinet closing; he heard the gentle whistle minutes later as the kettle began to boil. His mother returned with a couple of steaming mugs. He looked up at her, and an expression of pain briefly flitted across her face. He'd seen that before, too, on the steps of Dawit's store, when she had to explain to him that his father wasn't coming back. He remembered how she had stood in silence while Moss wailed in anger and grief, dropping to the cold concrete. Moss wished he could tear that card out of his mental Rolodex and shred it to pieces.

He hadn't broken down yet. He was certain that his mother was expecting him to. It was why she hovered so close to him, why she never strayed too far away, why she always kept him in her peripheral vision. *Maybe it's performance anxiety,* he thought, then wished he could make that joke out loud, but nothing felt right.

Moss ran a hand over the lumps on his legs. They were still warm, feverish. The one on his shin throbbed and pulsed, even when he wasn't moving, so he focused on it. Started counting each time he could feel his blood pump through and past it. One. Two. Three. Four.

"Did they find the cop?" Reg asked softly, breaking Moss's concentration.

Moss shook his head. "No. He disappeared after the . . . the . . ." He let the sentence dissipate.

His mother ran her hand down his arm. *You're still here,* she seemed to say with each touch. *You are here and you are alive.*

"How can someone just disappear like that?" Reg asked as the news began to report on traffic conditions, a welcome respite. "There were so many people there."

"I swear, he was sitting there when we were trying to get Moss up," Kaisha added. "Then he just *wasn't.*"

"At lot was happening," said Rawiya. "Maybe we just weren't paying attention when he left."

"He's not supposed to leave the scene of a crime, though, is he?" Kaisha asked. She shook her head and sighed. "I already know the answer to that."

"What were those . . . those *things?*" Reg asked. He shook his head. "Man, I have so many questions."

"What are they going to do now?" Esperanza asked. She sounded so worried, so afraid. "I mean, they're gonna stop the whole pilot program thing, right?"

"We don't have to talk about this," Wanda interjected, and she squeezed Moss's hand. "Moss, honey, we can watch something else. Talk about something else."

He shrugged. He was thankful that she cared how hard this conversation should have been for him, but he couldn't feel anything. "It's okay," he said. "Really. I don't know what else to do anyway."

"You just tell me the second you don't want to anymore," his mother said, then looked back up to Esperanza. "What were you saying?"

Esperanza smiled weakly at Moss; he didn't have it in him to respond. "Well, I was just wondering if this meant the end of that whole program at the school. It would have to, wouldn't it?"

"You'd be surprised at the lengths people will go to avoid responsibility," Wanda replied, and her voice was rough, but certain. Esperanza started to say something, but Wanda raised a hand to her. "I'm just sayin' that they're already spinning this on the news, aren't they? Listen to the damn language. It's all so *passive*. A police officer 'discharged' a weapon. A student was 'fatally injured.' It all sounds like separate events, you know? And that's how they start."

"Start what?" Esperanza said.

"Shifting how most people think about it. If it's presented to us in a way to make it sound like an accident, then most people won't try to hold the school itself responsible. If the walkout is portrayed as a chaotic riot—as it's already been—then most people will accept that the school had to do *something*. Sure, they'll shake their heads and say it was unfortunate that a kid got killed, but they ain't ready to commit to more than that."

"Javier," Moss said quietly.

"What's that, baby?" Wanda said, caressing his hand.

"His name is Javier." He swallowed hard. "Was. Is. I don't know."

She was nodding her head. "They won't use Javier's name," said Wanda, "at least not in positive statements. Watch how they'll refer to him as a 'suspect' or the 'trespassing student' instead of his name."

"And they're not even talking about what they did to us," said Njemile. "I have not seen one broadcast talk about that stuff that they shot on me. Or the weird thing that made Javier's friends vomit."

Kaisha rubbed Reg's arm. "I was doing some research before I came over," she said, "and . . . well, none of this is new."

"What do you mean?" Moss said, trying to keep up with the conversation, pushing past the throbbing in his legs. "I don't get it."

"There's all kind of technology out there," Wanda said, leaning forward. "Stuff I used to see back at protests before you were born. Tasers. Devices that would send out loud, piercing sounds."

"I wish I still had my phone," said Kaisha. "I found a whole bunch of stuff online about weapons used against protestors. I'm pretty sure the cops used something called a Mosquito against us."

"Great," said Njemile. "That doesn't sound terrible at *all*."

"You know," said Kaisha, her voice dropping, "they're gonna blame us. They're gonna blame the kids from Eastside, too. Say it was all our fault."

Wanda's face fell at that, and the next sentence out of her mouth was barely above a whisper. "Reminds me of all the people who blamed my husband for his own death."

"That's not *exactly* the same, is it?" Esperanza said. "Moss's dad was innocent!"

"Are you saying Javier wasn't?"

Moss leveled that one, and Esperanza shook her head. "No, no, of course not," she said, in a rush. "I just meant that it was pretty open-and-shut with your dad. No one questioned whether it was right or wrong."

"You weren't there," Moss said. "You didn't see all the news reports then."

Wanda was nodding. "He's right, Esperanza. You had them talking heads on TV, sayin' how it was a bad neighborhood, and how if he'd just put his hands in the air when asked, it wouldn't have happened."

"Which they always say," Reg added. "Sayin' that we don't got respect for cops. But his hands were full, remember?"

"But how can they do that?" Esperanza asked, frustration in her voice. "How can they just blame someone for something that isn't their fault?"

"Because they always get away with it," Moss shot back. "They always do."

"It can't be that simple," said Esperanza.

They all shot glares in her direction. Moss watched his mother start to say something, but she shut her mouth, pursing her lips.

Esperanza tried to recover. "But how can we get to this point where this just *happens*? First Shawna got assaulted, then Reg, and now Javier . . . how? It doesn't make sense to me!"

"It's an insidious thing," Wanda said. "It never happens overnight. This kind of thing crept into our community long ago. It latched on. It fed on prejudice. Selfishness. People's inability to see life through someone else's eyes. And it grew, bigger and bigger, until we got to a point where some people don't even question why a cop should be allowed to shoot first and ask questions later."

Esperanza went quiet after that, her gaze in her lap. She seemed unable to look at any of them, and it sent a bolt of anger through Moss. The thought coursed through him. *This isn't about you.* But he didn't say it.

"This is our reality," Wanda said softly. "It was back when Morris got killed, and it is now. The details are different, but it's exactly the same thing."

She wanted to say something more. Moss could see it. She wiped at her eyes, but kept quiet.

"I'm sorry," said Esperanza. "I really liked Javier."

Her voice broke on his name, and Moss felt the wall inside of him crumble. The tears came freely and the lump formed back in his throat. "I know," he croaked. "Me too."

Reg's eyes were red and glassy. "I know I already said it, man, but I'm so sorry," he said. "It's just so unfair."

"And I hate knowing that his killer is gonna get away with it," Kaisha added.

"You really think that's gonna happen?" Esperanza said, sniffling.

"How often have the cops killed someone in our city? In this *country*?" Kaisha asked. "How many times have they gotten off scot-free for it?"

"A lot," she admitted. "Practically every time."

"So why do you think that happens so regularly?" Kaisha asked her. "Who is allowing people to die like that?"

"I don't know," she said. "The police department. Maybe people in the local government."

"It's more far-reaching than that, though," said Wanda. "How many people are sitting in their homes right now, watching this same news report, and justifying death? Who else is deciding that Javier deserved to die?"

"When I went home, I logged into Facebook, and . . . it's a mess," said Kaisha. "I've already had to delete a few people because they want to believe that no one did anything wrong. Well, no one *except* Javier." She sighed. "I can't show you, though, cuz my phone is still busted. Same with all you?"

Reg, Moss, and Esperanza all grumbled an affirmative, and Rawiya held hers up. "Completely broken," she said. Moss's phone wouldn't turn on at all, and he hoped that he hadn't lost any of his old texts. The thought that he might have pushed Moss closer to the edge of panic, but his mother began to run her fingers over his scalp through his hair. It calmed him, as much as it could.

"When my husband was killed," Wanda said, "me and Moss constantly had people come up to us. In grocery stores. At the mall. While waiting for a bus. And they would come up to the two of us, and they would tell us how sorry they were, how sad it made them that Morris was dead, but did we think it was fair to blame the police?"

Esperanza's mouth dropped open. "Wait, really?" she said, staring directly at Moss.

"Yeah," he said, his voice hoarse. "All the time, Esperanza. I guess what's so messed up about how my dad died is that the whole thing *was* the fault of the police. They weren't even at the right store, and then they thought my dad was someone else. If anyone was in the wrong place at the wrong time, it was them, not my dad."

"But how did they get away with it?" said Esperanza.

"Do you think the cops aren't capable of just making shit up?" Kaisha said, anger filling her voice.

"Okay, that's not what I meant," she said. "I meant that it can't be that easy to just *lie* about people so openly."

"But they did, and they did it often," Wanda said. "The initial reports all said he had a gun and that it was self-defense when the officers shot him. Even after Dawit leaked the surveillance video."

"Months," Moss said, his voice cracking. "Months of me hearing about how he was a dangerous individual. Months of those Piedmont assholes teasing me at school, telling me he deserved it because he was a thug and the streets were cleaner without him. *Months,*" he said, emphasizing the word.

Esperanza wrung her hands together. "Oh my god," she said, and she was no longer looking at him. "I didn't know it was that bad."

Moss shrugged, but offered nothing else. Esperanza had always been good with his own anxiety and depression over the years, but he knew this was the one big thing she never seemed to get. More than ever before, he wished she just understood it without them having to explain everything.

"Can you imagine how bad it's gonna be for Javier?" Kaisha asked, and she fixed a frown on her face. "I don't even want to find out."

"Oh god," Moss groaned. "He's not from here. They're gonna use it." Wanda frowned. "What you mean, Moss?"

"Javier told me once that he and his mother did not come here legally. He's not technically a citizen."

Moss stared at Esperanza, watched the realization spread over her. She turned her head away, wiped at tears.

He stopped talking and watched the weather forecast, focusing on any detail he could. The broadcaster's tiny brooch. Was it an owl? He couldn't tell. He saw how her dark brown hair curled at the ends and watched as it bounced about each time she turned her head back to the camera. He watched her gesture about a map of the peninsula, rattling off various locations and their temperatures. He watched the two anchors exchange banter with each other. He wanted to make fun of their outfits with Javier.

I won't get to see him laugh like that again, Moss thought. His heart felt like lead, weighing down his chest, and it was like it was pulling him down to the floor. He just wanted to sleep and never wake up again. Then the pain in his legs and in his chest would stop, and he wouldn't have to ever worry about himself or his mother or his friends anymore.

But his mother leaned into him and the thoughts scurried away. The group in the living room all watched the television in silence. Moss used the armrest to give himself leverage and pushed himself to his feet, wincing as the pain laced through his left leg.

"Honey, where are you going?" Wanda said, rushing to help him stay upright.

"I can't watch this anymore," he said quietly, and he shuffled off toward his room. "Y'all can stay or leave, I don't care." He said nothing more, and he caught the look on Kaisha's face before he left the room. Her eyes were wide, vulnerable, and they darted away at once.

His mother was right behind him, following him much like their neighbors' pit bull did whenever Moss walked by their yard. Moss didn't bother closing the door to his room. He limped over to his bed and flopped down on it, burying his head in his pillow. Wanda sat on the bed and gingerly ran a hand along his back. "Oh, Moss, honey, I'm so sorry," she said.

He hated how hurt she sounded. "I know," he said into the pillow. He turned his head to the right and sucked in a deep breath. "I'm so tired of you being sorry, though."

Her hand stopped in the middle of his back. "I'm tired, too," he heard her say. "Tired of a lot of things." Another break. "I'm sorry you have to go through this." Pause. "Again."

He felt his throat begin to constrict at the thought of another person gone from this world, forgotten, because he knew that was what Javier would eventually become. What if he was nothing more than another statistic, or hashtag online? What if his name was forever stripped of all the wonderful memories that Moss had been gathering? That was the last thing Moss wanted. He wanted to remember Javier running his lips over Moss's jaw. He wanted to remember the last time they'd ridden their bikes together, a goofy smile etched onto Javier's face as Moss passed him. And every time Moss tried to center his thoughts on one of these memories, it would instead flash before him: the pop of the gun, Javier clutching his chest, the red blood dripping.

"What's happening to the world, Mama?" Moss said, his voice cracking on the last word. "Why does this keep happening?"

"Well," she said, her forehead crinkled with concern, "because people keep getting away with it."

"He's gonna get away with it, isn't he?" he asked her, and the tears spilled out and down his cheeks. Wanda raised a hand to brush some of them away, but it only made Moss cry harder. She pulled him into her lap and he clung to her as if she might disappear any second. The sobs shook his body, but his mother said nothing. She held Moss with a tenderness he craved, that he needed more than anything else in the world.

He finally sat up, sniffling every few seconds, his congestion getting the best of him. He crossed the room, leaving his mother on the bed, and grabbed a handkerchief off his desk so he could blow his nose. When he finally looked at his mom, tears were streaming down her face as well.

"I'm sorry, Mama," Moss said. "I didn't mean to make you sad."

"Baby, you know you can always talk to me," she insisted. "It's not *your* fault I feel this way."

"I just . . ." His voice broke again, and he felt his throat close as he fought the urge to start bawling. "I just thought . . . I could have loved him, Mama."

She stood and came to him, her arms out, and he let her hold him again. He liked the feel of her hands running up and down his back, so he tucked himself into her as close as he could. "I kinda figured," she said. "I could tell you felt something for that boy."

"I just want him back," he said, and then knew it was a pathetic thing to say.

"Me too," she said softly. She gently pushed herself back a bit. "You know we can't stop."

"Stop what?"

"What we started. It's more important than ever. We gotta get justice for Javier."

"Oh, damn," Moss said, sniffling again. "We need to go talk to his mom. I completely forgot."

"I know, baby. I understand. You've kind of had a lot on your plate, you know."

"But what else can we do?" he asked. "I don't even know where to start."

"Start with the small things," his mother said. She moved closer to him. "Visit Javier's mom. Make sure she's taken care of. You remember how expensive funerals were?" He nodded up at her. "I imagine it's even worse these days. So we need to get our community to raise some money. And then . . . we hit everyone else where it hurts. We need to organize something—I don't know what yet—to let them know that this can *never* happen again."

She moved away from him and began to pace back and forth in the room. "We need to find a way to get at them. In a way they can't ignore." Wanda was quiet again, and then she walked over to the door, stopping before she left the room. "I'm calling another meeting," she announced, then wiped her face. "Leave this part up to me."

His mother drifted out of the room, and Moss lay down on his bed, his eyes on the ceiling, his heart empty. He was more than willing just then to let someone else do the work.

24

When they arrived at Ms. Perez's home, Moss couldn't bring himself to climb the stairs. It would become real. *If I stay here,* he thought, *then I can still imagine that he's home.*

The man from downstairs peered out from his doorway. The screen creaked as he did so, and Moss locked eyes with him. The man was motionless, sadness all over his face. He must know. Moss realized he didn't even know the man's name. He was only the father from downstairs. Would it even matter? Would Moss ever have a reason to come back here again?

The man lowered his eyes. He said nothing. The door squeaked shut.

"Moss, honey, I'm right here."

He sucked in a lungful of air, and his gaze drifted up to the top of the stairs. Moss's memory filled in the blanks: Javier was at the top of those steps. He was going to spring out the door and stand there, waiting for Moss, that goofy smile twisting up his mouth, and when Moss got to the top, he'd offer to take his bike, but not before giving him one of those adorable kisses on the cheek. A kiss. Moss wanted to feel Javier's lips on his again, and the thought was a lance through his chest. He leaned into his mother's hand on his back, and she steadied him. Right as he felt a weakness in his knees, he heard the door at the top creak open. Without another thought, Moss bolted up the steps, his legs a quivering mess of nerves and soreness and his heart full of misguided hope. *Javier,* Moss thought. *It'll be just like it was before.*

"Moss!" his mother cried after him, but it was too late. Moss was at the top seconds later, and he swung open the screen door, only to find himself face-to-face with Javier's mother. It was then, staring at the emotional ruin of her face, the redness of her eyes, that the memory fizzled into the past. It was just that. A memory. A moment in time. It would never happen again.

Eugenia gestured to them to come inside, her lips tightly pursed. He embraced her without a word, hoping that was enough. Over her shoulder, he saw the table overflowing with flowers and balloons. *Already?* Moss thought. One of the balloons floated eerily above a bright vase full of irises. "Get Well Soon!" it urged, and the terrible inappropriateness of it forced him to stifle a giggle. The emotion made no sense to him. Where had the giddiness come from? Perhaps it was the irony. Would any of them *ever* be well again?

He let go of Javier's mom and moved into the room, giving his mother a chance to greet her. They embraced and then Eugenia succumbed to her sobs. They racked her body. Moss could see his mother's face over Eugenia's shoulder. Tears spilled down her cheeks, but her eyes were vacant. *Shit,* Moss thought. *This must remind her of Papa, too.*

The two women sat down on the couch, and Moss's mind flashed back to that afternoon. *Overwatch.* The kiss. Their bodies, so close. Moss moved away and wandered into the kitchen, placing his hands on the counter to steady himself. He could feel his throat constricting again, and he focused on that, knowing it kept him in one piece while he was here.

"Baby? You want to come join us?"

He heard his mother's voice, but he knew he couldn't even turn around to face them. What would happen to Javier's room now that he was gone? What would Ms. Perez do?

His mother's arms slid around his torso, and it sent him over the edge. His tears fell down onto the counter and he said, "It just isn't fair."

"It never is," she replied. "Never."

"I just want him here, Mama. Just right here."

He pulled away from her and twisted around. He saw Ms. Perez wringing her hands together on the couch, her own face wet with tears.

There was one thing he could do for her, though. He crossed the room, pulling Javier's beanie out of his back pocket. When he sat on the couch next to Ms. Perez, he held it out to her. She looked at it, then up to Moss's red eyes, and then she took it hesitantly, as if she were sure it would turn to dust if she touched it. She caressed it before bringing it to her face, inhaling. "It still smells like him," she said.

Moss nodded. He had wanted to keep it, to have something to remind him of what it felt like to be cradled against Javier's chest, but it wasn't right. She needed this more than Moss did.

"They didn't let me see him," she said, her accent even thicker now. "They said they had to do the autopsy first." Her voice cracked into another sob, and she fell to the side, right into Moss's arms. He provided what little comfort he could while his own mother watched quietly.

Eugenia stood up suddenly and made a beeline for Javier's room. She returned moments later with his bag, the one he wore when he was biking, and she handed it to Moss. It was heavy; his massive chain must have been inside it.

This was her offering. Moss accepted it, grateful that he would have a piece of Javier to keep for himself.

But it didn't feel real, like he had hoped it would. None of it did. Moss glanced over at the hallway and saw that the light in Javier's room was on. A panic darted through him, a trick of his mind. He had believed, just for a second, that Javier was still home, that this was all some cruel prank. The scene unfolded in his head. He'd yell at Javier, scold him for pulling such a vicious joke on them all. Javier would smile, that devilish grin filling up his face, and Moss would forgive him.

No matter what Moss did in the coming days, no matter what rallies he attended, no matter what revenge he got, Javier wouldn't come back. Couldn't, he corrected himself. He could not come back.

"Go," Eugenia said.

He shook his head at her. "What do you mean?"

"Go in his room," she explained. "Take something. Keep it." She sniffled. "Recuérdalo."

Wanda nodded at Moss, so he crossed the carpet slowly, his legs seemingly unable to move without conscious thought. When he pushed open the door, he realized that this was the first time he'd ever been in Javier's room. The lamp in the far corner cast a yellowish pall, a sickly vibe that weighed heavy on Moss's eyes. But there was so much vibrant color spread about that it overpowered the grimness of that lamp. Posters were tacked to the wall, almost haphazardly, as if Javier had tried to cover every bare surface with something he liked. There was a Wonder Woman poster that stretched over his bed, which overlapped one of Selena. There were gig flyers taped all underneath it, and Moss wanted to come back, to spend hours reading them all, to see if they'd ever been at the same show and didn't know it.

There was a poster for a movie called *But I'm a Cheerleader,* a young white girl looking at Moss from the center of it, a pensive expression on her face. He'd never seen it, but it seemed such an odd choice among everything else. *Maybe I'll watch it,* he thought, and he moved over to the tiny desk tucked into the corner to his left. Papers and note-books were spread over the top of it, as well as some scattered colored pencils and thin-tipped markers. He aimlessly moved the papers around, grabbed a black Moleskine journal and opened it.

Moss was staring at Javier's comic.

The coloring was light, clearly a draft done to block out scenes and placements. His eyes darted from one scene to the next, to the super-hero in the purple outfit and red cape. He thumbed back to the first page, ran down the long list of notes, and his finger stopped on one:

"Name character . . . El Gran Misterio? Ugh why, what is the mystery."

Then, two lines down:

"What if he is made of MIST or something."

Javier had crossed it out.

He flipped through the pages, admiring Javier's use of color, the way he seemed to know how to arrange scenes in all those square and rectangular frames. He looked at a scene where someone leapt off a building, and he could tell that Javier had erased one part of El Gran Misterio's leg over and over again, trying to get it right.

But he was trying. Moss flipped a few more pages. El Gran Misterio was removing his costume, hanging it in the closet, and Moss laughed. The main character had a stunning resemblance to Javier, and the laughter choked him as his throat began to close up again. *I can't even make fun of him for creating a Gary Stu.*

He turned the page. His tears hit the page, blurred the frame with the bed in it, and he saw that El Gran Misterio was no longer a superhero, no longer the man in purple spandex and a red cape, and then he was climbing into a bed with another man, whose skin was a deep, dark brown, who looked . . .

No, please don't let it be true, Moss thought, and then he was utterly unable to look at Javier's drawing of him, unable to fathom a world where so much potential had been snuffed out, unable to want anything else but Javier, right there and right now. He closed the notebook and clutched it to his chest as he collapsed on Javier's bed.

They must have heard him. Wanda shuffled into the room first, Eugenia behind her. His mother sat on the edge of the bed, ran a hand down his arm, but she seemed so reluctant. Uncertain. Even she was lost, and it sent him spiraling more. They were all lost.

Eugenia was there at his side, and she reached over to his face, put her hand on the side of it, touched him gingerly. "You have to get him," she choked out, then yanked her hand back and wiped the snot away from her nose. "Please."

"Get who?" Moss asked. He saw the heartbreak in her expression. *Does she mean Javier?*

"Get the diablo who did this, please," she begged. "Promise me you'll get him."

It was a goal. Something Moss could focus on, to make him forget that Javier wasn't here.

Moss nodded. "You have my word," he said. "We'll get him."

His mother didn't react. They sat in silence for the rest of the evening.

25

"Did you hear that, Mr. Jeffries?"

Moss looked up at Mrs. Torrance. Her eyes were red. His own head pounded something fierce, the pain hiding behind his eyes and in his sinuses. It was too bright in the room.

"I'm sorry," he said softly. "What did you say?"

She sighed. "We don't have to do this if you don't want to," she said. "You can step out if you want to."

He shook his head. "No, it's important," he said, and for the first time that morning, he smiled. "We all need to know."

She nodded back at him. "Classes for the morning have been changed," she explained, standing up. As she spoke, she paced back and forth. "We're on a limited schedule until lunch. Our homeroom classes are two hours this morning, and then you'll visit periods one through four for just half an hour each. Mr. Jacobs, our assistant principal, wanted to make sure that students had time to process what happened on Friday and talk to their teachers about it." She walked over to her desk and picked up a yellow piece of paper. "I'm supposed to read this statement to you from Mr. Elliot, but I suspect it'll anger y'all more than anything else."

"Oh, then you *definitely* need to read it," said Njemile, full of scorn. "Please. *Perform* it for us, Mrs. Torrance."

There were murmurs and grumbles about the classroom. Mrs. Torrance chuckled. "Well, it's short," she said. "I suspect that the school's lawyers aren't letting any of the administration say much."

"Figures," said Njemile. "Well, what does it say?"

"'To the esteemed student body at West Oakland High,'" she began, then she scoffed at the page. "*Now* he thinks you are all esteemed?

That's nice." There was scattered laughter about the room, more awkward than anything else. She continued. "'We are all deeply saddened by what occurred here on campus on Friday afternoon. The West Oakland High administration requests your patience and understanding as we try to deal with this situation as best we can. For the immediate future, our partnership with the Oakland Police Department has been suspended, and the metal detectors have been disabled. There will be a more detailed statement later this week.'"

"Well, that's not so bad," said Larry. "Hella fake, but not the worst thing I've ever heard."

"I'm not finished yet, Mr. Jackson," said Mrs. Torrance.

He groaned. "Why did I speak up?"

She grimaced as she silently reread the remainder of the note. She exhaled. "'I would like to personally remind students that trespassing is not tolerated on campus. If there are any disruptive incidents this week, they will be met with strict enforcement of our disciplinary policy.'"

Moss felt his stomach sink right as his class erupted in response. He heard a few students swear, which Mrs. Torrance usually did not tolerate. But her face was lost and exhausted. She dropped the note on her desk and raised her hands, waited for the class to quiet down. "I know, I know," she said. "This is all very confusing and deeply upsetting."

"That's an understatement," said Moss. The words came out with a bitterness, and he cringed. But Mrs. Torrance was looking at him. He saw it again: sympathy in her eyes, pity on her face.

"The faculty hasn't been briefed on anything," she said, "so all I know is what I saw and what others told me they saw. And it was pretty bad on our end."

Kaisha's hand shot up. "Permission to use my cell phone," she said. When Mrs. Torrance nodded, she added, "My *new* cell phone, since my old one doesn't work at all. Who else had a broken phone after Friday?"

Nearly every hand in the room shot up, including Moss's. He hadn't had time to get a new one or to find out if the information on his old one could be salvaged.

"I don't think that's an accident," Mrs. Torrance said. "But I have no explanation for it. They didn't tell the faculty anything."

"Well, I've been keeping track of everything," Kaisha said, scrolling down to something on her phone. "If you don't mind?" Mrs. Torrance silently gave her permission. "Well, here's what we know for sure. The final count: one hundred and seventeen students injured in total."

The silence was painful. It was worse for Moss because his fear had just come true. Javier was a number, unspoken in the count but still part of it. He would forever be part of a statistic, a fact read aloud to shock others, a part of a fractured history. As Kaisha began to talk about the injuries, as she shared quotes from the Oakland Police Department, from pundits and online blogs, as other students began to tell their own stories, show off their injuries and wounds, Moss's attention floated away. He couldn't hear it anymore. None of it was new to him. No one wanted to be accountable. No one wanted to take responsibility. And the more he heard about the school district distancing themselves from what had happened, the more certain he was that nothing would ever be fixed. They'd all get away with it. They'd all get to live their lives and go home to their families.

All of them but Javier.

It was Larry who brought Moss back. In the pained silence after Kaisha stopped reading, he cleared his throat loudly. "Mrs. Torrance," he said, his tone defeated and afraid, "I just don't understand. How can they do this? They killed someone. What are we supposed to do next?"

Mrs. Torrance sat on the edge of her desk and lowered her head, her dreads hanging down the sides of her face. "I don't know, Mr. Jackson," she said. There was no confidence in her voice. She was normally so sure, so certain, so snappy and purposeful. But now, she sounded like all of Moss's peers, and it left Moss feeling more dejected than before.

What *were* they supposed to do next?

26

Days passed. Moss was adrift in it all. He left his biology class on Wednesday afternoon, walked right past the hallway they'd run down to escape Daley after he had tripped. He saw a boy with a black beanie on his head, crooked, tilted to the side, and his mind betrayed him for just a second.

Moss rounded the corner. It was a freshman; he looked nothing like Javier.

He saw a ghost of Javier again on BART that night, a tall man with skin the same hue as he'd had, his black fixie leaning up against him. Moss did a double take. The man just glared back, angled his body away from Moss.

His brain kept filling in the chasm, the hole that was left behind. At dinner that night, his mother pushed her pad thai around the Styrofoam container. It sat there until the steam stopped rising, until the normally scrumptious smell of it disappeared.

"I'm going over to Eugenia's tonight," she said. Wanda closed the lid, shoved the box away from her. "You wanna come?"

His heart leapt. Javier would be there, wouldn't he—

He shook his head. "I can't," Moss said. "Not yet."

She nodded. "I'm setting up another meeting for Sunday. For the church. You wanna come to that?"

He sighed. "Yeah," he said, finally. "It's important."

"You don't have to talk or anything if you don't want to."

"I know. I probably should, though."

She reached out, her hand on top of his. "It'll get easier someday," she said.

Someday seemed a long way away.

27

It was Sunday night, and Blessed Way Church was overflowing.

Moss saw Martin at the main door, chatting with those who were struggling to get inside the space, but it was futile. There had to be nearly a hundred people on the steps and spilling out on either side of the building. Moss finished locking up his bike and headed straight toward his barber.

"We're setting up a speaker!" Martin yelled at the crowd, then winked quickly at Moss. "I promise, y'all will be able to hear everything from out here!"

Martin stretched his hand out and pulled Moss through the crowd. "Good to see you, man," he said, embracing Moss. He held Moss for a few seconds before pushing him in the direction of the doors. "Your ma's about to get started, so you better head up front."

"Thanks," said Moss, his voice dull and lifeless. He ducked inside quickly, eager to avoid socializing as much as he could. The patient excitement that Moss observed during the first meeting was gone now. People spoke loudly and coarsely to one another, and a nervous energy filled the room, as if any second, a spark would ignite the entire crowd. They were angry, frightened. He worked his way toward the front of the room, stopping to greet a few people he recognized. The Meyerses were there. Mrs. Torrance and her partner. Shamika, Dawit, and Bits were up near the stage, so he headed in their direction. Moss saw Rawiya deep in conversation with Mr. Roberts. He gave them a nod as he passed. "Didn't expect to see you here," he said to his biology teacher.

"There are a lot of us who are unhappy," Mr. Roberts said, frowning. He gestured with his head to somewhere behind Moss. The school nurse, the secretary, and two guidance counselors were chatting with one another not far away.

He saw more people he didn't expect. Tariq and Eloisa. (No dog, though.) Jasmine waved from the far end of one of the rows of pews. There was a group of young kids near her, and they held a banner above them. ASIAN-AMERICANS IN SOLIDARITY, it read, and he felt a burst of appreciation. It passed. He couldn't seem to hold on to anything for more than a few seconds.

Moss ascended the steps to the stage and found his mama crouched down behind the pulpit. "A good turnout, no?" she said as she rose.

"Yeah, it's a lot of people," he said. "Way more than I thought."

"It's a big night, baby. I'm proud of you, you know."

"For what?"

"Being willing to sit up here and talk," she said, and she kissed him on his temple. "It'll be a huge help to us."

"What do you want me to say tonight?" he asked, uncertain.

"Whatever you feel comfortable talking about," she said. "And I mean that. Moss, this hurts, and I know it's not fun to talk about. And you know I don't want anyone to exploit the tragedy of this just for the sake of activism."

"Neither do I," Moss said. He took a deep breath. "But I think I need to. To feel better about this." He looked out at the massive crowd. "It feels right."

She beamed at him. "I love you, Moss," his mother said, her voice small but proud.

And with that, she drifted across the stage toward Reverend Okonjo. He backed away and moved over to stage right, where someone had set up a table and a few microphones. Eugenia sat on the end farthest from Moss, and Reg was there, too. Moss leaned down and gave Javier's mother a kiss on the cheek, and she smiled in return. He greeted Reg with a big hug.

"Good to see ya, Moss," Reg said. "You seen Kaisha yet? She's supposed to be here, too."

Moss shook his head. "Nah, but it's hard to find anyone here. I didn't expect it to be so crowded."

Reg wiped the sweat off his forehead. "I'm a little nervous, man. What are we trying to do here?"

Moss sat down next to him. "I dunno. I was just gonna let my mom lead the show. She's so good at this."

"Yeah, I know. There's Esperanza!"

Reg pointed to someone coming up the center aisle, and she bounded up the steps and smothered Moss in an embrace. He gave her a smile, a genuine one, thankful for the moment that she was there.

"You doing okay?" she asked. "I feel like we haven't spoken much this week."

"I'm okay, given the circumstances. Sad all the time, but it has its highs and lows, you know?"

"I do," she said. "My parents are just confused by the whole thing. They don't really understand what happened, and to be honest . . . I don't even know how to explain it all to them."

"Are they not here?" he asked.

She pointed to the rear corner at the south end of the church. Rebecca and Jeff tentatively raised their hands, waved at Moss. He returned the gesture with a single wave.

"Well, at least they didn't turn this into one of their crusades," she said.

He shrugged. "Not like they could have done anything to help," he said.

"At least they're trying?"

She didn't sound convinced of what she was saying. "Maybe, but your parents can be pretty clueless every once in a while."

Esperanza frowned at him, and then sighed. "I hate agreeing with you," she said. "It feels like I'm betraying them."

The squeal of feedback from the microphones at center stage pulled their attention away from each other. Reverend Okonjo and Wanda stood at the pulpit together, and just their presence alone inspired the audience to quiet down. As Esperanza headed back down to her seat, Kaisha managed to get up onstage, and she planted a kiss on the top of Reg's head before sitting down between him and Ms. Perez.

Reverend Okonjo raised his hands, and the last few people chatting and gossiping quieted down. You could hear every shift in the seats in that church, every cough, every sniffle. "We have a difficult task ahead of us," the reverend said, his voice carrying throughout the room. "We are angry." There were shouts of affirmation. "We are in mourning. We are *tired*."

A few folks said "Amen!" in response, and he continued. "It is during this time that we ask for compassion. For understanding. For empathy." He cast a glance in Moss's direction, and Moss inclined his head. "It is going to be very easy for all of us to be consumed with rage over what has happened in this community. And I don't blame anyone for feeling despair and anger. I am not here to tell any of you what to feel. All I am asking"—he gestured to the entire room, his arms spread wide—"of all of you, is to have patience. Just for the moment. Just for the next few hours. Give one another a compassionate ear, and let those who wish to speak do so."

Moss gazed out at the sea of people. Teachers. Students. Parents. Administrators. Tax preparers and barbers, convenience-store owners and stay-at-home moms. They whispered to one another. Hands shot up, like those of eager students in a classroom.

"I know many of you are eager to speak," the reverend acknowledged, "but I'd like Ms. Wanda Jeffries to say a few words before we get started. She'll be leading the conversation, so we'd like to set a few ground rules now."

He stepped out of the way, and Moss's mother took her place at the pulpit. Her poise was firm, direct, and carried an authority to it. She didn't speak at first and instead cast a powerful gaze over the audience, taking in every face she could.

"I want to begin by thanking each of you for being here," she finally said, her hands softly gripping the sides of the pulpit, the muscles in her upper arms flexing. "You are part of something special, and right now, our community needs it." She let the mumbling and muttering that followed her words die down. "We may feel raw and desperate at this moment, but I believe that through a conversation between *all* of us, we can find a solution to this . . . this . . ."

In the quiet space of the sentence that died on her tongue, someone chimed in. "Nightmare."

Wanda nodded her head. "So let us take this one at a time, like we did before. It helps no one if we talk over each other, even if we agree. Please conduct yourselves with respect, and I promise, we will get to each of you. Jermaine has set up a microphone again, and we ask that you line up behind it if you want to speak."

She then turned to the four of them at the table. "I also want to introduce some people who will not only speak tonight, but who will be able to provide you with answers if you need them. I'm sure y'all remember my son, Morris Jeffries, Jr., or Moss, as he goes by."

Moss didn't know what to do. He awkwardly raised his hand to the crowd. *Lord, why don't they teach classes on this?* he thought.

"Next to him is Reg Phillips, who was the reason for our last meeting here, and many of you remember his partner Kaisha from that evening, too. If you don't mind, though, I want Ms. Eugenia Perez to go first." Wanda gestured to her. "Go ahead."

Eugenia pulled a piece of paper out of her pocket. As she unfolded it, it echoed through the church, amplified by the nearest microphone, and each pop and crinkle felt large and awkward. "Thank you, Wanda," she said, casting a glance at Moss's mother. "And thank you, Moss, for . . . for loving my son."

He had wanted to hold it together for the entire meeting, to present himself with confidence and certainty, to be the kind of person the community could depend on. He wanted to be like his mother. But Moss had never said that he loved Javier once, not to anyone, and yet as Eugenia said it, he knew it was true. He was in love with Javier. The stone in his throat came back, so sudden that he didn't know if he could hold it back.

"I lost my son a week ago," she said, and she didn't bother wiping her tears away. They dripped down onto the table, onto the statement she had handwritten and folded and brought with her. "He was taken from me by a man who has disappeared, who won't even show his face and admit that he shot my . . . my . . ." She coughed, too loud, and it was like she shrank before them all, became a smaller person somehow. She was throwing her soul into the world, uncertain she'd ever get it back.

"I don't know what to do without him. I am here to ask you for help." She broke into a full sob then, and Moss stood and dragged his chair with him, the sound of it scraping the stage loud and obnoxious, but he didn't care. He sat next to Javier's mother and wrapped an arm around her shoulder as she continued. "They have not even released his body to me," she said. "They still have it. I can't bury him. I don't know what to do."

She put the paper down on the table and pushed it away. "Please help me do something," she begged, her eyes on the crowd. "Help me do *anything*."

Martin sidled up to Moss and put a box of tissues and a pitcher of water on the table before dashing off. He handed a tissue to Eugenia and she blew her nose. "I'm sorry," she said. "This is too hard."

She stood, her chair scraping like Moss's had, and she moved into the wings, collapsing into a man's arms. Moss turned back to the crowd and could make out a number of people crying. *Hold on,* Moss told himself. *You have to be strong for them.* He remembered that morning in the quad, when he shoved down his terror for Shawna. *Do the same thing again.*

"So what do we do for Ms. Perez?" Wanda asked the crowd. She gestured toward the table. "Any of you?"

Moss felt the eyes of everyone in that room turn to him. It was instantaneous, and he didn't know how his mother didn't crumble under that kind of pressure. "I don't know," he said, his face too close to the microphone, and the feedback squealed at him. He moved back from it. "How do we get James Daley held accountable? That's what I want." He looked over to the wings, saw Eugenia still bent with grief. "I think that's what all of us want."

There was a shuffle in the back of the room, a hand thrust up in the air, a white sheet of paper in it. "I might be able to help!" The voice cut through the commotion, and Moss squinted as he watched a woman with short blond hair squeeze past people grouped in the aisles. She stumbled as she made it to the steps, but she recovered and headed straight to the pulpit, where Wanda and Reverend Okonjo stood. Her outfit was conservative, dress pants under a light blue blouse, her hair delicately swept back. She extended a hand to Wanda, who stared at it with confusion.

"Excuse me, but who are you?"

"Rachel Madsen," she said, and she smiled, a quick gesture with her lips pressed together. "Communications manager for the Oakland Police Department."

It was like someone had punched the entire room in the gut. Moss stood, and his heart leapt to this throat. "What are you doing here?" he shouted. "This isn't for *you*."

The words seemed to cut her deep. He saw the disappointment cross her features for just a second, but that smile returned. "I understand you might be upset, but I assure you—"

"*Might* be upset?" He grabbed the back of his chair to steady his legs, which shook from terror. "They killed her son!" He pointed back toward Javier's mother.

"I came because I have a statement from the Oakland Police Department that I wanted to read. We believe that it was best you heard it from us first before we released it to the public."

There was silence. It was painful. Moss looked to his mother, whose brows were creased in concern. She was shaking her head gently, but Rachel Madsen still stepped up to the pulpit. She laid out the paper she had, ran her hands over it as if to straighten it out. She looked up at the crowd, which sat frozen in horrified silence. He saw Esperanza in the front row, her mouth slightly agape, her body on the edge of her seat. Moss wanted to slump so badly, but he refused to look weak. *Not now,* he told himself. *Don't give it away.*

Rachel cleared her throat, gave another meaningless smile. "'On Friday, September twenty-first, at two twenty-one P.M., the Oakland Police Department responded to reports that there was a riot at West Oakland High School after multiple students allegedly tried to leave campus.'"

"You know that's a lie," Kaisha interrupted on her own microphone. "How can the police *respond* to something *they* started?"

"If you'll just let me read the statement—" Rachel said.

"No, I won't let you read it," Kaisha shot back. "I thought you said that you might be able to help."

Rachel pursed her lips, but did not say anything at first. "I am here to respond to claims that the Oakland Police Department acted outside the scope of their—"

The crowd got restless, and Moss lost his temper. "Why . . . are . . . you . . . here?" He clapped in between each word, eschewing the microphone, shouting as loud as he could.

Rachel flinched, then blinked at Moss. She looked down at the statement she had, then back up at Moss, then back down to the paper. She cleared her throat again. "'Officer James Daley then encountered Javier Perez, a student of Eastside High, who was trespassing at the time of—'"

She never got to finish. Moss picked up his chair and flung it toward the back of the stage, fury coursing through his veins. People in the audience sprang out of their seats and started shouting. Kaisha was at Moss's side and she held him as he glared at Rachel, who folded up the paper she had. That same little smile appeared again, the one where she didn't open her lips, where she pressed her mouth into a thin line, and it made the anger boil inside him, swirling in his chest and pulsing out into every inch of his body. But Kaisha reached down and grabbed his hand and whispered in his ear. "Not now."

They watched Rachel walk past them. She avoided their gaze and darted off into the shadows behind the stage.

Reverend Okonjo shuffled up to the pulpit, and he already looked exhausted. "Please," he said, and the microphone carried his voice throughout the room. "Please sit down."

Wanda was there, and she pulled Moss into a hug. "I'm sorry, I'm so sorry," she said, and squeezed tight. "I shouldn't have let her speak. I was just . . . shocked."

He stepped away from her, his heart racing. "It's not your fault,

Mama," Moss said. He felt a giddiness run through him, much like he did that night at Eugenia's place. "Well, I admit I didn't expect that."

His mother rolled her eyes, but the sadness was gone. It was as if the woman had given them all a jolt of energy to snap them to attention. "Yeah, I thought that the OPD might have a little more tact than that."

"Wanda?" Reverend Okonjo was gesturing toward her. "If you'd like to continue?"

She kissed Moss on the forehead, then headed back to the pulpit. Moss sat in the chair Eugenia had been in, taking in the audience as they tried to settle back down. He watched as his mother reclaimed the room with grace. "Well, that was interesting, wasn't it?" Wanda said, laughing.

Some folks responded with curses. A short black woman at the front of the line to speak tapped the microphone. "If you don't mind?" she said.

"Go ahead, Lanessa," Wanda said.

"I think we can already see how quickly they're going to blame other people for what they've done," she said.

"Tell 'em!" someone in the crowd yelled.

"I don't have any answers, but I run the community workspace down on 14th Street in downtown," she continued, "and I wanted to offer you a space. Somewhere you can print posters, plan rallies, anything. Anyone from West Oakland High can come down, show me their ID, and you can use the space for free as long as you need to."

There was a loud round of applause after that one, and Wanda thanked Lanessa. The woman stepped aside, and Moss's heart leapt. Rebecca stood at the microphone, and she reached down to adjust it, raise it higher. Moss looked down to Esperanza, who was typing on her phone. He snapped once, and her gaze flew up to him. He pointed toward her mother with his chin, and she turned to look. In the awkward silence, he heard Esperanza say, "Oh, no. . . ."

Rebecca cleared her throat. "Hello, Wanda, Moss," she said, smiling from ear to ear.

Wanda nodded at her. "Good to see you, Mrs. Miller. Did you have an idea?"

She shook her head. "More of a question about how those of us who are more privileged can help," she answered. "Because we *want* to help, even if this didn't happen in our neighborhood or to our daughter. And there are a lot of folks in Piedmont who want to help, but aren't sure what we can do that's most effective."

There was some light applause in appreciation of her words. "That's a good question, Rebecca," said Wanda. "I can't speak for everyone, but the easier answer I can give is that we need to fund-raise for Ms. Perez to help her with the costs associated with the funeral."

That got a louder round of applause, and Rebecca was nodding at that. "Is there anything some of us can do with the administration? Pressure we can apply there?"

"Perhaps," said Wanda, "but we should probably wait until we have a more concrete plan before any of us reach out to anyone at the school."

"Well, I would like to offer up myself as a resource, if that's okay." Rebecca seemed excited that she had a way to contribute. She puffed up, beamed toward the stage. Moss caught an eye roll from Esperanza and stifled a laugh.

"Of course," said Wanda. "We can talk later." She gestured as if to tell Rebecca to let the next person speak.

But Rebecca didn't move away from the microphone. "It's just that I have a connection of sorts to one of the people who runs West Oakland High," she said. "I actually taught the principal's son a few years back."

Moss looked back to Esperanza, whose face was crunched up in confusion. She shook her head at Moss, then mouthed, *I don't know.*

"Okay," said Wanda, her voice tentative, unsure. "If we need to utilize that, I'll let you know."

"Well, I've already talked to him about this matter once."

The gasps were audible. Moss felt his heart drop into his stomach, and Esperanza cried out. "What? What are you talking about, Mom?"

"It's not a big deal," she said. "I just called him up a few days ago to chat with him about the rally, to make sure he knew how hard the kids had been taking these new initiatives."

Moss stood slowly, the horror of realization spreading upward, planting itself in his chest, threatening to erupt out of his mouth. His mother had a question ready, though, and she lobbed it out.

"Exactly *when* did you talk to Mr. Elliot?"

Rebecca's initial response was to take a step away from the microphone, and she seemed suddenly aware that every eye in the room was on her. She cleared her throat. Again. "A couple of days before the rally," she answered, and this time, it was Esperanza who shot up.

"Mom, what are talking about? I told you not to get involved!"

"I just wanted to make sure that none of your friends were hurt!" Rebecca shot back, confusion spilling forth.

"You told him," Moss said, to himself at first, and the sound in the church began to rise, so the next words out of his mouth were at the top of his lungs. *"YOU FUCKING TOLD THEM!"*

Her mouth was agape. The crowd silenced. "What?" Rebecca said. "What do you mean?"

"They knew *everything*!" Kaisha exclaimed. "They knew about the walkout, about when we'd be leaving, and *you* told them? How could you?"

She sputtered for a couple of seconds. "It sounded like he already *knew*," she said. She turned back to look in the far corner, but Jeff was trying to hide his face. "He knew, honey, didn't he?"

Moss's heart pitched to his feet and the nausea rose in its place. He heard Kaisha and Reg say something to him, but he couldn't parse the words, and it was like all the oxygen in the room had been sucked out. He felt the blackness again, the dark blurs in the corner of his vision. "Please tell me you're kidding," he muttered, but it came out too loud and his shaking voice was sent out into the church.

"I thought I was *helping*," she said, and the worst part, Moss knew, was that she believed herself. "I didn't want them overreacting and hurting anyone."

"But look what you *did*!" Moss shrieked. "You told them our plans, and they got the police involved, and now he's *dead*, and it's *your* fault!"

She was drowned out at that, the crowd shouting at her, and Moss recognized the start of a wave of panic in Esperanza's mom. Rebecca stepped back up to the mic to say something, but he couldn't stand there. He couldn't listen to her. He swayed at first, and Reg's hand darted out, grabbing his arm, and Reg tried to help steady him, but momentum carried Moss toward the side of the stage. He backed away from the table, slowly at first, and then he was jogging down the steps, and he couldn't even bring himself to look at Esperanza, even though she was yelling his name. He pushed past all the people, and he flung open the doors at the back of the room, light spilling into the tense space. It was a cool night, and it felt good on his burning face, but the shame came rushing back as Moss saw just how many people were staring at him.

There were hundreds standing around the doors to the church. Some sat on the steps. He saw Shamika, shock on her face. Dawit rose and called in his direction, and he ignored him, too. He just started walking away, pushing past everyone, many of whom must have put two and two together and figured out that he was the kid onstage, the one whose life had just fallen apart. He could tell because they wore expressions of pity. Moss hated it and he just wanted to escape from them all.

Bad memories flooded back. The reporters outside Dawit's store, the way they crowded around Moss days after his father's death, their microphones in his face. "Do you think your father should have put his hands up?" Moss couldn't speak then, just as he couldn't speak now.

The Rolodex in his head flipped again. He and his mom were at the farmers' market, the one down by Jack London Square. A woman had swooped in so quickly that no one had any time to see her coming. "I'm glad your father is dead," she had said to Moss. "Less garbage on the streets."

Again.

Francis. On the playground during recess. He had pushed Moss down on the basketball court, and his palms hurt for days after that. "My daddy's a cop," he had said as he stood above Moss, his hands balled in fists. "I'll tell him to shoot you next."

Again. And again. All of the people who had told him and his mother that Morris deserved what he got. It was the same nightmare once more.

Except it wasn't a dream.

He hooked a sharp right at the end of the building, and he felt the ground drift away from him. He put his hand up against the stone facade of Blessed Way to steady himself, to stop the darkness from swallowing him whole. He squatted down, to get closer to the earth, and he crumpled there. His knees scraped against the concrete, and the brief flare of pain felt liberating. He hurt. It felt so lonely to think that, but it was his truth. That truth swallowed him up.

Javier was gone, and there was nothing he could do about it.

No clever speech would make Moss feel better. No plan to take down the Oakland Police Department would absolve his heart. Tears poured freely down his face. They felt immense on his cheeks, as if somehow he were crying harder than was humanly possible. He cried for a minute, two, maybe ten, and he didn't care. Moss choked on the spit and congestion and he then felt a hand on his back.

He looked up and into the face of Bits, whose own eyes were red. "Hey," they said. "Been watching you. Didn't know if there was a good time to interrupt."

Moss wiped his face with the back of his hand and cleared his throat. "It's okay," he said. He sat up and put his back against the church, but he couldn't look at his friend. How long had they been here? How loud had he been? "Everything okay in there?"

"I think so," Bits said. "It's pretty intense, though. There are a few people who agree with Esperanza's mom who're tryin' to argue that it's our fault the walkout ended so badly." They paused. "Someone brought up Javier's citizenship. It's honestly a nightmare."

Moss swore under his breath. "Is my mom okay?"

Bits smiled and sat down next to him. "Your mama is always okay, Moss. She's in her natural element in there."

He sniffed a few times, trying to clear up his sinuses. "Yeah, I hope so."

"She tried to leave to come get you," Bits said. "I told her to stay, that I'd do it."

"Really?" Moss said, looking up at his friend. "Thanks."

Bits seemed to recognize that maybe Moss didn't want to say anything. It comforted him.

Moss squeezed Bits's hand. "Thank you. For being here."

"You know I lost my dad, too, right?"

Moss shook his head at that, looking into Bits's eyes. He could tell they were holding back a rush of tears, so he looked away quickly, down at the hand that held his. Bits's was rough, not that much lighter than his own.

"A while back," Bits said. "Like, just at the end of fifth grade." They laughed, a rueful sound. "Actually, it was right after I met Njemile."

"How come I never heard about it?" Moss asked.

Bits shook their head. "I mean, I don't talk about it myself. Drive-by shooting over on Campbell. 'Collateral damage,' they called it." They wiped at one of their eyes. "He didn't even make it to the ambulance."

"Jesus," said Moss. "I'm sorry."

They smiled. "It's okay. You didn't know. I got pretty messed up after that. Joined the Willow Street gang not too long after, did some things I'm not proud of. I was young, maybe, but I didn't know what I was doing. What I got involved in."

"You?" Moss said, shocked. "In a gang?"

"I know, I know," they said. "Pretty surprising, right? I got jumped real bad once, around age twelve. Stopped talking much after that. I felt ashamed that I couldn't stand up for myself, like I was a disappointment. I stopped talking to Njemile during that time, but she never stopped being my friend." They spread their hands out in front of them dramatically. "That's where Bits came from."

"I can't believe I didn't know that."

"I only talk when I wanna talk," Bits said. "I'm just a lot more careful about myself these days."

"Well, I'm flattered," said Moss. He squeezed Bits's hand again. "Thanks."

Moss released Bits's hand and draped his arm around their shoulder, pulling Bits in closer to him.

"I only barely met Javier," said Bits. "You liked him a lot, didn't you?"

Moss nodded, his throat constricting again at the thought. His words felt tiny. "Yeah. A lot."

"It's hard to like someone. I try not to."

Bits then leaned into Moss and they sat together like that for another half hour, silent but calmed by the presence of each other. They watched cars go by on 23rd, heard the sound of amplified voices in the church, felt the cool fall wind rush down the street. And still Moss sat, unmoving, but with his friend's body next to him, warm and comforting.

A commotion spilled around the corner, and Moss pulled his arm back to push himself up off the ground. He helped Bits up, and they both saw people spilling out onto the streets.

"It must be over," said Moss. "Lemme go find my mama. You'll stick around, right?"

Bits nodded, and then Moss pulled them into a quick hug before sprinting off. He darted around the crowd forming on the steps and pushed his way into the church. People were still making their way outside, so he expected it would take a while for him to find his mother. But she stood up near the pulpit with Reverend Okonjo, Martin, Esperanza, and someone in a navy hoodie who had their back to Moss. He tried his best to be quick about the greetings he gave to all the familiar people he passed, but it was hard. Shawna stopped him to express her thanks again and say she was sorry about what had happened to Javier. Mrs. Torrance pulled him aside at one point, but she could tell that he was preoccupied. "I'll see you in class Monday, Mr. Jeffries," she said. "We all got your back." He was thankful.

He ascended the steps quickly, and Martin made room for Moss to join the group around the pulpit. When he did so, the man in the hoodie turned to look at him, and he smiled weakly.

It was Mr. Jacobs.

"What are you doing here?" Moss asked.

"Not so loud, honey," Wanda said, and she directed the group into the wings on stage left. She focused her gaze on Moss. "You okay?"

"I'm okay, I guess," he said, dismissing her. "A little shocked to see him here. How's your jaw?"

Mr. Jacobs's hand shot up to the bruise on his face. "I've had better days," he admitted. He sighed. "I know this doesn't mean much, but I'm really sorry about what happened to your friend."

There were other folks sitting on the edge of the stage, and Moss watched as Esperanza hovered nearby. *I can't talk to her right now or I'll explode.*

Instead, Moss looked directly at his mother. "What's going on, Mama? I don't understand. I just want to help."

"I know," she said. "And you did a fantastic job tonight."

"So why all the secrecy? What's going on?"

This time, Mr. Jacobs stepped close to him. "I got a chance to talk to your mom before this started, Morris, and—"

"Moss," Wanda corrected.

"Sorry. Yeah, of course. Anyway, I wanted to help because what happened last week was . . . awful. Really awful."

"I know," Moss said, his face burning as anger flared in him again. "You don't need to tell me. *Again.*"

It was quiet for a beat before Mr. Jacobs continued, pushing past the awkwardness. "Look, I know more about this than you think I do, and I told your mom everything I could, and she decided that it was best to share what I know with . . . a select few."

"A select few?" Moss turned to his mother. "A select few *what*?"

"People I trust," she said. "And I think you and some of your friends deserve to come along. You've done the work that's gotten us here."

Rawiya joined Moss at his side. "Okay, now I'm confused, too," she said. "What do you know?"

Mr. Jacobs cleared his throat. "I know everything," he said, and then he paused. "And where James Daley is."

Martin whistled as the others gaped at Mr. Jacobs in shock. Moss snickered, if only because he'd been shocked so many times that night that he had no surprise left in him.

"Well," said Moss. "You better start talking."

28

They sat down in the pews, before Mr. Jacobs began to talk. Moss curled up next to his mother and leaned his head on her arm, and Bits found a spot behind them. Rawiya sat across the aisle from them with her parents. Moss had never met them, and he marveled at how tall her mom was and how short her father was. He realized that Rawiya must be the exact median height between them, and it amused him.

Reg and Kaisha had stayed behind, along with Martin, Shamika, Njemile, and Njemile's moms, but Moss crossed his arms when he saw that Esperanza had not left.

"No," he said. "I love you, Esperanza, and I know this isn't your fault, but you can't be here."

"Moss," said Wanda, a harshness slipping into her tone.

"What if she says something to her parents and they go snitchin' to Mr. Elliot again?"

Wanda grimaced. "I can't really argue with that," she said. "Esperanza . . ."

She put her hands up. "I am just as pissed as all of you," she said. "Trust me, I'm not going to be speaking to my parents for a long time, so I can promise you that nothing said here will get back to them."

Moss sighed. Maybe this was Esperanza's chance to stand up to her parents, to get them to realize that they couldn't make everything about them. "Okay," he said reluctantly. "We can talk more about this later." He gazed at Mr. Jacobs. "This better be worth it."

Mr. Jacobs shook his head at first. "I didn't really think it would get so out of control," he said, shifting to cross his other leg. He looked so uncomfortable when he spoke, his gaze jumping from one person to the next. "I just wanted to—"

"To what?" Njemile said, ire in her words. "I'm really interested to hear what you have to say about what you did to us."

"Njemile." Wanda's voice was clear and sharp, and Moss had heard her speak like that on the rare occasion when he decided to get smart with her. If the atmosphere weren't so tense, he probably would have laughed as he watched Njemile's shoulders drop. He hid a smile in a yawn as his mom continued. "I know you're angry. We all are. But let's allow him to talk first."

"Thank you," Mr. Jacobs said.

"You're not off the hook," Wanda shot back. "Tell 'em what you told me."

Mr. Jacobs sheepishly picked a bag up off the floor in front of him, slowly opening it and pulling out a stack of manila folders filled with papers. "I made copies," he said, handing them to Wanda, "as much as I could before I left the office today."

She took the folders from him, but set them aside. "What are we going to find in here?"

Mr. Jacobs sighed. "I don't know that much of it will make sense. There's a lot of information about our contract with the Oakland Police Department, as well as the blueprints and whatnot for the metal detectors. It might give you some sort of answer to what's been going on at the school."

Wanda paged through one of the folders, and a thin bound book fell out of it. Kaisha darted in and out so quickly that Moss's mother couldn't stop her. She flipped it open and began to peruse the table of contents. "Now this is what I wanted to see," she said, running her finger down the page.

"It's just a—" Mr. Jacobs started to say.

"What is it?" said Shamika, her focus on Kaisha.

Kaisha turned to a page with a sketched diagram on it. "They lied to us," she said. "That was not a metal detector."

"*What?*" Esperanza said, and they all gathered around Kaisha.

"Look, I'm no expert, but that's a giant magnet here," she said, and she traced her fingers along the outline of the machine. "Not only that, but what is *that* thing?"

Moss looked to where she was pointing. "'Endo-bio-imaging plate,'" he read aloud.

"What does that mean?" said Wanda.

The group stared at Mr. Jacobs, who trembled under their glare. "It's part of the imaging mechanics of the machine," he explained. "So that we can see more than just what a person might be carrying."

"Like what?" asked Moss, and his pulse flared in his throat. "Is that why our phones don't work? I still can't get service on mine at all."

Mr. Jacobs nodded. "It was the magnetic band your friend just pointed to," he said. "Unless you had an older model, the machines destroyed the inside of all your phones."

Wanda cursed and it echoed throughout the church. "Don't repeat that, none of you," she said.

Mr. Jacobs didn't let anyone recover, though. "That's not the worst part. That imaging plate allows the school to scan bodies."

"Meaning what?" said Martin, who had stayed quiet throughout all of this. "Ain't you scannin' bodies anyway with those things?"

"We can scan inside them."

The silence that fell in the room sent a chill up Moss's spine. He shuddered as his mother flung herself upright.

"Inside? Mr. Jacobs, how can that be possible?" she demanded. "Do you realize what a huge violation of privacy that is?"

"You don't understand," he said. "The Oakland Police Department has access to stuff I never knew existed. They claim that they get a lot of it from the federal government. Surplus from all our country's military spending or something."

"Like . . . actual stuff used in *warfare*?" Esperanza said.

"Weapons," Reg said, and the realization spread through the group.

"You mean all that stuff they used on us?" Njemile said. "It's all from *wars*?"

"It's not exactly unheard of in activist circles," said Ekemeni, her chin in her hand, her head shaking from side to side. "I just never heard of it being used at a *school*."

"What do you mean?" Rawiya's father looked at Ekemeni with panic on his face. "Sorry for interrupting, but we haven't lived here long." He gestured to himself and then his wife. "Hishaam, Afnan. We're Rawiya's parents. What sort of stuff?"

"You remember those protests about the BART fares last year?" Wanda asked them.

Hishaam looked to his wife. "Afnan, do you remember?"

She tilted her head to the side. "Was that the one where they brought out the tank?"

"No, that was the BART police shooting two summers ago," said Martin.

"Wait, was that the time the National Guard got called out?" Afnan said.

"Nope," said Kaisha. "That was for the school shutdown in East Oakland."

"*Wallahi,* this city is a mess," said Rawiya. "I think we get your point."

"You wanted to know where everything came from," said Mr. Jacobs. "And what happened last week. Well, it's pretty much a lot worse than you imagined."

"But he hasn't told us anything, Mama," said Moss, and he stood up and wrung his hands together. He paced in the aisle, from one pew to another. "We haven't learned anything new from what he's said." He leveled the assistant principal with a glare. "So tell us something new, Mr. Jacobs. We're listening."

Mr. Jacobs visibly gulped. "Well, I know that the school was looking for an excuse to start the pilot program, and they used Shawna's assault as a means to justify its use."

"We knew that," said Kaisha. "It was obvious to anyone who went to that school that that was the case."

"Do you know *anything*?" Moss said. "Or are you just wasting our time?"

"I'm not, I swear!" Mr. Jacobs said, and he shifted nervously in his seat once more. "It's just that . . . look, I don't know what kind of trouble I'm going to get in for doing this. Not just for talking to you, but if I tell you everything."

"No one recognized you, right?" Kaisha said, her hand in Reg's. "So what are you worried about?"

"They did this all on *purpose*," Mr. Jacobs said. "None of this was an accident. None of it."

"Meaning *what*?" Wanda said.

He sighed again. "We knew that the metal detectors were of a higher grade, that they were intended for high-profile border checks. In *Afghanistan*. It's supposed to be for detecting *terrorists*. We knew that the walkout was happening, thanks to Mrs. Miller's phone call. It was embarrassing, really; Mr. Elliot was so thrilled with himself for feeling like he had 'insider knowledge,' as he put it."

Moss leveled Esperanza with a glare, and she refused to look him in the eye. The anger returned again, and he was certain in that moment that he would never talk to Rebecca or Jeff ever again.

"We knew when it was planned for, and we knew that the Oakland Police Department was going to use their full riot gear in order to stop it."

"What do you mean by 'full riot gear,' Mr. Jacobs?" Afnan asked. "What we heard from our daughter made it sound like there was a science fiction movie unfolding at the school."

He rubbed his temples with the fingers on his right hand. "Once Mr. Elliot contacted the Oakland Police Department, they came and met with us on Thursday evening, after no one was left on campus," he explained. "And I don't just mean a few low-level officers or sergeants or whatever. Top brass. People who make three or four times what I'll ever make in my life. We were given a complete briefing about how many officers would be on campus and what they'd be bringing with them. They told us that the metal detectors would be on, and that the magnetic band would be turned higher to break your phones."

"Wait a second," said Reg. "You're telling me that they *knew* that these magnets were there? The whole time?"

It was only then that recognition dawned on Mr. Jacobs's face. "Oh, damn," he said. "Your leg."

"Yes, my *leg*," he said. "I'm in this chair again now, probably forever, because of what those things did to me!"

"I know, I know," Mr. Jacobs said. "And I feel bad about that, I really do!"

"Man, I'm getting real tired about you feeling bad," said Moss. His mother turned to say something, but he cut her off. "I know, Mama, I know that he's supposed to be here to help us, but how long did he have to feel bad before he did something? Was Reg or Shawna getting hurt not enough? Did it have to take Javier *dying* for this man to actually *do* something?"

The words stung, and he knew it. Mr. Jacobs dropped his gaze down and didn't say anything for a few seconds. Moss's heart was raging in him, so he sat back down next to his mother. "I'm tired," he said. "Real tired."

"Well, I have some questions, too," said Njemile, "and I'm also bored of Mr. Jacobs here actin' like he's conflicted about telling the truth."

"I'm not *acting*," he said, his eyes wide in shock. "I promise you! I'm just worried that—I might lose my job over this."

"What about my leg?" Reg said. "Was it worth it to keep your job for that?"

"Javier lost his life," Moss sneered. "You feel any better?"

"Please," Wanda said, her hands raised up to silence them. "Njemile said she had questions, and frankly, I have a few of my own. Let him talk."

Mr. Jacobs did not thank her this time. He pursed his lips, then turned to look at Njemile.

"What made everyone's faces swell up?" Njemile said, frowning.

"A combination of pepper spray and tear gas," Mr. Jacobs said. "Deployed with aerosol cans. And portable . . . uh . . . grenades."

"*Grenades?*" That was Afnan. "Please tell me you're kidding."

"What were those other things they had?" Njemile asked. "The ones that looked like bullhorns."

Mr. Jacobs sighed. "How familiar are any of you with human physiology?"

He got silence in response. He motioned for Wanda to hand him back the folders that sat next to her and she obliged. Moss watched as he began to look through them, then pulled out a set of papers from the middle of the stack. "I didn't believe them until I saw it in action myself," he said, then folded one of the pages back and held it up. There on the paper was a diagram of one of the weapons that had been pointed at Moss and his friends in the science lab.

"That's it," Moss said. "That thing made some people throw up!"

"Apparently, there's a frequency that most adults can't hear," Mr. Jacobs explained, handing the document to Afnan, who began to examine it. "We lose the ability to as we get older. Just a natural part of aging I suppose."

"Okay, but what did that thing *do*?" Wanda said.

"What is this?" Afnan asked, fear in her voice. "Hishaam, did you see this?" She passed the page to her husband.

"It upsets your inner ear," Mr. Jacobs said. "It's kinda cool in a terrifying way, I guess. Messes with your sense of balance, apparently, all through a wave of high-frequency noise that most adults can't hear. It usually induces nausea in younger folks. The guy who showed it to me said they use it occasionally in protests to temper the crowd."

Mr. Jacobs spoke like a doctor listing routine symptoms, and Moss shuddered. *This can't be happening,* he told himself. He reached down and grabbed his mother's hand and she squeezed his. Hard.

"Are you telling me they shot that *thing* at my daughter?" Hishaam said loudly.

"But it didn't really work," Njemile interjected. "Remember, Moss?"

Moss nodded his head. "Yeah. In fact, only a couple people felt sick in that room. That's how we got out. Daley was distracted *because* it didn't do what it was supposed to."

"Yours is a generation of headphones," Mr. Jacobs said. "Meaning most of you damaged your hearing enough for it to not work." He smirked a little. "God bless iPods, I guess."

This isn't real for him. The though hit Moss suddenly, making so much sense that he couldn't believe he hadn't realized it before. Mr. Jacobs spoke with an easy detachment, a combination of fear and humor that only centered on himself. *He can't even fathom this happening to him,* Moss thought. *It's like he's telling a story.*

Moss squirmed in his seat, the uncomfortable epiphany still radiating through him. Would this man save his career at the expense of all of them? Moss stood up again, this time walking over to Mr. Jacobs and grabbing the remaining files as the man was explaining another diagram. "I think you should leave," he said.

"Moss!" Wanda said, rising herself. "We have more things to ask him—"

"And is he actually going to tell us anything we can't figure out ourselves?" Moss shot back. "He's sitting here all smug, making cute little jokes about iPods and talkin' 'bout how *scared* he is of losing his job, but is he actually helping?" He turned to Mr. Jacobs, a fire in his heart. "We can read through these ourselves. You better leave before someone catches you here."

"Oh, come on, Moss," said Esperanza, rising to grab his arm. "You should let him speak. It's only fair."

He yanked his arm away. "Whose side are you on, Esperanza? *Fair?* You're gonna tell me about *fair?*"

Mr. Jacobs sputtered, unable to form a sentence. "No, I just . . ." He sighed again. "It's just that—"

Kaisha laughed. "Man, Mr. Jacobs, you really don't get it, do you?"

"Course he don't," Reg said, shaking his head. "Do you expect us to thank you for all this?"

The assistant principal threw his hands up. "Why do you all have to be so difficult? I'm *trying* to help you."

"Well stop *trying* and start *doing* something!" Moss shouted, and the blood rushed to his face again, the heat rising in his cheeks. "He *died,* Mr. Jacobs! He is dead and he's not coming back and *you didn't stop it from happening!*"

Moss's voice echoed in Blessed Way, and the silence that followed it felt endless. He knew they were all staring at him, and he didn't care. He held up the files in his left hand.

"*This* has always been our lives, Mr. Jacobs. The police have *never* been on our side. So what if the technology is new? So what if it's now in our school? These people murdered my father years ago, lied about it, covered it up, and when the truth came out, they didn't even apologize to me and my mama." Moss looked over at Shamika and Martin, who sat together, their heads nodding up and down. They were there. They *knew.*

But he stepped closer to Mr. Jacobs, looked down on the man. "You think I'm the only one? Or that Javier is the only kid taken from this world by these monsters?"

"No, I never said that—" Mr. Jacobs said, and he scooted away from Moss.

"Go find old issues of the *Tribune.* Or search online for the last person killed by the Oakland Police Department. You won't have to go far back. I bet you can find at least a few of them from this summer."

"I don't get what this has to do with me," Mr. Jacobs said. "I didn't do any of that! Why can't you just thank me for this?"

"Because you let them on our campus!" Moss screamed. "You let them prey on us, and it was only after someone *died* that you felt compelled to say something." He paused, his rage in his throat. "You're supposed to be an adult, man. You're supposed to look out for us. We're just *kids.* Javier hadn't even turned seventeen, and now he's gone, and you're still here worried about your job. He won't even ever get to *have* one!"

Moss raised the files above his head and slammed them down on the ground. It was petulant, he knew it, but he still watched them spread out on the floor, their contents spilling everywhere, and it gave him a momentary sense of satisfaction.

"We don't need your help," Moss said. "Get out."

His face was wet. When had he started crying? He did it so much these days. Moss rubbed at his cheeks, and he didn't know if he had ever felt so angry in his whole life. This man sat there, his cowering, pale face filled with regret and fear, and at the end of the day, he would still get to go home. He'd still have a job and a life and goals and dreams and hopes, and what did Moss have?

He felt a hand in his. Bits. Their eyes locked with his. No pity. No sadness. He looked back at Mr. Jacobs, who stood awkwardly, legs shaking. The man said nothing else, only grabbed his jacket off the pew in front of him and walked quickly down the aisle. When the door shut behind him, the silence swallowed everyone.

Moss sniffled. "I may have overreacted there," he said, and he chuckled as a bolt of awkward energy surged in his chest.

Wanda was at his other side. "No, you didn't," she said. "Well, maybe throwing all those papers was a bit dramatic."

"Moss? *Dramatic*?" Rawiya said. "You don't say!"

A ripple of nervous laughter rolled through the church, a catharsis for Moss. He let go of Bits's hand and knelt down, gathering the pages scattered at his feet.

His mother knelt beside him to help as the others began to chatter away about what had just transpired. "I didn't realize this would be so upsetting for you," she said softly, and she ran a hand down his back. "I should have taken more control."

He smiled at her, but shook his head. "No, it's okay. I need to learn to deal with my anger better."

She handed him a sheaf of pages. "Do you, though?" Wanda asked him. "Mr. Jacobs needed to hear that."

He stopped. "You really think so?"

"I do," said Rawiya, who came over with her own pile. "So do my parents."

He looked to Afnan and Hishaam, who smiled at him. "That man was a smug asshole," Afnan said. "I bet no one has ever told him otherwise."

Wanda nodded. "Yeah, he may have been trying to help, but why wait so long? It's like he expected us to bake a batch of cookies for him."

Moss cast a glance at Esperanza. She was avoiding him, but he wouldn't let his irritation distract him. "So what *are* we supposed to do with all this?" Moss asked. "We don't even know what all of this stuff is."

"I can start reading it," said Kaisha. "There's gotta be something here we can use." She grabbed the pile from Moss and sat down near him. Without another word, she started to go through the files that Mr. Jacobs had handed them.

"For *what*, though?" Moss scratched his head. "I don't even know what the next step is supposed to be."

"Well, we gotta start planning," said Wanda. "We gotta go bigger."

"But what about Daley?" Moss asked. "We still don't know where he is." Moss groaned. "Mr. Jacobs said he knew where he was, and I chased him away."

"Don't worry about it," said Martin. "It's not like we could go kidnap him or anything." His eyes went wide. "Or *could* we . . ."

Shamika punched him in the arm playfully. "Shut up, man," she said. "You tryna get us all arrested with your plots of *kidnapping a cop*."

"Well," said Moss, "the longer we wait, the more likely it is that he gets away with this."

"Maybe," said Wanda. "But we've got to be patient and careful about this. We're dealing with some powerful people, Moss."

"It's not the first time folks in this city have gone after the police," said Shamika. "Just ask your mama about the cost of that."

He saw his mother shoot a pointed look at Shamika, and Shamika raised her hand to her mouth and grimaced.

"Wait, the cost of *what*?" Moss said.

"It's not that important," his mother said. "Ask me later." She turned away from him and wandered over to Kaisha.

He'd never seen his mother act so cagey about anything. "No, I saw that," he said. "You just gave Shamika that *look*. The one you give me when I'm runnin' my mouth and you want me to stop."

She sighed. "Look, Moss, it's not really the time for it," she said, briefly looking up from the files. "We need to focus on reading through this so we know what we have." His mother grabbed a few folders from out of the pile. "Who else has time to read?"

Njemile took a couple, and Rawiya and her parents each took another. Soon, each person in the group had part of the whole except for Moss, who still stood in the aisle, a suspicion creeping into him.

"You want something to read, Moss?" Wanda asked him.

"Mama, what aren't you telling me?" The nerves came back, and his anxiety started to climb up his body. "I don't like this."

"You need to be patient, honey," she said. "Let's get through this and figure out what we're doing with it, and then we can talk. Just you and I."

"No." He said it plainly, without hesitation. "No, I want to know now."

He saw the exasperation spread in his mother, saw the chasm grow between them. "Moss, I promise you, this is not the time. Please sit down and help us out."

"No, Mama. Not until you start talking."

"Can't this wait until later?" Esperanza said. "It sounds like something personal, Moss, and I'm sure your mom has her reasons for not sharing."

He glared at Esperanza, and for the first time during their entire friendship, he hated her. It was a bitter sensation, a sourness in his mouth and heart, and he knew he wore it all over his face. "You're not exactly unbiased when it comes to questioning your parents," he said, and he knew it was a petty, underhanded thing to say.

"Moss, come *on*," she said. "Parents are complicated, that's all."

"So that's your justification for your mom getting Javier killed?"

The anger spread over her this time. "My mom didn't do that," she said, "and you should take that back."

"No," he said, stepping up to her. "I *hate* your mother, and if her nosy, white savior ass hadn't called Mr. Elliot, Javier might be alive today. What was she thinking, getting herself involved?" He pointed a finger at her. "You even said it yourself: Your parents can't avoid making things about themselves."

She grimaced. "Moss, you're upset, I get it," she said. "But you don't need to take it out on me. I'm not the bad guy here."

He didn't even think about what he said as the words came spilling out. "You sound a whole lot like your parents."

Her mouth dropped open, then shut, hard. She grabbed her bag and stomped out of the room without another word.

He saw all the eyes locked on him. In another situation, he might have felt self-conscious, but his anger pushed him forward. "Why does no one want to tell me the truth?"

Wanda stood up and raised a hand in front of her, toward Moss. "Honey, please," she said, her voice shaky and uncertain. "I'm sorry, I should have been more considerate—"

He took a step away from her. "How long do I have to wait?" He looked at each of them, but no one said anything at first.

"Maybe we should just focus on one thing at a time," said Shamika, her eyes downturned, shame in her voice.

"Is that how you all feel?" Moss asked, and his hands shook at his sides. He clenched his fists, released, clenched them again.

"I don't know, man," said Reg. "I know this is a lot to handle sometimes, but maybe we should just like . . . I dunno. Just let your mom do this."

"This whole thing scares me," said Kaisha. "Maybe we should just rely on the adults here."

"It's not a bad idea," Rawiya chimed in. "They have experience with this sort of stuff. We should let them do it."

"Do *what*?" Moss shot back. "We have no plan. Y'all have all these secrets you won't tell me. What about how *I* feel?"

"No one's saying you can't feel anything," said Martin. "But your mama's got more experience with this, so maybe we should—"

Moss didn't let him finish. "Wait. Just wait. Is that what y'all are gonna say?" He started to move away from the group, a fear blossoming in the silence that followed. "I been waiting years for someone to take responsibility for Papa. I waited for school to get better. I waited for my brain to stop being broken. I'm gonna have to wait for this damn city to do something about Javier. And now I gotta wait for my own mother to just be *honest* with me?"

He backed up into his messenger bag, then quickly knelt down and scooped it up. He saw his mother try to leap over Njemile's leg, and Moss turned away from them. "I'm done waiting," he said, the rage spilling over, consuming him, and he bolted for the doors of Blessed Way Church and shoved his way outside. Moss ran to the corner and unlocked his bike as quick as he could, jamming Javier's bike chain in his bag, and he did not look back to see if anyone had followed him. He just rode.

29

He pedaled. He headed toward the lake for no specific reason, just because it was in front of him and he needed to keep moving. The breeze whipped at his face, and tears sprang to his eyes. The cityscape before Moss blurred, each of the lights twisting into a sparkle, its edges sharp. The stoplight at Grand flashed green and he pushed harder, spun his legs faster, enjoyed the burning sensation in his thighs. It made him forget about the pain from the knots on his knee and shin.

Someone hollered at him as he went by. He ignored them. It felt invigorating, even if it was nothing more than a simple distraction. He blew through the light at 20th. A car screeched to a stop, its horn blared, and Moss didn't even look. *What if they had hit me?* Moss wondered. *Maybe this nightmare would end.*

But he'd been through it before, and he knew what would come next. Wasn't it always going to be the same? He slammed on his own brakes, and they squealed in protest. Moss pulled up to a bus stop near Jackson and let his bike fall to the ground beside him. He was heavy with grief and anger, and he allowed the world to pull him down onto the sidewalk.

He was sick of crying, tired of feeling sad, but it was like second nature to him now. What was he supposed to do? How was he ever supposed to make this feel right? It hadn't worked when his father died; why would this be any different?

The moon reflected over the lake, which sat still in the darkness of the brisk night. Moss shuddered and remembered: the feeling of Javier lying on his chest, on the couch, in his arms, a body somehow cooler than his own. Moss had hated how warm he ran, how easy it was for him to wake up in the night, covered in sweat, and it was like Javier was meant for him. The perfect temperature to counter his own. But the world had shown Moss that he was not meant for Javier. If he had been, why was Javier now gone? He was consumed with sobs again. Moss wanted nothing more than for Javier to hold him, to see Javier's goofy face, to run his hands over his arms. The finality of it all was too overwhelming. *I have to accept this or I will never get over it.*

Moss pushed himself up from the curb and coughed. Wiping the snot and tears away, he closed his eyes and sucked in a deep breath, let it out. Once. Twice. Three times. He kept going until his heart settled down before he opened his eyes.

The lake still shimmered quietly in its own indifference to him. The world was still here. *He* was still here. He sucked in another frigid breath, felt the air fill him.

He was alive, still.

Moss leaned over and picked up his bike. He couldn't go back to the church, at least not yet. He couldn't face Esperanza, and the shame of yelling at his mother—Moss knew better than to do that—dulled the sadness. At least this was a new emotion, one he could focus on.

He shook his head as he turned on Jackson and headed toward 14th, rising to pedal up the hill. Moss knew he was going to have to apologize to his mother for his behavior at the very least. With Esperanza . . . he wasn't sure. He'd felt himself growing farther and farther from her in the last couple of weeks. They needed to talk, eventually, but he was fine to let her simmer in frustration for once.

But as Moss pulled up to a stop at 14th, he didn't feel so certain that his burst of anger was merely a tantrum.

He'd been through this cycle already with his father, and it *was* true that Moss had never gotten closure. How many times had he been taunted by Morris's death? How many people had told Moss that his father deserved it? After all these years, he wasn't any closer to a sense of justice, was he? It didn't seem like a feasible outcome, just some nebulous idea thrown about by people who had never experienced this kind of heartbreak. How was the horror of Javier any different this time around? It didn't matter how much evidence there was; it didn't matter that by hiding, Daley more or less confirmed his guilt. Even if Daley came forward, would it fix this?

Moss wished more than anything at that moment that he could

force the hand of the Oakland Police Department. The rally at his school had been a failure, and he didn't know how many people would be discouraged from future protests because of what had happened on campus. They'd won, hadn't they? There was no power in another walkout. The police would just do the same shit all over again, the cycle would continue, and it would pass to another family once the police killed someone else.

The light turned green and Moss pedaled through the intersection. A couple of guys walked hand in hand to his right, both of them black, wearing wide smiles on their faces. The taller one leaned his head back, and a deep laugh roared out of his mouth. Moss craned his neck to watch them. Were they newly in love? Had they maintained it for years? It felt unfair, to see two people so in love with each other when Moss had nothing. He knew it was unfair to judge them from a single moment. They had found something in one another, and it wasn't their fault that he was in so much pain.

It's not their fault. He thought it first, then said it aloud. "It's not their fault." They weren't responsible for what he was feeling. He pedaled harder, an idea forming in his mind, one that felt big and silly and ludicrous. A jolt shot down his spine, sending a chill through his skin, bumps rising on his arms. *Who's actually responsible?* Moss asked himself. *Who did this to us?*

He hooked a right turn as he passed by Madison Park. He'd been here before, years ago. There was a man who sold cha siu bao from a tiny cart on weekends, and his papa had taken him there after a morning at the Oakland Museum. He'd eaten four of them, one after another, his father laughing as Moss ate the last one slower than the others. "Your eyes are bigger than your stomach, mijo," he had said.

Moss filed the memory away, but it felt like a sign. He had remembered something new, and he let it wash over him. *This is what I need to do,* he thought, and he pedaled faster down 8th, through a Chinatown that was mostly asleep. A few people lingered outside one of the restaurants that was open late on the weekends, waiting for a table, but most of the shops were dark, their storefronts nothing but metal grates and silence. It was the perfect time, he realized. No one could betray him. Esperanza's parents couldn't foolishly intervene. His mother couldn't stop him. It was his idea, and Moss alone could pull it off.

The light was green at Broadway. He went left, and the building loomed ahead of him, a gray, white, and black monstrosity. He rushed through the light at 7th and rolled to a stop in front of it. He hated the sign that rested above the door: a large silver badge with a smaller, blue star in the center. It was so egregious and unnecessary.

Moss pulled his bike up to a rack on the sidewalk and locked it up with his U-lock. Then he swung his bag back and stood next to the tall flagpole that rose outside the front of the building. He gazed up at the sign. Was this an administrative building? A precinct? He wasn't sure, but it was right next to the freeway and on the busiest street in the city. It was perfect, wasn't it?

He unclipped his bag and swung it around, tearing it open. He pulled out the bike chain he'd inherited from Javier, and his heart leapt at the sound of the thick metal links clanging together. He looked back up at the building, then behind him. No one was anywhere near him. He dropped his bag next to the flagpole and took a deep breath. *Do it,* he thought. *If anything, they'll definitely notice you.*

He ran the chain around the flagpole, then turned to press his back against it. It was cold, but his body heat would warm it. He brought the two ends of the chain in front of him and slid the open end into the bulky yellow lock at the other end. He stood there a moment before he could close it. Was this what he wanted?

Moss didn't hesitate again. He lowered the chain so that it sat close to his waist. It might be a bit snug, but it didn't impede his breathing. For once, he was the right size around the middle. Moss snapped the lock shut, then slowly slid down the flagpole, his feet planted firm so he could start to squat. He struggled near the bottom, his thighs still burning from the ride over, but he balanced as best as he could, pushing his feet out until his legs rested against the chilly concrete, and then he sat there.

Moss wasn't going to move until the Oakland Police Department handed over James Daley.

30

He didn't know what to expect as he sat there, but for the first ten minutes, nothing happened. It was late at night, but people hadn't left the bars south of where he was, out toward Jack London Square. Moss wished he had had time to replace his phone, though he continued to worry about losing all his texts. He reached into his bag and pulled out the device, its screen still cracked, unable to turn on. He wished he could read everything Javier had said to him. Maybe a new phone would have helped time pass quicker. *Until what?* he thought. *What comes next?*

More minutes passed. His heart was still racing from the thrill of it all, and it left him warm, focused. It would only be a matter of time before someone saw him, and then, it would be inevitable. More people would find out, and they'd have to ask him what he was doing. Moss began to run through lines in his head. He had to have the right thing to say! He imagined himself in front of a reporter, a stoic, proud look on his face. "I'm protesting the injustice of the death of Javier Perez," he would say, his resolve unwavering. "I refuse to remove myself from this property until James Daley is arrested for the murder of my friend."

No, no, that wasn't right. Javier was more than a friend. Boyfriend? No, that was too much; they'd never even gotten to have *that* conversation before he was killed. Moss's excitement was slowly eclipsed by a sadness. If Javier had survived, would he still have wanted to be with Moss? He shook it away as best as he could. *No,* he told himself, *you have to focus. You are here for a reason.*

So what would he say? His lover? *Oh god,* he thought, *that makes me sound so white.* No, he had to say his "friend." It was true. Best friend, perhaps?

He thought then of Esperanza. Of Njemile and Bits and Reg and Kaisha and Rawiya. What were they doing? Was his mom panicking? Was Esperanza still mad at him? *Maybe I should check my phone,* he thought, then remembered how pointless that was. *That's gonna be a hard habit to break.*

He heard a scuffing sound to his left. He started and looked up at a man in black jeans and a flannel shirt, his brown hair ruffled and messy, his hand in his right pocket, digging around. He pulled something out of his pocket and tossed it at Moss, who flinched. Coins jingled as they hit the concrete. "Sorry," the guy said, smirking. "That's all I've got."

He walked off toward Jack London Square. Moss gaped in his direction. *Did he think I was homeless?* There were two quarters and a dime lying on the ground next to him. *Did he not see the chain?*

A panic rolled through him. What if no one knew he was here? What if he stayed here all night and no one stopped to ask him what he was doing? *This is a terrible plan!* Moss thought. *Terrible, terrible, what were you* thinking??? He fished in his own pocket and his fingers grazed his key ring, but he stopped. *No, you have to do this!*

The anxiety stretched out inside him as if preparing for a long haul, spreading from his chest up into his head and down through his torso. He hadn't planned this out at *all*! The impulsivity of the idea had been so attractive to him twenty minutes prior, but now it seemed silly. Trite. Meaningless. How was he ever going to survive the night? What if this stretched out for days? Weeks? Would it actually take this long for someone to react?

"I've made a mistake," he whispered, thinking that if he said it out loud, he'd feel more certain about it. But he didn't reach into his pocket to find the key. He didn't try to stand up. He remained exactly where he was.

"I can do this," he said, not in a whisper, but at a confident volume.

"What are you doing?"

The voice came from behind him, and Moss discovered that in his position, he didn't have enough leverage to turn around. So he stopped trying to twist about and looked straight forward. "I'm staying right here," he said, and his voice did not sound confident anymore. "I'm not moving until . . . until I—"

"Are you stuck to the pole or something?" Moss looked up to his right and terror pumped through his body. An Oakland police officer stood looking down on him, confusion twisting his face. He was middle-aged, a large man who seemed like a giant from where Moss sat. He ran a hand through his blond hair, then laid the hand on his hip as he inspected Moss. "Do you need any help, young man?"

Moss shook his head. "I am fine right where I am, sir," he replied.

He heard the rustle of clothing, the scuff of a boot on concrete. "Do your parents know you're out so late?"

"My mother trusts me," Moss replied. *Not exactly a lie,* he thought.

There was another scuff. "Son, what are you doing?"

Moss looked back up at him. "I'm protesting," he said. "I will remain here until my demands are met." He swallowed. "Sir."

Moss didn't recognize the sound he heard at first. He thought the cop had cleared his throat, but the smirk belied what it was. A *chuckle.* "Are you serious, young man? What on earth could you be protesting?"

"Of course I'm serious," Moss shot back. "Why would I lock myself to this flagpole if I wasn't?"

The cop moved behind Moss, and seconds later, he felt a gentle tug on the chain. It dug into his waist. The cop walked back around to stand in front of him, and the amusement was still on his face. "That a real lock?"

Moss nodded.

"And you're doing this for *what*?"

He gulped. "One of you killed my friend." He said it with the certainty he had wanted in his voice earlier. "And until his killer is arrested, I'm staying right here."

The cop chuckled again. "Okay, whatever you say," he muttered. "You want me to call your parents?"

"No," said Moss, "but you can bring out James Daley."

The effect was instant. The smirk on the cop's face disappeared. "What did you say?"

"James Daley killed my friend, Javier Perez, so I'm not moving until he's arrested."

The cop said nothing more. Moss heard the footsteps leading rapidly away from him. A door nearby slammed shut.

And the silence felt terrifying. It closed in around Moss. This was happening now, and he couldn't take it back. His mind swirled with horrible possibilities, with the fear that this would be it. Had he blown his chances already? Would they cut the chain and remove him? Arrest him? Something worse? The fear pulsed in his throat and it was hard to swallow, and he was tempted. Tempted to unlock himself and hop on his bike and just start pedaling, never looking back. It would be so much easier, wouldn't it?

The door squeaked open and Moss thought he was going to throw up. There were more steps this time, and he prepared himself. *Deep breaths,* he thought, and he sucked in a lungful of air, letting it escape slowly. *Don't give up.*

Two cops stepped in front of him. They were about the same height; one was white and not the same guy from before, and the other was black. They inspected Moss, looking him up and down, and he felt self-conscious, as if they were judging his appearance. He resisted the urge to stare them down and instead kept his eyes locked forward on their legs. The men said nothing for a few moments. What were they doing? Why weren't they saying anything?

"What's your name, son?"

Only then did Moss look back up at them. "Moss," he replied.

It was the black officer speaking. "We spoke with our colleague just a few minutes ago," he said, his voice gentle, his eyes dark and comforting. "He told us that you're here about your friend. Is that true?"

Moss nodded. "Yes, sir. And I'm not leaving."

The cops exchanged a look, but Moss couldn't read their expressions. "My name is Sergeant Moore, and this is my partner, Officer Vincent Childs," he said, gesturing to the white cop. "Excuse me, but if this seems condescending, I assure you it's not . . . but are you really locked to that flagpole?"

"Yeah," Moss said, and his voice quavered. Why did he feel so confused about this?

"Well, I gotta say . . . that's a first," said Moore. "You ever heard anything like that, Vincent?"

His partner shook his head. "Not in all my years here. And we've both seen some strange things in our time."

Moore nodded. "And you really plan on staying here?"

"Yep."

"All night?"

"As long as it takes."

"Until what?" Vincent asked. "I'm sorry, I just don't see what your endgame is here . . . Moss, is it?"

Moss lowered his head. His plan seemed so ambiguous and meaningless now, in front of these uniformed men. How could they ever understand what he was going through? Why weren't they taking him seriously? He cleared his throat, the sadness pressing on him. "He killed Javier right in front of me," he said softly. "Did you know that?" Moss raised his eyes up to the two cops, and he wanted so badly to be brave and calm, but his eyes blurred once more. Shame filled him anew; he felt more like a child at that moment than he had since this whole mess started.

"We didn't," Moore said. "I'm sorry you had to see that. It's never easy."

Moss scoffed at him. "I watched Daley fire on him, and Javier didn't have a weapon. He did it out of *spite*. And now Javier is gone because someone couldn't control their temper. Do you know what *that* feels like?"

Neither man said anything, and Moss felt a tear spill out of his eye. He kept going. "His mom is alone. She doesn't know what to do anymore. I lost someone I could have loved. And he hides from us. He hasn't even apologized or anything."

Vincent pivoted on his feet, and Moss could tell he would have rather been anywhere than right in front of him. "Well, I don't think there's anything we can do," he said. "Your friend shouldn't have been trespassing."

The air went out of Moss, and with it went all of the grief that had been piling up inside of his body. In flew the rage, and he actually *laughed* at the cops that stood there. "You are so predictable," Moss said, and his anger gave him the boldness he'd been looking for. "I knew it was only a matter of time before you blamed Javier."

"Now hold on, son," Moore said, raising his hands in a gesture of innocence. His thick brows were creased above his dark eyes. "We're not blaming anyone. What my partner was *trying* to say is that it's just not that simple."

"Maybe not to you," said Moss. "It seems real simple on my end. Your buddy shot someone and killed him and there was no justification for it in the first place. It *is* that simple."

Moore lowered his hands, but his mouth stayed shut. He exchanged another look with his partner; this time, Moss could see the concern. "You really aren't leaving, are you?" Moore said.

"No, I'm not."

"Jesus," Vincent muttered. The two stood there a few more seconds, and then they walked away without a word. It was then that Moss noticed what the two cops had been blocking:

A small crowd. He counted them—twelve people—and saw phones raised in front of a few of them. As the door behind Moss shut, two of the people darted across Broadway. One of them, a thin white woman with her hair pulled back from her face, lowered her phone as she approached Moss. "Are you okay?" The woman stood in the gutter, her phone at her side. "Do you need help?"

"I think I'm okay," Moss answered. "Just a little wired, that's all."

The second person, a brown man with long black hair that fell down his back, was shaking his head. He raised a skateboard up and tucked it behind his head. "They harassing you over something, man? You need backup?"

"Backup?" Moss shook his head. "Nah, I think I'm okay."

The man knelt beside him and reached out a hand gingerly, running his fingers over the thick links of the chain. "Wait, did *they* do this to you?"

Moss laughed at that one, thankful for the relief it gave him. "No, no, not at all. I did it myself."

"But why?" the woman asked.

Moss took a deep breath. "Javier . . . my friend was the kid who got killed last week at my school. During the walkout."

"Oh my god," she said, and then she sat down next to him and looped an arm behind his head, pulling him into a strange hug. "I'm so sorry. I read about that online."

"Are you protesting, dude?" The man's eyes got wide when he said it. "Oh man, that's *bold*. Respect." He held out his hand for a fist bump, and Moss smiled and obliged him.

"Thanks, I guess," Moss said. "I had to do something. They can't get away with it."

"Then I'll stay here with you," the other man replied, and he promptly sat down on his skateboard to Moss's right. "My name's Enrique."

"Moss," he said. "And you don't have to stay, man. This is my thing. I gotta do it by myself."

"Well, I'm staying too," the woman said, and she stuck her hand out. "Hayley. Nice to meet you, Moss."

"You're kidding me," he said as he shook her hand. "Seriously, you don't have to stay here."

Hayley leaned in and Moss had no time to pose for the selfie she took. "If you don't mind, I'm putting this on Twitter. More people need to know."

His mouth dropped open. "Wait, really?"

"Dude, that's such a good idea!" Enrique said, then pulled out his own phone. "You okay with that?"

Moss's head swirled, shocked by this turn of events. "Yeah . . . I guess, man. I hadn't really thought that far."

Enrique laughed. "You gotta use social media, amigo! How else are people gonna find out about what you're doing here?"

Amigo. He remembered Javier using that on him, but Hayley interrupted his thoughts.

"I'm already getting replies," Hayley said, and she turned her screen so that Moss could see the notifications coming through. "How long have you been here?"

"I don't know. An hour maybe? I kind of lost track." He looked up then, and people were now standing in the street in front of him, snapping photos. One woman was recording a video, and as she stepped closer, Moss could hear what she was saying. She was *narrating*.

"And I was just walkin' down the street, headin' to get a drink with my friends, and *this* is what I come upon." She pointed the camera at Moss's face, and he grimaced a little. "The cops were harassing him, but he's okay now. Aren't you?"

"Uh . . . I'm fine, yeah," Moss said.

"Why are you here?"

Moss gulped. He'd have to get used to repeating himself. "I'm asking for justice for Javier Perez," he said, thankful that he wasn't tripping over his words this time. "He was shot and killed by the Oakland Police Department at West Oakland High during a peaceful walkout."

The woman pressed something on the screen of her phone, then lowered it. "It's going up on Snapchat," she explained. "Thank you for what you're doing. Honestly. It's about time someone stood up to them."

Moss wanted to say, "But I'm not *doing* anything yet!" She was gone, though, and the crowd around him had grown. Where were people coming from?

Another phone was thrust in front of his face, and the flash went off. "Hey, be careful!" Enrique said. "Don't be like the paparazzi. That's not what this is for."

"Could everyone take a step back?" Moss asked. "This is a lot. I'm feeling a bit closed in."

Hayley stood up then, her arms stretched out protectively in front of her. "Everyone move up onto the sidewalk!" she ordered, waving people out of the street. "Please, give this young man some room."

"How is this happening?" Moss said quietly, watching as the group moved off the road.

"Did you think no one would notice you here?" Enrique said.

"No, of course not," he said. "I just didn't think it would happen so quickly."

"It might be a Sunday night, but you were bound to get some attention," Hayley said. "That's some good planning, Moss."

If only I had actually planned this in advance, he thought, but he kept it to himself. A couple came up to him to ask him what he was doing. He spoke to them for a few minutes before he realized it was the same couple he'd seen on his bike ride over. *Maybe this won't be so bad,* he thought, *and maybe I don't need to be so negative.*

He lost track of time. Enrique was talkative, full of stories about growing up in East Oakland. He told Moss about his uncle dying from a drive-by and then how the Oakland PD shot his brother during a traffic stop.

"They've never protected our neighborhood," Enrique explained. "Never. You know, we got robbed once, and my mama was scared as hell. These guys in ski masks had busted into our house, and I came home to her crying. Guess I just missed them."

"She ask you to call the cops?"

He nodded. "Yeah, and I told her it wasn't a good idea, not after what happened to my brother, but she just wanted to feel safe."

"What happened?" Hayley asked.

"They showed up six hours later. At like four in the morning. Banged on that door like it was a drug bust. Scared the shit out of all of us."

"Lemme guess," said Moss. "They weren't exactly helpful."

"Nah, man! They tried to tell us it was our fault for living in a bad neighborhood and that we shoulda had a better lock on our door."

"Yo, that's the same trash they told my pops," said one of the newcomers who stood behind Enrique. He was handsome, and Moss admired whoever had done his cornrows. "Except they said it was because his car drew too much attention to him."

"They told me my dress was too short."

They all looked over at Hayley, whose eyes seemed distant and vacant. "Happened last summer," she explained. "Some guy—super drunk, went to Cal, you know the type—cornered me in a bar over on Telegraph. Tried to put his hand up my skirt. I knocked him over the head, and he called the police. Guess which side they took?"

Enrique swore loudly and Moss reached out and squeezed Hayley's hand. "I'm sorry," he said. "Probably doesn't help at all, but if it matters, I'm glad you're here."

"Of course it matters," she said, and a smile flitted across her lips. "We all have our reasons for being here. So I'm glad *you're* here."

"I guess I just can't believe anyone would stick around for this," Moss admitted. "I don't know, I thought I was gonna be here all night by myself. That it was all going to be pointless."

"Most people don't care," said the guy with cornrows. "It's a lot easier to pretend the world will go on spinnin'."

Moss shifted his position. The pole at his back was starting to feel a little too hard. He stuck his legs out in front of him and leaned forward a bit, hoping that he could get a good stretch. He became aware of how his body felt in that moment: cramped and trapped. He swallowed hard and his throat was dry, so he pulled his messenger bag toward him to get some water. As he was doing so, a car screeched to a stop a few feet up the road from the growing crowd, and Moss recognized the blue Toyota. Martin's car. The passenger door was flung open, and his mother emerged from it, her mouth agape, and Moss dropped his bag at his side. *Oh no,* he thought. He hadn't figured out what he was going to tell her.

There was no anger on her face as she approached him, though. She came forward, slow and deliberate, and her eyes danced from one person to the next. She looked over at the group of young black girls who'd arrived ten minutes earlier; they held a sign that said, #JUSTICE-

ForJavier. They stood next to a group of older men who had set up a small table to play checkers, the same men who often played at Lowell Park. Most of these people were complete strangers to Moss, and he saw something in his mother that he recognized. This must have been what his own face looked like when he entered Blessed Way and seen what his mother had done.

He was nervous about what his mother was going to say, but a swell of pride swallowed up the anxiety. "Hi, Mama," he said, and he beamed up at her, hoping it would overpower the awkwardness that hung over everything. "I guess I stopped waiting."

Hayley moved out of the way as Wanda crouched down beside him. She reached down and grabbed his hand, caressed it, and gave him a look he'd never seen before. What was it? Anger? Concern? Something else?

"Morris Jeffries, Jr.," she said, soft and in awe, "what have you started?"

He felt a wave of bashfulness pass over him. "I don't know, Mama. I don't know."

"This is your mom?" Enrique asked, and a huge smile lit up his face. "Buenas noches. Your son is pretty amazing."

"Yes," she said. "He is."

31

"How'd you find out where I went?" Moss asked as his mother sat close to him. "I probably should have said something, but it was a . . . a momentary inspiration, I guess."

"You were upset," said Wanda. "I don't blame you for running out. And it was Kaisha who told me."

"Kaisha?"

"Yeah," said Martin, who had walked up to them. Next to him was Shamika, who looked around at the crowd with wonder in her eyes. "You know she's clued in on all that online stuff."

"Online stuff?" He turned to his mother. "What's he mean?"

"Baby, you're *everywhere*," she said, and he saw the twinkle in her eyes. She was serious.

"Yeah, Moss," said Shamika, grinning, her hoop earrings catching the streetlights and sparkling. "You're the whole reason that the whole JusticeForJavier thing is even happening."

"You're kidding me, right?" Moss said.

Wanda shook her head. "Kaisha found the hashtag on the trending page of Twitter. It was only a few minutes later before she figured out you were here."

"Pretty boss, man," said Martin, and he rubbed Moss's head. "Look how many people are here! And in just a few hours."

"It's not that many people," said Moss. "Maybe like thirty or so."

"You kidding?" Martin said, and he laughed. "Brotha, there's like a few *hundred* people here already."

"No way, man. That's not possible!"

"Maybe you can't see from where you are," his mother said. "Come on, let us help you stand up."

Wanda and Martin grabbed under Moss's arms, and his mother helped guide the chain up the pole. When he managed to get upright, he saw beyond the people who had been standing around them. The crowd stretched down Broadway, almost to the on-ramp to the 880. He looked in the other direction and saw people bunched up to his left, and they began to peter out closer to 8th Street. He heard voices behind him and craned his neck. He couldn't even catch a glimpse of the front door to the precinct if he wanted to.

"You did all this, Moss," Wanda said, and she planted a kiss on his temple. "Though next time, maybe tell your mama what you're about to do."

He blushed. "I'm sorry, I really am. I just got overwhelmed, that's all."

"We should talk, though. Soon. I do have some things to tell you. I was just worried that it wasn't the right time."

Moss danced from one foot to the other, hoping that the pins and needles that had come rushing in would go away. He had so much he wanted to say to her, but the crowd in front of him parted, and a pretty Latina woman walked through, straight up to Moss. She stretched her hand out and Moss gingerly shook it. "Sophia Morales," she said. "Sorry to barge in here, but I got wind of your protest from Twitter."

"Who are you?" Moss said, a little wary of her sudden arrival.

Shamika gently smacked him on the arm. "Moss, she's from NBC. You know, one of them big-name reporters?"

He thought she looked a little familiar. His nerves spiked. "What do you want?"

"You don't have to talk to me if you don't want to," she said. "I can't say the same for the other people who will inevitably show up. But I wanted to hear what you have to say. Your protest has already gotten a lot of attention."

She cast a glance over at Wanda. "I assume you're his mother. I won't interview him if either of you don't want to."

Wanda looked at Moss. He shrugged. "I want to do this," he explained. "I figured that if things went well, the media would show up."

His mother curled up her lip in concentration. "When you want this to stop, you just tell her. Or give me a look." She turned to Sophia. "Don't mess with my boy," she said.

"I won't, I promise," said Sophia, then she gestured to her camera guy, who'd been waiting on the outside of the crowd. He walked over to them as Wanda stepped away. Moss squinted as the bright light at the top of the camera flashed on. *You can do this,* he told himself. *Just be honest.*

The others moved away from him, and he caught Enrique nodding in his direction. "You got this, man," he said, his skateboard at his side. Sophia took a position next to Moss while the cameraman took a few lighting tests.

"Do you prefer to go by Moss?" Sophia asked.

He nodded. "Yeah. You can call me Moss Jeffries if you want."

"Have you ever been on camera like this before?"

"No, not at all," he said. "I'm a little nervous."

"That's okay," she said. "It'll keep you attentive. This is going to sound weird, but try your best to talk to me as if the camera isn't even here. I'll stand here and pivot your direction, so speak to me, not to Tyree over there."

Tyree handed over a body microphone to Sophia. She clipped one end to Moss's collar, then snaked the cord behind him and put the transmitter in his back pocket. "Just talk normally," she explained. "You don't need to speak into the mic. It'll pick everything up."

"Can I get you to say a few things, Moss?" Tyree said. Moss looked at the cameraman and was jealous of how thick his beard was.

He cleared his throat. "Uh . . . yeah. Testing. Check, check. My name is Moss. I live in West Oakland."

Tyree gave a thumbs-up.

"Now, this is for a live broadcast around eleven twenty P.M.," Sophia continued. "Don't worry about the live thing. I'm going to introduce the story, and then turn to you, ask you about why you're out here. I'll try not to surprise you too much, just ask open-ended questions to get you talking."

"Okay, okay," he said, rubbing his hands together. The temperature had dropped even more in the last hour, but he'd been so occupied that he'd not had a chance to think about it. He cupped his hands around his mouth to blow warm air on them and was then hit with a wave of self-conscious anxiety. "Wait, what do I do with my hands?"

She laughed at him. "Everyone has that same problem. Even I did when I started. You can keep them in your pockets at the start, but if you're expressive and like to talk with your hands, that's fine, too. Just don't bump the mic; it's very sensitive."

Moss sucked in a breath and looked over at his mother. She smiled, short and full, and inclined her head once. "I can do this, I can do this," he said to himself.

"You'll be fine, Moss, I promise," Sophia said.

"Sixty seconds to broadcast," said Tyree. "Moss, can you turn your body just a little bit to your right, so that you're facing Ms. Morales?"

He reached down and held the chain as he turned. It scraped against the pole, and he saw Tyree wince. "Yeah, make sure not to move around much. We don't want the mic to pick that up." He looked at his watch. "Thirty seconds."

It was like his heart had never beat faster in his whole life. He started to look around at the crowd—at his mother, at Shamika and Martin, at Enrique and Hayley, at the guy with cornrows, at all the nameless faces whose eyes were locked on to him—and Sophia put her arm out, touched him lightly on the shoulder. "Not them," she said. "Just look at me. You'll do just fine."

She straightened up, and Moss watched Tyree count down silently on his fingers. When he pointed at her to begin, she smiled at the camera. "Thank you, Ross, and yes, it's a very interesting scene here in downtown Oakland. Just an hour ago, we got word that there was a protestor outside the downtown administrative building for the Oakland Police Department. When I arrived here, I almost couldn't believe my eyes."

Tyree slowly panned the camera, and Moss stood as straight as he could, taking his eyes off Tyree, keeping his attention on Sophia, just as he had been asked.

"I have Moss Jeffries with me here, and I wanted to give our viewers an exclusive. Mr. Jeffries, when we saw the photos on Twitter and Instagram, we thought this was part of a prank. But you've *really* chained yourself to this flagpole, haven't you?"

He nodded. "Yes, ma'am," he said. "What I'm doing is not a joke."

"Why have you decided to do this? And why here, outside this building?"

His throat felt tiny, constricted, but he wouldn't let this stop him. "Last week, Javier Perez was shot and killed by James Daley, an Oakland police officer who was part of an unethical raid on my high school." The words felt right coming out of his mouth, and he mentally patted himself on the back for thinking of "raid" at the last second.

"What do you mean by that? What happened at your school?"

"I go to West Oakland High," he said. His voice shook for a second, but he took a breath and began again. "It's an okay school. Maybe not the best, but we try. Lots of kids try there. But our school administration signed a contract with the Oakland Police Department to put cops on our campus and to run us all through metal detectors, and it's disrupting our classes. We can't concentrate. We can't enjoy learning."

Sophia turned to the camera. "Now, for our viewers who might not know, this is the same school where Reginald Phillips was injured by a metal detector installed by the school not too long ago. Mr. Jeffries, do you know Mr. Phillips?"

"Yeah, of course," Moss said. "One of my closest friends. That's why we had decided to peacefully protest the police presence on our campus. So that no more people would get hurt."

"And you were there when Mr. Perez was shot, yes?"

Moss knew he'd have to talk about Javier, but the way she said it tripped him up. It sounded so official, so *detached*. His gaze dropped down, but Sophia ran her hand down his arm. "I'm sorry, Moss, I know this must be hard for you," she said.

"Yeah," he said, and he wasn't looking at her, but he kept talking. "It happened right in front of me. James Daley was the one who shot him. Right in the chest."

"And that's why you're here," she said. "But why this? Why chain yourself to this flagpole?"

"It was kind of a last-minute thing, honestly." He paused; his heart fluttered in his chest. He hadn't prepared anything to say, so he just went with the truth. "James Daley has disappeared. The police haven't spoken to any of us who were there, despite that we witnessed a murder. That seems kind of ridiculous. Isn't that, like, the one thing they're supposed to do?"

"Wait," Sophia said, her face wrinkled up in a mixture of horror and disgust, "are you saying that *none* of you were contacted by the Oakland Police Department about Mr. Perez's death?"

He raised an eyebrow. "Not one of us, ma'am. We don't get to tell our side of the story apparently."

"Then what do you hope to achieve with this protest, Moss? What do you want to happen?"

"I don't know that I have, like, a long-term plan, you know?" Moss said. "I haven't even graduated high school, and this is the kinda stuff we have to deal with already." He sighed. "Miss Morales, you ever been to my school?"

He could tell that he caught her off guard. She was so used to asking the questions that she tilted her head to the side. "No, I can't say I have."

"You should go sometime," he said, and he felt a momentum building in him, so he rode with it. "You can see how the paint peels around the front door. Or how many ceiling tiles are missin'." He paused again. "Can I show you something? I promise it's important."

She looked over at Tyree, and he motioned for her to keep going. "Certainly, Mr. Jeffries."

He gestured toward his messenger bag, which sat on the floor near

Martin's feet. Martin picked it up and tossed it to Moss, and he caught it with his left hand. "This is the book we're reading for my AP English class with Mrs. Torrance," he said, rummaging through the bag. He pulled out his tattered copy of *Things Fall Apart,* and the cover caught on something and tore off. "Damn," he said. He held up the remainder of the book in front of him. "This is what I gotta use to study. Our school is in pieces, Miss Morales, and instead of helping us, getting us books, they installed metal detectors. They hurt and scare my friends. They brought in the police, and they *brutalized* us. Why wouldn't I protest that?"

Moss had forgotten about the crowd, but a few people present clapped after that. Sophia had a hand up to her ear, and Moss could tell she was listening to something in her earpiece. "Okay, got it, Ross," she said, then looked back at Moss. "My colleague wanted to know about your connection to this place. Is it true that your own father was shot and killed by the Oakland police?"

As she said it, she must have seen Moss's face droop. She must have heard the gasps, the collective loss of breath in the crowd. "That's *cold,*" someone said. Moss's mouth dropped open, just slightly, and it was like his heart stopped. Like the world froze.

"Oh . . . oh my god, I'm sorry," Sophia was saying, her hand up, "I was just repeating what he said and—"

Wanda stepped in front of Moss. "This interview is over," she said, and she blocked Tyree for a moment, but the man switched off the light, lowered the camera, and gaped at his partner. He looked sick, his own mouth agape in horror.

Sophia put her face in her hands, and Moss felt like dropping to the ground. "I'm so sorry," she said again. "I shouldn't have hit you with that. It was senseless, and I can't apologize enough."

Moss's head swirled. *Think, think,* he told himself. *Get a grip, don't let this derail you.* He flipped through the Rolodex while he tried to fill his lungs with air, but they felt like concrete blocks in his chest. His mom was there, her hands on his face, caressing him, telling him that he was okay, that she wasn't going to leave his side, that what he was doing was brave and courageous and that Morris would have been so proud of him.

He flipped the deck. *That night in Mosswood Park.* No, no, he thought about that all the time. *The piraguas.* No, no, it wasn't right. *The pupusas in the Mission. The Christmas bike.*

"No, no, no," he said, soft at first, then rising in volume. "I can't. I can't."

"You can't what, baby?" His mother ran her hands over his head, down the sides of his face.

The picnic at the lake. The first day of school. The bus rides to Fremont.

"No, no, no, no!" Moss shouted, and the panic pushed at his throat, burst out of his eyes, pressed at his heart. "Mama, I can't remember. I can't remember anything new."

She stopped. She looked into his eyes, and Moss saw them examine his face. She was afraid. It terrified him.

Sophia backed away. She was still apologizing. Tyree pulled her into the crowd, and Moss saw the looks on their faces. Sadness. Pity.

They pitied him. He slumped down the pole, crumpled to the ground. He had never hated himself more.

32

"I messed up, didn't I?"

He tossed the question at his mother, but she was already refusing it, her head shaking furiously from side to side.

"No, no, not at all, baby," she said. She caressed him again. "You did *incredible,* Moss. It's that reporter's fault for surprising you like that."

"Don't be so hard on yourself," said Shamika, and she lowered herself down to sit on Moss's right side. "You heard how the crowd reacted. They were surprised, too. It was a low blow."

He continued to practice his breathing technique, and his heart rate finally started to subside from the painful thumping of the last few minutes. The crowd around him seemed to be giving him space for the moment, so he took the opportunity to direct a question toward his mother. "You think I did okay?"

"Yeah, definitely," said Wanda, and she smiled at him. "Real good."

"Reminded me of your mom there for a minute," said Martin, and he was grinning, too. "She definitely rubbed off on you. Which reminds me." He turned to Shamika, who handed him a paper bag. "This is for you."

Moss took the bag and peered inside it. He reached in and pulled out its contents: a bottle of water, a bag of almonds, an apple, and an empty sports drink bottle.

"What's this for?" Moss asked, holding up the empty container.

"Well," said Martin, "I had a realization. You're gonna be here for a while, right?"

Moss nodded. "I guess. It certainly looks like it."

"Well, I figured that eventually, you're going to need to . . . uh . . . well, you're going to need to fill that empty bottle . . . with . . . um—"

"Damn, Martin, just say it!" Shamika shouted, then turned to Moss with a giant smile on her face. "You're gonna have to take a *mean* piss eventually."

"It just sounds so silly!" Martin said. "In my defense, I got the bottle. My work is done."

"No, it's not," said Moss. "You gotta help form a wall around me if that's the case. And someone's gonna have to empty it."

"I do not volunteer as tribute," said Shamika. "I changed your diaper enough as a kid."

Moss flushed. "Please tell me you're not serious."

"Your father was *terrible* at it," said Wanda. "Shamika used to help a lot when the two of us got scheduled to work at the same time."

He gaped at his mother. He had known that Shamika was a long-time friend, but he assumed that she had not gotten close to Wanda until after Morris had died. "I had no idea," he said quietly. "Guess there's a lot I don't know."

Martin whistled at that one. The others went silent; even his mother looked away from him.

"Ah, I'm sorry," he said. "I wasn't trying to be passive-aggressive, Mama. It's just been a long day. My brain isn't running on a hundred percent."

"It's okay," said Wanda. "And it looks like we've got a long night ahead of us, so it might be best to kill some of that time." She breathed in deep. He watched her look at her two best friends. "So what do you want to know, Moss?"

He examined her face, saw that she looked at him without her usual defenses. She was vulnerable. Open. She meant it.

"You know there's only one thing I really want to know," he said.

"That's my fault," said Shamika. "Me and my big mouth."

"What happened?" Moss asked. "Shamika said that this isn't the first time our folks have gone up against the cops. Was she referring to us and Papa?"

"Well, sort of," Wanda said. "In a roundabout way. There's a reason I stopped organizing. Stopped going to rallies. Just got lost in work and you."

"You talkin' about the end of junior high? That time?"

"Not long before," she admitted, and she pursed her lips. She took Moss's hand in hers. "I've been ashamed to admit it, but I got scared. *Real* scared."

"We all did," said Martin, and he squatted down in front of Moss. "Trust when we say that for a time there, it seemed like there was a real ugly force in this city that was prepared to do anything to stay in power."

"Okay, now you're spooking *me* out," said Moss, and he shivered from a combination of the cold and the unnerving sensation of fear that rattled through him. "What are you talking about?"

"I know this isn't a surprise to you, but there's a long, violent history of resistance against the police in this city," said Wanda, and she squeezed his hand a little tighter. "Stretching all the way back to the Black Panthers. Probably further."

"And obviously not just here," said Martin. "All over the country."

Wanda nodded in agreement. "But here, it's an undeniable part of the fabric of Oakland. For as long as I can remember, there's always been people here ready to check the police, to keep them in line, to remind them that they are servants of the public, not the other way around."

"Doesn't seem to have worked," said Moss. "I mean, I've never known that to be the case."

"Well, maybe not, but there were plenty of us who tried," said Wanda. "Present party included. You know, that's how I met your English teacher! Mrs. Torrance."

"Oh!" Moss said. "Well, that explains *that*."

"Oh, Moss, you shoulda seen some of the shit your mama used to get up to!" Shamika laughed. "Before you were born, she and Morris were *huge* in this community. Organizing rallies. Helping to protest every time the police shot and killed someone. She got arrested. A *lot*."

"I kinda figured that one out," said Moss. "I mean, I've heard so much about all the people arrested at protests that it only made sense that you had to have been at some point. But . . . it's more than that, isn't it?"

Wanda didn't react at first. She sat still, her hand in Moss's, and it chilled him. His mother was always so certain, so sure, and he then saw the doubt creep over her. *Why doubt?* Moss thought.

"It's a lot more than that," she said, and she was quiet. Small. His mother, who was always so bigger-than-life, now seemed to shrink before Moss. "I think you were four when it happened. Her name was . . ." She let the sentence expire and looked up to her friends.

"Sherelle," said Martin softly. "I can't even remember her last name. God, has it been that long?"

"Have there been *that* many of them that we can't remember?" Shamika said. "Christ."

"Mama," said Moss. "Who was Sherelle?"

"She was shot down the street from our house," said Wanda. "In a traffic stop. You know how it goes. The cops claimed that she had a weapon and brandished it, so they fired on her. She died there in her car. They wouldn't even let the paramedics see her."

"That's awful," said Moss.

"Yeah, and I saw the whole thing," his mother said. "Because I filmed it all."

"Oh no," said Moss, the words spilling out of him like a ritual. He knew the rest of the story without her having to finish it. "What did they do to you?"

"Nothing at first," she said. "They didn't even know until a couple days later that *anyone* could dismantle their story. I gave the tape to the news after we found out . . . when we—"

His heart dropped. She had tears in her eyes. She looked up at Shamika, and Moss gazed at her. She was shaking her head. "Moss, she was just a couple months pregnant when they killed her."

When he looked back at his mother, he saw her shudder, and he let go of her hand, pulled her closer, but she resisted. She pulled away from him. "No, not yet," she said. "You have to hear it all before you decide anything."

He hated how uncomfortable he felt. "What do you mean, Mama? Decide *what*? I don't understand!"

Moss turned his attention to Martin and Shamika, but neither of them would make eye contact. They held their heads down, their gaze elsewhere. "Mama, what *happened*?"

She sniffled. "The department visited me. After the news broadcasts with my video, which showed that she never reached for any weapon, that she never did anything to warrant a display of force, that they just *murdered* her. It was like a month later."

She stopped again. Moss had never seen her like this. She was never so reluctant to talk. What did this mean?

"I never got their names. No badges. Three of them showed up, told me that I had better be careful, that I had painted a target on my back, on my whole family."

He felt it rise within him: that anger, that fury and rage that he tried so hard to control. "Mama, you did the right thing," he said, desperate to push away the boiling in his blood. "Please don't feel bad for it."

"I saw one of them again, baby, years later. I didn't recognize him at first."

He was shaking his head. "I don't get it."

She looked to Martin, and he said what she had not been able to say. "She saw him outside Dawit's shop. Standing over your father's body."

She wouldn't look at him. He felt a horror grow within him, and he was crying openly when she started speaking again. "I didn't know it at the time, but I recognized him that day outside Dawit's," she said. "And I can never prove it, not in a court of law, not even in the public eye. But I know in my heart why that man fired his gun that day."

He looked upon the others in desperation. Martin wouldn't bring his eyes to meet Moss, and Shamika's mascara had started to run down her cheeks.

"How long until you were gonna tell me?" Moss said, and the words came out as daggers, rough and purposeful. "How long?"

"We didn't know how," said Martin. "How do you even start that conversation?"

"Oh, I don't know," Moss shot back. "Maybe, 'Hey, Moss, we just want you to know that the police are scarier than you already think they are'? Something like that?"

He made himself look at his mother. Her lips trembled, the tears fell. "Please," she said, and she looked like a child about to beg forgiveness from a parent. "Please don't hate me."

He swallowed. "Mama, damn it, I could never hate you," he said, and he wiped the wetness off his face. "I wouldn't dream of blaming you for what happened to Papa. Ever."

"Really?" Wanda said, the relief spreading across her features.

"I just wanted the *truth*," he said. "I just want to know what I'm up against. And to not feel like I'm just some kid who has bit off more than he can chew."

"Well, that's probably always going to happen," his mother said. "At least when you're going up against such powerful people. But you're right. You deserved to know the truth. It's unfair. And I'm sorry."

She didn't resist when he pulled her in closer. He hugged her hard. "I'm sorry, too," he said. "I had no idea that Papa's death probably hurt you harder than I realized."

"I know it's irrational," his mother said. "These two have been telling me that for years, and I still can't believe them. But I feel responsible."

"No," said Moss. "That would be the man who pulled the trigger."

"Amen," said Martin.

"And I'm glad we've got that out of the way," said Moss, and he motioned for Martin and Wanda to help him up. "Because I've got to pee something fierce."

"Oooh, I am not gonna be here for this," said Shamika, standing up. "Anyone want some coffee? There's a shop up on 19th that's open twenty-four hours."

As people shouted out orders, Moss was helped up. He smiled at his mother, certain that he loved her more now than he did before. He refused any anger toward her; he rejected it because he could not be angry at the wrong person. He was now more determined than ever to get justice for Javier, for Reg and Shawna, for every person who had been harmed by the monsters who worked in the building behind him.

Martin said he would take one for the team, and so Moss watched him walk away with a nearly full bottle of urine to dump somewhere discreetly. The crowd had grown even larger, despite it being well past midnight. As people joined them, many came up to Moss to say hello, to shake his hand, to congratulate him for what he had accomplished. Some posed for selfies; a photographer for the Associated Press asked Moss for permission to snap a few photos, and then he thanked Moss for what he was doing, too.

It felt good. Surprising. He legs ached every so often, and the chain had started to dig into his waist. He was certainly uncomfortable, but the trade-off was already worth it. *How are there so many people here?* Moss thought. *What's it going to be like in the morning?*

They arrived sometime after one. Moss didn't recognize them at first, felt strange about how they lingered on the outside of the crowd. A black girl, her braids immaculate, two people cowering behind her. It was when Carlos poked his head around Chandra that Moss lit up. "Carlos?! Is that you?"

Carlos's smile ignited a joy on his face. He rushed up to Moss, who was still standing, and he threw himself into a hug. It briefly knocked the wind out of him, but Carlos wouldn't let go. He was crying now, his sobs muffled in Moss's torso, and Moss just held him, saying nothing.

"Thank you," Chandra said. "We didn't want the world to forget Javier."

"Or turn him into a reckless monster," said Sam. "He was the farthest thing from that." They turned away to wipe at their face.

"I'm sorry you lost your friend, too," he said. "And I'm sorry I didn't get a chance to come to Eastside to tell you that myself."

"'Sokay," said Chandra. "You've kind of had a lot to deal with."

"I'm working on something today, should be done soon cuz I'm not going to school tomorrow," Carlos said. "Been working on it all weekend and I'm heading over now to do more before morning. Just a li'l piece for Javier."

"Little?" Sam laughed at that. "Boy, that piece is the entire side of a building."

Carlos crinkled up his face. "It's okay. I just hope you like it."

Moss pulled the boy in for another hug. "I can't wait to see it," he said.

There was a commotion behind him, a rising chaos of voices and scuffling. Moss couldn't see what was happening, so he asked his mother.

She frowned. "Someone's coming," she said. "From inside the building."

He could see the crowd moving out of the way. A woman floated into his line of vision, and he watched her with concern. She looked a bit like Hayley, though she was taller, her hair lighter. Her attire was simple, all plain colors and straight lines, but she seemed frazzled. Unprepared. *She must have just been woken up,* Moss thought. She extended her hand to Moss, but he remained motionless.

"Johanna Thompson," she said. "I wanted to introduce myself; I'm the communications manager for the Oakland Police Department."

"Wait, *what*?" Moss said. "Isn't that someone else?" He gazed over at the others. "Wasn't it someone else at the church?"

"Rachel," said Wanda. "Her name was Rachel."

Johanna smiled, and Moss nearly burst into bitter laughter. She smiled *exactly* like Rachel did.

"Well, there's been a bit of an internal change," Johanna said, but Martin's whoops drowned her out.

"Are you telling me they fired that last woman *already*?" Martin slapped his knee. "That is the funniest thing I have heard this whole year."

"Well," said Johanna, ignoring Martin and staring straight at Moss. "I'm here on behalf of the Oakland Police Department to help facilitate a fair exchange of ideas."

"Ah," said Wanda, who stepped closer to her son. "So, you're here to craft a message."

"No, no, not at all," said Johanna. She smiled. Again. "Actually, I'm here because Moss's protest has worked. We would like to talk to him."

The silence that followed felt unreal. The crowd that surrounded him was still, unmoving, quiet, and it was eerie, like the world had been paused for this singular moment. He saw phones, video cameras, and the like raised up, all of them pointed at him and Johanna.

"What do you mean?" Moss asked. "Talk to me?"

"If you unchain yourself and come with me, I can guarantee a meeting with our current chief, as well as other members of the department." That smile. "You've impressed a lot of people tonight, Moss."

"No."

His mother dropped that one, and she said it with such a quickness and with such force that his only reaction was to giggle. It rolled up through him, and he couldn't stop it. Johanna grinned back, but it was forced. "Am I missing something?" Johanna asked.

"I'm not going *anywhere* with you!" Moss said. "You want me to just walk into that station and just *give up*?" He laughed again. "I have no guarantee whatsoever that you won't just arrest me as soon as I walk through those doors behind me."

"I can assure you that won't happen," said Johanna, but she didn't smile this time. She gritted her teeth once before she continued. "You got what you wanted, Moss. Why won't you take it?"

"What I *wanted*," he said, "was to see James Daley arrested for the murder of my friend. Can you guarantee me right now, in front of all my friends"—he gestured at the gathered crowd—"that you will arrest him and have him charged?"

"I can't make promises like that, and it's not in my power to—"

"Then I have nothing to say to you." Moss turned his head away from the woman, dropped his hands to his sides, and stared straight ahead. He could sense her, even though she wasn't saying anything. "Please leave."

He heard her scoff. "Well," she said, "if you're willing to talk, please let anyone here know. I'll be inside." There was a pause, and Moss knew she hadn't left. "I'm surprised you're letting him do this."

That got his attention. Moss whipped his head toward this vulture, but his mother beat him to the punch. "I am proud of what my son is doing," Wanda shot back. "And I'd gladly join him."

Johanna had not expected that response. He watched her face twitch for the briefest of moments, like she was weighing whether to respond or not. "I guess we just disagree about how to raise our sons," she said.

Martin's hand shot out in front of Wanda, stopping her. "Don't take the bait," he said. "She just wants to get a rise out of you."

"I know," said Wanda, and the glare she fixed on her face made another wave of amusement pass over Moss. *Oh, she is* finished, he thought. "I just hope she knows who she's dealing with."

"A child," Johanna said. "And his little tantrum is not going to last beyond the morning, I assure you of that." She looked directly into Moss's eyes. "You had your chance to be civil and respectful, Mr. Jeffries. Don't cry to me when this gets out of control."

The woman stormed off, her black heels clicking on the concrete, and the crowd began to yell things after her. Moss looked to his mother, to Shamika and Martin, and he sighed.

"Looks like I've caused some trouble," he said. "Y'all ready?"

"We're not leaving your side," said Martin, and he patted Moss on the shoulder. "We'll be here until the end."

Moss hoped that the end wasn't too soon.

33

Light broke over Oakland many hours later, and Moss struggled to keep his eyes open. He had braced himself for a confrontation that never came, and there was a part of him that wished something had happened. At least that would have kept the exhaustion at bay.

Much of the crowd was sitting or lying on the sidewalk. Hayley and Enrique were asleep off to Moss's right, both of them curled up with their heads resting on backpacks, a single blanket spread over the two of them. Shamika and his mother were sipping a second round of coffees and gossiping about all sorts of things, but Moss kept to himself.

He then turned to Martin, who sat beside him, nursing a cup of coffee himself. Jasmine had stopped by with breakfast for the group, and pink boxes of doughnuts had been passed around until they were devoured.

"I really hate this stuff, you know," Martin said, gesturing to his cup. "It tastes like dirt water."

"My mom loves it," said Moss. "I honestly don't get it."

"Your dad loved it, too. Used to bring it into the shop with him when he came for a new cut. Only guy I cut who drank coffee while I did it."

"Really? I figured most guys read or were on their phones."

"*Normal* people are like that. That stuff smells nasty."

Moss laughed. "So what was he like back then? When he first started coming to your shop."

Martin removed his hat and set it in his lap. "A goddamn fool," he said. "You remember that part of him. Always ready with a joke or some terrible story. But he was great. Brought up the energy in that shop every time he was there."

Moss shifted his position on the ground, trying to stretch his aching back and move it off the pole. Martin scooted closer to Moss to let him lean into his shoulder. "That better?" Martin said.

"Yeah. Thanks."

Martin was quiet for a minute or two. "I remember when Morris brought you in for the first time," he said, and took another drink of his coffee. "You were small. Maybe four, maybe five. You held your daddy's hand so tight when you walked in there. It was a Saturday morning, so the place was real loud, you know?"

Moss nodded, and Martin continued. "You know, you wouldn't say a word at first. Your eyes were dancing around the shop, looking at all the others gettin' their hair done, wincing if people laughed too loud. But when it came time to give you your first fade, you suddenly got *real* talkative."

Moss sat up and glanced over at Martin. "No, I didn't! I don't remember that at *all*."

Martin laughed. "Man, you were a mouthy kid," he said. "You know you refused to sit in a booster seat?"

"You're kidding, man."

Martin shook his head. "You said you wanted a seat like all the others. You were *grown,* you said. So you wanted a cut just like them. And your dad supported you, too. He loved how much it annoyed me."

"Sounds like Papa," Moss said, and he sighed. "I miss him so much."

"Me too, Moss," said Martin, and he sighed. "Me too."

"I don't remember that day," said Moss. "I guess there's a lot I don't know."

"We all have memories of your father," Martin said. "Good ones, too. You should just ask us next time to tell you stories if you want."

Silence fell again, and Moss watched his city wake up. Buses were already chugging down Broadway as the sun rose in the east. It cast long shadows over the street, and the nearby freeway roared with traffic. He saw a lot of confused faces gawking at the assembled crowd as they passed by. Some stopped to ask questions of others, but no one spoke to Moss himself. A little before seven, three separate news vans showed up, parked north of Moss's location. They set up in the lane closest to him, and before long, each of them began to broadcast live from the site of the protest. There was another local affiliate directly in front of Moss, but the reporter, a short man with close-cropped brown hair, never once looked at him.

Moss asked Martin for help to stand up; then Moss adjusted the chain around his waist and tried his best to listen to what the man was saying.

"Reports claimed that a protestor had chained themselves to the flagpole outside the downtown administrative building of the Oakland Police Department. As you'll see, Diane, there are a few hundred people gathered here, all to protest the apparent shooting of a local Oakland resident, Javier Perez."

"Apparent?" Martin said under his breath. "Like it didn't even happen."

"We're still unsure of the motivations of everyone here, but I think it's safe to say—"

"You could just ask me," Moss shouted. "I'm right here."

The reporter stopped and turned around, shock on his face. Moss was unsurprised that this particular man was white. "Excuse me?"

"You don't have to be 'unsure of motivations,'" Moss said, air quotes over the last phrase. "You can just ask me why I did this."

Flustered, the reporter stumbled through a few words before turning back around, ignoring Moss completely again. Moss waited then without interrupting, but as soon as the cameraman stopped rolling, the reporter spun around. "What gives? I was broadcasting live."

"Are you serious?" Moss said. "How can you report on *my* protest without even talking to me?"

"This is *yours*? I didn't know protests could belong to someone."

"My son started it," said Wanda, who now stood at Moss's side. "I think everyone here is aware of that and willing to give him credit."

More of the crowd was awake now, and many of them vocalized their support with claps and cheers. The reporter scowled at them, then walked off.

"It's gonna happen more," said Wanda while she watched the reporter leave. "You did fine, baby. You're really good at this, you know?"

"Nah, I think I'm just super petty," said Moss. "How he gonna talk about me while I'm standing right behind him?"

Wanda gestured with her head behind Moss. "You got some visitors on their way," she said.

He was overjoyed to turn around and see his friends walking toward him. Rawiya and Njemile were in the front, with Bits, Kaisha, and Reg following behind. "Hey, make some room, everyone!" Moss said, the excitement and affection spilling out of him. "Oh, I'm so glad to see you all."

"Moss, you *scoundrel,*" said Rawiya, and she ran to him, throwing her arms around him. "You've really outdone yourself."

"Imagine my surprise when my moms woke me up this morning," said Njemile. "They were screaming at me about you, trying to tell me that you were doing something stupid and amazing."

"That sounds more like Ogonna," said Moss. "Lemme guess: Ekemeni stood there, her arms crossed like this." Moss imitated one of Njemile's moms, and he fixed his face with a wrinkled frown. "'That Moss, he is too wild for you, Njemile. You need more stable friends.'"

"Eerily accurate," said Njemile, and then she hugged him, too. "As always."

He greeted his other friends one by one as they pushed to make space in the crowd. And then she appeared, standing at the rear of them all: Esperanza. She kept looking back down at the ground as if she was too ashamed to keep eye contact. He nodded at her, but it was awkward. Painful. A rage simmered in him, but he was not sure he wanted to confront her just yet. They'd been friends for so long, but *his* wounds were still raw. He turned back to the group. "How are you all here? Isn't class gonna start soon?"

"We're skipping," said Rawiya. "And I think a ton of other people are, too."

"You're kidding me," said Moss. "Aren't you all going to get in trouble?"

"Maybe," said Bits. "But it's worth it."

"Totally worth it," said Rawiya.

There was a break, and so Moss went for it. "Well, what about your parents, Esperanza?" Moss asked. "I'm guessing they're not too pleased with me right now."

She sighed. "I'm sure they don't even know. And besides, they wouldn't understand anyway. They truly don't think they've done anything wrong. I'm not gonna share some of the things they've said to me since last night, just to spare you the pain." She went quiet, and the awkwardness he had hoped to keep at bay rushed in. "And I'm sorry about yesterday, too," she added. "I really need to learn that sometimes it's best if I just *listen*. It's a compulsion of mine, always wanting to be involved." She laughed nervously, then conceded, "Just like my parents."

"I appreciate that," he said. Moss had more to say, but this wasn't the right time. He looked instead toward Kaisha, who stood behind Reg's wheelchair. "What's the online world like?"

"It's . . ." She hesitated. "It's a lot. I'm sure I don't have to tell you that the internet cannot talk about the police in any sensible way, and your protest has made people *mad*. I been blocking Nazis from Twitter all morning."

"How's the night been?" Bits asked. "Last night seems so far away."

"I know!" Moss said. "It's been okay. Long. Met a lot of people. Mostly, it feels like a dream or something."

"I can imagine," said Njemile. "Kaisha figured out what was happening last night, but most of us found out this morning. Dude, you *really* surprised us all. What a great idea!"

"Aw, damn," said Moss, and his face burned. "Don't make me blush, I swear."

"You think we're really gonna let you get off scot-free?" Rawiya said. "We're here to remind all these people that you're really just a big dork."

They all laughed, but it was cut short once someone shouted out, "Five oh!" It came from behind Moss, so he hiked up the chain a bit and tried to turn around. There were too many people on the sidewalk blocking his line of sight. Two of the cameramen from the news vans that still sat on Broadway scrambled through the crowd, pushing people aside.

"What is it, Mama?" Moss asked. "What's going on?"

"I can't see either, baby," she answered. "But something's about to happen."

The crowd parted a bit, and Moss caught a flash of hair, a black suit. There was another commotion, and then he saw the cops, three of them, all pushing people to one side or the other. Someone cried out, and then he saw her, Johanna, the communications manager. She was holding a piece of paper in her hands. The woman moved forward, and Moss struggled as hard as he could to turn himself around, and she came right up to him. They were flanked by cameras, and Moss's mother grabbed his arm. "I'm right here," she whispered in his ear, but he didn't dare turn around to look at her.

He stared straight at Johanna, who had stopped just a few feet from Moss. She smiled, and it stretched her face, and it was wrong. There was joy there, a giddiness that unsettled him and sent goose bumps down his arms.

"Good morning," she said. "I'm here to make a statement on behalf of the Oakland Police Department and their chief, Tom Berendht."

She made direct eye contact. She smiled.

"The Oakland Police Department sympathizes with the loss of life, with Morris Jeffries, Jr., and with the rest of this community. It is never easy to lose someone, and the department does not take this lightly."

He bristled, and the crowd around him seemed to hold their breath all at once. This could go in so many directions, but deep down, Moss knew the worst was about to come. He wanted to be optimistic, but she dropped another tight-lipped smile at him, and he knew that this was it. It was over.

"However, the Oakland Police Department cannot comment on pending investigations, nor can it subvert the rule of law in this city."

The cry that rose up pierced through Moss, forced Johanna to stop for a moment. Someone swore, loudly, and she raised a hand up. "Please, let me finish." She turned back to the statement. "Morris Jeffries, Jr. was offered a chance to speak with the chief, but refused it. Therefore, in order to make sure we can continue to serve the Oakland community as best as possible, we have no choice but to declare this an unlawful assembly. You have one hour to clear the premises."

He heard the roar, the screams all around him, and he watched Johanna fold the paper in her hands, without ever once looking at him. She leaned over to one of the cops and said something, and he saw her walk away, saw the cops raise their batons threateningly, saw the crowd close around him, felt his world shrink to nothing.

34

It was 7:34 A.M.

The panic set in immediately and not just in Moss. He saw the frantic looks on the faces around him, but he couldn't afford them the attention they needed. He grasped his mother's hand, hard, too hard, and he spit out his question. "Can they do this?"

"Of course they can," she shouted back. "It's probably the most common tactic they have."

Enrique sidled up to him. "What are you going to do, man? We can't bail, can we?"

Moss shook his head. "I'm scared, but I don't want to give up so easily. We *can't* give up."

"What are you thinking, Wanda?" Shamika asked. "What should we do?"

"No, that's not for me to decide," she said. "Moss, this is *your* protest, and it's only fair that you lead it. If I've learned anything, it's that I've got to trust you."

He let the warmth dominate him for a moment. "Should I make a statement or something? Get people riled up?"

She smiled at him. "Whatever you choose, you know we'll support you."

He looked to his friends. "What do you think?"

"What are you gonna say?" Rawiya asked. "I think we're all a little freaked out."

"Just tell the truth," said Esperanza. "That's what you're good at, Moss. *Real* good at it."

His palms were too sweaty and his heart was racing. If he was going to say anything, he had to now.

It was 7:37 A.M.

Do it, he told himself.

He nodded. "Okay," he said. "Let me get their attention."

Before he could do anything, Bits stepped in front. "Everybody, listen up!" Bits yelled, and their voice boomed over the crowd. "Moss has something to say!"

Moss gaped at Bits. "Didn't know you could get that loud," he said.

Bits smiled from ear to ear. "I'm full of surprises," they said. "Go get 'em."

The crowd had turned toward him, and as far as he could see, every eye was trained his way. Moss sucked in air, deep, and he let it out in one slow exhale. "Thank you for being here," he said, as loud as he could.

"Speak up!" It came from somewhere in the crowd to his right. He couldn't locate who said it.

"Thank you!" Moss repeated, perhaps louder than he'd ever been, and he saw people in the crowd nod at him, smile, raise their fists in the air. "We are here to demand justice for Javier Perez!"

He felt good saying Javier's name, to hear the cheers and whoops that came in response to it. He heard music muffled by the crowd— Jazmine Sullivan's "If You Dare"—and then people to his left parted. A bearish black man pushed a dolly with a speaker on it toward him. He was impressed, once more, by how resourceful this community was. He was handed a microphone, and he tapped it, then held it up to his mouth. "Better?" Moss said.

More cheering. He had never felt so electrified before.

It was 7:41 A.M.

"We've just been told that we have less than an hour left," he said, "before the Oakland police move in. " He was met with a wave of boos. "Are we going to leave?"

The crowd shouted, "NO!"

"Are we going to be intimidated?"

"NO!"

"And are we going to accept anything less than justice for Javier?"

"NO!"

The denial rang out loud and powerful, and Moss wished he could see how many people were beyond his line of sight. He wanted to be taller in that moment, but in a way, he *felt* taller, like he finally mattered.

"I loved Javier," Moss said, and as the words came out of his mouth, he believed it. It hurt to say them, but it was true. "And I'm not leaving until we get what we want. Are you with me?"

He was drowned out. First by the screams of solidarity, then by the group chanting, "Justice! Justice! Justice!" over and over again. His mother hugged him as he got lost in the spectacle before him.

"It's gonna get ugly soon," she said. "But I got you. I promise you."

"I got you, too," Moss said. "Thank you for this. For making it possible for me to believe that I could *actually* do something."

His mother waved a hand at him, dismissing his words. "You didn't need me," she said. "I needed you."

It was 7:45 A.M.

Martin had been suspiciously silent after Johanna had left, and he grabbed Wanda's arm and pulled her in close to Moss. "What are you doing?" Wanda said, alarmed.

"Be quiet," he said. "Both of you." He moved close to Moss's mother, whispered something in her ear. Her eyes went wide, then back to normal an instant later. "I vote for telling Moss," he added.

"Tell me *what*?" Moss tried to keep his voice down, but all the fear and anxiety came rolling back into his body.

"It's not good," his mother said. "But I trust you, Moss, and I'm trying to learn my lesson. You should be told the truth."

"I hate this already," he blurted out. "I take back any and all proclamations I made, right now."

She smirked at him. "They're bringing in a Silent Guardian."

He furrowed his brow. "Is that supposed to mean something to me?"

"Moss, it's the worst," said Martin, and for the first time since he'd arrived the night before, there was fear in his eyes. "And we might want to leave, or at least warn others."

"About *what*? What the hell is a 'Silent Guardian'?"

"Remember all that weird shit that the cops used against you and your friends?" Martin said. "This is like the king of them all. It's a device that makes you feel like you're on fire."

Moss balked at him. "You have to be messing with me. That's not a *thing*."

"Unfortunately, it is, and even worse, I know exactly what it feels like," said Wanda. "Your whole skin erupts in heat. It only lasts while the thing is pointed at you, but . . . it's not pleasant, honey. And there are a lot of people here."

"How do you know this?" Moss asked.

"I heard that Johanna chick say it," Martin said. "I was right next to her."

No, no, no! Moss thought.

It was 7:53 A.M.

"What do we do?" Moss said, trying to keep his voice down. "Give up? Try something else?"

"I'm personally willing to feel a little pain to make a point," said Martin, shrugging. "I think everyone who is sticking around feels the same way."

"We gotta tell 'em," said Moss. "You wanna do it, Mama?"

She nodded her head. "I'll make an announcement," she said, and she set off to find the speaker that had just disappeared. Moss's feet hurt; his stomach rumbled; his back was a mess of knots and soreness. He drank more water, hoping he was hydrated enough. He couldn't risk a migraine at this point.

A woman named Estelle, who wrote a local politics blog, came up to him and asked him his story, and he spent nearly fifteen minutes telling her about his father, about his father's death, about his school, about Javier. She looked like one of his father's aunts, the one he'd only met once, when she managed to come over for a week from Puerto Rico. Moss couldn't remember her name, but he saw her in the way

Estelle nodded her head when he spoke. In the way she focused her attention on him. In the way her dark hair curled tightly. He missed his father fiercely when the woman walked away.

It was 8:10 A.M.

Moss tried not to let his nerves get the best of him. They were creeping up on him, hiding in the shadows of his mind, poking and prodding him. He hated *any* interaction with the police, but now he was inviting them into his life in a way that seemed absurd. How could he actually do that? How could he stand up to a power that could take his life, or the lives of everyone around him? He aimed for distraction at the moment instead. He asked Kaisha to update him about what was happening on social media. Njemile regaled him with tales of her first foray into online dating. "It's approximately as bad as you think it is," she said. "I have spoken with two whole men—two!—who pretended to be lesbians just so they could talk to me, an actual lesbian."

"Ew, *why*?" Moss said. "That's so gross."

"Men are gross," said Njemile. "Are you at all surprised by your gender?"

"I should not be, but come *on*. What did these guys think the end result would be? That you'd renounce your sexuality just because they could catfish a lesbian really well?"

"Moss, it is sometimes impossible to analyze the mind of men," she said. "I refuse to do it."

"I had the same problem before me and Reg got together," Kaisha added, looking up from her phone and then rolling her eyes. "So many men thought that they were *the one* who could prove to me that I wasn't ace."

Moss thought that Esperanza was going to chime in with a story or two of her own, but she still stood awkwardly off to the side. He instead turned to Bits. "How are you? Handling this well?"

They shrugged. "I'm a little nervous," they said. "I don't know what's gonna happen. Isn't it almost an hour? Why aren't there any cops around?"

It was 8:22 A.M.

Moss shrugged. "I don't know. It seems eerie, doesn't it? Where's my mother, by the way?"

Someone tapped him on his shoulder, and then Sophia appeared in front of him, a sheepish look on her face. "Moss, I just want to—"

"You're kidding me!" Moss said. "I don't want to talk to you."

"I know, and I don't blame you!" Sophia was shaking her head, desperate. "I promise you, I had no intention of asking that question. One of the anchors asked it, and I'm so used to just acting as a go-between that I blurted it out without thinking. Please, I'm so sorry, Moss."

He stared at her. She looked sincere, but he had no reason not to be wary of her. "Why are you here?"

"Well, I wanted to apologize again," she said, "but I also wanted to offer you something in consolation." She paused and waved to someone to come over, and Tyree ambled up.

"I have something to show you," said Tyree, and Moss's friends moved aside for him.

"What's going on?" Rawiya asked. "Sorry, some of us aren't entirely up to speed yet."

"Later," said Moss. "I'll explain it all. It's been an interesting night." He turned to Tyree. "What's up? What do you have for me?"

Tyree brought his camera up and flipped open the viewscreen on the side. "Since you're kind of . . . well, incapable of moving right now, we figured you might want to know what you're unable to see."

"This is around the corner, on 8th," Sophia explained. "About two hundred yards down the street. Tyree captured this about five minutes ago."

"Excuse me," he heard a familiar voice say, and his mother squeezed through people to get back to him. She looked to Moss, then to Sophia, then frowned. "I couldn't find the speaker, so it can wait," she said. "What is *she* doing here?"

"Mama, they have something to show us."

Moss and his mother huddled around the camera with as many of the others as could fit, and Tyree started the playback. At first, Moss wasn't sure what he was looking at. The shot zoomed out, and he gasped. It was in the middle of a street somewhere. There were so many of them, all clad in solid black, many of them wearing the exact same gear he'd seen at school that day, and it was like his entire insides became jelly at once. They stood in ordered lines, and he couldn't count them. Objects hung from their belts, some familiar, most completely foreign. He pointed to them, his finger hitting the screen.

"That's what they had on campus, Mama," he said. "Well, at least some of it."

"Oh, great," said Rawiya. "This is just *great*."

"Where'd you say this was?" Wanda asked, her eyes locked on the images unfolding.

Sophia pointed north. "Down that street up there, to the west."

"And I don't know how much time we have until they arrive," said Tyree. "It looked like they were getting ready to leave."

It was 8:29 A.M.

"Mama, how long do you think we have?" Moss asked.

"I don't know, baby," she said. "I didn't get a chance to tell anyone about . . . well, that other thing."

"Should we tell the others to get ready?"

The squeal of feedback was his answer. Their heads snapped to the right, to the entrance to the department building, and the shouts and warnings began to roll through the crowd.

Moss couldn't see anyone, but he heard the words that erupted out of the bullhorn.

"This is an unlawful assembly," the voice said. "You were given a warning to clear this area out within the hour. Anyone who is not gone in the next five minutes will be arrested for trespassing and disturbing the peace."

It was now or never.

35

His body was telling him to run, to get as far away from this building as possible. But Moss couldn't. He couldn't run away from this fear.

"*No,*" he said out loud, fierce and angry. "Not *again.*"

"What do you mean?" Wanda said.

"I can't run from them again," he said. "I wanted to run and hide when they had killed Javier. But I can't do it anymore."

"I love you, baby, I really do," she said. "But I don't know that we *want* to be here, you know?" She turned around and seemed to be looking for a way out.

But he stopped her, his hand outstretched, wrapped around her right arm. "Mama, I have an idea. Do you trust me?"

Wanda kept her eyes on the cops by the entrance to the administration building, and he swore that he could feel the rage pumping through her. *Guess I'm much more like her than Papa,* he thought. She licked her lips. "Yes, baby. I do."

He reached into his pocket with his other hand, and he dug around in it. His fingers closed on what he wanted, and he produced the key to the chain around his waist.

"Moss," said Esperanza, the horror evident in her voice. "What are you doing?"

"The element of surprise has worked in my favor all night," he said. "So lemme surprise them again. Sophia, you wanna help me?"

She was startled by the offer. "What? Me?"

He nodded. "Tell Tyree to start recording," he said. "Your little mishap earlier just gave me an idea."

Moss twisted the chain around, and the scraping on the pole

reverberated up his spine. He put the key in the lock that kept it to-gether and opened it, letting one end drop to the ground. He felt a relief spread, and he let go of the other end. It clanked on the side-walk, and even in the midst of the noise of the crowd, it got the at-tention of people surrounding him. Moss didn't hesitate. He crossed the space between him and the three cops in a few steps, and he en-joyed the utter shock on the face of the cop who held the bullhorn.

Moss raised both his hands high. "I have no weapons on me, and you're free to search me," he said. "I just want to ask you something." He paused. "Is this what you really want?"

The cop looked from Moss to the camera trained on him from over Moss's shoulder, then back to Moss. His salt-and-pepper mustache twitched. "What?"

"Is this what you really want?" Moss asked the question with the same commitment and certainty as before.

The man lowered the bullhorn, and it hung at his side. "What are you talking about?"

"You took my father from me already. Why are you letting them take someone else I loved?"

Anger passed over the man's features for an instant, but his eyes shot to the camera again and he kept his expression neutral. "I don't know what you're talking about."

Moss laughed. He couldn't help it. He'd figured that the man would react this way. "Are you saying y'all don't remember the shoot-ing of Morris Jeffries six years ago?" He tapped his temple with his right index finger. "That's right. Y'all have shot so many people that you can't sort them out."

The reaction from the crowd was so satisfying to Moss in that mo-ment, and he had his friends to thank. He felt like he was back in middle school, when a good insult could make you king. Rawiya and Bits had their hands cupped around their mouths, droning out a long "Ohhhhhhhhhhh!"

He smiled at the cop, thankful for who had his back. "Well?" Moss asked. "Do you remember?"

He hesitated. "It's irrelevant," he said. "And get that camera out of here!"

He lunged, but Moss did not flinch. Sophia was now at his side. "Excuse me, Sophia Morales, NBC News. Is it true that this department is responsible for the death of this young man's father?"

The cop's face went pale. "I don't need to make a statement about this to anyone," he said. "All of you need to clear out before—"

"So you don't deny it, then?" Sophia asked. "Don't you think that's a little cruel? Everyone knew the name of the young protestor chained to the flagpole hours ago. Or can you really not remember?"

Moss had never seen panic personified, but that is what this man had become. He raised the bullhorn again, but it was like his lips couldn't form any words. He dropped it to his side again. "I don't have to do this," he said, and he turned around to head back into the building.

Sophia took a step forward. "Sir, it's a fair question. We just—"

"Get back!" The cop who yelled it stepped forward. Moss saw the baton raised in the air, but it happened so quickly that he couldn't shout out a warning in time. The baton rushed down through the air and connected with Sophia's right elbow as she began to bring it up to block the blow. The crack of her bone rang out clear in the horrible, nervous silence, and Sophia's wail of pain and terror was an alarm, a warning bell, the drop of a match on a pool of gasoline. She fell to the ground and Moss tried to rush to her side, but his mother practically tackled him.

"No, Moss, we need to go *now*!" Wanda shrieked, and then the first of the cops was upon them.

Moss felt the baton over his back, but it only grazed him as he twisted away, his hand in his mother's. They ran smack into Martin and Shamika and toppled over one another. Everything around him was a mess of screams and the thuds of batons on bodies. Someone pulled him up—was it one of the cops?—and his feet ached. He screamed for his mother, then saw her take a baton to the face. Something broke, he heard the snap, and blood gushed out of her nose, but she didn't hesitate. She pushed herself up and reached over for Moss, taking his hand. *Who's holding me?* He wrenched himself around and saw Martin's hat.

"Go, go, go!" Martin yelled. "Don't waste no time, y'all. Get out of here!"

Moss stumbled forward, his mother yanking him away from cops that had begun to march on the others. He couldn't focus on any one thing happening around him, though he was desperate to catch a glimpse of someone he recognized. Where were his friends? Was anyone else hurt?

He saw Rawiya, the fear in her eyes. "What do we do?" She screamed at Moss. A cop reached forward, grabbed ahold of her head scarf, and tried to pull it. She deftly darted away from him, and then tried to draw Moss toward her.

"Go!" Moss shouted at her. "Just get to safety!"

The crowd that had spilled out onto Broadway surged to the north at first. There were voices in Moss's ear shouting and screeching, and bodies pushed and rubbed up against him. He had already lost Rawiya. He called out to his mother, "Are you okay? Mama, are you hurt?"

They pushed forward again, and Wanda wiped the blood away from her mouth. "Moss, I'll be okay," she said, the words forced out through pain. "Just focus. Get us out of here."

They hit a wall then as the crowd stopped moving forward. Enrique was there, his skateboard raised above his head, a large gash running down one side of his face. "What's happening?" Enrique said, and he grimaced as the people behind him slammed into him.

"What happened to you?" Moss shouted.

"Tripped," he said. "Hit my head on a mailbox."

"Dude, that looks *bad*," said Moss, anxiety in his throat.

The crowd surged again, but Moss wasn't sure they actually made any progress at all. He tried to see over the heads of the people in front of him. Why had everyone stopped?

"We're going the wrong way," Moss said, quiet at first, and then he started screaming it as loud as he could. "We're going the wrong way! The police have officers all over 8th Street! Go back the other way!"

He tried to turn around, but he was so tightly wedged in the crowd that it was impossible. The motion of the crowd flowed north again, and then a sound overpowered everything. He had no frame of reference for it, no way for his brain to process just how horrible it was. The screams rose, first in volume, then in pitch, and then it sounded like a slaughter, like farm animals squealing and shrieking.

"What is that?" Moss yelled. "What's happening?"

"Silent Guardian," his mother said, and she pointed. He followed the direction of her finger, saw the white van at the end of the block, the sand-colored box on top of it. It was like a weapon out of Star Wars; it looked about, roving from one side of the crowd to the other. It didn't make a sound, and he saw nothing emitting from it. The people in front of him began to part ways, to push to either side instead of toward the sounds of human suffering, and then he saw it in action.

The antenna on the top of the box would move sluggishly, and as soon as it seemed to be pointing at someone, that person would drop to the ground. Hands scraped at skin. People clawed at their faces, sometimes drawing blood. He watched a young woman run headfirst into the side of a car, trying to escape the sensation that Martin had described to him, and she lay still on the ground.

There was blood. Bodies bent in ways they should not be. He wanted to turn around and run away, to save himself, and the urge sent shame through his body. But as more people succumbed to the Silent Guardian, the more certain he was that he didn't want to know what that thing felt like.

Yet there was nowhere for them to go. More people were rushing from the flagpole and running into the group, discovering the wall of other protesters and bystanders. For every inch Moss managed to push forward, he'd be shoved farther back toward 8th Street. "Stop it!" Moss yelled. "We have to go the other way!"

He felt it on the back of his neck first, like a sunburn that suddenly bloomed into a burst of heat. It seared his skin, and a memory popped in his head: putting his hand on top of the burner on the stove. But it wouldn't stop, and as Moss began to scream himself, he tried to climb over the people who were in his way.

It passed, like a wave, and those to his right began to scream now, and his mother yelled in his ear. "Go! *Go!*" They pushed, and the wall broke, and they made a run for it. Wanda had her arm over his shoulder, and he did his best to carry as much of her weight as possible as they kept up the pace, telling those they passed to turn around, to head south. He heard the echoes of a helicopter above him, and the crowd craned their necks up as they moved. "This is an unlawful assembly," blared a voice from the chopper. "Please leave or you will be arrested."

"Well, I tried," Moss said, his breath ragged. "I tried to do something."

"Moss, you did something incredible today," said his mother. "Please don't let this discourage you."

He wanted to believe her, but it was difficult at the moment. The shoving was the worst. His legs felt trapped, but people kept pushing. At one point he used his left arm to hoist himself up, and the momentum of the mass carried him forward. Something pressed on his chest, just below his ribs. Someone's elbow. Another person was shrieking in his ear, but he didn't even have enough room to turn around to see who it was.

"Don't stop," his mother slurred, and it was then that he realized just how many people had shown up over the night. It was a strange moment for the epiphany; only now, as they all struggled to escape the cops, did Moss know how influential he'd been.

He just wanted to breathe. He threw his head back again and tried in desperation to fill his lungs. *No, no!* Moss thought. *Not now!* He shot a glance at his mother and her face was unrecognizable, swollen and battered and twisted into a grimace of pain. His vision began to fade in the corners, and panic swept through him.

The momentum spilled forward and Moss landed on top of the

large man who had been in front of him. He scrambled up, apologizing while doing so, and he reached for his mother, pulling her out from
under the other protestors who had fallen as well.

"Move!" Wanda screamed, and her words sounded broken. She spat
out more blood, and Moss did as he was told. With his mother trailing behind him, he bolted down Broadway, the crowd slowly thin-
ning out. His eyes darted from one face to the next, but they were all
strangers. All of them. A profound sense of isolation grew in him as
he pushed onward, unable to find any of his friends in the swarm of
people. Someone darted across from him, their face swollen and red,
and he flashed back to that afternoon in West Oakland High, to the
hallways full of his brutalized peers, and he knew it was happening
all over again.

36

The morning sun disappeared as they rushed under the 880 overpass. Moss saw someone climb up onto the railing on the east side of Broadway, and they were promptly tackled by an officer clad all in black. A skateboard clattered to the ground. *Was that Enrique?* Moss thought. He couldn't stop to find out, and the sheer terror of what was coming from behind kept his feet moving. He wanted to rest so badly, the soles of his feet on fire with pain, his heart raging, his head pounding.

"Oh, no," he heard his mother say, and then she was no longer at his side, no longer holding his hand. He came to an abrupt stop and numerous people slammed into him, some of them shouting at him to move, others giving him a double take when they realized who he was. His mother stood upright on Broadway, just beyond the freeway overpass, and the sunlight spread over her body, and she was angelic there, even with the blood down the front of her shirt, even with her face bloated and wrong. He heard horns blaring to his left; cars were trapped at the light at 5th because of the throngs of people streaming by.

"Don't," she said, and she waved Moss toward her. "We can't go that way."

He glared at her, then turned to look back toward 4th. He saw people scattering about in either direction. "I don't get it!" Moss yelled. "Mama, come on, we gotta go!"

Another person collided with him, and they wrapped their arms around his body and nearly took him down. He yelped in shock, but they pulled themselves away, and it was Njemile, fear in her eyes. "Moss!" Njemile shouted. "Oh my god, I thought they had already nabbed you!"

Wanda strode up to them quickly, and Njemile cried out when she saw her. "You two, we need to go *now*," she said. "It's a trap."

"What?" Moss said. "How?"

"Kettling," Wanda said, and she grabbed them in each of her hands. "It's an old technique, and they're trapping us in."

"But *why*?" Njemile asked. "They just told us to leave!"

"That's the trick," Wanda said in between breaths. "They give us the option to leave, then trap us so that they can later use it against us and portray us as unreasonable. Irrational." She bent over, her hands on her knees, her breath rasping out of her throat. "It's so we look like an unruly mob."

"What is wrong with them?" Moss screamed. He let out a guttural shriek, rage pulsing in his face. "Why do they keep doing this to us?"

"Moss, baby," said his mother, and she rose as more people streamed by. "I would love to give you a complete history of protesting in modern America, but we don't have time. Look!"

He followed her finger and saw the line of cops in black gear, their batons out, their shields up, as they completely blocked Broadway at 4th Street. Moss watched in dismay as someone tried to leave and was promptly dropped by multiple baton swings. What if it was someone else he knew?

"Ms. Jeffries, what do we do?" Njemile said, and her voice cracked on the last word. "I'm *scared*. I can't get arrested. Do you know what they do to girls like me? Do you know where they put us?" Moss saw her face crinkle up in terror. "Please, please, *help me*."

"I got you, honey," said Wanda. She looked behind her, and they all heard the roar of the police chopper, the horns blaring, the crowd screaming. He could see her desperation; she was trying to find a way out. Moss glanced toward the south and saw more people trying to claw their way out of the line of cops that stretched across the street. Then he looked to their left.

"I have another terrible idea," said Moss.

"We don't have many options," said Wanda. "So say it, baby."

He pointed over his mother's left shoulder. "Let's go there."

His mother looked and he watched her face light up with humor. "Oh, Moss, you're too much," she said.

"I don't get it!" Njemile said. "The *freeway*?" But then realization dawned on her face, too. "Oh my god, we should go through the Alameda tunnel!"

From where they stood, a dual set of roads branched off to the east. One rose to join the freeway, but the other—that was where Moss wanted to go. It looped underneath the on-ramp and headed south toward Alameda. The tunnel dropped underneath the bay for nearly a quarter mile before it rose onto the island.

Moss nodded at Njemile as he processed the plan. "They're not going to expect anyone to go that way," he explained. "And there's that weird elevated sidewalk thing along one side."

"It's separated," Wanda said, understanding spreading rapidly across her features.

"Meaning that the northbound cars can't see us," said Moss. "If we're quick enough, no one will even know we've left!"

"You're brilliant," his mother said, and she kissed him on the forehead. "Njemile, do you want to lead people? I'll stay here and direct people to follow you."

"I'm staying, too," said Moss.

"No, you have to go," said Wanda. "I can risk getting arrested. You can't."

He shook his head. "Mama, this is my thing! I want to help, at least as long as I can."

Sirens blared from behind him, and they all turned to see three police vans, white and plain, roll up on 4th. The doors slid open, and more cops in black riot gear poured out.

"Fuck," Moss said, then clamped his hand over his mouth.

"I'll let that slide just this once," his mother said. "Go, Njemile, go!"

Njemile embraced Moss in a quick hug and said, "Good luck," then yelled out, "Follow me!"

"Do not go down to 4th!" Wanda shouted. "Go this way, now!"

She waved her arms in the direction of the Alameda Tube, and the reaction was instant. The folks who had been milling about in confusion now sprinted toward the entryway. Moss stood next to his mother, jumping up and down, screaming at people as loud as he could, pointing them toward the group that was now pouring off Broadway.

All the panic he felt began to wash away. A couple rushed by him, thanking him for what he'd done, then bolted toward the ramp. Bits and Esperanza sprinted up to them, their hands locked together. There was a large crack running down the right lens of Esperanza's glasses. "Moss, what do we *do*?" she screamed. "Please, I don't know what to do."

The thought that crept into his mind felt so bitter. *Maybe now she understands it.* He wiped his face with both hands, pushing through the fright, then pointed to the escape route he'd come up with. "You two," he said, "grab as many people as you can and lead them to Alameda." He reached over and put a hand on each of them. "Do *not* go anywhere south of here. We're trapped that way."

"Thank you," said Bits, then tugged on Esperanza. "Let's go."

"I'm sorry," she said, but she was gone, sprinting as fast as she could alongside Bits. What was she apologizing for? He didn't even know.

Less than a minute later, Moss was overjoyed to see Kaisha pushing Reg toward them. Tears ran down his cheeks as he hugged Reg. "How did you get out?" Moss asked.

Kaisha was shaking her head. "I don't honestly know," she said, and she was out of breath and covered in sweat. "It's a nightmare back there."

"Someone's dead."

Reg said it with no amusement or horror. It was plain, a statement of fact. His face was still, a mask of shock.

"What do you mean?" Wanda asked. "Who died?"

"We don't know," said Kaisha. "But they started shooting these canister things into the crowd. Tear gas, I think."

"You *serious*?" Moss said.

She nodded. "Some girl took one point-blank in the face. White girl. She went down and there's no way she survived it."

"Someone's dead," said Reg, his voice unchanged from before. "They killed someone right in front of us."

"Again," said Kaisha.

Moss stopped directing people toward the tunnel and looked to his mother. "Mama, what are we gonna do?"

"Do you want to leave, Moss?" She did not look upon him with guilt or an accusation in her eyes. "We can go right now."

"Did I fail everyone?" Moss asked. "Did I fail Javier?"

"Don't say that, man," said Reg, and now, his voice pitched up. "Look what you've *done*, Moss!"

"Caused a mess," he said, dejected.

"Moss, you helped organize a protest when most people wouldn't have done anything after I got hurt," Reg said. "You supported me even after you lost Javier. You still cared about me. So don't you dare say you failed us. You didn't fail *me*!"

"He's right, baby," said Wanda. "And we gotta decide soon what we're gonna do. The police line up there is moving towards us."

She gestured back toward the police station, and he saw that she was right. The thousands of people had been weeded down to a few hundred, many of whom were still trying to find a way out. *Does this make me a coward?* Moss wondered. *Would Javier be disappointed in me?*

"I've done what I can," Moss said. "Let's go."

The four of them jogged off Broadway toward the ramp, and Moss let relief take over. He had survived a long night; he had made a powerful statement; he had done everything he could. Maybe he could try something else if nothing came of this. His mother locked her fingers in his as they curved around toward the entrance to the Alameda Tube, and Moss gave her a look of appreciation. *We'll have to try again.*

They ran, then. His lungs hurt, burned with the fire of exertion, and his shins still throbbed from the bruises that Daley had given him, but it folded into the fabric of pain that Moss felt all over his body. He ran because he knew he had to stay alive.

He heard the screeching tires first, then the loud, bleating siren next. *What now?* Moss thought, and the blur of white rushed into his field of vision. His brain could not interpret what was happening at first. It solidified: a white police van. A door opened, and they poured out. He just saw a blackness heading toward him, and Kaisha screamed out in terror.

He saw the baton in the air. Moss ducked out of the way, but tripped over something on the ground. It was Reg, sprawled on the asphalt, his chair overturned a few feet away. He watched as Reg tried to lift himself up, but there was an officer's knee in Reg's back keeping him down and the sound of a crack against the ground. Moss reached out to his friend and a shiny boot slammed his own fingers down, too, and the rage and terror finally overwhelmed him. Stars of pain filled his eyes, and there was his mother, crawling toward them, her eye swollen shut, and she stopped, her face just inches from his. "Don't fight it, baby," she said, and she put her arms behind her back. "Please don't fight it." Her words were barely above a whisper, and the men shouted at them. Moss was pressed to the street with a foot in his back, and he couldn't breathe. "Please don't take him from me," said Wanda as loud as she could. "I'll cooperate, I promise."

"Stop resisting!" The voice was in his ear, but Moss couldn't even move if he'd wanted to. His body ached. His brain was so tired. They forced his arms back, looped a zip tie around his wrists and pulled it tight. Moss yelped when it dug into his arms, but the pain in his fingers quickly drowned it out.

"I love you, baby," said Wanda, and she was pulled upright and out of his line of sight. He couldn't see Reg or Kaisha, but he could hear them crying. Where was Esperanza? Bits? Njemile? Had they made it? Were they free?

A sob filled his throat and spilled out of his mouth. Moss had failed his friends. He had failed them all.

37

The van ride was too quiet. Moss wanted to say so many things—to tell his mother that he loved her, to express his admiration for Kaisha and Reg, or even to beg the silent cop who sat in the back with them to loosen the zip ties at his wrists—but he knew not to. His mother had instilled that in Moss a long time ago. "Never say a word if you're arrested," she had said. "Just stay quiet and ask for your phone call. Do everything you are asked, but don't say *anything*."

He leaned into his mother. Who was he supposed to make a phone call to *now*? He supposed that it didn't matter. His mother would figure it out. But what if they got separated? What should he do then?

Moss still kept quiet. He would figure that out when the time came. His mother's breathing—in and out, in and out—was a soothing rhythm, and it helped to distract him from the mounting dread inside of him. He locked eyes with Kaisha. She smiled, a quick burst, and it warmed him. But the coldness of his fear quickly returned. His life was over, wasn't it? This was it. He'd be thrown in jail. He'd be the department's example, and there was nothing he could do about it. It felt so final, so definitive, and Moss could not fathom hope.

The van made a sharp turn to the right and stopped. The officer in the back—his face blocked by the opaque black visor on his helmet—rose, and when he spoke, his voice was clear and sharp. "Don't make any sudden moves," he announced to the four other occupants. "Unless you don't want to get out of this van walking."

Moss wanted this to be over. He briefly considered disobeying the man. The idea seemed so attractive then: a momentary rebellion, a flash of anger and revenge, and then Moss would probably be dead. It felt like a sensible alternative to prison, to living like this for the rest of his life. Then the van slowed down for a second, and the cop leaned forward, and Moss saw his chance. Saw how he could throw himself at him. But the urge passed just as soon as it had arrived.

Moss was just too tired. Even for that.

He watched Kaisha and Reg sit as still as they could, saw the sweat on Reg's bloody face, felt his own pulse pounding in his head. Moss needed water, was sure the others did, too. He wanted to sleep. But he kept his eyes open and tried to stay as alert as he could.

The cop pointed his rifle toward the back of the van. When the doors burst open, light flooded in, and his friends winced. Tears jumped to his eyes, and Moss wished he could wipe them away. A body was tossed inside the van and thudded against the floor. A black woman, her face smeared with blood. She squirmed a few times, then rolled onto her back and gasped for air.

"Do you need medical attention?" Wanda asked, unmoving.

"Shut up and stay where you are," barked the cop at his mother. He reached down and grabbed the hood of the woman's sweater and dragged her backward, then propped her up next to Moss. He could hear the gurgling, the desperate attempts to breathe, but he didn't dare move his head to see if she was okay.

Three more people were shoved inside, and he heard someone gasp. "Moss?" It was Esperanza, but he couldn't look, wouldn't look at her.

He heard her scramble over and she loomed into his sight. "Are you okay?"

The cop's reaction was robotic. His foot shot out and he put the sole of his boot on Esperanza's right shoulder and pushed as hard as he could. She slammed into the side of the van, and Moss heard the air knocked out of her. He looked up. Her glasses had fallen off her face and lay broken on the floor of the van. There was a sniffle. Kaisha was crying. So was Reg.

It's over, Moss thought. *It's all over.*

The door slammed shut and Esperanza regained her breath. "I'm so sorry," she said.

"Don't talk," Moss's mother said, even and quiet. "Not a word, Esperanza."

"I'm sorry I never understood . . . until now," she said, and that got Moss to turn his head slightly, and he looked straight at her, saw the rawness and terror in her eyes, and he inclined his head. It was his way of saying: *Now you know.*

He watched her gasp for breath, watched her lean her head back, desperate for air, watched her cry openly. This was what it took. This was the line she had to cross. He didn't know if it was enough.

38

Maybe the ride was short, or maybe he was in so much pain that he couldn't remember it; Moss wasn't sure. It seemed like a few seconds passed before light filled the van and the cop in the back pushed each of them out, grasping them by their clothing to direct them toward the exit. Moss blinked to adjust his eyes; he was next to a tall gray building, just beyond a chain-link fence with razor wire curled around the top. There were more vans with OPD emblazoned on the side and a couple of cruisers. He saw people being unloaded from a van just like the one he'd been in, but didn't recognize any of them.

He walked forward, stumbled. His feet were on fire, his lower back was a mess of knotted muscles and tendons, his fingers throbbed. He said nothing about it; he just trudged on, toward the door that was held open for the line of the arrested. He walked up a ramp to the entryway, then passed down a long hallway of doors and windows into offices. As he moved farther along, he realized he could still hear the chaos: Pops. Bangs. Shouts. The blaring alarms, the echoing of the chopper off the buildings. Wherever they'd been taken, it couldn't have been far from the location of the protest.

The same thought repeated in his head: *My life is over.*

They were herded to a large room with a high ceiling, and Moss was taken aback by how full it was. Officers buzzed from one desk to another, some helping with the intake of prisoners. He watched a woman roll someone's fingers in a pad of ink, then turn them from side to side on a form of sorts.

Enrique was a few feet in front of him, clutching his left arm, his face drooping and tired. He was the only person there without cuffs on, and when Moss saw the unnatural angle at which his arm bent, he understood why. More protestors lined the walls, their hands zip-tied behind them, many of them bleeding or bruised. He saw another Latino kid, one who couldn't have been much older than himself, hunched over on a bench, blood on his jeans. Martin was next to him, seemingly uninjured, his head held high, defiance and ire on his face. Moss didn't see Rawiya, and he hoped that meant her getaway was successful. Njemile and Bits were nowhere to be found; had they escaped the cops and made it to Alameda? What about Esperanza? Where had she been taken?

Someone pushed Moss to the right and he turned, hoping to see his mother behind him, but she was taken to the other side of the room. Their eyes met for a moment, and she looked broken. Incomplete. He couldn't stop the tears that came then as the fear swept over his whole body. He started to shake as his eyes burned, his head pulsed, his heart broke. "Please don't separate us," he said, and he knew he wasn't supposed to talk, but he couldn't bear the thought of being away from her.

A cop came up to him. "Sit here," she said, gesturing to an open spot on a plain brown bench against the wall. On one side was a short Vietnamese woman, her hair strung over her face, dejection in her eyes. He recognized the man on the other side, but was too tired to feel any surprise. The paramedic whom Moss had seen . . . how long ago had that been? Why did it feel like an entire lifetime had passed in the past few weeks? He remembered the cold cement of the BART station, the hand grazing his, and he struggled to recall his name.

"Diego?" Moss said as he approached.

Diego looked up and smiled, then laughed. "Well, look who it is," he said, keeping his voice low so as not to draw attention to their conversation. "I'd say it's good to see you, but I think we'd both prefer not to be here."

Moss eased himself down onto the bench. "Why are you here?"

"Heard about you on the radio on my rounds this morning," he said. "Before this nightmare happened. Got off around seven thirty A.M., thought I'd swing by to give my support."

Moss sniffled. "Sorry it turned out so bad. You musta got there just as everything went to hell."

"Not your fault," said Diego. "And I think you did a fine thing with this."

"Really?" Heat rushed to his face. "Well . . . thanks, I guess." He looked at Diego's face, saw the blood above his right eyebrow. "How'd you get hurt?"

"Trying to help a woman who got shot," said Diego, and his head dropped down. "She took a tear-gas canister to her face after she tried to stop one of the cops from wailin' on some poor kid. I was showing my identification to another cop when someone tackled me from behind. Claimed I had a gun."

Moss didn't say anything at first. What *could* he say to that? Diego was a paramedic. His whole purpose was to help people, and even *that* had been used against him by the police. "I'm sorry," said Moss. "You know, because it happened to you."

Diego didn't respond for a few moments either. "It was worth it," he said, then fixed Moss with a stare. "I'd do it all over again."

Moss looked away. It overwhelmed him, and he couldn't look into the man's face while his own body was overrun with appreciation and shame. He felt Diego nudge him.

"You come in with anyone?"

Moss nodded. "My mama," he replied, then gestured with his head. "She's the woman over there, with the short hair and . . ." More words dead in his throat. He heard Diego gasp. He must have figured out which woman was his mother.

"She needs medical attention," he said, first to Moss, then with his voice raised. "Hey! That woman over there . . . I'm a paramedic. Let me look at her."

None of the cops in the station looked in their direction, but many of the protestors glanced over at Moss's mother. Diego leaned forward and stood up, his hands still zip-tied behind his back. "I'm serious," he said, his deep voice louder than anything else in the station. "Please let me look at her!"

The reaction was swift this time, and Moss's heart dropped. A tall and lanky man strode over to Diego, placed his hand on Diego's chest, and shoved him—a direct motion, one that was so quick that it stunned Moss how fast the cop's arm had darted out. Diego slammed into the wall and slumped down, the air rushing out of him just as it had from Esperanza minutes before.

"Shut *up*," the cop said, his face now inches from Diego's. When he spoke up, he addressed the entire room. "That goes for all of you! Unless you want more charges tacked on, I don't want any more interruptions."

Someone sobbed. Diego gasped for air, and Moss saw a rage settle within him, a fury in his features that sent a chill down Moss. Diego said nothing. He just kept his eyes locked on the white man who had shoved him.

In another context, in another world, it might have been entertaining for Moss to witness this. But the weight of the night pulled on Moss's body. He found himself leaning to the side, into Diego's shoulder, and he promptly fell asleep.

Moss's eyes darted open, the light too bright and painful, and his mother was there, her face not as swollen as before. He was shaking. "Moss, wake up," Wanda said. "They're letting us go."

It didn't register at first. He looked at his mother's face, so calm and serene, then around her. He was still at the station. Someone stood to his mother's right. Tall, brown, a thick mustache. Diego was gone, and the bench was empty. "Come on, son," the man said. "Can you stand up? I'd like to get those cuffs off you."

He sucked in air, blinked more, then pushed against the wall, trying to get his legs to work. They were tight and heavy, unwilling to cooperate. The cop put a hand under Moss's arm and lifted, and he stood. His head spun for a second or two, he heard a snipping behind him, and then his hands were free. He brought them in front of him; they were caked with dried blood from the zip tie that had cut into his wrists.

"You want to visit the bathroom first, Mr. Jeffries?" The cop gestured behind him. "You can clean up if you want."

Moss shook his head. "Just wanna go home," he said. "Sir," he added, instinct getting the best of him.

"Let's go, honey," his mother said, wrapping her arm in his.

The cop reached out and grabbed Moss's other arm. "Before you go, I just wanted to tell you . . ." He paused. Moss watched his face, saw his lip tremble. The man let go of Moss, brought a hand to his mouth and covered it for a moment. "I'm really sorry this happened to you."

I have to be dreaming, Moss thought. *I'm still asleep, aren't I?*

"It should not have happened," the man continued, his eyes red and watery. "I'm sorry about what was done to you."

"Did you do anything to stop it?" The words fell out of Moss's mouth before he could even think about what they meant. The cop's expression changed, morphed into shock and confusion. He had no response, and his mouth dropped open. It stayed that way as Wanda pulled on Moss's arm and led him away.

"What time is it?" Moss asked, rubbing the sleep out of his eyes.

"After one," she said. "In the afternoon."

He balked at her. "How long have I been asleep?"

"Later, baby," she said, moving them along. "Let's just get out of here."

They didn't make it to the exit. A woman stepped in front of them, just feet from the door that would lead them to freedom. It was *Johanna,* the communications manager from that morning. Moss fought an urge to shove her out of the way, but his body ached too much. He thought of his bed, of the familiarity of their couch and the scratched coffee table, and he wanted to be nowhere else.

"I wanted to invite you to a special press conference tomorrow," she said, and that smile, that goddamn smile, crept across her face. "City Hall. Nine A.M. Can you make it?"

"What for?" Wanda asked, her own voice sluggish.

"For an apology."

Now it was Moss's turn for shock. "I'm sorry, an apology for *what*?"

Johanna pursed her lips. "I can't say much now, but things did not go as well as we would have liked them to this morning," she said. "But I can tell you this: Your little protest? It worked."

"You already told me that," Moss said. "Last time. Remember? And look what happened with that."

His mother squeezed his arm tightly. "You're not joking," she said to Johanna.

"No, I am not," said Johanna. "If you'd like, meet us at the south entrance to City Hall at eight thirty A.M. We'll introduce you to the mayor and the chief of police, then give you an idea of the schedule for the press conference. That all right with you two?"

They nodded, but neither could find any words. The smirk came back one last time. She left them standing in the hallway, alone.

"Did that just happen?" Moss asked.

"Yep," his mother said.

He scraped at his face, felt the soreness where his cheek had slammed against the asphalt. It was real. This moment was *real*.

"Mama, I don't think I can deal with another thing happening right now. Can we go?"

"You bet your ass we're goin'," Wanda said, and Moss willingly let his mother drag him out of the station. The light was so bright, and it seemed wrong. In the wrong place in the sky. He blinked, tears in his eyes, and he rubbed at them.

Martin rushed up to them. "Hurry," he said, taking them both by the arm. "I'm parked illegally, and the press is around the corner."

Moss couldn't tell where they were at first, but then saw the Tribune building in the distance, heard the traffic from the 880 freeway. They were still downtown. Moss didn't want to waste anymore time, though. They piled into Martin's Toyota and then said nothing as he drove them home. Moss appreciated the silence, mostly because his head was full. His heart was weary. He didn't have the words for how he felt. The numbness throbbed in his body, and he knew he'd be aching the next day when he woke up.

The next day.

There was another day ahead. Just hours earlier, he had convinced himself that he was bound for prison. How was he on his way home now? Moss looked out the window, watched as they crossed over the highway, saw downtown Oakland change into West Oakland, a neighborhood that still persisted in the face of too many changes to recount.

Martin turned down Peralta, and the neighborhood felt familiar, but in a terribly distant sense, as if Moss had been away for years and was only just now returning. He stared out the window as the warehouses and lofts passed by. He saw kids kicking a soccer ball around in one yard. Saw people waiting at a bus stop. Knew that their days had continued as normal. Did they even know what had happened downtown? Did they even care?

He looked forward, then out the window again, and then he saw it.

"Stop!" He shouted it louder than he had intended, and he stuck his head out of the window, gaping back at it. "Stop the car!"

Martin slammed on the brakes and everyone jerked forward. "What is it?" Wanda said, and she turned around and reached out for Moss, but he was already getting out of the car.

His legs ached, a fierce burning sitting on top of a dull soreness. He ignored it, and he hobbled down the sidewalk, right up to the brick wall, and he ran his hands along it, then backed up, into the street, and a car was honking at him but he couldn't stop. He couldn't leave.

Javier's face looked down on him. He was painted on the side of a warehouse in grand colors, his skin that same golden brown, that black beanie propped to the side, his mouth open in a wide grin as if he was in the midst of a laugh. He was framed with a white border, like a scene in a comic book. A crown of roses circled his head, angelic and pure, and there was a banner curled below his neck, sitting across his chest.

JUSTICE FOR JAVIER, it said, in that same lettering from all the comics he'd grown up reading. Then, down in the corner, in black, a name in delicate script: *Carlos.*

Javier was immortalized, transformed into a something both spiritual and visceral, a reminder of this city's violence, a reminder of this city's compassion. Moss walked forward, and his mama and Martin were there, and Martin had his hands behind his head, tears streaming down his face, and Moss realized he had never seen him cry, not even after Morris died.

Moss touched the wall again, just at the point where Javier's blue flannel opened, and he remembered how soft Javier's skin had been, how he smelled, how his lips felt across his own. The wall was rough. Bumpy. Static.

Moss didn't say a word. He got back in the car, his throat constricted with the threat of tears. Martin and Wanda followed behind him, and when she got back into the passenger seat, she reached back and held his hand the entire way home.

They drove past Njemile's place, the driveway empty, and Moss hoped it was a sign that her mothers had found her in Alameda. He didn't want to assume the worst, but then they were on 12th, the market was there on the left, and then Martin turned on Chester, and Moss couldn't stop himself. He turned around and stared at the market, and he had never willed harder for his father to appear than that moment.

But Morris didn't. He was gone. They were both gone. Forever.

"Oh, *damn*," Martin said.

Moss faced forward again and wanted to expire at the sight that was before the car. He couldn't even count the news vans; they lined both sides of the street. A reporter stood directly in front of the gate in the chain-link fence, speaking rapidly into his microphone as the cameraperson panned around him. Martin hit the brakes without another word, put the car in reverse, and backed up to the corner.

"Go," he said. "Into Dawit's. *Now*."

Moss's body wouldn't move at first, but when he saw the reporters scurrying in his direction, his instinct kicked in. He unbuckled, the seat belt slamming into the side of the car, and then he bolted out the door. He made straight for Dawit's, heard his mother panting behind him, and then got to the steps and stopped.

"Go in!" Wanda shouted. "Is he there?"

Dawit stepped into the doorway, and his eyes went wide as he saw the rush of reporters. He pulled Wanda inside, then gestured for Moss to follow. "Come on!" Dawit yelled. "Get inside."

Moss couldn't make the step. He looked down at the concrete, its chipped edges, and he didn't think about it. Didn't plan it. He crouched over, all the muscles in his legs screaming at him, and he sat on the steps in front of Dawit's market. He reached down, the steps just as cool as they always were. Moss ran his fingers over them, feeling each nook, knowing them all by heart. It was exactly the same as it had been when this whole nightmare started. It remained unchanged, waiting for him to come back.

The reporters slowed as they approached. He recognized a couple of them, certain one of them had postulated on-air that Javier was an illegal and therefore deserving of suspicion. That man started to ask Moss about something, but Moss had already tuned him out. The questions kept coming, the cameras flashed, and Moss said nothing. He did not move from that spot. He just kept touching the step, thinking of his father, remembering the times Morris had brought his son Popsicles from Dawit's, remembering the scent of the aftershave Morris used, remembering the wrinkles in the corner of his father's eyes when he smiled. Moss cycled through the Rolodex. Maybe the memories weren't new, but they made him feel good.

After twenty minutes of silence, the last reporter left. Moss smiled.

39

Their living room became a headquarters.

People—friends, family—started filing in, one at a time, as they found freedom. Bits and Njemile were first; they'd had to hail a cab and have Ekemeni pay for it once they got to Njemile's house. Bits's mother, Dominique, was there, and it was the first time Moss had met her. She was big, warm, and her hair was short like his own mother's. She hugged Moss, told him she was sorry, that she was proud that her child had made such a good friend.

Shamika was next, and she burst into tears when she saw her best friend, saw the end result of the damage they'd done to Wanda's face and soul. Stitches lined one of his mother's cheeks, and a bandage was wrapped around her head. Shamika and Wanda had hugged a good long while before they broke apart and darted into the kitchen. The sound of their conversation filled Moss with a familiarity; he remembered suddenly how much time Shamika had spent at the house after his father had died.

Esperanza limped inside nearly an hour later, and the conversation stilled immediately. Moss bolted off the couch, but then stood there, staring at her. She had an arm crossed over her chest, and she wouldn't make eye contact with him. He made his way to her slowly, reached out and put a hand on the arm she held loose at her side.

"Are you okay?" It wasn't small talk. Moss couldn't tell and he wanted to know.

"Not really," she said. Her eyes shot up to him. They were red. He pulled her into him, and when she began to cry, he could tell she'd kept herself together until this moment.

He held her for practically a full minute while she sobbed. "I didn't believe it," she finally said. "I'm so sorry, Moss."

"I'm sorry you had to find out the hard way," he said. He pulled away from her. "Do you need anything? Are you hurt?"

Esperanza shook her head. "No," she said, then made her way to the couch and plopped down on it. "I lied. I don't even know what hurts anymore."

"All of it," Moss said, nodding. "Let's just say all of it."

She smiled, and he realized it felt good to earn that reaction. *It's a start,* Moss thought.

Others followed. Reg and Kaisha arrived not long after Esperanza, and Reg brought his parents, Lawrence and Judy, and his older brother, Reginald. Judy rushed to Moss, startling him. "I never got to thank you," she said, "for what you did for my son. You risked your life for him. Thank you. Thank you so much."

Lawrence Phillips shook his hand, his eyes red and watery. "We won't forget."

Rawiya was the last to make it. She did not bring her parents, and a pang of sadness hit Moss as he watched his friend walk through the door, her shoulders dropped down, bandages and stitches criss-crossing her face. She looked worse than anyone else, and when she said hello, her voice croaked out of her throat. "Sorry if I sound like I'm going through puberty," she said. "A boot to the throat will do that."

Moss rushed to her side, guided her to the couch. "What happened? Are you okay?"

"I mean . . . relatively?" Rawiya said, and she tried to grin, then descended into groaning. "No one tell jokes, it hurts too much to laugh."

Wanda had come into the room at the sound of Moss's alarm, and she gasped loudly. Rawiya raised a hand in greeting, her eyes shut as she winced in pain.

"You got an ice pack?" Rawiya asked. "Or how about four thousand painkillers? That would be great." She opened her eyes and groaned again. "Never mind, it's clear they got you, too."

"Stay there, honey," said Wanda as she headed toward the kitchen. "I got something for you."

"So how is everyone?" Rawiya asked, her head back, eyes up to the ceiling. "Please tell me no one got it worse than me."

Reg cleared his throat. "Uh, well . . . someone died."

Rawiya's head shot up, and she immediately clutched a hand to it and grimaced. "Oh god, who?" She looked around the room, and Moss watched her do a silent tally. "Wait a second . . ." Her voice dropped in volume.

"No, not any of us," said Moss. "Some other girl."

"Y'all scared me," said Rawiya. The frantic giggles were quick, and she leaned her head back again. "So they killed someone new. Why am I not surprised?"

"It's like they can't avoid it," said Kaisha. "We were literally there to protest against them using deadly force, so they responded with . . . deadly force. Incredible."

"You had one job," Reg joked, but it seemed the whole group was out of laughter.

"But we're all free," said Moss. "And in relatively one piece, so that's surprising. Did anyone get charged with anything?"

They shook their heads. No one said anything.

"I guess that's okay," said Moss. "Not actually what I expected." He paused. "And the protest may have even worked."

"What?" Esperanza said. "What do you mean?"

"That one lady stopped us before we left," he explained. "Told me and Mama that they're holding a press conference for us."

"Really?" Esperanza's face lit up with a smile. "Moss, that's great!"

"Is it?" Moss said. "Like, I don't even know what it's for. What if they're gonna sell us out again? Throw us under the bus?"

"That's . . . fair," said Esperanza. "I am going to try and learn my lesson and just *believe* you this time."

He smiled at her. "Y'all are welcome to come if you want," Moss said to the group. "Anyone who can, that is."

There was nervous laughter. "I'll have to ask my parents," said Kaisha.

Rawiya made a sickening noise. "My parents," she said. "They're gonna flip out." She smiled, clearly in pain, then said to Moss, "You realize how punk rock I look, right?"

"You should go to it," Judy said to Reg. Then, to Moss: "We'll be there. To support *you* this time."

His mother returned with bag of frozen peas for Rawiya. "Sorry, that took longer than I wanted to," she said. "Kept getting distracted."

Esperanza stood up then, swayed a bit, and used the edge of the couch to keep herself steady. "I think I need to get home," she said. "I have to talk to my parents about all of this."

"Yikes," said Rawiya, the peas planted on her face. "I mean, I am not looking forward to talking to my parents, but I don't envy you."

"I don't think I'll make it tomorrow, Moss," Esperanza said. "I want to real bad. To support you."

"It's okay," he said, standing to help her to the door. "It's last-minute. Don't worry about it."

"No, that's not it," she said. "I doubt my parents will let me. Not after all . . . all this."

He frowned. "Yeah, they're not going to take this well."

"But I need to talk to them about other things, too," Esperanza said. "And it won't be fun. It might be a while before I see you again."

"Take care of yourself first," he said. "I'm sure we're gonna have to have a difficult conversation someday, too. But . . . get better. Deal with those parents of yours."

"Thanks," she said, and this time, she went in for the hug. "I love you, Moss. I really do."

He squeezed her in the hug, then told her the truth. "I love you, too. Even if you piss me off sometimes."

"Don't the best kind of friends do that?" She smiled again, but it was weak. Her eyes drooped.

"Hey," said Moss to the group. "Can someone take her home?"

Esperanza tried to protest, but Martin leapt up to volunteer. The two of them left the Jeffries house with a wave. Moss stared at the closed door for a few seconds. *There's a cost for everything, isn't there?* Maybe his friendship with Esperanza would remain rocky, or maybe this was their chance to rebuild. To heal. To understand.

The room was already back in the swing of multiple conversations. He saw an opportunity as the rest of the living room was consumed with chatter. He made his way to his room, quietly and with purpose. He flicked on the light and closed the door behind him, careful not to let it slam. He needed a moment alone.

His room had remained unchanged, too. Javier's bag was on the bed, its contents spilled across the top sheet. An iPod. White headphones. Bike gloves, old and splitting. A copy of *Overwatch*. The Moleskine notebook. They were all Moss had left of Javier.

No. That was wrong. He lay down on his bed, and he made a new Rolodex within himself, just for Javier. *The way you kissed my jaw. The way sweat ran down your chest. The feel of the muscles in your arm, the scent of your breath, the blackness of your hair, the curled smile.*

Moss had a lot of memories to save.

Moss adjusted his tie. He hated wearing shirts with buttoned collars; his neck was so big that they all fit too tightly. His wrists throbbed as he pulled at the tie, so he dropped his hands to his side. Ms. Perez smiled at him.

"Stop fidgeting, baby," his mother said. "It's making me nervous."

He smoothed down the front of his shirt, but it felt too small. The buttons over his stomach bulged. If he had had more time, Moss would have begged his mother to take him to get a larger shirt.

He looked up at his mother. Her eye was bruised, yellow and purple, still swollen, though not as grotesquely as yesterday. He glanced at his wrists, red and scabbing; his back was stiff; his legs were sore; his fingers were swollen, but not broken. Moss hurt all over.

Yet the exhaustion in his head overpowered it all. He shifted from one foot to the other again; he just wanted to get this over with. Eugenia had met them at a coffee shop that morning so they could talk about the press conference. They had invited her, too, given her a call the afternoon before. But once she saw them, saw the state of their bodies, Eugenia couldn't talk of anything else. No one knew what the press conference would be about, so how could they prepare for a surprise? So they had sat there, nursing their drinks, ignorant and nervous. Moss kept looking to the door, a fear swimming over him, a certainty that at any moment, the cops would burst into the shop and take him away to finish the job.

So he asked to get out on the street where he didn't feel so cramped. They were next to the south entrance to City Hall, as they'd been instructed. The mayor and the chief of police had not shown up yet, and neither had Johanna. Moss pulled out his old phone, which had a new screen thanks to a friend of Martin's but still wouldn't catch a signal.

It was 8:54 A.M.

"She'll show up," Wanda said. "The news vans are already here, and they have a little podium set up out front."

"I know," said Moss. "I'm just nervous, that's all."

"I don't blame you."

"This can't actually be over, can it?" He tugged on the bottom of his shirt once more, trying to pull it past his belt. "It feels too easy."

"It's never going to be over, Moss," his mother said. Eugenia turned away after that, trying to pretend like no one had seen her start to cry.

Moss remembered the fear he'd had that day that he would never see Eugenia again. He reached over to her. "Will you come over today? For dinner."

"Me?" She seemed surprised to be asked the question, and she wiped at her face. "De veras?"

Wanda nodded. "We don't have to disappear from each other's lives," she said. "Please, if you're willing . . . we would love to have you over."

"I would like that," she said, quiet and small. "I would like that a lot."

Johanna arrived a couple of minutes later, her heels clicking on the sidewalk, her hands raised in a defensive position. "I'm sorry, I'm sorry," she blurted out. "It's just been so busy this morning, I couldn't get away early enough."

"So what now?" Moss asked. "Is the press conference still happening?"

"Absolutely!" Johanna said, maybe a little too excited. *She's overcompensating*, Moss thought. "Unfortunately, you won't get to meet with the mayor and the chief of police until afterwards. They've both been in meetings since six this morning. Lots of policy decisions being made."

Moss sighed, but said nothing.

"Cheer up!" Johanna said. "I think you'll be quite pleased with what you'll hear today."

"We'll see," his mother said. "You haven't been the bearer of good news so far."

Johanna coughed and pursed her lips. Moss could see the frustration forming before him, and it was so annoying. *How does she feel more inconvenienced than me?* He let the moment pass, and the three of them followed Johanna as she led them toward the front of City Hall.

The cameras started flashing immediately once they stepped onto the lawn of Frank H. Ogawa Plaza. It was bright that morning and the sun warmed Moss. He glanced out at the large crowd that had formed. At first, he saw mostly photographers and reporters, and then there was Enrique, his arm in a sling, his other holding his skateboard up in the air. Now that he had a chance to take in the crowd, he could tell that the reporters were well outnumbered by everyone else. Moss nodded at Enrique, then gaped at who stood nearby.

Njemile, whose mothers, tall and proud, stood behind her. She held hands with Shawna, who had a hand on Reg's wheelchair; Judy and Lawrence were behind him. Kaisha flashed a peace sign at him, and Rawiya jumped up and down, waving. Her parents were there, and he nearly broke into laughter at how excited Hishaam seemed, his hand waving back and forth frantically. There was Bits, too, a grin plastered on their face. *How?* Moss thought.

"I figured you could use some support," Wanda said as they ascended the steps at City Hall. "I made a few calls to their parents."

His heart swelled with affection and admiration. In a universe so cruel and unfair, so designed to torment him, he'd been given a mother who cared for him, deeply and completely.

Given the circumstances, Moss felt lucky.

The mayor stood on the far side of the podium, alongside the chief of police. They were both much shorter than Moss expected. The mayor nodded at him, tight-lipped, but the chief of police stood still and silent, staring out at the crowd. *Figures,* Moss thought. But he wasn't there for them. *They* were here for *him*.

At least he hoped so.

Mayor Barry Trent stepped up to the podium, and he gripped both sides of it, hard enough that Moss could see the whites of his knuckles on his already pale skin. He'd seen the man on the news a few times, but it was only now that he felt like a real person, not just a figure or an idea. Moss didn't know much about him; he'd been reelected the previous year, and most of the adults in Moss's life hated him. Moss stared at him, and realized that the sweaty, nervous mayor looked so . . . harmless.

It was 9:02 A.M.

"Good morning, Oakland," Mayor Trent said. "Thank you for coming out this morning. The events that have unfolded over the last twenty-four hours in our city are disturbing and unacceptable. Oakland has a long and proud history of resistance and progressivism. These values were tarnished yesterday, and I am ashamed."

He breathed in deeply. "I am here this morning to announce that my office will be working intimately with the chief of police, Tom Berendht, to develop an effective and fair system to guarantee the right to peaceably assemble and the right to protest in Oakland. It is unfortunate that it took recent events to spur us into action."

There was a smattering of applause. A sound of clicking camera shutters. Moss looked over at his friends, saw Martin, Dawit, and Shamika there, too. They wore scowls, and it amused Moss.

"Mr. Jeffries."

Moss turned to Mayor Trent, who now stared directly at him, his eyes glassy, his face twisted with concern.

"I wanted to apologize personally for what happened to you. For how you were treated by this city." The mayor was not reading from any notes; he did not break eye contact with Moss. "You came to us in grief over the loss of your friend, and you were not listened to. You were treated with disrespect, with condescension, with violence. You did not deserve this. I am so sorry for that."

Moss couldn't help it. His eyes darted directly to Johanna, and it seemed like she'd never held her lips shut tighter. He nearly broke out in a round of laughter. He stayed quiet and controlled the urge.

The mayor stepped aside without another word or a glance at the other man who stood next to him. The chief of police stepped up to the microphone, and Moss thought he looked annoyed that he'd not been introduced. Berendht did not look in Moss's direction. His white cheeks were flushed, and he rubbed at his nose before he spoke. "Good morning," he said. "The Oakland Police Department would like to make a statement."

Moss braced himself. He was surprised by what the mayor had said; he had not expected an apology, certainly not one that felt real. But as he watched Berendht fidget at the podium, he was electric with anxiety.

The chief coughed into his left shoulder, then reached into a coat pocket and pulled out a white piece of paper folded in fourths. It crackled into the microphone as Berendht cleared his throat again. "The Oakland Police Department is committed to the safety and security of its residents."

"Bullshit!" The cry came from somewhere near the back of the crowd, and a rustling of voices passed toward the front. The chief of police looked up, but did not acknowledge the comment. His focus returned to the block of text on the page, too small for Moss to read from where he stood.

"I believe in the integrity and professionalism of our officers." Some of those in the gathered crowd groaned, while others shouted, incoherent, their words colliding with what others yelled. "In the execution of our duty, we try to treat each situation as unique and devise a plan that protects the safety of others and our own officers."

"Get to the point!" The exclamation evoked scattered applause.

Was that Martin? Moss wondered. He saw him and that red cap, and Martin's right hand was raised high, his middle finger a sign of defiance in a sea of anticipation.

Berendht pressed on. "Yesterday, in our attempt to best deal with the situation outside our administration building, a young woman, Hayley Simpson, was killed by one of our officers."

Hayley, Moss thought. *Oh god, it was* her? But the thought faded out of his mind as a rumble of voices passed through the gathered crowd. Moss's sadness fell to the background, dulled by a growing rage. *This can't be happening.*

"It was an unfortunate mistake," Berendht continued, "and the officer responsible will have to submit to our rigorous internal review, as well as possibly face criminal charges."

"Possibly?" That was Rawiya, and he saw her step forward as she pushed between two reporters. "What about Javier Perez?"

Her question set off a chain reaction, a chorus of voices shouting and screaming at Berendht, who seemed to get more and more uncomfortable, more rigid. He seemed like he was about to say something, but stopped. He looked so unsure.

"Are you telling me a *white girl* had to get killed for you to finally pay attention?" Wanda said, stern and certain. "*Now* someone will get held accountable?"

The chief answered none of their questions. He just looked back down to his wrinkled paper.

"The Oakland Police Department is also ceasing its pilot program at West Oakland High as of this morning. The metal detectors will be removed by the end of the week."

A roar spilled out of that crowd. Clapping, yelling, whoops of joy. Moss was stunned, his eyes taking in the jubilation in the crowd. *Oh my god,* he thought. *I did it.* But he couldn't form words, couldn't conceptualize this as a victory. It didn't *feel* like a victory. Yet Moss saw the excitement on his friend's faces, saw Shamika point at him and smile, felt his mother embrace him in a hug. It was real, wasn't it? This was *real*.

"We have also established a victims' fund," Berendht continued, "that will help offset the costs incurred by the actions of our officers. These funds will go towards Ms. Perez for funeral costs and to those injured at West Oakland High over the past month. We offer our apology to Ms. Shawna Meyers, to Reg Phillips, and to anyone else hurt."

"On a final note, the Oakland Police Department would like to extend a sincere apology to Morris Jeffries, Jr., for his treatment yesterday." Now, Berendht gazed toward Moss, his words seeming to be a sack of bricks in his throat. "We pledge to do better by our citizens, and we are sorry that you were harmed while trying to exercise your First Amendment rights."

He said all of that without any inflection, without any sincerity, without any meaning. Berendht folded the paper up meticulously, then tucked it back into his pocket.

Moss had no idea what the protocol was here. Was he supposed to thank this man? It was clear that someone else—probably Johanna—had written the statement and that he had been compelled to read it to defuse the situation. Why should Moss express gratitude for that?

Berendht had not moved. He was now glaring at Moss, his eyes searing into him. "As a sign of our support," he said, turning back to the crowd, "and as a gesture of goodwill towards the community, we have asked Lieutenant James Daley to make a statement."

This was a freight train. This was a wrecking ball. It was the force of the universe dropping on them. Moss's knees buckled, and then the smug, white face of James Daley was there, right next to the mayor and the chief.

Where had he come from? Why didn't Johanna tell him?

Moss's blood boiled, an instantaneous fury spreading so fully within him that tears leapt to his eyes. "*No,*" he said, to himself more than anything else, and then he shouted it. "NO!"

Wanda did not hold him back, too shocked herself. It was Eugenia, standing behind Moss, who grabbed the back of his shirt and pulled. He deflated in an instant, embarrassed that he had forgotten about her presence, but it didn't quell his rage. Why? Why was Daley here? What could he possibly do to help anyone?

He looked to Eugenia, saw an anger spread over her face that reminded him of his own. How was she ever going to deal with seeing her son's killer? But Eugenia's face was set in a determined rage.

"He's mine," she said, nearly under her breath, but Moss heard it, understood what this meant to her.

His mom looped her arm around Moss, and he took Eugenia's hand. The three of them stood still and faced James Daley, the man who had ruined all of their lives.

He had lost weight, Moss realized. Daley seemed so small next to that podium, as if the world had crushed him down in the last couple of weeks. There was no smile on that pasty face; his close-cropped haircut was gone, his hair now puffy and uneven.

"Good morning," James Daley said, and there was no humor in his voice, no arrogance, none of the fury Moss had heard the last time. "After the events of the last two weeks, I have decided to voluntarily surrender myself to the Oakland Police Department."

Eugenia started to sob. Moss didn't know what it was. Sadness? Relief? Rage? His own throat tightened.

"The city prosecutor has already spoken to Chief Berendht, and she will be making a statement later today. But I wanted to preempt that, to show that I am ready to take responsibility for what happened at West Oakland High."

How was he so calm? *This has to be a dream,* Moss thought. The crowd was too quiet. This wasn't happening, was it?

"I wanted to apologize to Ms. Perez. Your son is gone because of me. I am sorry for that."

Eugenia sobbed harder, collapsing into Moss's shoulder, and Moss wasn't certain he could stay upright much longer. There was so much pressure weighing down his arm, and he stole a glance at Javier's mother. There was no sadness on her face. *No*, he realized, *she wants to kill him*. The anger coursed over her features, twisted her mouth, and her eyes were piercing.

"And I wanted to apologize to Moss Jeffries. I took Javier away from you, and you were right to protest what happened to him."

"You did," Moss said, and he felt Eugenia squeeze him tighter. "*You* happened to Javier!"

Daley looked at the three of them. He was crying, and it enraged Moss. He had nothing to cry over.

"Yes, you're right," Daley said. "And I hope that you will find it in your heart to forgive me."

He stepped away from the podium and toward them, and Moss took a step back. James Daley stretched his hand out, the same hand that had held the gun that so easily killed Javier. The man walked over to them, right to Moss, his pale hand there in the space between them. Moss stared at it, then up at Daley, whose face was contorted in sadness and *hope*. The man had hope, that he had taken the necessary steps, that this apology was welcomed, that his world would eventually return to normal someday.

Javier was gone. He wasn't ever coming back.

Moss spat directly into Daley's face.

He ignored the cries and shouts around them. Moss was sure he wouldn't be heard over the noise, but he had to say something, anything—the last thing.

"You don't deserve my—*our*—forgiveness."

The three of them—Moss, Eugenia, his mother—backed away, then turned and walked down the steps. The mayor was calling after him, telling them to come back, and Johanna tried to follow, her heels clicking and clicking. But his family didn't stop. They walked onto the grass on Frank Ogawa Plaza, and Moss went straight for his friends. Rawiya held Moss for a few seconds, and then Bits was there, their eyes alight in pride and respect, and Moss hugged them, hard and sincere, before leading them all away.

The reporters followed and Moss tried to ignore their presence, tried to pretend that they didn't matter. They were like the mosquitoes that would buzz in his ears on summer nights when he left the window open. But then *she* darted out in front of him, her arm in a sling like Enrique's, and he stopped. Sophia Morales had an appreciative smile on her face. Moss returned it quickly, and Tyree hovered into view off to the side.

"Mr. Jeffries, good to see you again," she said, and he knew she wasn't posturing, wasn't pretending. "I just have one question for you."

He nodded his consent.

"What should the Oakland Police Department do next?"

Next? Moss thought.

There wasn't a next in his head. Javier was dead. Nothing the police did would bring him back or heal him or Eugenia or Reg or Shawna. Nothing would ever make Moss trust them again.

So the answer Moss gave was the only thing he could think of.

"Stop killing us."

Then Moss walked away from it all.

Author's Note

Moss's story will never be over. Those of us who have been the victims of state-sanctioned violence know this reality on some intrinsic level. We are frequently reminded of what happened to us, and we live with the fear that in a split second, it could occur all over again. Even when I was first plotting out Moss's journey, back in 2012—when *Anger Is a Gift* had a different title and also used to be the first book in a science fiction trilogy—I knew that this young man could never truly have closure, that he could never be part of a story that concluded with perfectly wrapped bows atop a pristine present. It did not seem honest.

That is not to say that we do not—or will not—experience happiness or joy ever again, or that justice is impossible. It is, rather, an attempt to talk about the ghosts that remain, that hide in the shadows of even the brightest mornings.

But this is not the end. For you, this might very well be the beginning.

This reading list is not complete; it is not all-encompassing; it is not without limitations; and it is not an attempt to give you a comprehensive look at the structural issues that people face in cities like West Oakland. Ferguson. The South Side of Chicago. Watts. Compton. Boston. New York. Atlanta. Austin. Instead, it is a start: An opening of a door. A flicker of an idea. A spark of inspiration.

Some of these books comprised my research, other pieces informed the politics of this manuscript, and all took my breath away. In some way, they all taught me that anger is indeed a gift, and that to wield that gift is an awesome experience.

I like to imagine that in another world, very much like our own, Moss found a tree in Oakland. Maybe it's in Splash Pad Park, or maybe it's somewhere down near Fruitvale. He locked Javier's chain up around it, and he visits it when he needs a reminder. On his way to his small home, painted like yellowed eggshells, he passes the mural Carlos painted. It's never been tagged. Defaced. Stained. It stands there still, to remind the community of loss and possibility.

It's a gift.

The New Jim Crow: Mass Incarceration in the Age of Colorblindness, Michelle Alexander

Critical Race Theory: The Key Writings That Formed the Movement, Kimberlé Crenshaw, editor

Race and Police Brutality: Roots of an Urban Dilemma, Malcolm D. Holmes and Brad W. Smith

Always Running: La Vida Loca: Gang Days in L.A., Luis J. Rodriguez

Brotherhood of Corruption: A Cop Breaks the Silence on Police Abuse, Brutality, and Racial Profiling, Juan Antonio Juarez

Our Enemies in Blue: Police and Power in America, Kristian Williams

Don't Shut Me Out!: Some Thoughts on How to Move a Group of People From One Point to Another OR Some Basic Steps Toward Becoming a Good Political Organizer!, James Forman

"Phantom Negro Weapons," Julian Abagond (abagond.wordpress.com/2012/12/06/phantom-negro-weapons/)

Angels with Dirty Faces: Three Stories of Crime, Prison, and Redemption, Walidah Imarisha

Notes of a Native Son, James Baldwin

No Name in the Street, James Baldwin

Time on Two Crosses: The Collected Writings of Bayard Rustin,
  Devon W. Carbado and Donald Weise, editors

One of the main motivations behind *Anger Is a Gift* was a desire to write a book that I wish I'd had available to read as a teenager. Fiction was my way of engaging with the outside world when I was growing up, but I desired so much more than what I had. It has been an inspiring and overwhelming treat to watch YA fiction begin to reflect the greater world that we live in. I know that there are now kids in libraries and bookstores who are picking up books in which they can finally see themselves. I have *The House on Mango Street* to thank for this (as well as the name for a character), and so I'd like to recognize, too, the books below. These works either changed my world or gave me hope for the future, knowing that teenagers around the world will get to read them, too.

Parable of the Sower, Octavia Butler
Parable of the Talents, Octavia Butler
Little Brother, Cory Doctorow
The House on Mango Street, Sandra Cisneros
The Hate U Give, Angie Thomas
Dear Martin, Nic Stone
All American Boys, Jason Reynolds and Brendan Kiely
How It Went Down, Kekla Magoon
Shadowshaper, Daniel José Older
They Both Die at the End, Adam Silvera
Ash and *Huntress*, Malinda Lo

Acknowledgments

First and foremost: thank you to the Mark Does Stuff community. Over eight years ago, I found an odd fame on the internet yelling about books I had never read before. I survived a bitter break-up, a relocation to Oakland, and getting laid off, and through that, I found out that I could make a living while yelling about books and television online. Without those years of support, I would not have felt confident enough to start *Anger Is a Gift*. I am utterly pleased that for once, all of you are not prepared. Much thanks must also be given to the incredible team of moderators and friends who help me make the Mark Does Stuff community what it is.

Thank you to my partner and love, Baize White. I hid this manuscript from you and begged you not to read it until I'd drafted it multiple times. I was most nervous about your thoughts on it because I knew you wouldn't pull any punches. You have helped shape this book in numerous ways, but you've also believed in me and this story of mine. Thank you for who you are.

I attended my first Worldcon in 2013, and it was there I met Miriam Weinberg, who insisted that we get away from everyone and go talk about anime in an empty pool. I knew that day that we would be fast friends, but I also quietly resolved to one day work with you. After *Anger Is a Gift* went through a dramatic change in genre, I experienced only one regret about the process: I wouldn't get to pitch the novel to you. I am glad that this turned out not to be true because I could not imagine an editor I'd want to work with more. You are hilarious, insightful, and incredibly fucking brilliant. What you've done with this book shows me that you got what I was trying to do from the very beginning, but also that you *cared*. There are lots of great editors in this industry, but there are very few who care about the world as fiercely as you do. *Anger Is a Gift* needed you to be complete.

In the summer of 2016, amidst a batch of querying and rejections, DongWon was the sole agent to give me the advice I needed. His urging that I focus on Moss's voice and story is what convinced me that I needed to pursue a book that was YA contemporary, not science fiction. While I will one day bring back the world of murder robots hiding underneath a city, I owe an immense debt to you, DongWon. Your vision and passion changed my life, and I would not be living out my dream without you. You are the best agent I could possibly have, so thank you for the gift that you've given to me.

My eternal thanks go out to E. K. Johnston, who had started following my Mark Does Stuff projects years before I actually met her. At ConFusion in 2017, she was responsible for a whirlwind period in my life where a major editor became interested in this story. Because of her, I ended up reconnecting with DongWon, and just over twenty-four hours later, he asked me to be one of his clients. Then, just over three weeks later, *Anger Is a Gift* was sold. I would not have traveled this journey if E. K. Johnston had not knocked over that first domino, and I will forever appreciate what she did for me.

I would be remiss if I did not also thank the large batch of beta readers/editors who read the very first draft of *Anger Is a Gift,* back when it was called *An Insidious Thing.* My eternal thanks to Jeeyon Shim, Jesi Lipp, Kelsey Polovina, Olivia Dolphin, Christopher Brathwaite, Meg Frank, Maggie Brevig, and quite a few others who gave me feedback years ago. All of you helped me write a better book, and most of you have heard me read from it a billion times. Thank you.

I've been lucky enough to gain the respect and support of a number of writers, creators, editors, and publishers since I first started doing Mark Does Stuff back in 2009. These people have cheered me on; given me invaluable advice; steered me toward my agent; promoted my nonfiction work; hired me to write or edit for them; and have generally made this queer Latinx dude feel like he could succeed in a world that usually makes people like me feel hopeless.

Thank you to: Lindsay Ribar; N. K. Jemisin; K. Tempest Bradford; Daniel José Older; Justina Ireland; Monica Valentinelli; Kate Elliott; Seanan McGuire; Victoria Schwab; Alyssa Wong; Sarah Gailey; John Scalzi; Diane Duane; Tamora Pierce; Libba Bray; Lily Meade; Danika Stone; Jay Coles; Susan Denard; Justine Larbalestier; Danny Lore; Brandon Taylor; Charlie Jane Anders; Dhonielle Clayton; Wendy Xu; L.L. McKinney; Zoraida Córdova; Sarah Hannah Gómez; Tiffany Jackson; Ashley Woodfolk; Teri Clarke; Adrienne Young; Tessa Gratton, Natalie C. Parker, and everyone who makes Madcap Retreats as special as they are; John Rogers; Javier Grillo-Marxuach; Zoë Quinn; Michael Damian Thomas, Lynne M. Thomas, Michi Trota, and the entire *Uncanny* team; John Joseph Adams; Tammy Coxen; Tanya DePass; Rakeem, John, Rene, Baize, and *Podcast of Color*; Navah Wolfe; Mischief Management; ConFusion; Arisia; WisCon; all of Team DongWon, because there are so many of us and we're taking over the world; the entire Brooklyn Speculative Fiction Writers group; and to anyone I forgot at the time I wrote this. You are still appreciated.

Thank you to Tor Teen and Tor Books for making my dream a reality, which included being published specifically by you at some point in my life. Specifically, I need to thank those involved in the initial stages of *Anger Is a Gift*. I know I'll have more people to thank later on, but my gratitude goes to Kathleen Doherty, Anita Okoye, and Zohra Ashpari, who welcomed me to Tor with open arms, creativity, and excitement. You made me feel like I fit right in.

And thank you, dear reader, for going on this journey with me.

Mark